BREAKOUT

Chris Ryan was born in Newcastle. In 1984 he joined 22 SAS. After completing the year-long Alpine Guides Course, he was the troop guide for B Squadron Mountain Troop. He completed three tours with the anti-terrorist team, serving as an assaulter, sniper and finally Sniper Team Commander.

Chris was part of the SAS eight-man team chosen for the famous Bravo Two Zero mission during the 1991 Gulf War. He was the only member of the unit to escape from Iraq, where three of his colleagues were killed and four captured, for which he was awarded the Military Medal. Chris wrote about his experiences in his book *The One That Got Away*, which became an immediate bestseller. Since then he has written over fifty books and presented a number of very successful TV programmes.

To hear more about Chris Ryan's books, sign up to his Readers' Club at bit.ly/ChrisRyanClub

You can also follow him on social media:
X: @exSASChrisRyan
Instagram: @exsaschrisryan
Facebook: ChrisRyanBooks

Also by Chris Ryan

Manhunter
Outcast
Cold Red
Traitor
Second Strike

CHRIS RYAN

BREAKOUT

ZAFFRE

First published in the UK in 2026 by
ZAFFRE
An imprint of Bonnier Books UK
5th Floor, HYLO, 105 Bunhill Row,
London, EC1Y 8LZ

A CIP catalogue record for this book is available from the British Library.

Hardback ISBN: 978-1-83877-984-9
Trade Paperback ISBN: 978-1-83877-985-6

Also available as an ebook and an audiobook

1 3 5 7 9 10 8 6 4 2

Design and Typeset by (Data Connection) Ltd
Printed and bound in Great Britain by CPI (UK) Ltd, Croydon CR0 4YY

The authorised representative in the EEA is Bonnier Books
UK (Ireland) Limited.
Registered office address:
Block B, The Crescent Building
Northwood, Santry
Dublin 9, D09 C6X8
Ireland
compliance@bonnierbooks.ie
www.bonnierbooks.co.uk

One

St James's, London. May 2025

David Hawkins took a long pull of his beer, glanced out of the rain-spattered window, and wondered how much shittier his life could get.

The one-time hero of 22 SAS was sitting at the bar in an old-fashioned boozer nestled amid the wankified art galleries, wine bars and private intelligence firms that infested this corner of the city. The Pheasant and Hound looked like it hadn't changed since the Blitz. Light seeped through the leadwork windows. The air was thick with the stench of stale beer and greasy food; the wainscoting needed several million licks of paint.

The place is a relic, thought Hawkins.

I know the bloody feeling.

The pub was packed. Thursday evening in central London. The new end to the working week. Everyone was getting in a few rounds before decamping to the suburbs.

Hawkins recognised a few faces in the crowd. Colleagues from the DeepSpear Defence Industries head office down the road. Well-groomed men in tailored suits sipping bottles of zero-per-cent lager. Older blokes with bellies straining against shirt buttons. Fake-browed women in pencil skirts and dark jackets, periodically ducking outside to take hits from their vape pens.

None of them paid Hawkins any attention. Fine by him. He wasn't here for the ambience or idle chit-chat. He just wanted to sit and drink until he could no longer feel his face.

Seven years ago, before the bastards at Hereford had taken what was left of his army career and fed it into the shredder, Hawkins had been a Tier One operator. One of the best warriors in the Regiment. A first-class door-kicker. He'd done the business in Iraq, Afghanistan. A whole bunch of other places.

Now he was a glorified desk jockey. Head of security for DeepSpear, an emerging player in the defence business. He'd traded a world of room clearances and vehicle interdictions for Zoom meetings and PowerPoint presentations. Eight hours a day sitting at a desk in an air-conditioned box, staring at a screen.

Not the worst job in the world. Steady. A quiet number. The kind of work Hawkins could do with his eyes closed. The pay was good. More than good. A hundred and twenty grand per year, annual bonus, company pension and expenses account. He even had the use of a company flat off High Street Kensington.

But still. A big comedown from life as a Blade.

For a while, Hawkins had gone through the motions. He'd ignored the looks from the junior employees, the barbed remarks muttered behind his back, mocking him as a Regimental dinosaur, a washed-up ex-soldier unfit for life on Civvy Street. He kept his head down and got on with the job.

The one bright spot in his life was his relationship with Zoe.

Hawkins had always had a difficult relationship with his daughter. The divorce had only made things worse, driving Zoe further away from him. But last autumn he had been given an unexpected opportunity to reconnect with her. At first things had been awkward but over time Zoe had welcomed him back into her life. Hawkins relished the moments they spent together. Going for walks along the river, helping her set up her gallery space. Zoe was twenty-three now. A grown woman, a promising artist. Getting to know her again had been the great joy of his life.

Then everything had gone to shit.

Hawkins was on his twelfth pint by now, or was it fourteenth? He couldn't remember, decided he didn't give a toss either way. He got up to go for a piss, staggered towards the toilets. The world seemed to have canted slightly to one side. Like walking on the deck of a ship being tossed about in a squall. Hawkins bumped into a thickly bearded bloke in a gingham shirt, knocking the tray of drinks he was carrying and spilling beer down his front.

'Oi, watch it, mate,' the guy cried.

'Fuck off,' Hawkins growled.

The man hesitated. He saw the black rage stamped on Hawkins's face. The look of a trained killer. Closed his mouth and moved quietly on.

Hawkins returned from the toilets, stumbled back over to the bar. The Hound had started to thin out. Commuters were necking their drinks before leaving to catch trains. Heading back to their partners and families. Back to weekend football matches and trips to the cinema and the million stupid little things that made life bearable.

Hawkins propped himself on the stool. Went back to drinking himself into oblivion.

The previous autumn, Hawkins and another ex-Blade on the DeepSpear payroll, John Bald, had risked everything to prevent a devastating attack on Britain's nuclear missile stockpiles at Coulport. In the wake of the op, they had expected to be praised as heroes. Instead they had been taken to one side and informed that there would be a company investigation into their conduct.

They were both facing serious allegations, the company HR director had told them. A restaurant owner in Plymouth had reportedly had his right hand shoved into a deep-fat fryer. There had been a number of fatalities aboard a fishing trawler off the coast of Liverpool. Some of the victims showed signs of torture. Millions of pounds' worth of damage had been caused during the firefight at Coulport.

Questions needed to be answered. Arses covered. The bods at DeepSpear seemed more worried about corporate blowback than rewarding the efforts of two men who had helped to save Britain from disaster.

Worse had soon followed.

A few months after the Coulport job, Zoe had announced that she was leaving London to open a gallery in Devon. Her girlfriend, Alex Millar, a cyber-security expert at DeepSpear, had quit the company to follow Zoe west. Suddenly Hawkins found himself alone. Again.

Just him and the bottle.

He tried to visit Zoe occasionally, but she always seemed to be busy, and he felt as if he was just in the way. Understandable. Zoe had her whole life in front of her. She had friends, a long-term partner, a flourishing career. He was just a middle-aged bloke whose best days were already in the rear-view.

Then came the sucker punch.

Eight weeks ago, Zoe and Alex had announced their engagement. A date had been set for the big day in the autumn, and Hawkins had been looking forward to walking his daughter down the aisle, the proudest man in the world.

Earlier that afternoon, Zoe had called him up at work.

'It's Mum,' Zoe had said. 'It's no good. She's refusing to go if you're there, Dad. She won't budge.'

Hawkins had sat at his desk gripping the phone so hard he thought the case might shatter. Zoe's mother. His ex. Michelle. She was living with a new bloke, some arrogant twat with a massive house in Gloucester, a kitchen island the size of an aircraft carrier and a hundred-grand SUV parked in the front driveway. Someone who had made something of his life and hadn't fucked it up.

Michelle and her partner were both adamant that Hawkins couldn't attend the reception. 'Mum says she's afraid of you,' she'd added, but Hawkins knew that wasn't the real reason.

She doesn't want me there because she thinks I'm an embarrassment. She's worried I'll cause a scene.

Zoe had argued his case, pleading with her mum to change her mind. But her efforts had ended in failure. In the end, Zoe had reluctantly come down on her mother's side. That was why she had called Hawkins at the office. To deliver the news he had been dreading. He wouldn't be going to the wedding.

I'm being cut out of my daughter's big day. I'm losing her all over again.

Hawkins had snapped. He'd grabbed his jacket, shut down his computer and stormed out of the office early. Headed straight for the Hound, determined to drink himself into oblivion.

He had a million reasons to be angry with life. His daughter's wedding, his dull-as-fuck job. The ongoing investigation into the Coulport attack.

I put my neck on the line for those bastards.

Now they're treating me like I'm the bloody enemy.

His old mucker Bald had already jumped ship. He'd taken early retirement a month ago. Full pension plus a generous lump sum in exchange for keeping his mouth shut on the Coulport attack. With his army pension topped up with the occasional gig on the Circuit, Bald reckoned he would be set up for life.

'Telling you, Geordie,' Bald had said after he'd handed in his notice. 'You need to get out of that place. Get yourself a tidy severance package. Take a leaf out of my book and play the old PTSD card. Tell 'em you've been traumatised since Iraq and you're thinking of going to the press with what you know. Those pricks will shit themselves when they hear that.'

Hawkins had dismissed the idea out of hand. He wasn't like Bald. He couldn't pull a fast one on his employers. It wasn't moral, he'd argued.

'Fuck morality,' Bald had replied. 'Those defence companies have got cash to burn. Rolling in it. You need to screw them bastards over while you still can. Before they come after you.'

Hawkins had asked what he'd meant.

'There's a lot of heat on the Coulport job,' Bald had explained. 'The press are all over it, Geordie. Flies on shit. They smell a cover-up. If they keep digging, it'll all come out in the wash sooner or later. The bods at DeepSpear will need a scapegoat to save their own arses. Someone they can pin the blame on. Who do you think that's going to be? Some exec with a big old pile in the Cotswolds? Or you, the head of security?'

Hawkins had listened doubtfully. He didn't think DeepSpear would throw him to the wolves. He'd stopped an attack that might have toppled the British government. That had to count for something. At the debrief there had been talk of awarding both Hawkins and Bald the George Cross.

Besides, Hawkins thought, *what else am I going to do?*

He could always find a job on the private military circuit. Ex-Reg lads were in high demand with security contractors. But that kind of work was dull. Worse than the DeepSpear gig, even. Six months on a training package in some shithole part of the world, living in an ISO container with a bunch of Yanks and South Africans telling each other made-up war stories. Hawkins was done with that life. Might as well stick it out in London. At least here he could live in a degree of comfort.

Hawkins necked the dregs of his overpriced Czech piss, held up his glass to the barman, making the universal sign for another.

The barman didn't see him. He stood at the other end of the counter, wiping down the surface with a filthy rag. Hawkins called out again, raising his voice above the low chatter and the indie music dribbling out of the sound system.

'I said, give us a beer, mate,' Hawkins slurred in his heavy Geordie accent.

The barman blanked him. He fetched a couple of packets of crisps for the bearded twat in the gingham shirt. The latter tapped his phone against the reader.

'Hey,' Hawkins called out, louder this time. 'Over here, fella.'

The barman sighed audibly as he approached. He was a wokey-looking fucker, Hawkins decided. Late twenties or thereabouts.

Dark hair tied in a man bun. Thin straggly beard. He wore a loose plaid shirt over a shabby white tee with 'WELFARE NOT WARFARE' stamped on the front in big bold lettering.

'You deaf?' Hawkins said. 'Give us a pint.'

'Sorry, mate,' the barman said in a flat, even tone. 'Can't serve you.'

'Why the fuck not?'

The barman rolled his eyes and pointed to a sign behind the bar. Golden writing set against a black background. Hawkins leaned forward, squinting as he struggled to focus on the words.

'It says right here,' the barman droned on self-importantly, 'we are under instructions to refuse to serve anyone we suspect of being drunk. And you've definitely had too much. I can tell.'

The barman glanced at the bouncer perched on a stool beside the entrance. A shaven-headed slab of muscle sheathed in a bomber jacket and cargos, with a hi-vis armband straining around his right bicep.

'Piss on that,' Hawkins said. 'Give us a beer, man.'

The barman sighed again and gave Hawkins a pitying look. 'Call it a night. Go home.'

Hawkins felt a sudden urge to give the barman a slap.

'I ain't even that drunk. For fuck's sake, I've only had a few.'

'Look, I've told you already. I can't serve you,' the barman replied, raising his voice. 'That's final.'

The bouncer must have overheard him. Because he slid off the stool and waded slowly over to the counter, arms swinging at his sides like a couple of wrecking balls, thighs the approximate width of ballistic missiles. He glanced quickly at Mr Woke, cocked his chin at Hawkins.

'Is there a problem, sir?' he asked in a thick Eastern European accent.

Hawkins swung round to face the bouncer. He was big and heavy and bull-necked. His skin had the wax-like texture of a lifelong roid addict. Hawkins guessed he weighed around a hundred and thirty kilos, maybe one-forty. A good fifty kilos heavier than Hawkins. But most of the bouncer's muscle mass was slow-twitch fibre. The kind of bulk you gained from long hours on the bench press and busting out one-rep-max deadlifts. A lot of strength, probably. But no speed. No explosive energy.

'Sir?' the bouncer repeated.

'No problem,' Hawkins said. 'Just waiting for this useless prick to do his job.'

The patrons at the nearest table had stopped talking and were staring at him. Hawkins knew what they were thinking, but he didn't give a crap. He just wanted a drink.

The bouncer exchanged a quick look with Mr Woke. He slid his tiny black eyes back to Hawkins.

'I think it's time you left,' he said.

'Fuck off.'

'I'm calling the police,' Mr Woke said nervously. He backed away from Hawkins, dug out his phone from his jeans pocket.

Hawkins gritted his teeth. He briefly considered flooring the pair of them. Easy enough for someone of his abilities, even with a bellyful of drink. He'd deal with the bouncer first. A quick head-butt, followed by a hard punch to the kidneys and the guy would drop faster than AI stock. Then Hawkins could turn his attention to Mr Woke. Give him a few sharp digs to the ribs. There would be a certain pleasure to be had from that.

He decided against it. Too much trouble. Better to leave this dump, decamp to another pub. He thought he might try his luck down Whitehall. Or strike west down Piccadilly. Plenty of boozers in either direction.

'Fuck you, then.' He shrugged off the bouncer's hand. 'Fuck off, the pair of yous.'

He started uneasily across the bar. He was much drunker than he'd thought. The world was swimming. Everything seemed distorted and out of focus. Like trying to pick his way through a hall of mirrors in the darkness. Just putting one foot in front of the other required serious concentration.

Hawkins felt the other drinkers staring at him as he shuffled towards the entrance. Fuck them. Fuck them all. They hadn't walked a mile in his boots. Didn't know what he'd been through.

He wrenched open the door, stepped outside. It had stopped raining. Rainwater gurgled in overflowing drains, dripped down from the window boxes mounted to the wrought-iron railings of the townhouses across the street. Cyclists hummed past on e-bikes. A couple of old boys in bin-liner suits were standing outside the pub, sucking on cigarettes and putting the world to rights.

Hawkins started down the street – and realised he needed a piss.

His mistake. He'd broken the seal too early. Now he was caught short. He couldn't duck back inside the Hound. The steroid-munching bouncer and the wokey idiot behind the bar would probably kick up a fuss. There was the private gentlemen's club down the road, but they'd never let Hawkins in. More chance of getting a seat in the House of Lords.

Christ, he really needed to take a slash. He could feel the pressure in his bladder building with every step.

Hawkins staggered past the pub, turned right down a one-way side street, started towards a row of slick-looking cars parked twenty metres away in front of a sculpture gallery.

This'll do just fine.

He carried on a short distance, passed a wine bar, moving further away from the noise and bustle behind him on Argyll Street. The nearest vehicle was a silver Peugeot minivan, but his eye was drawn to the hulking SUV parked directly ahead. A big boxy wagon, all futuristic lines and tinted windows, with tyres the size of Ferris wheels and a pair of carbon fibre snorkels mounted to the front fenders. The kind of vehicle you only ever saw being driven by Turkish gangsters through the streets of Tottenham. Or housewives in Chelsea.

His ex-wife's new partner owned the same model, Hawkins recalled. The massively successful bloke with the investment portfolio and the kitchen island.

A compulsive desire seized hold of Hawkins.

He looked round again, making sure he was alone.

At eleven o'clock at night the street was dark, and quiet. There was a homeless guy across the road, tucked up in a sleeping bag beside the entrance to a rare bookshop. Not another soul in sight. There were probably security cameras all over the place, but Hawkins was past giving a crap.

I just really need a piss.

He shambled along, stopped beside the SUV.

Unzipped.

Hot piss splashed against the rear wheel, ran in streaks down the diamond-cut alloy. Hawkins leaned back slightly, arching his hips as he hosed down the rear body panel just for the hell of it.

Jesus, that felt good.

'What the bloody hell do you think you're doing?' someone rasped.

Hawkins looked towards the voice.

A lean guy in a dark grey suit stood on the pavement outside the wine bar. He had a long, thin face, a rust-coloured chinstrap beard and a pair of oversized glasses. The man looked on in disgust as Hawkins relieved himself against the wagon.

'Christ, man, stop that!'

Hawkins had the vague feeling that he recognised the guy from somewhere, but in the dense fog of drunkenness he couldn't quite place him. One of the regulars at the Hound, maybe. From one of the big mining companies or recruitment firms based in St James's. He didn't care one way or the other.

Hawkins shook out the last few drops, zipped himself up.

Ahh. Better.

'Right, that's it. I'm reporting you.'

Hawkins turned towards Mr Chinstrap. The guy had dug out a phone from somewhere. He started tapping out a number.

'Put that fucking thing down,' Hawkins demanded. He took a step towards Mr Chinstrap, hands clenched into fists like cement.

'Piss off. You're in big trouble,' Mr Chinstrap replied. 'Fucking disgrace, man.'

Hawkins tensed. He saw red. All the rage and resentment of the past few months suddenly exploded inside his chest, sweeping like a river through his veins. He was on Mr Chinstrap in an instant, unloading a flurry of blows to the other man's body. Hawkins was too drunk to aim his punches, so he just went for quantity instead, swinging left and right, hammering his opponent's rib cage before he could throw up his arms to defend himself. Turning Mr Chinstrap into a human punchbag.

Mr Chinstrap grunted and fell backwards, arms clawing at thin air. He dropped his leather satchel and hit the pavement with a wet slap, groaning in agony. Hawkins pounced on him before he could get up, punching downward. There was a crunch as his knuckles slammed into nasal cartilage, shattering his glasses. Hawkins followed it up with a swift kick to the groin, like a striker smashing a penalty into the top corner of the net.

He stepped back, catching his breath.

Mr Chinstrap lay moaning in agony, pawing at his face. Hawkins picked up the guy's phone and lobbed it across the street. Then he gave his back to Mr Chinstrap and hurried away down the road. Voices called out behind him, shouting for help. Hawkins quickened his stride, headed down a series of backstreets. He took another right turn, carried on through another side street, hung a left. Started west down Piccadilly, heading in the general direction of the company flat.

By the time he hit Hyde Park Corner the anger had drained out of him. A tiny voice at the back of his mind whispered an uncomfortable truth. *You shouldn't have done that.*

You should have walked away. That would have been the smart move.

Now look what you've done.

He had fucked up. No question. There would be CCTV footage of the incident. Witnesses. Some of the more upmarket electric vehicles had dashcams. He should have kept his temper in check. Instead, he'd thumped the shit out of a civilian. A serious offence. Much worse than urinating in public.

Hawkins mentally reviewed the scene. The street had been poorly lit. The police would probably be unable to identify him from security footage alone. No one had actually seen him hit Mr Chinstrap. He just needed to keep a low profile for a while. Avoid the pubs around St James's.

Hawkins had been a hero at Hereford. He'd saved countless lives, dropped the bad guys. But on Civvy Street that seemingly counted for nothing. The world had treated him like a virus. Now Hawkins had had enough. He was sick of being pushed around.

I'm not taking it anymore.

The skies opened up as he took a winding route back to his flat. Huge raindrops the size of needles fell slantwise across the city, splashing down like mortars on the pavement, running in rivers down the road. By the time he reached the apartment block he was soaked to the bone.

He stumbled through the lobby, climbed the stairs to the third floor. Fumbled with the lock, shrugged off his dripping wet jacket. Found a bottle of Jameson's triple distilled in the tiny kitchen.

Hawkins unscrewed the cap and poured himself a generous measure in a dirty glass. Dropped himself onto the armchair and reached for the remote. His knuckles were torn and bloody from striking

Mr Chinstrap in the face. He'd have to clean that up. Plus any blood on his clothing. Get rid of the evidence.

Hawkins sipped his whiskey and watched the news. The Russians were up to their old tricks again, sabotaging electricity cables in the Baltic Sea. Inflation was up. Jobs were down. Some Silicon Valley tech bro was forecast to become the world's first trillionaire. Talks between Iran and the US over nuclear disarmament had stalled. The US Secretary for War had put out a statement warning Tehran of dire consequences if they acquired a nuclear weapon.

Everything was slowly going to shit.

Nothing changes, thought Hawkins.

A while later a numb heaviness settled over him. Christ, he was tired. He set down his empty glass. Closed his eyes. He forgot about the pain in his hand. The many problems in his life. The darkness slowly smothered him, and then he felt nothing.

Nothing at all.

TWO

Hawkins woke to the humming of his phone and a relentless pounding inside his head.

It was morning. Sunlight sheared in through the gaps in the shutters, stabbing Hawkins in the face. Pain seared between his temples, as if someone had taken a hammer drill to the side of his head and squeezed the trigger. His eyes hurt like fuck.

Bed, Hawkins realised groggily. *I'm lying in my bed.*

He guessed he must have got up for a piss in the middle of the night and stumbled into his bedroom afterwards, though he had no recollection of doing so. There was a whiskey tumbler on the bedside table, a bottle of Jameson's. Painkillers. A foil blister pack of Sertraline.

His phone buzzed again.

Hawkins stumbled out of bed. He was completely naked. His clothes lay in a pile on the carpet.

He felt terrible. Like a bag of shit reheated twice over. He rubbed his face and tried recalling the previous night. What the fuck had happened? He remembered being kicked out of the Hound, but after that he had only jumbled fragments of memory. Like stills from a film whose plot he couldn't remember. Had he pissed on someone's car? He might have done, though he couldn't be sure. There had been some kind of scuffle, but the details were hazy. Everything felt scrambled.

He began to shiver. His stomach churned horribly. He thought he might vomit. Christ, when had he last eaten? Yesterday lunchtime?

His phone kept on vibrating.

Hawkins glanced down at his G-Shock Mudmaster. 9.49. He'd slept in. He reached for his handset, fighting to suppress another wave of nausea.

Gracey.

Tom Gracey was calling him.

Shit.

Gracey was global director of security at DeepSpear. Hawkins's immediate boss. A corporate yes-man who jealously guarded his position, Gracey despised anyone who didn't toe the company line. He constantly sought to undermine Hawkins around the office, taking the piss out of him in front of his co-workers, imitating his Geordie accent and giving him all the crap jobs.

Before Bald had left the country, he'd warned Hawkins that Gracey would use any excuse to get rid of him.

Watch that one, Bald had told him. *That bastard hates blokes like us on a molecular level.*

Hawkins had nine missed calls.

All from Gracey.

What the hell does he want?

He was tempted to let the call go through to his voicemail. Tap out a message, telling Gracey he was sick and wouldn't be in. Roll back into bed and sleep off the hangover. It was a Friday, after all. Ninety per cent of DeepSpear's employees would be working from home today.

Except Gracey never called him. Ever.

He swiped to answer.

'David, where the hell are you?' Gracey had a typical private schoolboy accent. Charming and smooth, but with a hard edge to it. 'Why haven't you been answering your phone?'

'I'm at home. Feeling a bit rough, like.'

'Too bad. You're going to have to come in immediately. There's something we really need to discuss.'

Hawkins felt a sharp pain hammering against the sides of his skull.

'What's going on?' he asked.

'Not on the phone. Just get your arse down here. Right now.'

He clicked off.

Hawkins tried to piece his thoughts together. Gracey had sounded tetchy. More so than usual. Like he was pissed off about something.

Have I fucked up? Hawkins wondered.

He clinched his eyes shut, tried to gather his thoughts. Not an easy thing to do, in his condition. Had he done anything wrong lately? Made any inappropriate remarks to colleagues? He didn't think so.

Then it hit him.

The Coulport investigation.

Some hack must have got hold of the inside story. He thought back to what Bald had told him shortly after he'd quit the company.

There's a lot of heat on the Coulport job.

The press are all over it. Flies on shit.

It'll come out sooner or later.

Bald had been right to warn him. And now his bosses were summoning him to the office so they could throw him to the wolves.

He needed a drink. Badly. He reached for the Jameson's. Empty. Not a drop left.

Fuck.

Hawkins stumbled over to the bathroom, bollock naked, the sick feeling spreading through his guts. He wrenched open the cabinet above the grotty sink, grabbed hold of the mouthwash. Tore off the cap and took a long gulp. Swallowed. It tasted rancid, but the alcohol would take the edge off the hangover.

Christ knows, I'm going to need it today.

Twenty minutes later he checked out of the flat.

* * *

Hawkins reached the DeepSpear office at Cadmon House a few minutes before ten o'clock. By which point he felt almost human again. A combination of alcohol-based mouthwash, painkillers and two mugs of strong black coffee had blunted the worst of the hangover. The pain in his head was still there, but it had dialled down to a faint rhythmic pulsing. He stowed his company-issue Mercedes in the underground parking garage, climbed the stairs to the ground floor and crossed the lobby towards the speed gates. Slapped his security pass against the barrier reader.

The alarm squawked and flashed red.

The gates didn't open.

Hawkins stopped.

He checked his security pass. Wondered if maybe there was something wrong with it. He wiped the pass with his shirt sleeve, tried again. Got the same response.

No entry.

The alarm beeped.

Hawkins swore under his breath.

A security guard came over from behind the reception desk. A heavy-set guy with thinning grey hair, meaty hands and bags under his eyes as big as rubble sacks. Ex-Met, Hawkins reckoned. He had never bothered to learn the guy's name.

'Can I see your pass please, sir?' the guard asked gruffly.

Hawkins thrust the ID card at him. The guard inspected it for a long moment then circled back over to the main desk and showed the pass to a humourless-looking colleague sitting at a computer terminal. The latter tapped away at the keyboard. Peered at some sort of message on the screen. A slight groove formed above his brow.

'Can you confirm your name, sir?'

'David Hawkins.'

'I'm sorry, sir. Your pass has been revoked.'

Hawkins said, 'There must be a mistake. I work here, for fuck's sake.'

The guard shrugged. 'You need to come with me, sir. They're waiting for you up on the third floor.'

Third floor, Hawkins thought. *HR*. A summons from those guys was never a good sign.

The thumping pain in his head flared up again.

'What the fuck is going on?' he demanded.

'Just come with me, sir.'

Hawkins bit back his anger. He followed the grey-haired guard through the gates, past a throng of lanyarded DeepSpear employees making their way to the office canteen.

They took the next lift to the third floor and emerged to a brightly lit corridor furnished like an airport lounge, all hard-wearing carpet, fake pot plants and bland artwork. The pounding in Hawkins's head became louder as the guard led him past a labyrinth of open-plan desks towards a glass-walled meeting room located at the far end of the floor. A frosted band ran along the glass at eye level, affording the occupants a degree of privacy.

The guard rapped his knuckles twice against the door, levered the chrome handle. Gestured for Hawkins to step inside.

Hawkins brushed past the guy and entered. Three figures were sitting around an oval-shaped conference table in the middle of a sparsely furnished room. None of them rose to greet him.

Hawkins had the feeling something was very wrong.

Tom Gracey, his boss, was sitting at one end of the table, staring at Hawkins with a grave expression. Like a doctor about to tell a patient they had stage-four cancer. Next to him sat a professional-looking woman in her late twenties. She had scraped-back hair, dimpled cheeks and small mouse-like features. A pair of arched brows perched above fierce green eyes. Hawkins had seen her about the office occasionally. Leanne Briggs. DeepSpear's in-house legal counsel.

Then his gaze landed on the third figure, and Hawkins did a treble-take.

He was looking at a skinny guy with a thinning nest of ginger hair and a close-trimmed beard. Forty or so, with the rangy physique of a hardcore cyclist. Hawkins had seen the guy before, but it took a few moments to recognise him. Mostly because of the extensive damage to his face.

A large plaster covered the man's nasal ridge. He had a painful-looking gash on his forehead, bruises under both eyes, a purpled lower lip. He glared at Hawkins with undisguised contempt.

'Sit down please, David,' Gracey said. 'This won't take long.'

The guard backtracked, closed the door behind him. Hawkins planted himself in a chair opposite Gracey. Nausea surged in his throat. He wondered what the fuck was happening.

Gracey coughed and said, 'I've invited Leanne to join us this morning. And you know Adam Driscoll, of course.'

He waved a hand, indicating the middle-aged guy with the busted face.

Hawkins automatically tensed. Driscoll was DeepSpear's HR director. Hawkins had bumped into him at a few corporate events in the past, although the two of them had never seen eye-to-eye. He was the CEO's attack dog. Someone who wasn't afraid to roll up his sleeves and get his hands dirty in order to protect the big boss.

Hawkins had encountered guys like that during his time at Hereford. Troop commanders with their heads rammed firmly up the arses of the top brass. Guys who cared more about climbing the greasy pole than doing the business on ops. They were the ones who survived the longest, in Hawkins's experience. The pole-climbers always outlasted the decent operators. He had never really understood why.

He said, 'What's this all about?'

'You really don't remember?' Driscoll threw up his arms in exasperation. 'Jesus Christ, you make me sick.'

Gracey held up a hand in a placatory gesture. 'Adam, please,' he said. 'Let's do this properly, shall we?'

Hawkins stared levelly at Driscoll, gears slowly turning in his head. A scrap of memory floated to the surface. Yesterday evening.

A dimly lit side street near the Pheasant and Hound. A man shouting at Hawkins while he pissed against the wheels of a sleek SUV.

A long-faced guy with oversized glasses and a chinstrap beard.

Calling him a fucking disgrace.

'I'll cut to it, David,' Gracey continued. 'Adam has made some deeply concerning allegations against you. Specifically, he claims that last night at around eleven o'clock, after leaving a meeting with a client at Trummer's wine bar, he spotted you behaving in, shall we say, an inappropriate manner in public.'

'I was taking a piss,' Hawkins admitted. 'What's wrong with that? We've all been caught short before, haven't we?'

He wasn't going to confess to anything more serious than that. Not until he found out how much they knew.

'I'm afraid there's more,' Gracey said. 'Adam further alleges that when he confronted you regarding your behaviour, you became aggressive and threatening. He decided to report you to the police. Public indecency. You then physically assaulted Adam, causing extensive bruising to his ribs and face.'

The memories came flooding back to Hawkins, spearing through the tattered fog of his hangover. He remembered now. Punches had been thrown. Several of them. Aimed at Driscoll's midriff. He had an image of the HR director tumbling to the pavement. A pained groan.

Hawkins driving a fist at his face.

He glanced down at the torn skin on his right hand. Anxiety twisted like a knife in his guts.

Jesus, he thought. *I must have been totally off my face last night. I battered the HR chief, and I didn't even recognise him at the time.*

He understood something else, too.

I'm in big trouble.

'There's no point in denying it,' Gracey carried on briskly. 'We've got two witnesses who reported seeing a man matching your description flee the scene. Furthermore a junior member of staff confirms that you were kicked out of the Pheasant and Hound pub just before the alleged incident. The barman refused to serve you, apparently. Excessive consumption of alcohol. The streets in question are covered with CCTV cameras, of course. We could go through the proper channels and obtain the footage, but I think we both know what we'd find. Don't we?'

Hawkins said nothing. The pain kept on drumming inside his skull.

Gracey continued.

'So here's the deal, David. Tell us what you know, right now, or we'll go straight to the police. They'll take statements, interview you and seize the security footage. You're no doubt looking at a criminal record. Common assault, battery. Public order violation. At a minimum. That means jail time. Inevitable, really, given your background. You can forget about ever finding work again.'

Gracey eased back and folded his arms across his front.

Waiting.

Hawkins noticed Driscoll staring at him, eyes blazing with suppressed excitement. The guy was enjoying himself. Hawkins fought a temptation to lunge across the room, plant a right hook on his jaw. Finish what he'd started the previous night.

If Bald was here, he thought, *he'd know how to wriggle out of this one.*

Jock knew all the tricks in the book, and some that weren't. That guy could argue his way out of a firing squad.

But Hawkins wasn't Bald.

Plus there was the matter of the camera footage. Hawkins felt certain that Gracey wasn't bluffing on that score. The area around St James's was riddled with CCTV. All the big galleries and auction houses carried multiple security systems, covering the surrounding streets. There would be doorbell cameras, too. Car dashcams.

All of it supporting Driscoll's version of events.

'Well?' Gracey asked.

'Aye, it was me,' Hawkins said finally. 'I had a momentary lapse of judgement.'

'Rubbish, man,' Driscoll said. 'You're nothing but a stupid brute. A bloody menace and an embarrassment. You've been a liability to this company from the day you joined.'

Hawkins glowered at the HR man but kept his mouth shut. He visualised rearranging Driscoll's face, smashing his teeth apart. Blood all over the fucking place.

Gracey leaned forward and laced his smooth hands together. Conveying the impression of a serious man, getting down to brass tacks.

'I've discussed this with the board already,' he said. 'This is what's going to happen. You'll resign, effective immediately. No severance package. No notice period to serve out. Leanne has drafted all the necessary paperwork. We'll put out a statement that you're quitting on grounds of poor physical health. Frankly, anyone who takes one look at you wouldn't find that hard to believe. You'll surrender your company car and laptop, your security pass. We'll give you three months to vacate the flat.'

'What about my pension? Jesus, my bonus is due next month.'

'Not now it isn't. You'll leave with nothing, David. Fuck all. Zilch.'

Hawkins felt the blood pounding in his ears. 'You can't fucking do that. I've got rights.'

Gracey laughed and said, 'You pissed away your rights the moment you decided to attack a colleague.'

He leaned closer to Hawkins, dropping his voice.

'But I'm warning you now. Try to kick up a fuss, or fight us on this one, and we'll be obliged to instigate formal disciplinary proceedings and report the incident to the police. You'll end up doing time in Wormwood Scrubs with a bunch of convicted terrorists for company. Even an ex-army man like yourself wouldn't last long there. Is that clear enough, you thick Geordie bastard?'

Hawkins stared at his manager, his jaw clenched so tight it started to ache.

One punch, he thought. *That's all I'd need. One clean strike at this smug prick and I could put him in hospital. It would be almost worth the aggro that would follow.*

Almost.

Instead, Hawkins gave a grudging nod. He was in deep shit already. No sense in adding to it.

'Aye,' he said. 'Crystal.'

Gracey gestured towards Briggs, who slid a sheaf of stapled documents towards Hawkins and an expensive-looking pen.

'Sign it, man,' Gracey said.

Hawkins leafed through the pages, scrawling his signature in the relevant places. There was a pre-drafted resignation letter. Waiver of claims. Non-disclosure agreement. Confidentiality letter. A lot of paperwork. He should have had a lawyer present, but he was past caring. At that moment, he just wanted to get it over and done with. Leave the building.

Get back on the booze.

Briggs diligently checked through the documents one by one. Gracey glanced impatiently at his Breitling watch. Hawkins sat stewing. The end of his career, and quite possibly his working life.

Hawkins had always imagined he would bow out in a blaze of glory. Instead he was being shoved out of the door without a penny to his name. He almost laughed at the absurdity of it.

'Is there something funny?' Driscoll asked.

'Aye, there is,' Hawkins said. 'Your fucking face. I didn't think it was possible for you to get any uglier. Looks like I was wrong.'

Driscoll glared at him spitefully, but then he spread his lips into a smile, because he knew he had won. Briggs announced that everything was in order; Gracey eased up from his chair and cocked his head at the door. Hawkins looked past his shoulder. A pair of burly security guards stood waiting outside. One of them cradled a cardboard box filled with the handful of personal items from his desk. There wasn't much.

'These gentlemen will escort you from the premises,' Gracey said. 'Show your face here again, David, and you'll live to regret it. Mark my words. Now get the hell out of my sight.'

Three

Three weeks later

Ten minutes past twelve on a rain-slicked Wednesday afternoon. The middle of the working week. In a gloomy corner of the Golden Fleece, Hawkins sat alone, nursing his first pint of the day.

The Fleece was a dump. The food was revolting, the threadbare carpet was scarred with decades-old cigarette burns and the door to the toilets had several notices warning customers against taking or dealing Class A drugs. But it was quiet, the beer was cheap and he preferred it to the posh gastropubs off Kensington High Street.

The other drinkers kept to themselves. Mostly old-timers who had nowhere else to go, a few younger blokes in hi-vis jackets letting off steam at the end of a shift, reading the *Sun* or watching the horse-racing on a TV so low-res it probably pre-dated the Enlightenment. A few benighted souls popped in from the bookies next door. Celebrating their winnings or – more often – drowning their sorrows over jars of cheap lager.

Hawkins had been a regular at the Fleece since he'd been forced to resign from his job at DeepSpear. The place suited him. Somewhere he could drink by himself, and forget about his mounting problems for a short while.

And I've got a bloody lot of them.

He had no job, and few prospects of getting one anytime soon. None of the big defence companies were hiring, and even if they were, none of them would consider Hawkins. The industry was small and promiscuous. Everyone knew everybody else. Prospective employers would know about his exit from DeepSpear.

Hawkins is damaged goods. Don't go anywhere near that guy.

In desperation he had tried looking for work as a private contractor. But the few ex-Regiment lads he'd kept in touch with told him it was slim pickings on the Circuit. There was some work in Ukraine, but most of the lads weren't willing to touch that one. Too dicey. There was a chance you'd get identified by the enemy – and the Russians had long memories. Ten years from now you might go out for a jog one morning and take a bullet to the back of the head.

But Hawkins needed *something*. He was almost penniless.

The money at DeepSpear had been good, even though the taxman had gobbled up half his wages. But Hawkins had saved nothing. He'd spent everything he had on Zoe, buying up gallery space, giving her rent money and helping to pay off her crippling student loan. Whatever he had left had been spent on settling his own debts. Car payments. Overdraft.

Hawkins had been living the high life. Now he was paying the price for that recklessness. He had a month's salary left in the bank. After that, he would have to survive on his army pension. He thought back to his last conversation with Bald.

Get out of that place, Bald had said.

Screw them bastards over while you still can.

Before they come after you.

Hawkins should have taken his advice. Negotiated a settlement with the higher-ups. Instead, he'd tried to do the decent thing. Now it was too late. He was out on his arse, with barely a pot to piss in.

His own fault.

In a couple of months, his old employers would evict him from the Kensington flat. Hawkins had no idea what he would do after that. He couldn't afford rent for a place of his own, not on his pitiful income. He had no family, no place to go. Both his parents were dead; his younger brother Jacob had perished several years ago on SAS Selection. In the past he might have been able to go to Michelle for help. His ex. Get her to put him up, if only for a short while.

But she wanted nothing to do with him now. Couldn't even bear to be in the same room as him, Zoe had said.

That was when the voice had returned. The one that preyed on Hawkins in his darkest moments.

For several months Hawkins had managed to block the voice out. He'd kept it locked away in the box in his head, got on with his life. But the voice couldn't be shut away forever. Now it had crept back into his life. Like some sort of invasive weed. A low, soft murmuring in his ear. Telling him that he should stop fighting. Raise the white flag.

Why keep up the struggle?

There's nothing left for you here, Davey Boy.

Hawkins had started to wonder if the voice was right.

Time to face facts. The bastards had won. Hawkins had always tried to do things by the book. He'd kept to the straight and narrow, followed the rules. Stuck to his moral code. And look where he'd ended up. A middle-aged bloke with no career, no mates or family. Banned from his own daughter's wedding.

A few years earlier Hawkins had attended the funeral of an old mucker from the same troop. As he sat listening to the service, a bleak realisation had struck him like a fist. Every other operator from his old troop was dead. Some had taken their own lives. Others had been killed in tragic accidents, or succumbed to illness or disease.

They're all gone. All except me.

So maybe it's time I joined them. Drink myself to death, or pop a few pills. Better than trying to limp along.

It would be easy enough to end it. All he had to do was go back to his flat, swallow the pills, chase them down with a bottle of vodka. Close his eyes and drift off. Like falling into the world's deepest sleep.

All of his problems would magically disappear.

And Zoe?

She doesn't need you anymore, the voice had said. *Zoe has got her own life now. Besides, you'd be doing her a favour. Spare her getting entangled in any more of your shit.*

You're a bloody menace and an embarrassment, Driscoll had said back at the office.

Well, maybe the guy had been right.

Hawkins shook his head angrily. He tipped more beer down his throat, trying to smother the voice.

On the Iron Age TV the horse-racing had finished. The bored-looking woman behind the bar stabbed buttons on the remote control and channel-hopped until she landed on BBC News. Hawkins drank and watched Britain gently sliding into the sea. There was a report on a riot outside a migrant hotel in Norfolk. People in hoodies were tethering St George's flags to lamp-posts. Another northern factory had closed down. A grim-faced Prime Minister announced that taxes would have to go up again.

The rest of the world wasn't faring much better. Israeli airstrikes had hit a bunch of targets in Iran, knocking out a number of military and nuclear sites. The US President had given Tehran two weeks to return to the negotiating table, the report said. If they refused, he said, he'd send in the bombers. Another town in eastern Ukraine had fallen to the Russian meat-grinder. More swathes of the Amazon had been deforested.

Hawkins necked the rest of his pint and started to get up. Figured he might as well order another jar.

Then the door flew open, and two burly figures swept inside.

They weren't regulars. Hawkins could tell just by looking at them. They both wore shapeless navy suits and black polished lace-ups. One of them was built like a rugby prop gone to seed. Huge hands swung by his sides like a couple of shovels. A paunch showed beneath his crumpled white shirt.

The second guy was three or four inches taller than his companion and at least a decade older. He had skin like parchment, a brow with more lines in it than a Tube map and a nest of greying hair the texture of steel wool.

Shovel Hands and Parchment paused just inside the doorway while they scanned the bar. As if they were looking for somebody. Then Shovel Hands pointed towards Hawkins, sitting alone in the corner, and the two of them beelined straight for his table.

Parchment drew to a halt in front of him.

'David Hawkins?' he asked.

Hawkins set down his empty pint glass and lifted his gaze to the two guys standing in front of him.

Cheap suits, he thought. *Arrogant swagger. Faces that haven't cracked a smile since the dotcom crash.*

'Aye?'

'We're with Six, sir,' Parchment said. 'You need to come with us.'

Hawkins recognised their type. He'd seen plenty of them during his time in the Regiment. UKNs. As in, United Kingdom Nationals. British citizens, working for Vauxhall on a strictly freelance basis. They did all the low-level jobs. Sweeping rooms for bugs, ferrying people to and from meetings. Running surveillance.

Which could only mean one thing.

Six had been watching him.

Hawkins wasn't completely surprised. At Hereford it was common knowledge that the intelligence service kept track of every lad who left the Regiment. Where they were living, where they'd recently travelled, where they worked. People they associated with. The skillsets of a highly trained SAS man could be deadly if they were turned against Britain. But the UKNs had known where to find Hawkins at twelve o'clock on a weekday. Therefore, they must have had eyes on him for several days. Tracking his movements. Watching his flat. Shadowing him to and from the boozer.

'Mister Hawkins,' Parchment repeated, a note of minor irritation creeping into his gruff voice. A gentle reminder that things could turn ugly very quickly if Hawkins didn't behave himself.

'Come with us,' he repeated. 'Now, please.'

There was no point asking these two flunkies what Six wanted with him. UKNs were on the very bottom rung of the intelligence ladder. They wouldn't have been told anything more than they needed to know. Vauxhall compartmentalisation.

Parchment took a step closer.

'We have a car waiting outside,' he added, more forcefully. 'This way.'

Hawkins took a beat. He could tell the flunkies to go fuck themselves. Go back to drinking himself to death. The path of least resistance. But he was outnumbered two-to-one, and Parchment and Shovel Hands were both big lads. Dumb muscle, but they'd know how to throw a punch. Not great odds.

Besides, he was intrigued by Six's sudden interest in his life. Apprehensive, but also grateful that someone at Legoland considered him important enough to bring in.

Better to go along. Hear Six out.

Not like I've got anything else going on in my life.

Hawkins snatched up his phone and stood up. 'All right, fellas. You win. Let's go.'

Four

Parchment led the way out of the Fleece. Hawkins followed, with Shovel Hands bringing up the rear. A tactical decision, he presumed. Shovel Hands would be well placed to drop Hawkins if he tried to make a run for it.

They stepped outside to the retina-blinding sunlight of a London afternoon in early June. The air was rich with the smell of hot rain on asphalt, mingling with the stench of fried chicken from the takeaway shops further down the street. Plastic bags and junk-food wrappers tumbleweeded along in the faint breath of wind.

The lead flunky, Parchment, crossed the road and made for a deep blue saloon parked downwind of the Fleece. A BMW 8 Series grand coupé with blacked-out windows and a muscular front end terminating in a pair of chrome kidney grilles. Seventy-grand-plus of high-end vehicle. Hawkins doubted it was owned by Six. The bods in the intelligence service were notoriously tight-fisted. Every penny had to be accounted for, every cost justified. Their budget wouldn't stretch to a fleet of luxury motors. Most likely the Beemer was a rental. Paid for through one of the many front companies operated by Six.

Layers of deniability and a shoestring budget. The Vauxhall way.

Shovel Hands remote unlocked the car and deposited himself behind the steering wheel. Parchment circled round to the other side and sprang open the rear driver-side door.

'Get in.'

Hawkins got in. A plain navy jacket hung from the grab-handle above his head.

They coasted north then east out of Paddington. Shovel Hands kept the Beemer humming along at twenty miles per. A hard left brought them onto the grotty Bayswater Road and they joined the traffic slow-crawling east towards Marble Arch, skating around the edges of Hyde Park. Hawkins assumed they were taking him to Six's headquarters south of the river. They'd stash the 8 Series in the underground garage and escort him to a soundproofed room.

They veered south past Marble Arch and cantered down Park Lane, joining the chaotic throng of e-bike riders, double-decker buses and black cabs. Around them was a tableau of modern Britain. Five-star hotels and posh restaurants to their left, tented homeless encampment on their right. A sprawling site littered with sleeping bags and shopping trolleys, bin bags filled with clothes.

Shovel Hands downshifted to second gear as he approached Hyde Park corner, whereupon he made a left turn and arrowed north-east along Piccadilly, pointing the 8 Series away from Victoria and Vauxhall Bridge Road.

Away from Six's headquarters.

Hawkins sat up with a start. He leaned forward, glaring at the two flunkies.

'Where are you taking us?' he asked.

Parchment met his angry gaze in the rear-view mirror. He indicated the jacket hanging from the grab handle.

'Put that on, sir. I think you'll find it's your size.'

'What the fuck do I need a jacket for?'

'Just do it, sir.' Parchment twisted round in his seat, looked Hawkins up and down. Like a butcher assessing cattle at a market. His brow creased with mild disapproval.

'You'll need to tuck in your top, sir,' he added. 'What shoes are you wearing?'

'Brogues. Why?'

'That'll do. Now put on the jacket, sir. We'll be there in a few minutes.'

Hawkins pulled the woollen jacket from the hanger. It was a tailored piece, herringbone-patterned, with a velvet trim and brass buttons on the sleeves and front. He struggled into it, stuffed the bottom of his short-sleeved polo into his chinos and wondered once more where the fuck the UKNs were taking him.

Shovel Hands right-turned off Piccadilly past The Ritz, cutting south on St James's Street. With a sudden pang of anxiety Hawkins realised they were heading in the direction of DeepSpear's head office. He had a vision of the flunkies hauling him inside the building. His old bosses and Six working together. Throwing him to the wolves over the Coulport attack. A sacrificial lamb. Then they motored on past King Street, and the fear subsided.

They hit Pall Mall and bowled along the wide thoroughfare, flanked on either side by private members' clubs and dreary office blocks. After several hundred metres Shovel Hands eased the wheel to the left, dropped his speed and turned onto a quiet square encircled by Georgian townhouses. They looped around the central public garden in a clockwise direction until Shovel Hands eased to a halt on the north-eastern side of the square.

'This is us,' Parchment said.

A grandiose building dominated the street. One of the private clubs, Hawkins assumed. Four storeys high and dressed in Portland stone. From the outside it looked like a Greek temple. Or the official residence of a South American dictator. A series of immense stone columns soared up from the roof of the entryway and terminated in a carved frieze surmounted by an ornately decorated pediment. A doorman stood in front of the four-metre-high entrance, dressed in a knee-length coat trimmed with gold and a pair of gloves as white as his feathery hair.

Shovel Hands killed the engine. Parchment debussed, moved round to the rear passenger door. Wrenched it open.

'Get out,' he said.

Hawkins got out. The flunkies ushered him towards the entrance.

'What the fuck are we doing here?' asked Hawkins.

They didn't answer. Maybe their brain cells had overheated.

The flunkies marched him through the loggia, across a marble-floored atrium. Beautiful men and women in fine clothes sat in a cocktail bar to the left of the rotunda, sipping champagne. Hawkins felt uncomfortable in his cheap chinos, worn polo T-shirt and faded brogues. He looked towards Parchment.

'Don't I need to wear a tie in this place?'

'It's not compulsory, sir. People think it is, but it's not. This way.'

They took the stairs, descended into the bowels of the club-house, marched down a corridor lined with antique furniture. Paintings hung from the walls, expensive-looking pieces. There were portraits of club chairmen and black-and-white photographs of the building down the years. They passed a snooker room, a library. Another set of stairs led down to a swimming pool, sauna and gym.

Hawkins had the sense he was an intruder in a hostile environment. He'd trespassed into a secret world populated by ex-army Ruperts and Tory MPs and shadowy financiers. People with fingers in every dirty hole going. The other guests smiled at him but he could tell from the looks in their eyes that they knew he didn't belong. As if they could smell his working-class upbringing.

At length they reached a private room at the far end of the corridor. Shovel Hands held back while Parchment steered Hawkins into a wide high-ceilinged space furnished with leather armchairs and crystal chandeliers. Artworks hung from wood-panelled walls trimmed with gold leaf. At the back stood a bar stocked with luxury spirits. Ten-grand whiskies and rare brandies. Soft jazz played quietly in the background.

At first glance the room looked empty. Then Hawkins spotted the two figures. A man and a woman. They were sitting on a Chesterfield beside a marble-framed fireplace. The man wore a three-piece tweed suit and a grey tie. Receding ginger hair had been combed back from his shiny crown. The woman looked slightly older, with hair the colour of straw and a round face framed by a pair of cat-eye glasses. She was dressed in a dark cardigan over a plain blouse; tasselled loafers showed beneath her ankle-length red skirt.

Parchment beat a path over to the Chesterfield, Hawkins at his six o'clock. The man and woman simultaneously rose to greet him.

'Hello, David,' the man said in a voice as smooth as mulberry silk. 'Please, take a seat.' He waved a slender hand at the armchair opposite.

Century-old leather groaned in protest as Hawkins dropped into the chair. The balding man nodded at Parchment; the latter heeled round and trudged back out of the dining room, joining Shovel Hands in the corridor. The pair of them forming a human blockade. To stop anyone from entering. Or leaving.

'Can I get you anything?' the balding man asked. 'Coffee? Tea?'

'I'm fine, thanks,' Hawkins said. He could have murdered a pint but he didn't want to spend a moment longer than necessary in this place.

'Right,' the man with the slicked-back hair said, getting down to business. 'Let's get the introductions out of the way, shall we? I'm Peter Cruttwell. This is my colleague, Chantelle Jackson. We're with Vauxhall, but I suspect you've worked that out already.'

Hawkins studied the officers. He guessed Cruttwell was in his mid-forties. Blue-green eyes peered out from under heavy lids; his lips were as thin as boning knives. There was something of the devil about the guy, thought Hawkins. The unearned arrogance and privilege of old money. One of the Old Etonian dynasts at Six, probably, with a pied-à-terre in Millbank and a big pile in the stockbroker belt around the Surrey Hills. Hawkins had encountered his kind before. They had once dominated the upper echelons of Six but all that had started to change in recent years. Privilege was being forced aside. The old making way for the new. Cruttwell and his tribe belonged to a world that no longer existed.

Jackson was harder to read. She sat perched on the edge of the sofa, a notebook resting on her lap, like a secretary preparing to take down the company minutes. She had thin pointed features and a neutral expression, but the deep blue eyes were quick and alert. The kind of person who could take the temperature of a room within five seconds of entering it.

Hawkins wasn't intimidated by Cruttwell. He'd dealt with plenty of rich bastards before. But Jackson was different. She unnerved him. When she looked at Hawkins, he had the strange sense that she was staring deep into his soul. Reading his mind.

Cruttwell stretched his lips into a polite smile.

'Apologies for dragging you here at short notice,' he said. 'But we had no choice, you understand. Time is of the essence on this one.'

Hawkins said, 'You've been keeping tabs on me.'

Jackson shrugged. 'It's our business to keep track of every man who leaves Hereford.'

Cruttwell said, 'We heard about your difficulties at DeepSpear. That unpleasant business with your co-worker. A shame to end one's career like that. Though we weren't greatly surprised.'

'What's that supposed to mean?'

'This isn't the first time you've let your temper get the better of you, is it? That incident with the chief instructor on Selection seven years ago. You put him in the hospital. You're an angry chap.'

'Just tell us what's going on.'

Cruttwell dropped his smile and glanced deferentially at Jackson. Giving her the floor, perhaps. Or seeking permission.

Jackson said, 'We'll get straight to it. We've brought you here to brief you on a mission. One that requires your particular skills.'

She spoke with the clipped middle-class inflection of a BBC newsreader. Impossible to place, geographically. Hawkins had the strong suspicion that Jackson had worked hard to remove any trace of her native accent. Then something else occurred to him and he glanced warily round the room.

'Don't worry, it's been swept for bugs,' Jackson carried on in her articulate voice. 'We can talk freely.'

A question needled Hawkins. *Why are we meeting here, rather than across the river at Vauxhall?* He could think of only one reason that made any sense. They didn't want him to be seen around the building. Which meant that whatever Jackson and Cruttwell wanted to discuss with him was strictly off the books.

This isn't an officially sanctioned MI6 operation.

'What's the mission?' he asked.

Cruttwell exchanged a quick look with Jackson. Cruttwell crossed his legs and said, 'What we're about to discuss is not to leave this room under any circumstances. Breathe a word of this to anyone else and we'll make it our personal mission to ruin you. Understood?'

'Fine,' said Hawkins. He'd heard variations of the same speech before. Heavy-handed threats delivered by well-dressed men with public school educations didn't bother him. 'Tell us the craic.'

Jackson stared at him with those soul-piercing eyes. She said, 'How much do you know about Lance Kettler?'

'Kettler?' Hawkins repeated, puffing his cheeks. 'Bloody hell. I've not heard that name in a while.'

'You know him, then?'

'Aye. He's ex-Reg. South African fella. Rich, like.' He looked pointedly at Cruttwell. 'Served as a troop commander in Afghanistan for a couple of years. Took out a lot of high-level bomb-makers. Had the respect of his men.'

'Did you know him at all?'

'Not personally. Kettler cut around with a different crew. A few of my mates fought under him, but our paths never really crossed.'

Hawkins looked towards Jackson. 'Why are you asking me this? Isn't all of this in your files?'

'We're asking the questions here,' Cruttwell said sharply.

Hawkins shot him a hard, flinty look.

Jackson said, 'As you may know, Kettler left the army under a cloud six years ago. Allegations had been made against him concerning his time in Afghanistan with the SAS.'

Hawkins nodded. 'The missing pallets.'

He'd heard the stories around Hereford. There had been a bunch of ISO containers full of US dollars at the Regimental base of operations in Afghanistan. Money supplied by the CIA and intended for the tribal warlords. Partly to buy their loyalty, but also to encourage them to share intelligence on Taliban activity. Kettler and the guys in his troop were rumoured to have helped themselves to the cash, stuffing their rucksacks full with bricks of fifty-dollar bills. Millions had reportedly been stolen. Smuggled back to the UK in the coffins of dead soldiers.

Hawkins hadn't paid too much attention to the whispers at the time. But later on some of the guys who'd served under Kettler had been seen cutting around in flashy sports cars, or putting down deposits on lavish homes. Living well beyond the means of a standard Regiment salary.

Jackson said, 'There was an investigation, of course. But we were never able to prove anything. Kettler covered his tracks well. He was careful, and he had paid off a lot of people to look the other way. Air crews, base guards. We're talking about a highly sophisticated operation.'

Hawkins said nothing. In truth he didn't care about some of the lads helping themselves to a five-finger discount. If they had managed to steal the loot and get away with it, fair play to them. Life in the Regiment was hard enough, and once you walked out of the gates you were lucky if you could get a decent job these days. He'd heard of guys going to work as mercenaries for a pittance.

Two grand a month to risk your life in the arse-end of the world. The Ruperts were happy to stick their noses in the trough, but they hated it whenever the lads followed suit.

Cruttwell went on.

'Kettler resigned soon after Afghanistan. Whitehall had started asking questions and he didn't want to stick around to face the heat. He took his early pension and returned to South Africa. This was six years ago. After your time, I believe.'

Hawkins said, 'What has any of this got to do with me? I can't help you nail Kettler for the money if that's what you're after. That's all ancient history now.'

'That's not our interest in him,' Jackson said. She was writing something in a notebook.

Cruttwell shifted awkwardly. Something in Jackson's tone told Hawkins she was the brains behind the operation. The one calling the shots. Cruttwell was just the mouthpiece.

'Kettler runs a private military company in Pretoria now,' Cruttwell cut in. 'Goes by the name of Kopryon Security.'

'Never heard of it,' Hawkins said.

'You wouldn't,' Cruttwell replied airily. 'Kopryon is a small outfit. Discreet. No public accounts. Only a handful of employees. Kettler likes it that way. He prefers to work in the shadows. Friends in high places. Hands on lots of levers. The sort of chap who greases the wheel, gets people in a room together and makes deals happen.'

Hawkins nodded along and pretended to give one half of a shit. He wondered where this was going.

'Five days ago,' Cruttwell went on, 'we received credible intelligence regarding an operation led by Kopryon Security. One far bigger than anything Kettler and his gang have attempted before.'

That caught Hawkins's attention. He sat up.

'What's the op?'

Cruttwell paused. He looked towards Jackson. Deferring to his boss. She had set aside her notebook and looked evenly at Hawkins.

'Kettler is planning a heist,' she said. 'In Iran. At a place called Fordow, approximately a hundred miles south of Tehran. One of the regime's major nuclear enrichment sites. Two weeks from now, he's going to steal two hundred kilos of enriched uranium and sell it on to a third party. And we want you to stop him.'

Five

Hawkins stared at the two officers for a beat. He could barely believe what he was hearing. He'd known that Lance Kettler had been involved in some shady dealings in the past, but this was on a whole other level. Lifting a few bands of US dollars from an unguarded ISO container didn't hurt anyone. A victimless crime, more or less. Worst-case scenario, a tribal warlord had to settle for a slightly smaller penthouse in Dubai. Stealing nuclear material and flogging it – that was some very dark shit.

Questions swirled around his mind. A bunch of them. He reached for the most obvious one.

'How the fuck is Kettler going to break into Fordow? I thought that place was hidden under them mountains.'

Cruttwell nodded. 'It is. The site is buried deep underground. Eighty metres beneath a solid mass of rock and soil, to be precise.'

Hawkins considered briefly. 'Can't be done. Suicide job. That place will be heavily guarded. You'd need a fucking army to get in.'

'Kettler isn't planning to attack the bunker. He doesn't need to.'

'The US President,' Cruttwell said, 'is coming under heavy pressure from his cabinet to destroy Iran's nuclear enrichment programme before they develop a nuclear weapon. Last night he publicly threatened to bomb the enrichment sites. Specifically, Natanz, Esfahan and Fordow.'

Hawkins nodded. 'I've seen the reports.'

He thought back to the Fleece. The news coverage. President Brian Farrell standing in front of the cameras in the Rose Garden with his slicked-back silvery hair and his salt-and-pepper beard. Bumping his gums and making all sorts of threats in his native Southern twang.

Cruttwell hitched up an eyebrow. 'A soldier who keeps himself abreast of world affairs? I thought you squaddies spent all your time down the bookies or getting pissed.'

'Fuck off.'

Jackson said, 'As you probably know, Farrell has given the Iranians two weeks to resume talks over handing over their uranium stockpiles. If they refuse, he'll send in the B-2s.'

Hawkins nodded again. Northrop B-2 Spirits. Heavy stealth bombers. One of the few aircraft capable of carrying the Massive Ordnance Penetrator. A huge precision-guided bomb. Six metres long and packing enough explosive force to punch deep into the side of a mountain. The only kind of weapon capable of taking out an underground nuclear facility.

'None of this is top-secret, of course,' Cruttwell said. 'The President is, for want of a better term, verbally incontinent. Posts his every thought on social media. Rather like my teenage daughter.'

He chuckled at his own weak joke.

'What has any of this got to do with the heist?' Hawkins asked.

Cruttwell said, 'We've learned through our source that the Iranians are preparing to smuggle the uranium out of Fordow before the deadline expires. A military convoy is going to transport the material to a secure new site elsewhere in the country.'

'Where?'

'We don't know. Neither does our source. But it"ll be somewhere secure. Somewhere even the Americans don't know about.'

'We think that's when Kettler will make his move,' Jackson interjected. 'Once the transports are on the road. Most probably on one of the major highways.'

Hawkins scratched his jaw and thought. An ambush deep in a hostile state. Targeting a convoy carrying a load of highly enriched uranium. Right now the country would be on high alert. State of emergency. Guards everywhere. Police. State security. Air cover.

Border patrols. A high-risk job, unquestionably. But less hairy than trying to storm a nuclear bunker in the mountains.

'It might be done,' Hawkins said. 'But they'd need eyes on the target. Intelligence. Mapping. Ammunition, weaponry, transportation. Comms gear. Infil and exfil routes. All of that.'

Jackson nodded. 'Kettler has people on the ground in Iran.'

'Who?'

'Local assets on the Kopryon payroll,' she replied. 'People with a vested interest in helping him steal the uranium. They'll tip him off when it's about to be moved.'

Hawkins nodded. It would be easy enough to recruit a couple of senior figures in the Iranian military or security services. People disillusioned with the regime for one reason or another and willing to betray their country for a few quid.

He said, 'Why haven't the Iranians shifted the uranium already?'

'You can't just stick that stuff on the back of a truck,' Cruttwell replied superciliously. 'You need a great deal of specialised equipment. Lifting machinery. Engineers, scientists. Roads have to be made good, routes checked and secured in advance, troops prepared. It's a security and logistics nightmare. Especially when you're trying to do it without attracting the attention of the NSA.'

Jackson said, 'The Iranians won't want to move the material unless absolutely necessary. They'll want to exhaust all their diplomatic efforts with Washington before they give the order to relocate.'

'How long until the convoy is on the road?' asked Hawkins.

'Our information suggests the transfer will happen in the next ten to twelve days. Shortly before Farrell's deadline. Which means Kettler will have to be in position before then.'

Jackson saw the doubtful look casting like a shadow across Hawkins's face.

'The int is solid,' she carried on, as if she'd probed his mind. 'It's gold-plated. This is definitely happening. Our source is at the very highest level within the Iranian military, and we've got him in the bag.'

'You trust him?'

'The source is as credible as they come. Everything he's told us so far tracks.'

Hawkins nodded. Useless to press Six further on that front. He knew the score. Vauxhall never discussed their sources with guys like him. Division of labour. He was a lowly door-kicker. Hired muscle. The man on the ground, doing the dirty work. They were big-picture guys. He would be expected to stay in his lane. Take it on good faith that the int had been verified.

Which Hawkins was prepared to do, within limits. He had a grudging professional respect for Six. They were cut-throat and callous, and they would drop you like a hot brick once you had served your purpose. But they were also brilliant at their craft. Maybe the best in the game. They had a unique ability to seduce people into acting against their own best interests. To betray their countries, even if it meant putting themselves in danger. That took a certain mindset. You had to be both charming and ruthless. Whoever Six had flipped in the Iranian regime, they would have him bang to rights.

Another question chiselled away at the back of Hawkins's mind.

'If you know all this stuff, why not go to the Americans? Tell them what you've found out. Get them to flatten the mountain before the Iranians can smuggle the goods out. Problem sorted.'

Jackson and Cruttwell traded a knowing look.

'That's not an option for us,' Jackson said.

'Why not?'

Cruttwell said, 'We know that Kettler and his gang are planning this heist. We also know the attack will happen in a specific window, and that Kettler has people on the inside feeding him information. But we don't know the identity of the prospective buyers.'

Jackson said, 'Someone out there is prepared to pay big bucks to acquire a large quantity of enriched uranium on the black market.

Someone willing to suffer international opprobrium, maybe even sanctions.'

Hawkins said, 'Could be ISIS. Them fuckers are on the rise again. They'd be keen to get hold of that shit.'

'That's one possibility. Equally it could be a state actor with a track record of financing terror. A rebel group. Or some other party that hasn't been on anyone's radar before. A new movement, looking to make a name for themselves by going nuclear.'

'We do know one thing, of course,' Cruttwell pointed out. 'Whoever is funding the deal has deep pockets.'

'How deep?' Hawkins said.

'We're not sure. But on the black market, to the right seller, we're probably talking hundreds of millions of dollars.'

'Jesus Christ.'

'We need to know who's involved in the deal,' Cruttwell said. 'Who they are – and what they intend to do with the uranium.'

Jackson said, 'Right now, we're in control of events. But if we take our findings to the Americans, they'll act on it in one way or another, and the buyer will go to ground. This is our only chance to identify them, stop whatever it is they're planning.'

'Which is where you come in, laddie,' Cruttwell remarked. His thin smile cut like a machete through primary jungle.

Jackson said, 'We need you to get on Kettler's team. Piggy back onto the operation in Iran, hit the convoy and track the goods until you can establish the identity of the purchaser.'

Hawkins puffed his cheeks and exhaled.

'That won't be easy. Like I told you already, I don't know the guy. We never met. Why the fuck would he put me on his team?'

'You don't know Kettler, but you know one of his men,' Cruttwell replied. 'Someone who owes you a debt of gratitude, in fact. Chap by the name of Rory Steyn. He's Kettler's second-in-command at Kopryon. A fellow South African. I believe the two of you became acquainted in Iraq.'

Hawkins nodded. The Second Gulf War. Seventeen years ago. Another lifetime. Before his brother had frozen to death on the side of a hill in the Brecon Beacons. Before he'd been forced out of the Regiment.

Hawkins had been posted to Baghdad as part of Task Force Black. A special unit bringing together 22 SAS and Delta, with orders to take down the insurgent groups running riot across the country at the time. The workload of the Regiment guys had increased a hundred-fold. They went from doing one op every couple of months to doing three or four every single night.

Hawkins had been burning the candle at both ends, studying for his courses during the day. At night he'd go out on ops with the other lads. Get on a Black Hawk, swoop in, arrest a high-value target, move on to the next job. Counter-terrorism warfare on an industrial scale. Gruelling. But effective. Hawkins had had the time of his life.

He had been in-country for a few months when the liaison officer had called them in for an urgent briefing. A team of South African contractors had been ambushed while ferrying a VIP to a meeting across the city. In the firefight that followed the VIP had been killed and the South Africans had been captured and handed over to the Sheikh of the Slaughters, Abu Musab al-Zarqawi. The guy who was number one on the target list. The Americans had learned that al-Zarqawi and his gang were holding the prisoners at a compound in the desert. Hawkins and the other lads had been sent in to rescue them.

He remembered the op vividly. Twenty-four guys riding in a couple of Black Hawks. Blades thumping as they screamed through the desert at night. Rounds coming in as they deboarded the choppers. They had swept through the stronghold, dropping targets. Doing the business. The main group of hostages had been located in a central part of the compound, but one of the South Africans was missing. By that time enemy reinforcements had been spotted making their approach and the troop commander had ordered everyone back onto the choppers.

Hawkins had ignored the command. He was already rushing over to clear the last building. A crudely built shed on the far side of the compound. Hawkins kicked in the door, single-handedly brassed up the two AQI fighters waiting on the other side, dropping them before they could squeeze a round off. Then he'd lowered his gaze to the floor.

He'd located the missing hostage in a corner of the cell, dressed in an orange jumpsuit. Hands bound behind his back. Hawkins recognised his face from the briefing packet. Rory Steyn. A thickset South African with a horseshoe moustache. A video camera had been mounted on a tripod in front of Steyn. There was a knife resting on the floor. A black flag with white Arabic text hung from the bare wall to his rear. The enemy had been moments away from parting Steyn's head from his shoulders.

Hawkins had paced over to Steyn. Calmly. Controlled. Like a guy taking a Sunday morning stroll. He'd sliced through the rope with the knife. Got on the comms and called back the second Black Hawk.

Then Hawkins thrust out his left hand and helped the South African to his feet.

'Come on,' he said. 'Come with me.'

The two of them had emerged from the gloom of the shed, Steyn limping along barefoot as they made for the returning chopper. They had staggered on board, the Black Hawk climbing above the compound a few moments before the first reinforcements had rocked up outside the gate.

Thirty minutes later they were back at base, sipping Diet Cokes and celebrating a job well done.

One of the NCOs had later told Hawkins he should have been given an MBE for his actions that day. Hawkins didn't care.

He wasn't interested in gongs. Way he saw it, he hadn't joined 22 SAS to add to his medal collection. He just wanted to soldier.

Cruttwell was speaking again.

'Rory Steyn joined Kopryon Security four years ago. He's close to Kettler. Very. The two of them are thick as thieves, as the old saying goes.'

'Most importantly, Steyn owes you. He's only alive today because you saved him,' Jackson said. 'That gives you leverage.'

Hawkins wasn't surprised that Six knew the innermost details of the rescue op. Those fuckers always knew absolutely everything, in his experience. They probably had a file on what brand of toothpaste he used.

'You're forgetting one thing,' he pointed out.

'What's that?' Jackson asked.

'Kettler might not be actively recruiting for the job. He might have his team sorted already.'

'We think that's unlikely. Kettler has had to move very fast on this one. Like building a plane in mid-flight. From what we've heard, he's still looking for bodies.'

'This isn't some training package in DR Congo,' Cruttwell chipped in. 'Kettler can't rely on his usual roster of retired police officers and squaddies. He needs highly skilled men for this job. Ex-SF soldiers with no scruples. Guys he can trust absolutely. He's fishing in a very small pool.'

Hawkins said, 'That doesn't solve the problem of getting on the team. I can't just ring up Steyn out of the blue asking for a job. He'll smell a rat.'

'We've already thought of that,' said Cruttwell.

He looked towards Jackson, who said, 'We're going to arrange an accidental meeting between you and Steyn.'

Cruttwell said, 'Steyn travels a lot. He's the point-man for any Kopryon business abroad. Right now, he's in Dubai, meeting with a local contact. He's due to fly back tomorrow with British Airways.

He'll land at Heathrow and catch a connecting BA flight to Johannesburg. Layover of around four hours. Should give you more than enough time to get reacquainted.'

'You'll lay it on thick,' Cruttwell went on. 'Tell him you're destitute and in danger of being made homeless. A real sob story. Steyn will buy it, naturally, because it happens to be the truth.'

'Steyn will take pity on you,' Jackson added. 'He'll see at once that you're the ideal man for the team and recommend you to Kettler. That's the plan.'

'What's my cover story?' asked Hawkins. 'I can't just turn up at the airport without a good reason.'

Jackson said, 'There's a media event this weekend in Italy. At Ventanola. A limited-edition supercar is being unveiled. You're going to fly out there as part of the security team. A three-day job. Two hundred quid a day plus expenses. Somewhat below your station, of course, but it's the only thing we could find at short notice.'

'Ought to add to your tragic circumstances,' Cruttwell said. 'An elite SAS warrior, reduced to working for pennies at a luxury car show. Quite the comedown.'

He smiled mockingly. Hawkins ground his teeth and imagined snapping his neck.

Jackson said, 'That means getting on the plane to Ventanola and doing the job, naturally. We should assume that Kettler will do his homework. Make sure your story checks out. It's important you stay visible while you're out there.'

'How am I supposed to do that?'

'Be creative. Put in a video call to Steyn with the cars in the background. Make sure you're in the shot whenever the paparazzi are lurking about. Just make sure Kettler has hard evidence that you're physically at the show.'

Cruttwell said, 'Once you've got the job, you'll likely be flown out to South Africa. Kettler has a mansion in a private compound near Pretoria. He's assembling his team there. You'll link up with the others and await the green light for the mission. At that point, you're on your own.'

'What if I need to contact you?' Hawkins asked.

Jackson inclined her head at Cruttwell. A subtle gesture. But also an order.

Cruttwell obeyed. He reached into his inside jacket pocket. Plucked out a smartphone and handed it over to Hawkins. Some sort of knock-off Chinese brand Hawkins had never heard of before. Similar to his personal phone, roughly the same size and layout, but a poorer build quality.

'I assume you've heard of false-screen phones,' Cruttwell said.

Hawkins nodded. False-screen phones functioned just like ordinary handsets. But if you opened a certain app and punched in a particular combination, it unlocked a secret channel, with hidden apps for highly encrypted comms. Vauxhall increasingly relied on them for covert ops.

'All your information has been scraped from your phone and uploaded to this handset,' Cruttwell continued. 'Photos, emails, text messages and so forth. To unlock the secret screen, tap open the calculator app and enter the combination two-one-nine-seven-four-two. Remember that, because it won't be written down anywhere. There's a messaging app which feeds into Vauxhall, unbreakable encryption. Plus an emergency SOS beacon. Activate that only if you find yourself in serious trouble, and we'll do our best to bail you out.'

'From the middle of fucking Iran?' Hawkins asked doubtfully.

Jackson shrugged. 'We don't have a big presence out there, but we'll do what we can, within reason.'

Cruttwell said, 'Ticket for your return flight to Italy has been purchased and preloaded onto the phone wallet. You're on a BA to Bologna. Five o'clock tomorrow evening. Economy class. You've also got a pass to the Star Lounge at Heathrow. Terminal Five. Steyn is booked into the same one.'

'When is he due to get there?'

'He's scheduled to get in from Dubai shortly before two o'clock. He's got around four hours to burn before his onward flight to South Africa. We expect he'll hit the lounge at around two-thirty.'

'You'll find several emails in your inbox,' Jackson said. 'From the company in charge of running security at the Ventanola event, confirming the terms of your employment and so on.'

'What about accommodation?'

'We've booked you in to the San Giardino Hotel. Walking distance from the corporate office. Four nights. Paid for through the agency.'

'Obviously,' Cruttwell said, 'you'll need to get a taxi from Bologna to the car show. Keep any receipts and we'll reimburse you once the mission is complete. The earnings from the Ventanola gig will be deposited in your current account at the end of the month. You can keep those. Questions?'

'Just one,' Hawkins said. 'What am I getting out of this?'

'You get to help your country,' Cruttwell replied haughtily. 'A chance to do your bit. That should be reason enough.'

Hawkins shook his head. 'Look, you want my help to stop this deal from going down, fine. I'll do it. But you need to give us something in return. I've got bills to pay.'

Cruttwell screwed up his face. 'You'll do it,' he said. 'You'll do it, because you don't have a choice, you ungrateful sod. Look at your life. A bloody joke. Turn us down and you've got nowhere else to go. You'll be living under a bridge before long.'

'Maybe,' Hawkins conceded. 'But on the plus side, I wouldn't have to deal with cunts like you anymore.'

Cruttwell drew in a sharp breath. His face was twitching with naked hostility.

Jackson said, 'I'm afraid we can't offer you much in the way of money,' she said, gently but firmly. 'This is the British government, not a Saudi investment fund. But we can perhaps compensate you for your time.'

'How much?'

'Four thousand a month. Paid through one of our front companies. Twelve-month contract.'

Hawkins crunched the numbers. Four times twelve. Forty-eight grand for the year. Not a massive amount. Not after the taxman had taken his share. Less than half what Hawkins had been on at DeepSpear. But with his army pension it would be enough to see him through to next Christmas.

'This is about more than just the money, David,' Jackson went on. 'We're talking about stopping the uranium from ending up in the hands of people who wish to do us tremendous harm.'

Hawkins pondered. He understood the stakes. He didn't like the idea of letting the bad guys win. And if he succeeded, he figured the mission might open doors for him. Six would never admit to their involvement in the op, but there might be future opportunities with them. He wouldn't be making big money, but it was better than the alternative. Better than begging for a job on Civvy Street.

'Don't pretend to mull over it, for God's sake,' Cruttwell said. 'We know you're desperate.'

Jackson was watching him closely. Analysing him. Picking up on every little detail, but giving absolutely nothing away. Like a psychologist evaluating a patient. Hawkins reckoned that she was a hundred times smarter than Cruttwell. One of the smartest people at Vauxhall, maybe. Talent still counted for something over there. Privilege and a private education could only carry you so far.

It was the same deal in the Regiment. A meritocracy. Flawed, in many respects. But ultimately it didn't matter where you came from, or how much money your family had in the bank. You still needed the minerals to get the job done.

Hawkins had flourished in that system. Then the system had turned on him. Fucked him over.

He'd tried his luck on Civvy Street, but modern society had no role for a washed-up ex-Blade. Hawkins had grown angry and bitter. He felt rootless. Cast adrift. The company investigation into the Coulport attack, the condescending attitudes of his former colleagues, the scrap with the HR director: all of it confirmed what he had long ago begun to suspect.

I don't belong here.

I'm only good at one thing in this life.

Killing.

'Well?' Jackson asked.

'Fine,' Hawkins said at last. 'I'll do it.'

'Good.'

Jackson stood up and gestured towards the doorway. Shovel Hands and Parchment came wading over. Hawkins surrendered his personal phone to Cruttwell, stuffed the false-screen handset into his jeans pocket.

'These gentlemen will escort you back to your flat. I suggest you hurry up and start packing. You've got a long journey ahead of you tomorrow.'

Six

Heathrow, London

At exactly two o'clock the following afternoon, Hawkins strolled up to the entrance to the Star Lounge. He was dressed in a pair of 5.11 Defender jeans, Timberland boots and a plain tee under a tank-green utility overshirt, clutching a dark leather holdall in his left hand. The unofficial uniform of ex-SF guys everywhere. He flashed the flight pass on his phone at the smooth-complexioned agent prowling the reception and waited while the guy consulted a computer screen. There was a long pause, and then the agent gave Hawkins his best customer-facing smile and waved him through.

The lounge was cramped. Maybe seventy people herded into a space the size of two tennis courts. Like a chain restaurant, squeezing in as many diners as possible to make ends meet. Hawkins threaded his way past the steady stream of guests heading up to the breakfast bar or returning with plates of cold eggs and dried-out pastries, found a spot at the end of the long marble-top counter overlooking the tarmac apron. He planted himself on a stool, dumped his bag between his feet. Checked his Mudmaster.

Twenty-eight minutes until Rory Steyn was due to show up.

From his position Hawkins had an unobstructed view of the lounge. Most of the guests were older couples and families. Mums in slob clothes trying to soothe moody toddlers. Harassed-looking dads rooting through bags in search of a clean nappy or a rattle toy. Kids watching noisy cartoons on their iPads. Hawkins spotted a few solitary travellers. Business types tapping away on laptops. At one table a group of blokes in matching stag do T-shirts were already on the beers.

Hawkins helped himself to a pint of bitter from the row of taps along the bar. He sipped his drink. Scanned the lounge.

Waited.

Since leaving the clubhouse on Pall Mall the previous day, Hawkins had been puzzling over the identity of the uranium buyers. He wasn't an expert, but he reckoned the international market for stolen nuclear material had to be fairly small. A handful of states at best. He could think of a few countries that would be keen to get hold of a nuclear bomb, but the enriched uranium would be useless without the had the means of weaponising it. And any state with that capability would almost certainly have their own enrichment facilities. They wouldn't need to acquire the stuff on the black market.

It could be a state actor with a track record of financing terror, Jackson had said back at the meeting. *A rebel group. A new movement, looking to make a name for themselves.*

Someone willing to suffer international opprobrium.

Maybe even sanctions.

But also someone with deep pockets, Hawkins reminded himself. Someone with access to several hundred million dollars.

So maybe the buyer wasn't a country at all. Maybe it was going to end up in the hands of a proxy. ISIS, or a similar group. Sponsored and funded by a wealthy Middle Eastern state. Someone playing both sides. Supplying the bad guys with deadly uranium but also coming over to London by private jet to buy up football clubs and press the flesh with backbench MPs.

Whoever was behind the deal, Hawkins could guess easily enough at their motive. With two hundred kilos of highly enriched uranium, a terror group could wreak havoc in Israel, throwing the region into chaos. Or they might go straight to the source and carry out a targeted attack in the West. Detonate a bomb in London or Paris. Massive casualties. A new era of nuclear terrorism.

Hawkins turned his mind to Kettler. Back at Hereford the guy had a reputation as a brilliant soldier. A charismatic warrior who commanded the absolute loyalty of his troop. First off the chopper, first man through the door. Fighting shoulder-to-shoulder with the lads, taking incoming and putting down rounds. Some Ruperts preferred to sit behind a desk, but not Kettler.

In Afghanistan his troop had been tasked with going after the Taliban's network of bomb-makers. At the time soldiers had been getting fragged on a daily basis. Guys ripped limb from limb or blown to pieces by a bunch of cowards rigging up IEDs. All that had changed after Kettler had arrived in-country. He'd gone after the enemy aggressively, storming their hide outs and making hard arrests. Anyone connected to the bomb-makers had been targeted. In a few months his troop had neutralised the threat. Lives had been saved.

So when the rumours had started circulating about Kettler and his guys lining their pockets, a lot of people back home had been prepared to look the other way. There was a deep respect for what they had achieved in Afghanistan. No one was going to shed a tear over an Afghan warlord being left out of pocket.

Still, Hawkins reflected, there was a big difference between pilfering bundles of US currency and ambushing a convoy of uranium. Kettler was playing a very dangerous game. High-stakes. But also high reward.

They were playing a dangerous game over at Vauxhall, too. If the Americans ever found out that Britain had kept quiet about the plan to evacuate the uranium from Fordow, and Kettler's heist, there would be hell to pay. Farrell was notoriously thin-skinned. Keeping high-level int from his administration was bound to piss him off.

Hawkins gulped down the dregs of his beer and helped himself to another.

He glanced again at his Mudmaster.

14.34.

Across the room the guys on the stag party necked their lagers and left to catch their flights. The smooth-faced lounge agent clocked off. A short, dark-haired woman with pouty lips took his place at the desk.

There was still no sign of Steyn.

Hawkins frowned. He'd checked the arrivals board shortly before heading up to Star Lounge and he knew that Steyn's flight from Dubai had got in on time. Steyn was travelling business class to Johannesburg. He'd want to use the lounge facilities. No way he'd slum it with the economy-class brigade downstairs.

The guy should be here by now. So where the fuck is he?

The number of guests in the lounge dwindled. The families checked out, along with most of the retirees. Hawkins sipped his bitter and waited some more.

He was confident that Steyn would remember him. Iraq had been seventeen years ago, but the pair of them had kept in touch for years after the Baghdad op. Exchanging text messages. Checking in every once in a while. Most of the activity came from Steyn's end. Boasting about the Springboks' latest victory over England, or sharing a dirty joke he'd heard from a mate on the Circuit.

Hawkins had never really cared much for Steyn. Hard as nails, maybe. But he was arrogant and huffy, with a very high opinion of himself. Hawkins had run into plenty of guys like that in Iraq. Huge fellas cutting around as if they were invincible. They failed to understand a simple truth: a 7.62mm round doesn't care how big you are, or where you've come from. It'll drop you just the same. Steyn and the other South Africans had underestimated the enemy. They had gone into Baghdad thinking they were better than the bad guys. Big mistake. One that had very nearly cost them their heads.

Four minutes later Rory Steyn strolled into the lounge.

Hawkins recognised him immediately. The previous evening Jackson had sent him a message on the false-screen phone. A photograph of Steyn taken a few years ago, scraped from his private social media account. The man standing a few metres away was identical to the face in that snap.

Steyn hadn't changed much over the years. A little heavier around the midriff, thicker in the arms and shoulders. The dark hair had almost completely receded. But he still had the horseshoe moustache. The same meaty physique. He wore a Springboks jersey over a pair of khaki chinos and dust-caked boots.

Hawkins pretended to read an article on his phone as he tracked Steyn out of the tail of his eye. The heavyset South African scanned the lounge before his gaze landed on Hawkins.

Steyn called out to him: 'Holy shit. Geordie fucking Hawkins! Bra!'

He came barrelling over to the bar, wheeling his carry-on luggage behind him. Hawkins looked up, feigning surprise. Steyn thrust out an arm the size of a hanging ham. They shook hands.

'Fucking hell, bra,' Steyn added in his thick Boer accent. He had a coarse, outdoorsy way about him. Like he'd just returned from hunting game in the veldt. 'It's been a minute, right?'

'Aye. It has.' Hawkins made a face. 'Christ, mate. You've put on a few pounds since I last saw you.'

'This?' Steyn patted his stomach. 'This is pure muscle, bra.'

'Lifting cookies out of the jar,' Hawkins said, 'ain't a workout.'

Steyn laughed heartily. 'Fucking English. Got to admire your sense of humour. Guess you've got to have something, though. Not like your boys have got piss-all chance of winning the World Cup, hey?'

'Two years to go, mate. Still time.'

'Yeah, there is. Time for you lot to practise polishing your silver gongs.' Steyn grinned, revealing a set of wonky yellowed teeth.

He grabbed a bottle of Johnnie Walker red label from the counter, filled a pair of tumblers to the brim, handed one to Hawkins. Deposited his immense bulk on the stool next to him.

'Cheers, bra. Good to see you.'

'Likewise,' Hawkins said.

They drank their spirits and shot the breeze for a while. They talked rugby. Ukraine. The shocking state of the SAS and the

British army in general. Putting the world to rights over double-measures of Scotch. Hawkins was happy to keep the conversation ticking along. He thought: *I'm supposed to be looking for a job on the Circuit.* Any ex-Regiment man in that position wouldn't plunge straight in and beg for work. Too degrading. Better to soften Steyn up first. Pretend to be best mates, wait for the right moment to bring it up.

They finished their drinks. Steyn refilled their glasses. Hawkins bided his time, sipping his whisky and waiting until Steyn was suitably relaxed and well-oiled before he made his move.

'How's business?' he asked.

'Same as ever,' Steyn replied. 'You know how it is. There's work, but it ain't like it used to be in Iraq, when you had fellas making money hand over fist. Glory days, bra. But we've got some new stuff lined up. Could be a big payday.' He knocked back a slug of Johnnie Walker and spoke again.

'How about yourself? Last time I heard, you were with that defence company. BigSpear, or whatever.'

'DeepSpear,' Hawkins corrected. 'I ain't there now.'

'What the fuck happened?'

Hawkins gave him the shortened version of events. The drinking. The ritual humiliations at the hands of the younger, university-educated colleagues at the office. Beating up the HR director. He left out the sensitive stuff about the Coulport op.

When he had finished, Steyn said, 'You need to be better at staying in touch, my friend. Should have told us about this. That's what mates are for.'

'Aye, I know,' Hawkins said.

He thought: *We're not fucking mates.*

'What are you doing here, anyway?' Steyn swept an arm around him, gesturing to the lounge. 'Off for a dirty weekend? Got a bit on the side?'

'No such luck. Security job. Three days down in Ventanola.'

'The car event?' Steyn puckered his brow. 'Fuck, bra. They can't be paying you much for that.'

'Pennies. But I need the money.'

Steyn gave him a searching look. 'Things are really that bad?'

'Worse,' said Hawkins. 'I'm in a shit state.'

Hawkins paused. He was aware that the entire mission hung on the next few minutes. He had to lay it on thick. Convince Steyn that he was the right candidate for the Iran job without making him suspicious. Hawkins figured the best way to win him over was to appeal to his massive ego. Steyn would surely relish the idea of being Hawkins's saviour.

'I haven't got a pot to piss in,' he began. 'Michelle took everything in the divorce and them bastards at DeepSpear screwed me over on my severance. I've got a roof over my head for now, but in a few months I'll be out on my arse with nowhere to go. All I've got is my army pension, and that doesn't go very far these days.'

'You've got your qualifications. Can't you go elsewhere?'

'No one's hiring, and they wouldn't take us on anyway. Not after I lamped that twat in HR.'

'That's a rough deal, bra.' There was a note of genuine concern in Steyn's voice. 'What are you gonna do?'

'I don't know. But I need work.' Hawkins sighed in frustration. 'If something doesn't turn up soon, I'll end up stacking shelves in the supermarket.'

Steyn looked at him thoughtfully. 'How long did you say this job in Ventanola lasts?'

'Three days. Then I'm back home again. Why?'

'And you've got nothing going on after that? Nothing at all?'

'Fuck all. Like I said, no one's hiring.'

Steyn pursed his lips. 'What if I could help you out?'

'Thanks, mate. But I don't need your charity,' Hawkins said. Playing the role of a middle-aged ex-Blade broken by life.

He thought grimly: *I've been living that role for the past few weeks.*

'I ain't talking about lending you money, bra. I'm talking a job.'

Hawkins lifted his head and looked expectantly at the South African. 'What sort of job?'

Steyn glanced round, as if making sure that no one was listening in. Then he leaned closer to Hawkins, lowered his voice to an undertone.

'I can't go into specifics. Not here. But it's something big. Pays good money, too. Overseas work. I can put a word in, if you're interested.'

Hawkins suppressed a pang of excitement and relief. Steyn had fallen for it. He said, hopefully, 'You would do that for us?'

'We're brother warriors. Got to look out for one another. Not like any other prick is gonna do that for us, is it? Besides, you did me a good turn once. About time I returned the favour.'

Steyn looked pityingly at him. Hawkins felt a sting of humiliation. *Seventeen years ago*, he thought, *I saved this idiot's life*. Now the roles had been reversed. Steyn was playing the hero, coming to the rescue of a soldier fallen on hard times.

'I don't know what to say,' Hawkins said, falteringly. 'That would be amazing, mate. You're a lifesaver.'

He was appealing to Steyn's ego, laying it on thick.

'Don't thank me just yet, bra. I'll have to raise it with the boss man first.'

'Would he agree to it?'

'Reckon so.' Steyn added, proudly, 'I've known the bloke for a long time. We're best mates. He trusts my judgement.' He tipped his head at Hawkins. 'You might know him, actually. Lance Kettler.'

'I know the name, but we've never crossed paths. He was in Afghanistan with G Squadron. Air Troop. Years ago.'

Steyn said, 'He's a big deal these days. Lots of fingers in lots of pies. Very well connected. He's looking for manpower. Solid lads. Fellas with experience in the game. You'd fit the bill, I reckon.'

Hawkins swallowed his dignity and said, 'Thanks, mate. I can't believe you're doing this for me.'

'It's no big deal. Anyway, like I said. The boss needs a good man for the team, and capable guys are hard to find these days. Too many idiots on the Circuit. Know what I mean, bra?'

'Aye. I do.'

They chatted some more. Moving the conversation back to more familiar territory. Steyn did most of the talking, bragging about jobs he'd done in the past. People he'd met. Places he'd visited. Women he'd shagged. He showed Hawkins photos of the latest watch he'd bought. A limited-edition Breitling Chronograph. A cool thirty grand. Steyn owned several of them, he said. He planned to get a Patek Philippe with his share of the next payday.

After a while Hawkins glanced over at the departures board mounted on the wall. The five o'clock to Bologna had started boarding. He tipped the rest of the Johnnie Walker down his throat and got up to leave.

'Are you still on the same number?' Steyn asked. He was scrolling through his contacts on his phone. 'The one ending in – let me see – nine-six-four?'

'That's the one.'

The false-screen phone had been set up to relay all messages and calls from his personal device. Six had thought of everything.

Steyn said, 'I'll be in touch.'

'When?'

'A day or two. I'll speak to the boss as soon as I'm back in Joburg. See if I can get this thing rubber-stamped. Soon as I know, I'll give you the heads-up.'

'Roger that.' Hawkins paused. He went on, 'Thanks again. I mean it. This means a fucking lot.'

Steyn swatted away his gratitude and poured himself a refill. Hawkins grabbed his holdall. Steyn slapped a hairy paw on his shoulder.

'One thing, Geordie. Keep this to yourself,' he said quietly. 'Not a word to anyone else. The job is extremely sensitive. Boss man doesn't want word getting around. You understand.'

'No worries, mate. I'll keep my mouth shut.'

'Good man.' Steyn offered his hand. Hawkins gripped it. 'See you around, bra.'

'I hope so,' Hawkins said. 'I really hope so.'

Hawkins left the lounge and followed the signs to the gate for the Bologna flight.

Going cap-in-hand to Steyn had been a humiliating experience. He hoped it had done the trick. Steyn had seemed confident that he could secure a place for Hawkins on the Kopryon team. Part of him wondered if he had done enough, but there was no point worrying about that now.

All I can do is wait, Hawkins told himself. *Do the job in Italy and wait for the phone to ring.*

And hope to fuck that Kettler agrees to bring me onto the team.

Seven

Ventanola, Italy. Two days later

A few minutes after six o'clock, on an evening of thick heat and rain, Hawkins stepped through the entrance to the San Giardino Hotel on Via Carlo Costa. He crossed the reception, blanked the moody bloke manning the reception desk and rode the single working lift to his room on the third floor. Hawkins had followed the same routine every day since he'd arrived in Ventanola. He'd finish his four-hour shift working security at the company headquarters down the road, head back to his grubby hotel room. Change out of his suit, grab his phone and hit the expat bar across the street. Get on the beers.

The job was boring. The kind of work Hawkins could have done with his eyes closed. Four hours a day getting crap money to guard a prototype of the company's latest supercar. Sentry duty. Standing like a performing seal next to the stanchions encircling the vehicle, keeping an eye on the invitees and the press pack. Making sure no one else got near enough to mark or damage it in any way. Mainly he was on the lookout for eco-warriors trying to sneak through the scrum. Students with cans of paint and too much time on their hands.

The car was a limited-edition model, the company's chief of security had told Hawkins when he'd first reported to the office two days earlier. Two hundred and fifty would be manufactured and offered to a select group of VIPs. Loyal customers. Lifelong fans of the brand. Oligarchs and Arab princes, billionaire athletes. The kind of people who could afford to drop the thick end of two million quid on a car they'd never drive. The motors would sit in their collection for a while, the chief said, gaining in value. Because of the exclusivity. Five or six years from now, that same car would be worth six million. An impressive return. Better than any pension scheme. More than Hawkins would earn in ten lifetimes.

He had followed Six's instructions to the letter. On the first day he'd put in a video call to Steyn. Checking in with his new bestie while he undertook a recce of the conference space. Hawkins had panned the camera round, giving Steyn the remote tour. *Here you go*, he'd said as he zoomed in on the prototype. *This is my principal, mate. It's got four fucking wheels.*

The next day, Hawkins had taken up a position next to the velvet rope while the paps took a zillion shots of the scantily clad celebrity models hired for the grand unveiling. Getting his mug in plenty of snaps. The girls and the supercar. Hawkins in the background, dressed in a drab suit and tie.

Only one more day to get through, he reminded himself. Tomorrow there would be a shakedown on the private circuit abutting the company offices. A test driver would spin out a few laps in the supercar while the throng of journalists and models and influencers looked on. Then it would be over.

But there had still been no news from Steyn on the meeting.

At first Hawkins hadn't been worried. Kettler wouldn't make a snap decision on whether to hire Hawkins. He might have his own candidate in mind. Steyn would have to win him over. *This guy has done the business, boss. He saved my life once. We can trust him. Let's bring him on.*

There would be various background checks, too. Off-the-record chats. Hawkins didn't know Kettler personally, but he assumed the guy would be cautious. He was planning an op to steal Iran's precious stores of uranium. Kettler would do his due diligence before bringing a new guy onto the team. He'd reach out to his old Hereford connections. Lads who had served in his troop. *Do you know Hawkins? What's he like? Is he loyal?* Building up a detailed profile of his character. Kettler might have contacts in the defence sector as well. They would confirm the story behind Hawkins's abrupt departure from DeepSpear.

The guy punched a colleague in the face. Lucky he didn't end up in a police cell. Last I heard he's out of work now.

They might even check in with the agency in charge of running security for the Ventanola event. Get someone to pose as a relative or an old friend. *I'm trying to get hold of David. Someone told me he's out in Ventanola at the moment, is that true?*

All of which would take time. That was understandable. People might not respond to the inquiries immediately. Or Kettler might want to think it over before committing himself either way.

But two full days had passed since he'd bumped into Steyn. Still Hawkins had heard nothing.

He shook off his jacket and tie, slumped on the armchair, woke up his false-screen phone. He opened the calculator app. Punched in the number he'd committed to memory. 219742. Then he hit divide, followed by 0, then the equals symbol.

The phone reverted to a bog-standard home screen. Like he'd just done a factory reset of his device. Default wallpaper in the background, default apps. Except two additional apps were stored inside the Extras folder. The encrypted texting app with a direct line to Vauxhall, and the SOS beacon.

Hawkins tapped open the secret chat icon. He had a new message from Cruttwell.

Have you heard anything yet?

Hawkins stared at the screen. He thought: *Six is getting impatient, too*. Presumably they were having the same internal debates at their end. Asking themselves why Steyn hadn't come through yet with the job offer. He drew in a breath and typed out a response.

No. Not a peep.

Hawkins pressed send.

The typing bubbles at the bottom of the screen bobbed up and down as Cruttwell wrote a reply. Thirty seconds later a new message popped up.

You're sure the conversation with Steyn went well?

Hawkins had been asking himself the same question. He'd replayed the chat in his mind several times, searching for something that could have been taken the wrong way. Some inconsistency in his cover story that might have caused Kettler's antennae to twitch. Couldn't think of anything.

So maybe there had been another problem. Something unrelated to his airport-lounge interview with Steyn. An external factor, beyond his control. Possibly Kettler had already hired someone else for the job. Someone from the old troop. Or perhaps he'd changed his mind about the mission and called the whole thing off. He might have been fed intelligence by someone on the inside. *You've been compromised. Vauxhall knows what you're planning to do.* Equally, the buyer might have got cold feet. Or they might have wanted to renegotiate the terms of the deal. Any number of things could have scuppered the op.

In which case I'm back to square one. Jobless and broke. Another Regiment dinosaur chucked onto the dunghill of life.

Hawkins wrote back:

The meeting was fine. Nothing bad. S said he'd speak to K.
He sounded hopeful. That was it.

Hawkins sent the message. Then he added, hastily:

Should I chase S? Find out what's going on?

The typing bubbles joggled again. Hawkins waited. Sixty seconds later the reply came through from Cruttwell.

Absolutely not. Do not pester him under ANY circumstances.
We sit tight and wait. Do not fuck this one up. Understood?

Hawkins could almost hear the venom in Cruttwell's voice. He quickly replied:

Fine. I'll let you know.

He sent the message, closed down the app. Entered the code into the calculator app again and pressed the equals function. The display reverted back to the ordinary home screen. The one with the picture of Zoe smiling on her fourteenth birthday. He took a quick shower, threw on his 5.11s and a clean shirt. Resigned himself to another day of drudgery at the car showcase. Close protection for a high-end car. The ultimate humiliation. He suddenly felt the need for a stiff drink.

Hawkins snatched up his room keycard and phone and made for the door, levering the door handle. He was about to step outside when his handset vibrated.

He stopped on the threshold, frowning at the digits glowing on the screen. Unknown number. Hawkins recognised the first two digits. An international caller. The plus sign, followed by '27'.

The country code for South Africa.

Hawkins stepped back from the door. Closed it.

He retreated into the room, swiped his index finger lengthwise across the screen. Heard a beat of dead air on the other end of the line.

'Hello?' Hawkins said.

'Geordie, bra,' a familiar voice said. 'It's Rory.'

Anticipation twinged in his guts. This was it. The call he had been waiting for. He forced himself to reply chummily to Steyn.

Playing the role of a guy on the downhill slope of life. Someone who had lost their pride a long time ago.

I should be buttering Steyn up. Trying to be best mates with him, doing anything that might help get me on the team.

'Listen, bra, I've spoken to the boss,' Steyn said after a few minutes of aimless chit-chat.

'OK,' Hawkins replied, just to fill the silence.

'He's not a guy who makes decisions in a hurry. Likes to recce the terrain before he commits his troops. Had to check some stuff out first. That's why I couldn't get back to you before now.'

Hawkins said nothing. Steyn paused to clear his throat. Hawkins felt like a contestant on a second-rate talent show, waiting for the judges' verdict.

'Long story short, you're on. You're on the team, bra.'

Relief flooded through Hawkins's veins. 'That's fucking brilliant news, mate.' He remembered his cover story and added, hastily, 'You're a legend, doing this for me. I'll owe you massively after this one. I can't thank you enough.'

'Listen, the boss man wants you to get down here. Pretoria. Things are moving fast.'

'Fine by me,' Hawkins said. He wasn't keen on sticking around Ventanola for a moment longer than necessary.

Steyn continued: 'There's a flight from Bologna tomorrow morning. Six-thirty. KLM. Connection at Schiphol. Short layover, then a straight hop down to Joburg. Gets in at dead-on ten o'clock tomorrow evening. Book yourself onto that one. Got it?'

Hawkins was about to agree, then checked himself. He said, 'I can't afford the fare. I told you before, I'm flat fucking broke. You're gonna have to front me the money.'

'Wait one.'

There was a long pause. Hawkins heard muffled voices in the background. More than one of them. Steyn was presumably checking in with someone else. Kettler, maybe. Someone higher up the chain of command. Then Steyn came back on the line.

'Right, this is what we'll do. We'll put your ticket on the company credit card. Send us your details and a scan of your passport, I'll sort everything at our end.'

Hawkins thanked him again.

'Don't mention it. Just get your arse on that plane tomorrow morning, bra. I'll wait for you at the terminal. Then we'll go and meet the big man.'

Eight

For the second time in four days, Hawkins travelled in style on someone else's dime. He checked out of the hotel in Ventanola at four-thirty in the morning. Took a prepaid taxi to Bologna Guglielmo Marconi Airport and caught the six-thirty short haul KLM to Amsterdam. Two hours later he touched down at Schiphol. He pissed away half an hour at a garishly lit pub, scrolling through the news on his phone while he grazed on a plate of lukewarm eggs and bacon washed down with mugs of foul-tasting coffee. The headlines were dominated by the situation in Iran. The President's deadline was edging closer. Five days had passed since Farrell had issued his public threat to the Ayatollah. *We're looking at sending in the B-2s. It's on the table. Everything depends on the Iranians now.* Defence correspondents and military experts were being wheeled out to discuss what the President might do. The consensus seemed to be that Farrell was bluffing. Acting the madman. Some sort of last-minute compromise would be reached, the experts confidently asserted, allowing both sides to back down without losing face. Hawkins wasn't so sure. The hawks in Farrell's cabinet would be whispering in his ear. Urging him to act now, before it was too late. Telling him that if they did nothing, Iran would get its hands on a nuclear bomb. The nightmare scenario.

We have a small window of opportunity, sir. Either we do this now, or we're looking at all-out war.

Which would influence the decisions being made in Iran. Their generals would be accelerating their plan to remove the uranium from Fordow. Straining every sinew to beat Farrell's deadline. A rush job. Mistakes would get made. Security protocols would be overlooked. *That could work in our favour,* Hawkins thought.

At nine-thirty he settled the bill and made his way to the gate for the onward flight to Johannesburg. He boarded a commercial airliner three times the size of the short-haul hopper and dropped into a reclining seat with more legroom than the average London studio flat. A stewardess with immaculate white teeth sauntered over and handed him a complimentary flute of champagne and a menu curated by a Michelin-starred chef.

Hawkins had spent a lifetime slumming it in cattle class, on the rare occasions he could actually afford to fly. He decided he could get used to this.

The attendants went through the usual pre-flight routine, the twin turbofan engines howled as they rocketed along the runway. A few minutes later they were clawing their way through the grey clouds blanketing the skies above Amsterdam.

Hawkins quaffed champagne, flicked through the crap movies on offer on the entertainment system. He gave up and turned his mind back to the conversation with Steyn the previous evening.

The boss man wants you to get down here. Things are moving fast.

Ten days until Farrell's deadline. But Kettler would have to strike before then. Because the Iranians were operating on a different timetable. Six expected Tehran to make the transfer soon. Between six and eight days from now. The team would need a full day to fly out from Pretoria and move into position. Maybe longer. Which gave them only a few days to plan a complex military operation. Tough, but not impossible. In Iraq the lads sometimes had to plan an op while they were on the choppers and heading out towards a target.

This also explained why Kettler had brought an unknown quantity into the team at short notice. Because he was working against the clock. If he was going to carry out the job, he needed manpower. Tier One operators. Guys with a track record of performing to a high level, who wouldn't baulk at the prospect of nicking a shit ton of uranium.

Kettler would have taken a deep dive into his background. He would have learned about Hawkins's multiple tours in Iraq and Afghanistan. The rescue op in Baghdad. The death of his younger brother, Jacob, on winter selection. Hawkins's assault on the bullying instructor responsible. How the head shed had turned him into a Regiment outcast, banishing him from the camp. The wasted years up in Manchester, sitting behind a desk and instructing the TA SAS squadron, before he had finally left to work in the private defence sector. His troubles at DeepSpear.

All of it painting a picture of an SAS hero who had been stiffed by a system that despised him, and guys like him. The ideal candidate for the job.

Five days ago, he thought, *I was drinking myself to death.*

Now I'm flying out to meet a shadowy ex-Regiment legend.

The lights dimmed. Around him the other business-class passengers reclined in their seats or settled back to watch the shows on their phones or tablets. Hawkins popped in his earphones, dug out the false-screen phone and jumped onto the Wi-Fi. He didn't read much, but he was a big fan of podcasts. Anything to do with military history. He was currently halfway through a series on the Napoleonic Wars. A couple of middle-aged blokes talking for three-plus hours about the Peninsula campaign and the march on Moscow. His kind of thing. Epic battles, the fates of nations decided by men on the ground. Hawkins felt like he could listen to them all day.

Nine hours later he landed in Johannesburg.

* * *

Steyn was waiting for him in the arrivals hall. Hawkins caught sight of him as he emerged from baggage collection behind the other weary travellers. The squat South African with the horseshoe moustache was standing next to a shuttered kiosk, a short distance away from the loose knot of scruffy-looking chauffeurs with their meet-and-greet signs and beaming smiles.

Next to Steyn stood the biggest guy Hawkins had ever seen.

The guy stood at about six-six or six-seven. Hard black muscles bulged beneath an olive-green T-shirt the size of a circus tent. His legs were as wide as a couple of Corinthian columns. Steyn looked tiny next to him. Like Goliath had paired up with David for a tag-team wrestling match. Hawkins made straight for them, shook hands with Steyn. The latter gestured towards his giant companion.

'This is Moussa. He's with the team. Eritrean. Served with the boss man in the Emirates. He ran one of the mercenary outfits working for the sheikhs.'

Hawkins had heard stories about the mercenary battalions. Western security contractors tasked with bringing in guys from Sudan, Eritrea and Chad. Young men shaped by constant war and hardship. Once in-country the new recruits were put through a training package run by the contractors before being sent out to fight in proxy wars in Libya and Yemen. A way for the sheikhs to exert their influence without getting their own hands dirty. That line of work seemed to fit with the Kettler mythos.

He's a big deal these days, Steyn had told him back at Heathrow. *Lots of fingers in lots of pies. Very well connected.*

He turned his attention to Moussa. The guy was a genetic freak. Like something out of a superhero comic book. His fingers were the size of mortar rockets; his biceps were like sets of kettle bells stuffed in a hessian sack. Tiny dark eyes studded the immense granite face, like openings in a carved wooden mask. A pinkish scar ran zigzaggedly down his cheek.

'All right, mate,' Hawkins said.

Moussa stared at him but made no reply.

'The big man don't say much,' Steyn remarked. He glanced quickly at Moussa. The look in his eyes told Hawkins that Steyn didn't like him.

'This way,' Steyn said, motioning towards the exit.

They stepped out into the cool darkness. A gentle breeze blew in, thrusting through Hawkins's hair as he followed Steyn and Moussa towards a mud-spattered Toyota Land Cruiser ZX. Hawkins deposited his holdall in the boot and hauled himself into the front passenger seat while Steyn jumped behind the wheel. Moussa somehow crammed his frame into the middle row. The guy was so big the smooth dome of his skull was pressed against the roof.

There was an AK-47 rifle shoved barrel-down into the footwell near the gearstick. 'Protection,' said Steyn. 'In case anyone jumps us at a red light. Happens more than you'd think.'

Steyn fired up the engine, reversed out of the spot and pulled away from the terminal building. He took a circuitous route out of the airport before they mounted the five-lane freeway shuttling them north through a sprawl of industrial sites and stockyards.

Steyn liked to talk. When he wasn't speaking, he would hum along to the country music on the radio, drumming his fingers on the steering wheel. He was the kind of guy who had to always be emitting some sort of noise. Like some sort of condition. Hawkins braced himself for a long journey.

Moussa didn't say a word. He just stared out at the flat, featureless veldt ribboning the freeway. The brightly lit scrapyards and rubbish-strewn verges.

Steyn said, 'The boss is keen to meet you. I'll introduce you as soon as we get to his place. The other lads are already there.'

'How many on the team?'

'Six in total. Me, you, Moussa. Three other blokes. Foreigners. Good lads. You'll get on well with them, I reckon.'

'Kettler isn't going on the op?'

'He doesn't go on any of them now. Age is catching up with him. That's why he needs us young bucks. We do all the heavy lifting.'

Hawkins said, 'Can you tell us anything about the job?'

He was feigning ignorance. Acting like he had no idea what Kettler was planning. Sticking to his cover story. The hard-up Brit grateful for an opportunity to get his creditors off his back.

'Sorry, bra,' Steyn replied. 'Sworn to secrecy. Orders from the boss man. He wants this one locked up tighter than a witch's tit. He'll explain everything at the briefing tomorrow. But it's going to be big. We're gonna get rich, bra.'

A broad grin split Steyn's brutal face. Like an axe biting into wood.

'Once this is done you might want to think about moving down here, Geordie. Get the fuck out of rainy Britain. Buy up a place in one of the estates round this way. I've got a mate who can get you a good deal. We could end up as neighbours.'

Hawkins thought: *I'd rather peel my eyelids off than live next door to you, you cunt.*

He said, 'I'm grateful, mate. Really.'

'You should be.' Steyn picked his nose. 'It wasn't easy to swing this one with the boss. He had his doubts.'

'About me?'

Steyn nodded. 'The boss is concerned about leaks. He doesn't trust anyone right now. He wasn't thrilled about the idea of bringing in an outsider. Said you might be working for someone else, for all we know.'

Hawkins was silent for a beat. Working himself up into a confected rage.

He said, 'If your man Kettler has got a problem, he can come and talk to me. I'll soon set him straight. We served in the Regiment at the same time, for fuck's sake. We might not be mates but he'll know my reputation. He'll know what those cunts did to me. Why the hell would I help the system that fucked me over?'

'Hey, I'm on your side, bra.'

Hawkins snorted and said, angrily, 'Maybe this was a mistake. If your boss doesn't trust me then I'm better off heading back home.'

'Fuck that, bra. You're here, aren't you? I got you on the team. Took a while but I won the boss round. That's all that matters now.'

Hawkins fell quiet as they rolled on through the darkness, hoping his faked outrage had quelled any doubts Steyn might be having. But Steyn wasn't the big problem. From what the guy had told him, Kettler was paranoid. On edge. Hawkins would have to tread carefully from now on. Very carefully. Kettler would be keeping a close eye on him. Watching his every move. The slightest mistake and he'd end up taking a bullet between the eyes.

One thing's for sure.

This job just got a lot more dangerous.

Nine

They continued north out of Kempton Park. Steyn kept the Land Cruiser bowling along for eight miles before he de-ramped from the motorway near a place called Irene. Then the landscape shifted, and they shuttled north-east along a nearly empty road flanked by parcels of gently rolling farmland, pale grey beneath the pallid moonlight. Clusters of lights glowed on the horizon. Private estates, Steyn explained. Gated communities where the wealthy inhabitants of Pretoria lived in a luxury daydream. He was planning to move there himself once the op was done.

Steyn hung a left at a T-junction, flying through the red lights. He turned right at the next intersection. The road broadened again, as if it was exhaling. They were gliding through the eastern fringes of Pretoria now, past the concrete shells of unfinished apartment blocks, the two-metre-high brick walls topped with razor wire and security cameras. Beyond them Hawkins glimpsed the terracotta roofs of large villas, half-hidden behind screens of cypress trees and giant palms. Rough tracks straddled the grass verges; billboards advertised the services of private security firms, golf estate memberships. Others carried the smiling faces of real estate agents promising to find Hawkins's dream home.

After another mile Steyn abruptly veered off the main road, rolling down an unpaved track leading into an unlit slum. Hawkins looked questioningly at Steyn.

'Where the fuck are you taking us, mate?'

'Got to make a quick pit stop. Get in the entertainment for tonight. Then we'll be on our way again. Won't take long. The estate's only a couple of minutes away from here.'

'Entertainment?' Hawkins repeated.

'You'll see.' Steyn grinned slyly and nodded at the glovebox. 'Do us a favour. There are a couple of pistols in there. Get them out. One for you and one for the big fucker in the back.'

Hawkins popped open the compartment. He retrieved a pair of semi-automatics nestled inside. Vektor SP1s. South African pieces. Nine-millis, chambered for the 9x19mm Parabellum round. Fifteen bullets to a clip. A solid tool. Not much stopping power, but enough to wound or temporarily force a target to take cover.

Hawkins passed the second weapon back to Moussa and thought: *A long in the footwell, two pistols.*

A lot of hardware. But understandable. They were driving into a slum in one of the most dangerous cities in the world. They wouldn't want to take any chances.

Steyn kept the Toyota to under twenty per as he steered down the rutted dirt track. Hawkins stared out of the window at the teeming jumble of tin-roofed dwellings, many constructed from plastic or bits of cardboard. Some looked like they were about to collapse. In the glare of the headlamps Hawkins saw bedraggled figures rooting through an ocean of rubbish. Scrawny goats searched for food amid the tangle of scrap metal, discarded water bottles and worn car tyres. Chickens pecked at the dirt. Men sat on upturned beer crates, smoking cigarettes while they stared at their phones. Toddlers squatted in the doorways of flimsy shacks, playing with sticks or just staring at the white faces rolling past in the Land Cruiser. A rancid smell of raw sewage seeped in through the vents, filling the wagon.

Not a slum.

An inner circle of hell.

'Everyone calls it "Little Zimbabwe",' Steyn said, giving Hawkins the grand tour of human despair. 'They all come down from Harare looking for work in the compounds. Place is a shithole. No running water, no electricity. Every so often a fire breaks out and half the shacks burn down. Then you've got the gangs pissing bullets at each other. Kids getting plugged in the crossfire. Cops won't come near the place. Life is cheap here, bra.'

They carried on down a maze of narrow tracks lined with rusting old bangers and brightly painted shipping containers housing barbershops and phone repair businesses and grocery stores. Steyn seemed to know where he was going, which made Hawkins think he knew Little Zimbabwe pretty well.

They came to a stop on the corner of a muddied street, next to a crumbling shack with sheets of plastic taped over the exposed windows. Nearby, a trio of underfed kids in football shirts played next to a pile of rubble. On the other side of the road stood a one-storey breeze-block building with sturdy metal bars on the door and a sign painted above the entrance: 'No. 1 Best Cosmetics'.

Three women stood beside the shop, clutching handbags and chewing gum. They had the look of street prostitutes, Hawkins thought. With a pimp lurking somewhere nearby, he assumed, making sure that they didn't fleece him. One of them wore a red latex skirt and a puffer jacket. Next to her stood a petite big-boned woman in leopard-print leggings and a patterned plunge blouse.

The third woman was younger than the others. And stunningly beautiful. The kind of face you only ever saw on the cover of fashion mags or adverts for designer perfume brands. She was dressed in a pair of dark leather trousers and a tight-fitting red crop-top. Her colourful braided hair ran down past her shoulders.

Steyn buzzed down his window, beckoned to the three women loitering across the street. The short, well-built woman in the tight-fitting leopard-print leggings glanced quickly at her two companions before she sauntered over to the Toyota.

'Best whores in South Africa, bra,' Steyn said, pointing them out. 'Cheap as you like, and they let you do anything you want to them. Anything at all.' Steyn grinned again. 'You'll need to wear a rubber, though. These girls put all kinds of shit in their bodies.

Best not to go into battle without the right armour on. Know what I mean, bra?'

Hawkins kept his mouth shut.

Anger pounding between his temples.

We're supposed to be preparing for a highly dangerous op. And these idiots are more interested in getting a load of whores in for the night.

A moment later Leopard Print drew to a halt next to the driver-side door. She leaned in, arms resting on the beltline, her ample dark mounds visible beneath the cut of her blouse. Her fingernails were as long as claws and painted various shades of green. A strong scent of cheap perfume violated Hawkins's nostrils.

'What you want, boy?' Leopard Print asked Steyn, chewing her gum loudly.

'Take a wild guess, sweetheart. Get in the wagon. You and the others.'

'It's gonna cost you more this time. For the extras.'

'How much?'

'Double the normal price. Five thousand rand each. OK?'

'Fine. I'll square it with the boss. Five thou a piece. Get in.'

Leopard Print glanced over her shoulder at the others. Gesturing to them. The woman in the red latex skirt approached the Toyota, but the younger woman with the rainbow braids stayed still, watching her friends.

'Her, too,' Steyn said. Pointing a finger at Braids. 'We want that one.'

Leopard Print clicked her tongue. 'She doesn't want to come. Not after last time. She's afraid.'

'That's too bad. Tell her to get a fucking move on. We ain't got all night.'

Leopard Print called out to Braids. A brief exchange followed. Braids shook her head forcefully and stood her ground, arms folded defiantly across her chest.

Steyn glanced at Moussa in the rear-view. A knowing look passed between them. An unspoken order. Moussa unfolded himself from the back row of the Land Cruiser, stuffed the nine-milli down the waistband of his trousers, stalked across the street.

Towards Braids.

One of the kids playing football caught sight of Moussa and pointed him out to his two friends. Shouting something Hawkins didn't catch. All three of them abandoned their game and scuttled into the nearest alleyway, yelling at the tops of their voices. As if they were afraid of Moussa.

The giant Eritrean grabbed hold of Braids by her skinny arm. She started to scream for help. Moussa struck her hard across the face, silencing her. He dragged her back over to the Toyota, Braids whimpering and pleading with him.

In the next moment a throaty voice split the air. A podgy guy burst out of the doorway of the shack next to the cosmetics store, pointing and yelling at Moussa. Charging over to him. The pimp, Hawkins guessed. Protesting at the attempted theft of his merchandise. Moussa shoved the hooker towards the Toyota, spun round and dropped the pimp with a hard drive to the torso. Liver shot. The quickest way to end a fight. The pimp folded at the waist and dropped to the ground like a collapsing push puppet.

Moussa gave his back to the pimp. He marched back over to Braids, wrenched open the rear passenger-side door on the Land Cruiser, levered the middle row of seats forward, shoved her roughly into the back. Leopard Print and Latex Skirt both stood frozen for a moment. Then they saw the pitiless expression stamped on Moussa's face and climbed into the wagon, dropping into the seats beside Braids.

Moussa pulled the door shut. Planted himself on the row in front of the hookers. Steyn floored the pedal, the Toyota shot forward, gaining speed as they shuddered over loose gravel and potholes the size of T-rex footprints.

They carried on in a broad northerly direction through the slum. Two minutes they turned back onto the main road, continued east then south out of Pretoria.

Steyn said, 'We're gonna have some fun with these ones tonight. You're in for a treat, Geordie.'

'Not for me, mate,' said Hawkins. 'Not my bag.'

Steyn gave him a funny look. 'Something wrong, bra?'

'It could have gone noisy back there,' Hawkins said through gritted teeth. 'It wasn't necessary.'

Steyn laughed. 'No one would have laid a finger on us. Because of him.'

He indicated Moussa in the rear-view.

'All the locals are terrified of the bloke,' Steyn went on. 'Think he's a jinn or something. They've got another name for it, though.'

'Why the fuck would they think that?' Hawkins asked.

'These people believe all kinds of stupidity. Shamans, healers. Ghosts. Folklore stuff. The gang leaders are afraid of him too. Trust me, we were safe as houses back there.'

Hawkins stared out of the window, fuming at the stupidity of Steyn. Driving into the slum had been a senseless act of bravado. He decided he would have to keep a close eye on the rest of the team. They were clearly lacking in discipline. That was usually why ops went wrong, in his experience. Guys got slack. They took their eyes off the ball. Thought with their little heads instead of their big ones. They made mistakes, neglected the minor details. The difference between surviving a mission and getting double-tapped. When you were operating at the tip of the military spear, you needed to have your soldier's hat on twenty-four-seven. Anything less than that and you were asking for trouble.

Hawkins lifted his gaze to the rear-view mirror, looking at the three whores in the back row. Braids stared dead ahead, her face stricken with terror.

Steyn drove south for two kilometres. He took the next left, steered down a wide ribbon of tarmac lined with neat grass verges and pillared with leafy palms. Bare jacaranda branches interlaced above the street, forming a nearly continuous arch. Like rib vaulting in a cathedral. Every hundred metres they passed a prefabricated pillbox with a couple of uniformed guards milling about in front of it.

They carried on for a kilometre. Then Steyn took a right turn and the landscape shifted once more. The road degraded. The streetlamps disappeared. Isolated farmhouses and steel wire-mesh fencing replaced the rows of luxury properties. In a matter of minutes they had gone from the high-end suburbs to semi-rural Pretoria. Further on Steyn crossed a beam bridge running over a slow-moving river, thirty metres wide. Several dark shapes, some of them four or five metres long, dozed on the sandy bank, faintly illuminated by the moonlight. Hawkins craned his neck, straining to get a good view of them as they passed over.

'Is that what I think it is?' he asked.

Steyn said, 'Nile crocodiles. Get shitloads of them in these parts. Don't see them much at this time of year, though.'

'Why not?'

'It's our winter, bra. They're cold-blooded. When it's warm enough they'll bask on the banks. Spend the rest of their time sheltering in their burrows.'

They drove on for five hundred metres before Steyn stopped in front of a galvanised steel gate with a pair of eagle statues mounted on the stone pillars either side. Kettler's mansion, Steyn said. Once owned by one of South Africa's richest men. Multi-layered security system, he added. Doing the hard sell. Security cameras, guard dogs, back-up generator system, panic rooms. Seismic sensors dotted along the perimeter to detect any attempts to burrow under the defences. High-voltage electric wires mounted on top of the wall, ready to fry anyone who tried to scale it.

A pair of guards in drab brown uniforms stepped out of a concrete gatehouse beside the entrance. Both were carrying shoulder-slung longs and belt-holstered pistols.

One of the guards, a skinny guy in a baseball cap, paced over to Steyn's window, scanned the faces inside. He gave Steyn a curt nod, signalled to his colleague. A few beats later the gate opened, the guard stepped back and Steyn pointed the Land Cruiser down a wide tree-lined avenue that climbed towards a low rise in the land. Security lights softly illuminated the grounds either side of the approach. At his left, off to the north, he noticed several manèges and paddocks, along with a stable. Next to it stood a massive barn-like structure.

Steyn noticed his interest and said, 'Indoor riding school.'

'I know,' said Hawkins. Steyn gave him a puzzled look. 'My daughter, she was big into the riding as a kid,' he added by way of explanation. 'Used to take her to lessons in a place outside Hereford.'

'I didn't know you had a daughter.'

'She wasn't a part of my life for a while. Her choice, not mine.'

'Complicated, is it, bra?'

'Something like that, aye.'

Hawkins fell silent again, shutting the conversation down.

To his right, at his three o'clock, fifty metres away, stood a cluster of single-storey bungalows organised in a broad semi-circle around a central outdoor area covered by a thatched roof supported by stout wooden poles. Like a bandstand designed by a Zulu chief.

Two figures sat around the fire-pit, while a third man strode over from the direction of the bar. Hawkins was too far away to make out the guy's face, but something about his gait was oddly familiar.

I've seen that walk somewhere before.

I'm bloody sure of it.

The Land Cruiser neared the crest. There was still no sign of the mansion itself. Just an endless expanse of land merging with the blackness in both directions.

'Fuck me,' Hawkins said. 'How big is this place?'

'Four thousand acres in total. Basement cinema, swimming pool. Tennis courts, clay and hardcourt. Shooting range. Walled garden off to the rear. Boss has even got his own private golf course.'

'Jesus,' Hawkins said. 'I'm in the wrong line of work.'

'Ah, this is nothing compared to the place he's got in Monaco. You should fucking see it. Incredible, bra. Best view of the race-track in the town. Then he's got his apartment in Dubai, his town-house in Chelsea, and the chalet up in Courchevel. For the skiing in winter,' he added, stupidly.

A thought struck Hawkins. 'If he's got this much dough, why is he still running bang-average security jobs?'

Steyn gave a wry smile and said, 'The boss says it's never enough. He always needs more cash.'

Which made sense, Hawkins supposed. If you were moving in the same circles as billionaires, a few hundred million quid might not seem like that much money. You might even start to feel skint. You'd think to yourself: *Life's not fair. I've got this house and that place, but I don't have my own superyacht or my own private jet.* Both of which were unbelievably expensive to run. Or maybe you wanted a bigger penthouse in Dubai. One with a bigger footprint and a better view of the sea. All of a sudden, you needed more money to move up to the next rung on the wealth ladder.

Beyond the rise the drive sloped gently down towards a carriage circle with an ornate water fountain at its centre. Kettler's mansion stood due east of the circle. It was even bigger than Hawkins had imagined. Like a palace. Or something out of a fairy tale. It made the clubhouse in London look like a corner shop. Greek columns as tall as wind turbines supported the porticoed entrance. A pair of white-stuccoed wings extended either side of the central block, each one roughly the size of an Amazon warehouse.

To the left, twenty metres away, was a separate two-storey garage. Steyn pointed to it and said, 'That's where the boss keeps his supercar collection. He's got a dozen of them in there. Bentleys, Lotuses. All sorts. Rare models. Worth a fucking fortune. A big one.'

Hawkins said, 'How many guys on security here?'

'Six. Them two you saw at the front, two more on patrol in the grounds. Two more to cover the rear. Working in twelve-hour shifts. Plus you've got the chefs, gardeners, stable hands and maids. Total staff of twenty-eight, plus a few irregulars. You see what I mean about the money?'

Hawkins pretended to feel sympathetic towards a rich bastard suffering his own cost-of-living crisis. 'A lot of salaries to cover. Must be hard.'

'Like I said. The boss thinks he's never rich enough. He's always looking out for the next big payday.'

They steered clockwise round the turning circle, pulled up next to the steps leading up to the grand entrance. Hawkins debussed, fetched his holdall from the boot. Moussa ordered the hookers to get out.

A lean figure emerged from the mansion, puffing on a stubby cigar as he trotted down the steps. He was tall and severe-looking, decked out in a pair of beige trousers, a matching jacket over a plain polo.

Hawkins recognised Lance Kettler immediately. He knew the face. He'd seen the guy around the camp at Hereford on a few occasions, and although that had been nearly ten years ago Kettler still had the same wiry physique, the same hard features. But the neck had started to sag, liver spots corroded the weatherbeaten face. Grey streaks now jetted the cropped dark hair and wispy goatee. A Richard Mille watch worth more than Hawkins's lifetime earnings girded his left wrist.

Kettler stepped forward, wedged the cigar between his teeth as he greeted Steyn and Moussa. He glanced disapprovingly at the hookers, then shifted his gaze towards Hawkins. Hooded eyes looked him up and down. There was something about him that reminded Hawkins of a bird sizing up its prey. He flashed a quick, cold smile, revealing a set of immaculate white teeth.

'You must be Hawkins,' Kettler said. He had a strange accent; South African hardness fused with English public schoolboy formality. Probably a result of his years of service with the British Army. Like all Ruperts, he was in the habit of referring to men by their surnames. 'I've heard a great deal about you. Call me boss.'

Hawkins shook the offered hand. A brisk, businesslike handshake, conveying the impression of an important man with heavy demands on his time and a lack of tolerance for frivolity. Kettler swivelled his hawk-like gaze towards Steyn.

'Make sure none of those fuckers go anywhere near the house,' he said. He didn't look at the women, but the implication was readily understood by all. 'Is that understood?'

'Yes, boss,' Steyn replied meekly. 'Don't worry. We'll keep them away.'

'Good.' He took a long draw on the cigar. Tapped ash onto the ground. The hooded eyes skated back towards Hawkins.

'Come with me, Hawkins,' Kettler said. 'I want to show you something. Moussa will take your luggage.'

An order, dressed up in the language of a polite request.

'OK, boss,' Hawkins said.

He passed the leather holdall to the Eritrean, who took it and promptly set off with Steyn and the hookers down the flagstoned path leading towards the semi-circle of bungalows and the thatched-roof bar a hundred metres to the south.

Kettler had already started back up the steps, moving along at a fast clip, cloud of cigar smoke trailing in his wake. Kettler had been out of the army for six years, but he still had the bearing of a Rupert. Confident, brisk stride. No-nonsense attitude. Like an officer on the Western Front, preparing to lead his men across no-man's land. Hawkins had met guys like him before in the Regiment. They were the ones who invited you round to their home for a glass of sherry, then told you to light up the wood-burner as if you were nothing more than a lowly servant.

Hawkins caught up with Kettler as they approached the entrance. Three hours since his last glug of booze on the flight. God, he needed a drink. He wondered if Kettler had a wine cellar. Or a collection of fine whiskies.

Right now, anything will do.

'You'll be quartered in the guest accommodation, of course, with the other chaps,' Kettler continued, waving a hand in the direction of the bungalows.

He didn't give an explanation, but Hawkins guessed it had something to do with the twenty-eight members of staff. A lot of ears potentially eavesdropping in on private conversations. Especially if you were worried that the CIA or MI6 might have planted someone in your inner circle. Better to have the discussions off-site. Somewhere well away from the domestic workforce.

'I'm afraid the chefs have finished for the day,' Kettler went on. 'But if you're hungry speak to the bar staff. They can rustle something up for you in the kitchen.'

Hawkins nodded along, though he had no appetite. He had been sitting on his backside for the past sixteen hours. One of the rules he tried to live by: only replace what you've burnt off. A rule that had kept him in reasonable nick, despite the years of hard drinking.

They swept through the doorway and moved down a dome-ceilinged atrium. A chandelier festooned in diamonds loomed over the main space. Like a UFO making its final descent. Two grand staircases on either side of the space ran up towards the first-floor landing. There was a living room off to the left, a dining room to his right, both decorated with antique furniture and gold-leafed wallpaper. Hawkins was getting definite Versailles vibes.

Kettler pushed further down the hall until he stopped outside an open doorway.

'My office,' Kettler said, motioning for Hawkins to enter.

Hawkins stepped into the study, wondering what the fuck Kettler was so eager to show him. A fearful thought flashed across his mind. What if Kettler had uncovered his links with Vauxhall? What if they had lured Hawkins to the compound to torture him? He swiftly dismissed that possibility. Aside from Cruttwell and Jackson, no one else knew about the op.

So why has Kettler brought me here?

Hawkins looked round the room. There was a walnut desk at the far end of the space, bare except for a laptop and a thin stack of papers. An executive swivel-chair behind it. In one corner he spotted a mid-century reading chair, a teak sidebar with a whisky decanter, a couple of glasses on a drinks tray.

Then Hawkins noticed the photographs.

The walls were covered with them. Hundreds of snaps. Most of them featured Kettler meeting with various dignitaries. Hawkins recognised some of the faces – lesser members of the royal family, Cabinet ministers, a couple of undistinguished former Prime Ministers. In some of the photos Kettler was pictured with a dark-haired woman about his age. His wife, Hawkins assumed.

Kettler set his half-smoked cigar down on a glass ashtray, poured himself a whisky. He didn't offer Hawkins a drink. Didn't reach for the other glass. Instead he walked right up to a group of shots showing Kettler in army gear. Presumably dating from his time in the Regiment. He made a broad sweeping gesture with his right arm.

'Recognise any of these chaps?'

Hawkins moved closer, raking his eyes over the faces in the snaps. He pointed out a framed shot of Kettler standing in front of a dusty track. Mountains in the background. Afghanistan. Kettler and another man looking stern-faced towards the camera, both kitted out with swept-back helmets, modified weaponry, Crye Precision combat trousers and jackets. The other guy was gripping a GPMG. Otherwise known as the General-Purpose Machine Gun. The weapon favoured by SAS men over several decades.

Hawkins said, 'I know this fella. That's Peter Woodruff-Hill. He was in G Squadron.' He jabbed a finger at a face in another photo. 'This one here is Jonty Hillard. He was in A Squadron. He went on to become OC after I left.'

Kettler nodded. 'Both good friends of mine. Although Jonty is no longer at Hereford. Works in Whitehall now. Next in line to become DSF now, actually.'

DSF. *Director Special Forces*, thought Hawkins. The person in overall charge of UK SF. One of the most senior figures in the British army. *Bloody hell. Steyn was right. This guy has got more connections than Network Rail.*

'You were in D Squadron, I believe,' said Kettler.

'That's right,' Hawkins replied.

'Who was your commander?'

'Depends what year you're talking about, boss. When I joined it was Simpson-Purcell. Then he left and Drake-Thomas took over. When I left it was Stanforth-Lee.'

A lot of double-barrelled names, thought Hawkins.

A lot of rich bastards.

Kettler said, 'Oh, I know Drake-Thomas. I bump into him at the Jockey Club occasionally. Lovely chap. Simpson-Purcell went into politics, you know. Serves as an ambassador. Somewhere in the east. I forget which country. Stanforth sits on the board of one of the defence giants these days. Developing the next generation of underwater drones, I gather. Doing rather well for himself.'

'Good for him,' Hawkins said.

Christ, I really could do with a drink.

'Do you stay in touch with any of them?' asked Kettler.

'Me?' Hawkins laughed. 'No chance, boss. They're in a different social world to me. Different solar system.'

'I see. Well, they're all good friends of mine.'

Kettler stared meaningfully at him.

So that's why he brought me here, Hawkins realised. Kettler was demonstrating his credentials. Establishing dominance. A way of telling Hawkins: *I'm a serious player. I move in the same circles as the big beasts.*

If you're loyal to me, I can make things happen for you.

Try to fuck with me, and I'll bury you alive.

Kettler seemed to lose interest in him. As if Hawkins had disappointed him somehow. He glanced at his Richard Mille and said, 'It's rather late. I imagine you're pretty shagged out. Can you find your way back to the bungalows?'

'Aye, boss. I know the way.'

'Good man. You'll find the rest of the guys there. Beers and braai, that's their metier. Yours too, I should think.'

Kettler looked at him for what felt like several seconds. Studying Hawkins. As if trying to weigh him up. *Can I trust him, or is he working for the enemy? Is he friend or foe?* Then Kettler abruptly turned and ushered Hawkins out of the room. Escorted him back down the atrium, past the Versailles-tribute décor, towards the entry foyer.

'I'll see you tomorrow morning, then,' Kettler said as he tugged open the main door. 'Operational briefing, nine o'clock sharp. Suggest you get a good night's kip, Hawkins.'

'Roger that, boss.'

The door snicked shut. Hawkins descended the steps, passed the central fountain and started down the paved walkway leading to the guest lodges.

A wave of smoky heat wrapped its arms around Hawkins as he approached the thatched-roof bar. What the South Africans called a lapa. Which was basically an outdoor hangout, somewhere for people to cook, drink and socialise. Outdoor electrical heaters mounted above the tables glowed like branding irons. In one corner a rugby match was showing on a projector screen. The British Lions versus Argentina.

Five guys were seated on a set of rattan chairs close to the fire-pit. They looked on as Red Latex and Leopard Print danced lazily in front of them. Putting on a private show. The third woman, Braids, sat on a sofa, arms crossed in a defensive posture. Steyn had draped an arm around her. His thick Boer voice carried across the lapa as he called out to the two dancers. Making a lewd request.

The three other guys slapped their thighs, roaring.

Foreigners, Steyn had said.

Good lads. You'll get on well with them.

One of the recruits had a sculpted face topped with a wave of sandy-blond hair and eyes so cold you could have frozen meat with them. The second guy was solid and bull-necked, with a rust-coloured beard as long as a spade and sleeves of tattoos running down both forearms.

The third guy had his back to Hawkins.

Ten metres away, a black bloke in a crisp white shirt manned the bar. Rows of high-end spirits on the shelves behind him.

Thank Jesus. A drink. At long bloody last. Hawkins had never been so thirsty in his life.

A second bar worker tended to a brick braai. Coals smouldered in the firebox, searing the T-bone steaks and sausages on the metal grid above. Smoke eddied out of the chimney built into the reed thatching. A smell of grilled meat hung thick in the air.

Steyn caught sight of Hawkins, levered himself up from his chair and lumbered over to the Briton. Moussa stared greedily at Red Latex. Mentally undressing her. She was grinding against Leopard Print now, the men cheering their approval.

Steyn spread his arms wide and said, 'Welcome to the lapa, bra. Party's just getting started. Get you a beer?'

Hawkins didn't reply. His eyes were locked on the fifth figure in the group. The guy who had been sitting with his back to Hawkins. He was on his feet now, turning away from the hookers. Looking towards Hawkins. Ready to greet the latest addition to the team.

He had a grizzled face with a widow's peak of silvery hair. The craggy lines were as deep as trench pits; the glow of the flames reflected in the cruel greying eyes. It was the face of a man who had done terrible things in his life, and might do more in the future, and never lose a moment's sleep over any of it. A man who would cut the throat of his best mate if it added a few zeroes to his bank account.

A face Hawkins knew well. One he had last seen two months ago.

His old mucker.

John Bald.

Ten

Silence hung in the air. Like meat from a hook. Hawkins stood dumbstruck. Bald looked at him with an expression that fell somewhere between surprise and wariness.

'Jock,' Hawkins said. 'What the fuck are you doing here?'

'I could ask you the same question, Geordie,' Bald hit back in his thick Scottish brogue.

Steyn looked from Bald to Hawkins, eyes darting between the two ex-Regiment operators. Realisation slowly dawning on his bovine face. 'You know each other?'

'Aye,' said Hawkins. 'We do.'

Bald didn't reply. At his side, Moussa and the other two recruits had switched their attention to the ex-Blades. Leopard Print and Red Latex had stopped gyrating. They had been deprived of their audience. Braids still sat in a tight defensive posture. She looked afraid.

Steyn said, stupidly, 'I didn't realise you were mates.'

'We were in the Regiment together,' Bald said, keeping his gaze fixed on Hawkins. 'Not for long, mind. Geordie came from a later intake. I was out of there soon after he got his winged dagger beret. Didn't see the cunt for years until we ended up working security together at DeepSpear.'

Hawkins nodded but stayed quiet. Thoughts whirlwinded inside his head. *Is Jock working for Six too? Have they planted him on the team without telling me?*

Hawkins knew how Vauxhall worked. They had form for that sort of thing. They might have decided to hedge their bets. Insert a second man onto the team as an insurance policy, in case the first guy's cover was blown. In which case Six would want to silo their assets, keeping both men in the dark, so that neither would know that the service had put a second plant on the team. That way, if one of them was compromised and tortured, they wouldn't be in a position to expose the other asset. The smart move. But cynical. It had Jackson's fingerprints all over it.

There was another possibility, though. Bald might not be connected to Six at all. He might have joined the team for the money. Hawkins remembered some of the rumours he'd hear from fellow Hereford men. Jock Bald. The hero of the Regiment. A legendary operator who had gone rogue. There had been stories of Bald getting caught up in all kinds of evil shit. Drug-trafficking in South America. Weapon deals with the Albanian mafia. Diamond theft.

Bald didn't give a crap about anyone but himself. That was practically the guy's MO. Someone should chisel that on his gravestone. He wouldn't lose any sleep working for a shifty operator like Kettler.

Hawkins tried to think back to their last conversation. Eight long weeks ago. Back when he still had a future at DeepSpear, and his name was still on the invite list for his daughter's wedding. Before he'd gone on a bender and roughed up the company HR chief. Before his life had gone badly south, and Cruttwell and Jackson had made him an offer he couldn't refuse.

Over a few pints Bald had boasted about landing a new gig on the Circuit. At the time Hawkins hadn't paid much attention. He'd assumed it was more of the same old Jock Bald bollocks. Now the guy was standing in front of him.

Hawkins made a snap decision. He had no way of knowing where Bald's loyalties lay. Of course, Bald might have his own suspicions about Hawkins's presence on the team, but there was nothing he could do about that. He would just have to play it straight. Stick to his cover story. Focus on his own situation and hope for the best.

Steyn beckoned to the other two recruits beside Moussa. The man with the sandy hair and the bigger guy with the inkwork arms and the spade beard. They both stood up. Behind them Leopard Print stood watching the men, hands resting on her wide hips. Red Latex had retrieved her phone from her handbag and was scrolling disinterestedly.

Steyn made the introductions.

'This is Geordie Hawkins,' he said, addressing Bald and the two other recruits. 'He's ex-Hereford. He'll be on the job with us.'

The recruits stared at Hawkins. Making quick and dirty assessments of the new man. Steyn took a pull from his beer and tipped the bottle towards the sandy-haired guy with the frozen blue eyes.

'Geordie, this is Paul Martel,' he carried on. 'German lad. Munich born and bred. Served with the KSK.'

KSK, thought Hawkins. As in: Kommando Spezialkräfte. A relatively new addition to the global SF community. Hawkins had bumped into a few of them during his time in Afghanistan. They were efficient and professional, although some of them held questionable political views. Later on, the KSK had been partly disbanded in an effort to weed out the far-right extremists in the ranks. Not the best SF unit in the world, in his opinion. A step below the lads in Delta and the Regiment. But not the worst, either.

Hawkins muttered a greeting at Martel. The German's lips were curled up into a faint sneer, as if he found something vaguely amusing about the Brit. His face radiated a smug superiority. A quality that came with almost every German SF operator Hawkins had met. Like software preloaded onto a laptop.

Steyn cleared his throat and flapped a hand in the direction of the bull-necked guy with the spade beard and the elaborate arm-ink.

'Terry Devaney,' Steyn said. 'He's worked with us before. Eight years in the Irish Army Ranger Wing, wasn't it, Terry?'

'Nine,' Devaney said. 'Nine years. Eight before that with the Royal Irish.'

He took a step towards Hawkins. His breath reeked of beer. A pair of wild eyebrows slanted down at forty-five degree angles, forming a prominent 'V' above the bridge of his nose. Hawkins took one look at the guy and decided right away he didn't like him.

'Another fucking Brit,' Devaney said with a snarl. 'Just what we need. Can't get rid of you lot, can we? Like fucking cockroaches.'

Hawkins gave him a hard stare. 'Royal Irish? You must know some of the lads taken hostage in Sierra Leone.'

'My brother was with them, as it happens. What of it?'

'You should be thanking us, mate. Our squadron pulled the Irish out of the shit that day. Your brother and all his Paddy cunt mates.'

Devaney's face paled with rage. Steyn cut in before he could reply, slapping the Irishman cheerfully on the back.

'Easy, Terry. Let's keep it friendly, eh? No need for any of that shit.'

Devaney eyeballed Hawkins for a few moments. Getting in the last stony stare. Then he turned and headed back over to the fire-pit, snapping at the hookers.

'What are youse two looking at? Get back to your fucking dancing.'

The hookers resumed their bored routine. Martel and Moussa settled back into their chairs. Making themselves comfortable for the next performance.

'Help yourself to drinks,' said Steyn. 'There's chow going too, bra. Steaks and such. You're in bungalow four, by the way. Your stuff is all in there.'

Steyn returned to his spot next to Martel. Moussa had his arm around Braids, fondling an exposed breast. Bald watched them for a beat, then turned to Hawkins.

'Come on, Geordie. Let's get a drink.'

They swung round the tables, approached the counter. The black guy in the crisp white shirt was busy restocking the beer fridge.

'Whisky,' Bald said, bluntly. 'None of that cheap shite, either,' he added as the barman started to reach for a bottle of bog-standard Kentucky bourbon. 'Give us the stuff on the top shelf, you cheeky fucker. Two large ones.'

The barman reached up and retrieved a bottle of Macallan twenty-five-year-old single malt. He unscrewed the cap, poured a generous measure into a pair of patterned tumblers. Bald snatched up one glass, handed the other to Hawkins.

Hawkins took a sip of his drink. The booze swept through his bloodstream, taking the edge off. Easing his strained nerves.

Bald said, 'What's going on, Geordie? I thought you were still dodging papercuts over at DeepSpear.'

'Not anymore. They kicked us out.'

'Fuck happened?'

Hawkins gave him the same story he'd told Steyn. The drunken scrap outside the pub in St James's. The summons from Tom Gracey the next morning. Gracey's threat to involve the police unless Hawkins agreed to their terms. No pay-off. No notice period. No company pension.

'Those bastards left us with nothing, Jock. I needed money. Ended up taking on a job in Ventanola on crap wages. Had no idea what I was going to do after that. That's when I bumped into Steyn. He said he'd have a word with Kettler about getting us on the team. One thing led to another, and here I am.'

Bald stared intently at him. 'I thought you hated the idea of working on the Circuit. What you told me.'

'I need money. Haven't got a fucking penny to my name.'

Bald snorted his contempt. 'You're a mug, Geordie. I warned you not to stick around that place. Them bods at DeepSpear were just waiting for a chance to get rid. Should have taken a leaf out of my book and played the PTSD card. Bled them fucking dry.'

'It wasn't that easy. I had Zoe to think about. I couldn't just walk.'

Bald saw straight through his lame excuse. 'Bollocks. You're weak, man. Coasting through life instead of sticking up for yourself. Look how that's worked out for you.'

'I don't see you doing much better. We're both in the same boat here.'

'Like fuck we are. This here,' Bald swept his arm in a broad arc across the lapa, 'this is just the icing on the cake for me. Pocket money. I've still got my full pension, my Regiment pension, the tidy sum DeepSpear put in my account when I left. Made for life, son. Never have to work again if I don't want to. You – you're just a sad cunt hoping for a few crumbs from the top table.'

'I made a mistake,' Hawkins said defensively. 'That's all. Could have happened to anyone.'

'No, mate. You're a liability. An ex-Reg pisshead. Should tell your story to the new intakes. Cautionary tale. What happens if you get slack.'

'You're not exactly the poster boy for Dry January yourself.'

'Yeah, but I can handle it. Stomach of iron, son.' Bald patted his rock-hard abs. 'None of that blackout drunk bollocks. Either hold your drink or throw away the bottle.'

'I've got it under control,' Hawkins insisted. 'There's no problem.'

'You'd better fucking hope so. Because if things go Pete Tong on this one, you're on your own. I won't be risking my neck to pull your sorry arse out of the fire. No bloody way.'

'It won't come to that. I've still got what it takes.'

'Doesn't look that way to me, Geordie. Christ, look at the state of you. Are you sure you're up to this job?'

Hot anger simmered in Hawkins's chest. 'You're forgetting something.'

'What's that?'

'I saved your arse back at Coulport. Remember? If it wasn't for me that gunman would have put a hole in your head.'

'Nine months ago,' Bald replied dismissively. 'Ancient history. You've let yourself go since then.'

Hawkins didn't respond. Mostly because he knew Bald had a point. The truth was he'd been slack the past few months. The bouts of heavy drinking. The anger. He could still soldier, because a

Regiment man never forgot those ingrained skillsets. But he'd lost his sharpness. All the hard edges blunted by his lifestyle choices.

On the projector screen, the Lions were celebrating a try. Over by the fire-pit, Braids screamed in protest as Moussa dragged her to her feet. As if he was handling a rag doll. He marched the hooker away from her companions, ignoring her frantic pleas as he shoved her down the separate path leading to the guest quarters, Steyn and Devaney whooping their encouragement. A few moments later Braids and Moussa disappeared inside the nearest bungalow.

Hawkins took another hit of whisky. Part of him hated Bald. The guy could be absolutely ruthless. In his view there was no place for weakness or pity. You were either the person being gutted, or the one sinking the knife into the stomach. But Hawkins respected him on a professional level. Bald knew how to operate better than anyone. Thirty years of hard soldiering had filed down every last trace of softness in the body. The weathered face and cold eyes gave the impression of a man permanently at war with himself and the world around him.

With Jock on the team, we might just stand a chance of pulling this thing off.

A short distance away, Steyn was shouting at Leopard Print and Red Latex. Ordering the two hookers to take their clothes off. Taking the entertainment to the next level. Martel and Devaney hollered in excitement as Leopard Print removed her plunge blouse, revealing a pair of large breasts.

Hawkins heard a noise coming from beyond the lapa. From the direction of Moussa's bungalow. A series of screams and sobs. Piercing the night sky. He looked round but no one else seemed to notice it. They were too busy gawping at Leopard Print's tits.

'How long have you been working with Kettler?' he asked Bald.

'Not long after I quit DeepSpear. One of the lads in G Squadron reached out to us a couple of weeks ago. Said his old troop commander was running a company down this way and looking to put a team together for some sort of job at short notice. Told us that Kettler was in need of a few good lads, but he couldn't confirm the job until closer to the time. He was waiting for a green light from elsewhere. I threw my hat in the ring and got the call six days ago. Took the first plane out.'

Two weeks ago, Hawkins thought. Which meant that Kettler must have been tipped off about the planned movement of the enriched uranium out of Fordow before then. Before President Farrell had announced his deadline. *Nothing is confirmed yet. All options are on the table. We'll make a decision in the next two weeks.*

Hawkins solved another piece of the puzzle he had been building in his head. He remembered the news reports several weeks ago. Talks between the US and Tehran over dismantling Iran's nuclear stockpiles. Discussions had dragged on for months without any signs of progress. The Iranians must have made the decision back then to relocate the uranium. The smart play. Stall for time, plan for the worst-case scenario. Farrell could be an unpredictable foe. Kettler's source would have alerted the South African to the plans at an early stage. *This might be happening. Get a team on standby. I'll let you know as soon as I do.*

'What about the others?' said Hawkins. 'What's their deal?'

'Steyn and Devaney are capable enough. They're solid. Thick as fuck, but they can kick in a door and pull a trigger as well as anyone. Devaney's a bit huffy, but I've worked with worse. A lot fucking worse. We both have.'

'And Martel?'

'Clever. Too clever by half, that one. Thinks the sun shines out of his arse. As for Moussa, he never says a word. The guy's a mute. But I wouldn't pick a fight with him.'

'Do you think they're on the level?'

'Why wouldn't they be?'

Hawkins pursed his lips. 'Steyn reckons Kettler is worried about plants on the team. Any one of this lot might be sharing int with someone else.'

'What for? The job's probably a run-of-the-mill training package. A couple of months on site, teaching Botswana's finest how to shoot straight. No one's going to give a shit about that.'

Hawkins looked carefully at his old colleague. He was thinking about Bald and Six. If Jock had been co-opted by Vauxhall, they would have surely briefed him on the Iran op. But there was no sign of a tell on his face.

So maybe Jock was telling the truth. Maybe he had joined the team for the quick payday. But there was another explanation. *What if Bald is playing the same game as me? Secretly working for MI6 whilst feeding me his cover story, pretending he knows nothing about the mission?*

Bald drained his glass in one gulp. Downing fine Speyside whisky as if it was water. The bartender reached for the bottle to pour him another measure, but Bald raised his palm as if stopping traffic.

'Fuck that. Just give us the bottle, mate.'

The bartender didn't argue. He just handed Bald the Macallan. Two grand of high-end Scotch. Bald said, 'You and your mate can fuck off now. You're finished for the night. Private party. Off you go, sunshine.'

The black guy nodded and called out to his colleague, addressing him in a sing-song dialect. The short bloke working the braai stand hung up the tongs, left the meat sizzling on the grid, joined the barman at the edge of the lapa. The two workers tramped up the dimly lit pathway leading back to the main house.

Leopard Print was fully naked. Red Latex had stripped down to a high-legged lace thong. She toyed playfully with Leopard Print's breasts, caressing a nipple with her pierced tongue while Steyn, Devaney and Martel cheered rowdily.

Hawkins and Bald drank for a while. Trading gossip on old Regiment comrades. Towards one o'clock in the morning Hawkins decided to call it a night. He was wiped out after the long journey from Ventanola. He knocked back the dregs of his drink, unglued himself from the stool, left Bald with the half-empty bottle of Macallan for company. Plodded his way across the lapa towards the path leading to the bungalows.

The screams coming from Moussa's billet had faded to a soft intermittent sobbing, barely audible above the boisterous shouts coming from the other side of the bar.

He knew Bald's style. The guy would have no interest in the sex workers. Not an ethical thing. That word didn't exist in Bald's universe. But given a choice between spending time with a cheap hooker and a fine bottle of Macallan, there was only one winner. He'd sit at the bar until he'd polished off the Scotch. Tomorrow morning he'd roll up for the briefing looking fresh as new paint.

A voice called out to Hawkins.

'Fuck do you think you're going, pal?'

Hawkins stopped. He turned towards the party beside the firepit. He saw Devaney rising to his feet. The Irishman swigged his lager, wiped beery lips with the back of a tattooed forearm and stomped over to Hawkins.

'Party's just getting started,' Devaney said. 'Take a seat. You won't want to miss this shit.'

'Another time,' Hawkins replied. 'I'm off to get my head down.'

'Nah, sod that. Get back here. We're celebrating.'

'I said no,' Hawkins said, more firmly this time.

Devaney knitted his eyebrows together. Drops of beer glistened on the spade beard.

'You got a problem, English?'

'Yeah, I do.' Hawkins threw a hand in the direction of the hookers. Red Latex had slipped off her thong, revealing a patch of dark pubic hair. 'In my world, we celebrate after the op. Not before.'

Devaney glared at him. He wore a face like he'd just swallowed arsenic.

'Who the fuck do you think youse are, telling us what to do?'

'I'm trying to save you from a trip to the clinic. If one of them rubbers bursts, six months from now you'll be losing weight faster than the jab.'

Devaney stepped towards him. 'I ain't having no bastard English tell me what to do.'

The guy was pumped up with drunken aggression. The veins on his neck bulged like anchor cables. His hands were balled into hard fists.

'Got a big family back home?' Hawkins asked.

'None of your fucking business.'

Hawkins shrugged. 'Maybe not. I'm just wondering how many cousins you've got left. Reckon I've dropped more than a few of them down the years.'

He stepped into Devaney's face.

'Carry on like this,' Hawkins said, 'and I'll drop you too.'

Devaney's eyes bulged in their sockets. He trembled with fury. Hawkins was trying to goad the Irishman into attacking him. Then he'd floor the fucker. Claim he was acting in self-defence. Shut him up without jeopardising his place on the team.

Devaney backed down. Some primitive biological instinct at work, warning him off. Fifty thousand years of evolution kicking in. He wheeled away and plodded back over to the hookers, muttering under his breath.

Hawkins made the short trek from the lapa to the bungalows. He found the until with a brushed-brass '4' fitted to the front door, twisted the handle, stepped into a spacious front room. Small kitchen, wet room and bedroom. All of it furnished to a surprisingly high standard. But perhaps not that surprising, on balance.

The guest block would have been designed to put up Kettler's mates whenever they stayed over for the night. They would expect a certain degree of comfort.

Moussa had dumped the leather holdall on the king-sized bed. Hawkins kicked off his boots and did a quick recce. Searching the rooms for any hidden cameras or microphones. He checked the power sockets. Ran his hands under the study table and looked behind the pictures hanging from the wall. He inspected the Wi-Fi hub and speakers, closely examined the light fittings and curtain rods and the corners of the ceiling.

He found nothing.

Hawkins retrieved his false-screen phone. He entered the code to flip over to the private messaging app. Started typing. Considered asking his handlers about Bald. Demand answers. He decided against it. Vauxhall wouldn't level with him, even if Bald was working for them. In the end he settled for a simple two-word note.

I'm in.

He switched the phone back to its normal screen, stuck it on charge. Tried to shut out the black thoughts crowding in on his mind. The ones that always came back to him when he didn't have a drink in his hand.

Jock's right, the voice muttered. *You're a liability.*

Hawkins left the bungalow. The lapa was quiet at this hour, and empty. He could hear a distant chorus of voices from one of the other bungalow as Steyn and Devaney continued their private party with the hookers. He couldn't hear anything at all from Moussa's pad.

He swung round the bar, swiped a bottle of Finnish vodka. Headed back to his lodgings. Seated himself on the armchair in the front room, switched on the TV, tore off the voddie cap.

He drank until the voice had gone silent, until the blackness no longer mattered.

On the news, various defence experts in suits were poring over detailed images of the targets. There was a big debate over the B-2 bombs. Whether they were capable of destroying the nuclear sites. A fifty-fifty chance of success, one expert claimed. Parts of the infrastructure at Fordow were located deep underground. Too deep even for the bunker-busters to penetrate. They might only cause limited damage to the facility. A minor setback to Tehran's nuclear dreamland.

His tired mind drifted back to the mission. Stealing uranium from under the noses of the Iranians. A dangerous assignment. Any number of things could go wrong. The team might get cut down in the assault. Or killed during their escape. They might be betrayed, or captured by the enemy.

Which would be the worst of all outcomes, Hawkins reflected. The interrogators in the Iranian Revolutionary Guard would show them no mercy. There would be no one coming to rescue them, despite what Cruttwell had told him back at the clubhouse. No cavalry to bring them back home. He hoped to fuck Kettler had a good plan.

Otherwise we'll be heading to our deaths.

Eleven

The next morning, a few minutes before nine o'clock, Hawkins left his bungalow. He beat a path towards the lapa, his eyes gritty from lack of sleep, the hangover scraping claw-like down the sides of his skull. Not the worst he'd ever felt. Bearable. But there all the same. A subdued pain, stabbing behind his pupils, fogging his mind. He needed strong coffee. Lots of it.

Workers were milling about the grounds. Hawkins counted a dozen of them. Gardeners watering plants and pulling out weeds and pruning bushes. A maid swept down the steps in front of the main house. Someone else was cleaning the windows. To the north, a handful of grooms exercised the horses in one of the paddocks.

Kettler's private workforce. Impressive. But also ruinously expensive.

The boss thinks he's never rich enough. He's always looking out for the next big payday.

The other team members had already taken their places either side of a long table facing the retractable projector screen. Martel was polishing off a plate of eggs and bacon. Moussa stayed perfectly still, as if he was posing for a life-drawing class. Devaney sat next to him, staring daggers at Hawkins. Steyn was rigging up a laptop to the projector unit. The two black guys were behind the bar, cleaning glasses and chatting.

Hawkins crossed the lapa, helped himself to a brew from the drip machine behind the counter. He migrated back over to the table, dropped into the empty chair beside Bald. Drank his coffee while Jock gave him a look of withering contempt.

'Jesus, mate. What the fuck happened to you?'

'Had a couple of slugs last night,' Hawkins said. 'It's nothing.'

'Bollocks. You're hanging out of your arse. That breath of yours could put down an elephant.'

'I said it ain't a problem. I just need a few ibuprofen and I'll be good to go.'

'Fuck that, Geordie. I've been down that same road a few times myself. This is no way to operate. Either drink a lot more or cut it out.'

'I don't need a fucking lecture.'

'I'm giving you friendly advice, you idiot. Sort your shit out. I mean it.'

Steyn said, 'Fellas. Boss man is coming.'

Hawkins gazed across the estate. Kettler bounded over from the direction of the mansion, decked out in a striped shirt, dark jeans and a pair of leather boots. Like a banker on casual Friday. The bar staff hastily cleared away the clutter from the table while Steyn finished setting up the laptop. He dug out a key-fob-sized laser pointer from his back pocket, set it down next to the computer.

Kettler swept into the lapa. He halted beside the projector screen, plucked a Montecristo from his shirt pocket, sliced off the cap end with a guillotine cutter, pulled a Zippo lighter from his trouser pocket. Held the flame to the open end of the cigar and took a couple of slow puffs while he looked round the table. Like a punctilious officer conducting an inspection of his troops.

Kettler's gaze lingered on Hawkins for an uncomfortably long beat. Then he turned to Steyn.

'Has this place been swept?'

'Yes, boss. Did it first thing this morning. It's clean.'

'The hookers?'

'Left before dawn, boss. Moussa ferried them back to Little Zimbabwe.'

'That's it from now on. I want no more unauthorised personnel coming through that gate. No one comes or goes without my express fucking permission. Is that clear?'

Kettler looked calm, though there was a note of menace in the public schoolboy accent.

'Yes, boss,' Steyn replied quickly.

'Good.' Kettler turned his gaze towards the bar staff. 'You two. Get lost.'

The two workers left the dirty glasses on the counter and walked double-quick out of the lapa. Once they were out of earshot Steyn fetched the remote control from another table. He stabbed a button, lowering the projector screen. There was a short pause while Steyn punched in his login creds on the laptop. The home screen flashed up on the hundred-inch canvas, shielded from the sunlight by the reed-thatched canopy.

Steyn passed the laser pointer to Kettler. Steyn returned to his seat, drawing the laptop towards him, while Kettler addressed the team between draws on his Montecristo.

'I'll make this short. We've got a lot to hack through, and not much time. I'll give you the overall plan, then Rory will talk you through the details. Hardware, infil and exfil routes and so forth.

'Gentlemen, in a few days we're going to undertake an operation that will make us all extremely rich. Richer than you could ever have dreamt. I warn you now. The job won't be easy. There are multiple complications and risks, but if we pull this one off, none of you will ever have to work ever again. You'll live like kings for the rest of your days.'

Kettler gestured towards Steyn. The latter hit a key on the laptop. A satellite image popped up on the projector screen. A barren mountainside. There was a wedge-shaped structure on the slope, ringed by several access roads.

'This is the Fordow enrichment plant. Thirty kilometres north of Qom. A hundred kilometres south of Tehran. No doubt you've all heard of it, what with everything that's been going on.'

'That's the one buried deep underground,' Bald observed. 'The one the Israelis are pressuring Farrell to blow to fuckery.'

'One of them,' Kettler corrected. 'One of three. The sites at Natanz and Esfahan are also on the Pentagon menu, but Fordow is the biggest plant. Our target is contained within this facility. Two hundred kilograms of sixty per cent highly enriched uranium. Or HEU as it's usually called. We're going to steal it.'

Devaney raised a paw. 'How the fuck are we supposed to hit that bastard, boss? No offence, but I didn't sign on for no suicide job.'

'This isn't anything of the sort,' Kettler replied smoothly. 'Rory, slide.'

Steyn punched more keys on the laptop. He clicked open a folder on the right-hand side of the main screen. A new window sprang up displaying a column of thumbnail images arranged in some sort of order. Steyn double-clicked on the top one. Another satellite shot filled the screen. A wider-lens view of the landscape around Fordow, taking in Qom and the surrounding hills, salt flats and arid plateaus.

Kettler said, 'A few days from now – shortly before the US deadline expires – the Iranians are going to move the HEU out of Fordow and relocate it to a top-secret site in the north-east of the country. A newly constructed enrichment facility somewhere in Semnan province. Location unknown. This place is so secret even the Americans don't know about it. But the material will never reach its destination. Because we're going to attack it en route, wallop the escort troops, lift the HEU and smuggle it out of the country. Then we're going to sell it.'

Kettler smiled thinly, letting his words sink in. He smoked his cigar and went on.

'In advance of this mission I've negotiated a deal with a foreign buyer. Someone with extremely wealthy backers. We've shaken hands on the headline terms. The delivery of the HEU to a pre-designated RV across the border in Turkmenistan, in exchange for an agreed price.'

'How much?' Martel asked.

'Two hundred million dollars.'

A stunned silence fell over the lapa. Hawkins glanced round at the others. Gauging the reactions of his accomplices. Bald stared at the screen, his brow scrunched in thought. Moussa and Devaney were rubbing their hands in greedy anticipation. Martel wore his usual arrogant smirk.

Bald said, 'Who's the buyer?'

'That's for me to know, sonny, and me alone,' Kettler responded. 'Someone with access to sufficient funds to make the deal happen. That's all you need to know.'

'What's the split, boss?' asked Devaney.

'Ten million dollars for each of you. Clean money, untraceable, deposited in bank accounts in Dubai registered in your respective names upon completion of the mission.'

Moussa and Martel looked at one another, grinning with excitement at the thought of the huge wad coming their way.

Bald said, 'What's the craic with the ambush?'

Kettler trained the laser pointer on the main road due east of the Fordow site. A three-lane motorway running north past the rim of a massive salt lake.

'Rory will run through everything with you shortly. But you're looking at an ambush on this highway. Route Seven. Also known as the Persian Gulf Highway.

'The convoy will depart Fordow via the main access road before mounting the highway north of Baqerabad. From there it will proceed north along Route Seven towards the cloverleaf at Zavarshahr. You'll strike before it reaches that point.'

Steyn fiddled with the laptop again and brought up the next satellite image. A zoomed-out shot of Iran with the Caspian Sea to the north and the mountainous border crossing with Turkmenistan in the north-east.

Kettler said, 'Infil is via Turkmenistan. Rory has done a site recce so he's best placed to run through that with you. Exfil will be in the same direction, with a few route changes, back across the Turkmen border to a prearranged RV. I'll be waiting for you there, ready to organise the handover of the material to the buyer for onward transportation to its final destination. Once that's done, we're home and dry.'

'Where's all this int coming from?' said Bald.

'We have a man on the inside.'

'Who?'

'A senior general. Highly respected figure within the Iranian military. One of his subordinates is in charge of the security arrangements at Fordow. A young colonel. Rising star. The general was his mentor for several years. He's going to tip off the general in advance of the movement of the uranium.'

'Why the fuck would those guys help us?'

'The general lost his brother last year. Executed in a purge of the ranks by the hardliners. He knows they'll be coming for him next. If he sticks around, he'll end up swinging from a crane in a town square. He wants out, before everything turns to shit, and he's willing to betray his country. For a price, of course.'

'How much?'

'Enough to feather his nest in exile.'

'And the colonel?' said Hawkins.

'He's in on it too. Same reason. The regime will train its sights on him before long. Because of his long-standing friendship with the general.'

'What's in it for him?'

'Safety. Freedom. The general has promised the colonel and his family a new life in Dubai once this is over.'

Bald grimaced. 'Even with their help, it's gonna be fucking hard to pull this thing off. The Americans and Israelis will have eyes on Fordow twenty-four-seven. Satellites, drones. They're going to be alerted as soon as we hit the convoy.'

'I've taken care of that,' Kettler said. 'The general has been drip-feeding false information to the CIA and Mossad over the past few weeks. He's told them that the uranium has already been moved from Fordow to a holding site, prior to its onward transportation to the new facility in Semnan province. They'll be watching that holding point. The general has convinced them that Fordow is empty.'

'And they believe him?'

'No reason not to. The general is a high-value source with close links to the Iranian leadership. He's credible.'

'How does that help us, though?' said Devaney.

Kettler blew out cigar smoke and said, 'Right now, the Americans and Israelis are laser-focused on the fourth site. The limited number of satellites they have in the area will be watching that place. Which means no one will be monitoring Fordow, or the area around it, when the attack on the convoy goes down. Smoke and mirrors.'

Martel said, 'What about the British?'

'The general has fed them the same bullshit. They've been hoodwinked. When the attack begins, no one will be aware of what's really going on. Not for a few hours, at any rate. Which should be all the time we need.'

Hawkins listened with a growing sense of alarm. He thought back to the clubhouse. The briefing with the MI6 officers. *Our source is at the very highest level within the Iranian military*, Jackson had told him.

It's the general, Hawkins realised.

He must be Six's source.

He's double-dipping. Taking Kettler's coin while tipping off Vauxhall.

The guy was playing a dangerous game. One wrong move and he'd end up getting fed into the woodchipper. Six had obviously forced his hand. No other reason why the general would spill his guts to them. Blackmail, or a threat to kill his family unless he cooperated. Possibly they had encouraged the general to deceive the Americans and Israelis, keeping them in the dark about Fordow. They would want to give Kettler and his gang the best possible chance of pulling off the op. That was MI6's only hope of finding out who was bankrolling the uranium deal.

Kettler was staring at him curiously. 'Something wrong, Hawkins?'

'No, boss. No problem.'

'Good.'

His gaze lingered on Hawkins a moment longer.

Bald said, 'What if the general is lying to us? He might just take the dough and throw us under the bus anyway.'

Kettler said, 'Unlikely. He's a greedy fucker. Spends his downtime in Dubai. Likes his Western women and liquor. That sort of lifestyle doesn't come cheap, of course. He's received an initial payment, but he won't get the big bucks until the job's over.'

'But why come to us with this int in the first place? Why not take it to the Americans?' said Hawkins.

'Money. If he approached the Americans, they'd thank him for his patriotism and send in the bombers. Best-case scenario he gets to live in a backwater in Bumfuck, Vermont, doing part-time work for a military think-tank and wondering what the hell happened to his life. This way, he gets to stick the middle finger up to the clerics and enjoy an early retirement in Dubai shagging escorts and knocking back Lagavulin.'

'Know which one I'd rather go for,' Steyn said with a sly grin. 'Am I right, boys?'

Devaney and Martel shared a dirty laugh. Moussa said nothing. Perfecting his impression of a Zen master.

Bald said, 'How far is the airhead from the enrichment plant?'

Kettler deferred to Steyn, who said, 'Nine hundred kilometres. Some of the route goes through steep mountain passes. We're looking at a journey time of around fourteen hours, depending on the precise route.'

'What about the flight from that airstrip to Turkmenistan?'

'Sixteen hours, give or take. Including the stop to refuel.'

'What's your point, Jock?' asked Hawkins.

Bald shrugged. 'We're going to need plenty of warning before that convoy gets on the road. Thirty hours at the very minimum. More, if there are any fuck-ups or unforeseen obstacles along the way.'

'There won't be,' Steyn replied confidently. 'The planning on this one is nailed down, bra.'

Bald laughed weakly. 'There are always fuck-ups, mate. First rule of any mission. Murphy's law.'

Kettler said, 'The timing isn't going to be an issue. Transporting containers of HEU on public roads is a major ball-ache. The regime won't want to move the uranium until the last minute.'

'Which is when?' Hawkins asked.

'Seven days from now. Two days before Farrell's public deadline.'

'Once the colonel gets the heads-up, it'll take time for the convoy to mobilise and reach Fordow. Then there's the actual loading of the HEU onto the trucks. Not a straightforward process. There are security protocols. Bottlenecks. Equipment checks. The Iranians will take their time, even though the clock is ticking, because the last thing they want is for the cylinders to suffer any kind of damage en route to the new facility. The colonel has been advised that it will take a full twenty-four hours to prepare and load the cylinders. We should have around thirty-four hours' notice.'

'That's still cutting it bloody close,' Hawkins muttered.

Devaney turned to Moussa, grinning.

'Looks like the big brave SAS soldier is getting jumpy. Reckon you should have stayed at home, Grandad. Stick to your pipe and slippers. Leave the hot work to the young bucks.'

Hawkins gave him a flinty stare. 'I might not be a spring chicken, but I could teach you a thing or two about how to soldier.'

'The Englishman has a point, I think,' Martel said. 'They know how to fight. They had an empire once.'

'*Had*.' Devaney spat on the ground. 'Good fucking riddance. English cunt.'

He stared stonily at Hawkins. His skin stretched like dried leather, his whole face boiling with hatred. Hawkins imagined his right fist connecting with the Irishman's face. Blood and shattered teeth all over the place. A happy thought.

Kettler said, 'The timing is tight, but it can't be helped. Just make sure your go-bags are packed. Soon as the general gets word at his end, he'll let us know. We'll have vehicles ready to ferry you down to the airstrip, so there shouldn't be any delays at our end.'

He paused while he looked round the table. 'Any questions before I hand over to Rory?'

Devaney raised a tattooed arm.

'Yes, Terry?' Kettler said.

'Ten million each, you say?'

'That's right.'

'For six of us.'

'Yes.'

'But that only makes sixty million. Out of two hundred.'

Kettler's eyes narrowed. 'What are you alluding to, exactly?'

'Where's the rest of it going? Your back pocket, I'll bet.'

'This is my operation,' Kettler said matter-of-factly. 'I've negotiated the sale of the material. My cut reflects that.'

Devaney stood his ground. 'We should be getting more, boss. We're the ones having to put our balls on the line. What if it goes wrong? We'll be fucked while you get to sit on your arse smoking a fine cigar.'

Kettler said, flatly, 'Ten million is what's on the table. That's what you're going to get. Not a penny more.'

'Bullshit. It ain't proportionate.'

An ugly laugh escaped Kettler's throat. 'That's a very long word for a bog-hopping Irishman.'

'Fuck off.'

'No, son, you fuck off.' Kettler flicked ash onto the stone floor and gave the Irishman a filthy look. 'Let me educate you about how the world works, since you obviously haven't got a clue. I've got as much resting as you on this thing. More, in fact. I've had to front serious money for the operation. Down payments to people on the ground in Turkmenistan and Iran. The general needs his share, plus the colonel. Not to mention the equipment costs, weaponry, cargo plane rental. If the mission goes tits-up, I'm left out of pocket. But if you're really not happy, you know where the gate is. I fucking mean it. Piss off and your cut will be shared between the rest of the guys. I'm sure they'd be happy with that arrangement.'

'I didn't mean it like that, boss.'

'Then what did you mean, Terry?'

There was a cold glint in the hooded Kettler eyes. The kind of look that could have skinned a stag.

'Nothing, boss,' said Devaney, meekly. 'It was a heavy night last night, that's all. I'm not thinking straight.'

'So you're happy with your cut?'

'Yes, boss.'

'Anyone else have a fucking problem?' Kettler swept his gaze round the table.

Everyone stayed silent.

'Good.' Kettler straightened up and carried on. 'One more thing before Rory goes through the nitty-gritty. It goes without saying that the opsec on this one must be watertight. That means no personal phone calls or messages, no social media posts. From now on, you'll stay offline and stay in this compound. No one comes in or leaves without my say-so.

'If you get bored, you've got free use of the weights room and cardio equipment in the basement. Shooting range. Every satellite channel under the sun. There's a library, too. Treat your stay here like an all-inclusive holiday. Except when you get on that plane, gentlemen, you're not going back to a shitty mid-terrace in Slough. You're going to pull off the crime of the century.'

Ten million, thought Hawkins. For an ex-soldier, a life-changing sum. He could feel the pull of the money himself. Only a fraction of what Kettler stood to bank from the sale, but more than any of them could have hoped to have earned on the Circuit. Two or three million to put down on a nice house and car, the rest sitting in an account in Dubai, accruing interest. Live on that. Women and drink on tap.

The high life.

'Rory will walk you through the details,' Kettler said. 'Then we'll wait for the signal from the general. Succeed, and a few days from now you'll all be rich men. Fail, allow yourself to be captured, and you'll end up rotting in an Iranian prison cell. Make sure that doesn't happen. Otherwise the size of your cut will be the least of your worries.'

Twelve

Kettler lowered himself into the chair at the far end of the table. Giving the floor to Steyn. Kettler would take a back seat to the detailed mission briefing, but sit on in the discussions, on hand to answer any questions or weigh in on any proposed changes to the plan. He sat with his long hands resting in his lap, the drooped eyes focused on Steyn as the latter picked up the laser pointer and aimed it at the satellite image.

'Infil route is via Gorakan,' Steyn began. The green dot floated over a point roughly three hundred kilometres from the Iranian border.

'We'll fly out from this estate. Boss has a chartered aircraft hidden on his golf course. Chartered cargo plane fuelled and ready to go. One of the old Russian Antonov AN-72s. Wheels up as soon as we have the word from the general. Crew are local contractors. Two pilots and an engineer. They've worked with us before; one of them flies the boss's private jet. So they're dependable.'

'Hidden?' Bald asked.

'You'll see, bra.'

Steyn grinned and went on.

'We'll make a short stop en route at Djibouti to refuel. Then we'll fly straight to Gorakan. Cargo is listed on the manifest as farm machinery. Humanitarian flight. We're logged as engineers and charity reps, going out to provide the local peasantry with much-needed farm equipment. Except there won't be anything on board.'

Hawkins said, 'It would be better if we landed at night.'

'How's that, bra?'

'That airstrip will be quieter in the evening. If we land in the daytime, there's a chance someone might see us. A journalist, for example.'

Devaney pulled a face. 'Why the fuck would some hack be hanging out in the arse end of Turkmenistan?'

'They might be waiting for a local flight. Might be working for a business journal, covering the oil sector. Could be a travel writer researching the wonders of Central Asia. Any number of things. But if they spot a bunch of burly ex-soldiers filing into a hangar, it's going to set off alarm bells. You'd know that, if you were a half-decent operator, instead of a useless Paddy bastard.'

Devaney's expression hardened. He stared at Hawkins, his two brain cells working overtime as he tried to think of a witty comeback.

Kettler said, confidently, 'There won't be anyone at the airfield. Place went to rack and ruin years ago. Back in Soviet times it serviced a nearby gas field, bringing workers and equipment, but the facility shut down twenty years ago. Been abandoned ever since. There isn't even a full-time manager. Just a fuel manager. A handful of long-haul cargo planes use it as a refuelling stop, and the Turkmen President sometimes lands there, but that's it.'

That drew a bemused look from Bald. 'The President?'

'There's a gas crater. Near the old gas field. Been burning for decades. Soviet engineers set fire to it after it collapsed, to stop any poisonous fumes leaking out. Locals call it the Mouth of Hell. The President likes to fly in on his jet, do a few doughnuts in his rally car around the edge of the crater. Posts the videos on his social. It's a big tourist attraction.'

'That could be a problem, boss,' Hawkins said. 'What if we land in full view of a bunch of influencers?'

'Not going to happen. The airfield is at the edges of the Kara-kum desert. You get sandstorms in the spring and early summer. Tourists tend to flock there in the autumn, when the temperature is cooler. This time of year it'll be empty.'

'What about our weaponry?' asked Martel.

'Hardware will be waiting for us at Gorakan,' Steyn replied. 'In the hangar next to the tarmac apron. Fuel manager will look after it for us.'

'Is he trustworthy?'

'He's getting paid to look the other way,' Kettler said. 'A generous sum. He won't be a problem.'

He smiled, but something in his expression made Hawkins think that the fuel manager wasn't going to live long enough to enjoy his new wealth.

Steyn said, 'Hardware was delivered six days ago. RPGs, two of them. Couple of Dragunov sniper rifles. AK-47s, six each, plus ammunition. Four pistols.'

Hawkins said, 'Where's all this stuff coming from?'

'We've got an interlink with one of the drug-smuggling cartels in Turkmenistan. They've sourced everything. Russian-made kit, but it'll be in good nick.'

'Explosives?'

'Plastique. PVV-5A. Russian version of C4. Couple of kilograms. Initiators will be clackers. Similar to the Claymores.'

'We'll need comms gear, too,' Martel said.

Steyn said, 'We'll have a set of HF walkie-talkies. Half a dozen of them, stashed with the rest of the kit. Military-grade units. Power banks in case we need to juice the batteries.'

'Range?'

'Four kilometres. A lot less than that in the mountains, but that'll be fine for our purposes. We won't need to use them much once it goes noisy.'

Devaney said, 'What about vehicles?'

'Two Unimogs. For transportation of the HEU from the attack site to the RV. Plus a technical in support. Toyota pickup. All waiting for us at the airhead. Extra tanks on the wagons and jerry cans of diesel for the technical. Enough juice to cover the journey there and back, with plenty to spare.'

Hawkins nodded approvingly. Unimog trucks. The big beast of the off-road world. More adaptable than a Swiss army knife. You could steer it up steep trails, clear snow with it or drive it across a deep river.

Steyn went on, 'There's an articulated lorry waiting for us at Gorakan, too. Stolen to order. Trailer's filled with rubble. We'll be using that for the highway ambush.'

Steyn swivelled round to face the projector screen. He homed in on the airfield with the laser pointer, outlined a route cutting south-west on the highway towards the border.

'As soon as we've touched down we'll grab the hardware and vehicles and get straight on the road down to the Iranian border. We're looking at a five-hour drive. Crossing point is at Incheh Borun, near the foothills of the Kopet Dag mountain range.'

'What's our cover story?' asked Martel.

'We don't need one. It's been fixed so we'll be waved straight through.'

Kettler said, 'The border force commander is a close friend of the general. They came up together through the ranks in the Revolutionary Guard. Both served in the Quds Force and by all accounts formed a close bond. It so happens that the chap was overlooked for a big promotion a few years ago. Now he's taking the same path as the general. Selling out so he can start a new life abroad.'

Hawkins puffed out his cheeks. 'Bloody hell. How many of them fuckers are playing both sides?'

'Everyone has their price, Hawkins.'

Kettler looked fixedly at him. Weighing him up. Hawkins felt a twinge of anxiety in his bowels. Not for the first time, he wondered if Kettler suspected him of being a plant.

Steyn continued, 'Once we're across the border we'll make straight for the ambush point. Which is here.'

He punched another key on the laptop, bringing up a fourth satellite shot. A two-kilometre section of Route Seven running north past the salt lake. Twenty kilometres beyond Fordow, thirty south of the cloverleaf at Zavarshahr. Steyn trained the green laser dot over the point where a slip road joined the highway. An off-ramp two hundred metres further along coiled round in a broad circle and ran under a flyover before it merged with a dual carriageway running west to east.

Steyn pointed to the on-ramp and said, 'We'll pre-position the Unimogs on this slipway. It's on a slight depression, near a large mound of rocks, so we won't be visible to traffic passing along the highway. Meanwhile the artic will be on the hard shoulder further up the main route, waiting for the convoy. Engine running, hazards on. Anyone passing by will assume the driver has broken down.

'We'll have a spotter here, in the technical,' Steyn continued, lasering a dirt patch on the hard shoulder south of the slip road. 'Binos on the highway, watching for any sign of the convoy. Once we have it in sight, that will be the signal for the artic to hit the gas and swing it round so it's blocking all three lanes.

'Meanwhile we'll drive up behind the transports, debus and wipe out the infantry guard using the RPGs and longs. Half the team will commandeer the wagons with the uranium and load the containers onto the Unimogs, rear team gets into a defensive position. Two guys brassing up anything that comes at them while the other tows the troop transports back round to block the approach from the south. Once that's done, we'll shoot out the tyres and put a few rounds in the engine blocks. Set them on fire. That'll create a bottleneck, delaying the arrival of the Quick Reaction Force coming up from Fordow.

'The artic driver will open up a space for us to pass through, reposition the vehicle and blow it with explosive charges. Seal off the highway in both directions. No other slipways for twenty kilometres on either side, so there's not a cat in hell's chance of anyone getting through that mess. Not without bringing in some heavy lifting equipment.

'Then we'll dive back into the wagons, leave the artic to burn, race down the off-ramp, tool under the flyover and take the dual carriageway away from Fordow. From there it's a straight run back across the border to the pre-designated RV.'

'It's a good plan,' Martel said after a pause.

'Course it is, bra. I came up with it, didn't I?'

Bald said, 'I've done something similar before. In Geneva. Once you seal off that motorway, there's no escape for the convoy. We'll have the bastards trapped.'

Hawkins gave his mucker a guarded look. 'When was this?'

'Donkey's years ago, son. Before your time, Geordie.'

Hawkins flicked his attention back to the projector screen. Running through the plan in his head. A play-by-play movie. Looking for any weak points in the attack. 'How busy does that road get?'

Steyn said, 'It's the main link between Qom and Tehran. We're anticipating heavy traffic in the day, less so in the evenings.'

'What's your fucking point, English?' Devaney said.

Hawkins said, 'We're going to be operating in an area with a lot of civilians. That could mean trouble. They'll be calling the police, filming us on their phones. Some of them might try and intervene.'

'If they do,' Kettler said, 'you'll have to drop them. No other choice. Collateral damage.' He looked inquiringly at Hawkins. 'Is that a problem for you?'

'No, boss. No problem.'

Kettler nodded. 'The main thing is that you get out of there as quickly as possible. Once the attack goes down, the Americans are going to realise very quickly that they've been tricked by the general and switch their attention from the holding facility back to Fordow. You need to be well clear of the attack site before that happens.'

'How much time will we have?' Martel asked. 'Before that happens?'

'Depends,' Kettler replied. 'Best-case scenario, you'll have fifteen minutes to make the attack and get back on the road. Anything more than that and you're in trouble.'

'Fuck me,' Bald said. 'This thing is getting more difficult by the minute.'

'It's one job, mate,' Steyn said. 'We pull this off, we're rich as Croesus. Just like the boss man said.'

'Of course,' Kettler said, 'if anyone fails to make it back alive, their share will be divided equally among the survivors.'

A wicked grin flashed across Bald's face. Martel and Devaney looked at one another knowingly. Moussa sat immobile, his expression giving nothing away. Like a mannequin on roids.

Hawkins said, 'Any settlements nearby?'

'A small village. Six kilometres away,' Steyn said. 'A dot on a map. Handful of farmers and goat-herders. No local police presence. It's a good spot. As good a spot as any.'

'How many vehicles in that convoy?' asked Bald.

'Six, according to the general. Two Neinava trucks in the front, two in the rear. Plus a couple of modified civilian wagons carrying the uranium. Each one transporting eight twenty-five-kilo cylinders stored in boron-lined casks. To guard against any accidents en route.'

Martel said, 'I might be wrong. But isn't uranium usually transported in much larger containers?'

'Ordinarily, yes,' Kettler conceded. 'But the Iranians don't want to draw attention to the fact that they're smuggling it out of Fordow. Remember, they believe that the NSA and Mossad have got round-the-clock satellite surveillance on that facility. They don't know the general has misdirected them. If they start bringing in specialist machinery and lifting two-tonne drums onto the backs of lorries, it's going to raise red flags. A few small cases of equipment being loaded on the trucks is much less suspicious.'

'Still,' Bald said, 'it's gonna be a hair-raising drive on the way back, carrying them cylinders.'

'Not as bad as you think,' Steyn said. 'We'll transport them in Laycorn storage boxes. Lead-lined and foam-padded and secured with ratchet straps. Four crates per wagon. Ought to stop 'em knocking around.'

'Why not just steal the Iranian trucks themselves?' Devaney wondered aloud. 'Simpler than transferring that shite over.'

'Too slow. Those vehicles have been modified. Maximum speed of sixty kilometres. Because of the sensitive cargo. If it comes down to a getaway, the Unimogs are a better bet.'

'What about troops?' asked Hawkins.

Steyn said, 'Sixteen in total, we believe. Iranian army.'

'Kit?'

'Heckler and Koch G3 longs. Ballistic helmets and Kevlar vests. Poor quality, as you might expect for troops on escort duty. The QRF is a much bigger threat. Those guys are from the Saberin Unit.'

'I've heard of them,' Martel said. 'They're trained to a good standard. Some of the best operators in the Iranian military.'

'How many lads are we talking, roughly?' said Bald.

'Battalion-sized force. Three hundred men,' Steyn replied.

'Better make sure we're out of there before those fuckers rock up, then,' Devaney said. 'Don't know about you fellas, but I don't intend to get in a firefight with that mob.'

They took a short break, getting in more coffees and stretching their legs. A pair of maids brought over breakfast platters from the main house. Pastries, bagels, eggs, meat, yoghurts and bowls of fresh fruit. Hawkins tucked into a ham-and-cheese croissant, devoured a plate of sausages, inhaled another mug of strong black coffee and felt marginally less shitty. Ten minutes later they gathered round the table while Steyn walked them through the exfil route, which would take the gang down the main trunk road running east along the Alborz mountain range. A longer journey than the infil, Steyn said. An extra hour or two. But essential.

'We must avoid Tehran at all costs. Police and military units will be out in force across the capital.'

'What if we run into any checkpoints?' asked Martel.

'The guys in front of the wagons will roam ahead, searching for threats. If there's a roadblock, they'll radio back to the drivers, telling them to take the next slipway or turn off the road, and we'll box our way round. If there's nowhere to turn off, we'll reverse and head back on ourselves until we can find another way through. Worst-case scenario, we'll have to blast our way through.'

'Maybe we should stick to the back roads,' Devaney said. 'Get off the big highways. Safer that way. Less chance of running into a roadblock.'

Steyn said, 'Can't be done. The secondary road network east of Tehran is piss-poor. Roads aren't well maintained. Carrying the cargo on unmetalled tracks is asking for trouble.'

'We're better off on the highways,' Bald agreed. 'Those back roads might knacker the vehicles. Them Unimogs hit a pothole, or go over some loose rocks, it'll fuck the tyres. Might even damage the undercarriage.'

'Anyway,' said Steyn, 'the nuclear sites are scattered across central and western Iran. The further east we go, the more distance we put between ourselves and Fordow, the less likely we are to run into any major obstacles. The main thing is avoiding Tehran.'

They moved on to the plan once they had made it back across the border with Turkmenistan. Meeting Kettler at an RV south of Gorakan. Followed by a handover to the group purchasing the uranium. From there they would make their way to the airfield, board the Antonov and fly back to Pretoria.

A grim realisation slowly dawned on Hawkins as he listened. Six had tasked him with establishing the identities of the individuals or group buying the uranium from Kettler. But that wasn't going to be easy. The purchaser would be in a rush to ferry the cylinders on to their final destination. Hawkins would have only a narrow window of opportunity to alert Cruttwell and Jackson before the buyers went underground.

Hawkins checked himself. He was thinking too far ahead. *Cross that bridge when you come to it. Worry about it later. Deal with the first problem first.*

They wrapped up the briefing. Then Kettler produced a loose bundle of papers and passed them round the table.

He said, 'Take a pen and write down your details. Sign and date in the relevant boxes. I'll need one form of ID from each of you as well. Passport or driving licence will do.'

'What the fuck are these, boss?' Devaney asked.

'Application forms. Remote-opening of your checking accounts in Dubai. Funds will be deposited ten days after completion of the mission.'

Hawkins took a black biro, scribbled in the relevant boxes. Opening an account for a great whack of money he would probably never get his hands on. Or this could be a ruse. A simple trick to convince the lads that they would be getting their money instead of a double-tap to the head. It had crossed his mind that Kettler might be planning to eliminate the team once the dust had settled on the job. The most effective way of making sure no one found out about Kettler's link to the heists. No loose tongues.

Or maybe Hawkins was just jumping at shadows.

I don't know.

But I'm sure of one thing. I can't trust anyone.

In the periphery of his vision he noticed Kettler staring at him. Wearing that same inscrutable look on his liver-spotted face.

Kettler waited until they had completed their forms. He gathered in the papers and stood up.

'That's it, guys. My accountant will get the paperwork processed straight away. In the meantime, you'll remain here on standby. Get some rest while you still can. As soon as we get the green light, we're wheels up and the mission is go.'

And then, thought Hawkins, *there's no going back.*

Thirteen

Kettler left the lapa and headed back to the mansion. A hundred metres away a couple of uniformed maids were hauling black bin bags down the front steps and dumping them at the edge of the carriage circle. They bowed their heads dutifully as Kettler approached. Like serfs on a feudal manor, acknowledging their lord. Kettler breezed past them, vaulted up the steps, disappeared inside the main residence.

Steyn pressed his paddle-like hands together as he looked round the table.

'How about we put down a few rounds at the pistol range, guys? Pass a bit of time before the rugger's on.'

'Sod it. Why not,' Devaney said. 'Get these two grandpas to pop a few rounds off. See if they've still got what it takes,' he added, indicating Bald and Hawkins.

Bald said, 'Son, you never lose those skill sets. We might be getting on, but we can still teach you a trick or two.'

Devaney laughed. 'The only thing you'll be teaching us is how to use a colostomy bag, old man.'

Bald stared at the Irishman, his jaw set firm.

Steyn said, 'What do you say, Geordie? Dust off a few cobwebs?'

Hawkins considered. He would have preferred to spend the afternoon sipping expensive whisky and thinking about how the fuck he was going to make it through the next few days without getting himself slotted. He needed to reach out to Six, too. Update them on the plan Kettler and Steyn had laid out at the briefing. The highway ambush. Smuggling the uranium across the border to Turkmenistan. The RV Kettler had arranged with the buyer near to the airhead. The potential difficulties

Hawkins faced in establishing their identities before they went underground.

He could think of a billion things he would rather be doing than heading down to the range with Devaney. Emergency root canal surgery, perhaps. Stage-four cancer treatment. Taking a degree in corporate tax law. But if he tried ducking out of it, Bald would probably give him grief. Maybe another lecture on his drinking.

'Fine by me,' Hawkins said. 'I can give a demonstration to Paddy. Show him how I plugged his cousins.'

Devaney's expression tightened into a scowl. 'SAS wanker. English prick. No one gives a toss about you lot anymore. Bunch of has-beens.'

'See this?' Hawkins pointed to his face. 'This is me looking wounded.'

'Fucking English. You should leave us alone. Ireland for the Irish.'

'We would, mate. But we keep having to pull thick Irish squaddies out of the jungle.'

Devaney glowered at him. Rage was surging within the guy. He was breathing noisily through flared nostrils, wearing a face like he was chewing cement.

Steyn glanced at the Breitling clasped around his wrist and said, 'Right, lads. Get your shit sorted. Bin collection is due in an hour. Any rubbish, leave it outside your front door. Meet back here in ten.'

They retreated to their bungalows. Hawkins hastily pinged off another message to Cruttwell and Jackson on the false-screen phone. A quick summary of the plan laid out to them by Steyn and Kettler. The wait for the general to give them the signal. More news to follow when he had it.

Nine minutes later Hawkins left the bungalow and made his way back to the lapa. Bald, Martel, Devaney and Moussa were milling around, waiting for Steyn, who was nowhere to be seen. Gone to fetch the weapons from Kettler's armoury, Hawkins supposed. The two bar workers had magically reappeared while the guys had been dossing in their billets. The bartender restocking the drinks fridge, his mucker handing him bottles from a crate.

Steyn emerged from the main house lugging a pair of black gun range bags, one in each hand. He stomped over to the lapa, handed one of the bags to Moussa, then led the team down a separate path winding south-east across the estate, walled garden on their right, a pair of hard tennis courts on their left. A little further on they passed the golf course clubhouse. Beyond which lay a patchwork of immaculate fairways, bunkers and roughs.

After four hundred metres they arrived at the edge of the range. Which was essentially a wide depression set into the ground, surrounded by a wall of exotic bushes and native mahogany trees. Two-metre-high stacks of worn car tyres filled with sand had been arranged in a U-shape around three sides of the dip; a series of four-by-four wooden target holders stood in a rough line at the far end of the range, fifteen metres downwind from Hawkins and the others.

Steyn dumped his gun bag and made for a small shed built to one side of the range for the storage of equipment and tools. Like a shelter beside an English bowling green. Steyn tugged open the door, slipped inside, retrieved a foldable table. He laid it on the ground, prised open the metal legs, grabbed the table with both hands and flipped it over, setting it down beside the shed.

Steyn ducked back inside the shelter while Moussa emptied the gun bags. The Eritrean laid out a selection of pistols, holsters and boxes of ammo on the scuffed laminate. A wide variety of different calibres. All of them instantly familiar to Hawkins from his time at Hereford. There was a Colt 1911, chambered for the .45 ACP round. The old workhorse of the American army. A Glock 22 chambered in the slightly smaller .40 Smith & Wesson.

Two FN pistols, both using 9x19mm Parabellum. A Heckler &
Koch USP Tactical, also supporting the .45 platform. Five hand-
guns in total.

Steyn re-emerged from the shed with a stash of paper bullseye
targets pasted onto strips of plywood. He strode over to the timber
holders at the far end of the range, fitted the targetry into the post
slots. Paced back over to the team.

'How about a shooting competition?' he suggested. 'We could
put some money on it. Make it a bit tastier, like.'

Devaney's eyes lit up like a couple of halogen lamps. 'Grand
fucking idea. I'll go first. Take this dickhead on.' He hard-stared at
Hawkins as he spoke. 'Show the old bastard how it's done.'

'Geordie? You up for that?' asked Steyn.

'What's the challenge?'

'Twelve rounds from, say, ten metres. Fifty bucks for the best
shooter.'

'Make it a hundred,' said Hawkins.

Steyn looked towards Devaney. Taking on the role of referee for
the occasion. 'You happy with that, Terry?'

'Am I fuck. Easiest hundred bucks I'll ever make. Bring it on.'

'Right, then. Choose your pieces and put in a few warmers, lads.'

Hawkins followed Devaney over to the gun table. The Irishman
selected a Glock 22 chambered for the .40 S&W. Hawkins went for
the USP Tactical. Weapon of choice for the US SF community. He
depressed the mag release button, eased out the magazine. Empty.
He pulled the slider back, checking to see if there was a bullet in
the snout, retrieved twelve rounds of .45 ammunition from one
of the boxes. Started thumbing them one by one into the double-
stack clip. Then he slid the magazine back into the underside of the
pistol, fastened a side holster to his belt and secured the USP snug
in the moulded polymer casing.

Devaney was midway through his warm-up. He was standing
almost square-on, six metres back from the paper targetry, hands

closed around the pistol grip as he fired two shots at one of the bullseyes. Getting a feel for the weapon. He backtracked a couple of steps, squeezed off another couple of .40 rounds. When he had discharged his last round he ejected the empty magazine, slapped in a fresh one.

'Fuck are you waiting for, pal?' he called out to Hawkins. 'Scared of losing, are youse?'

Hawkins finished shoving rounds into a second mag. He stuffed that one into his back pocket, started towards the range. Before he could move away Bald reached out and seized him by the bicep.

'Don't bite, Geordie,' he said in a low voice. 'Don't give that prick the satisfaction. It's not worth it. A few days from now, you'll never have to see his face again. Remember that.'

'Fuck off. I know what I'm doing, Jock.'

He shrugged off Bald's grip and approached the targetry, Devaney giving him a screw-face. Hawkins had worked with plenty of blokes he'd disliked in the past. It was the nature of life in the Regiment. You were operating in small-sized teams, working in close proximity for weeks or even months, sometimes with people you didn't get on with. Ninety-nine per cent of the time that wasn't a problem. You learned to be professional. Control your emotions and get on with the job.

But once in a while you'd meet someone you hated at first sight. A mutual animosity based on nothing more than the way a person looked or the sound of their voice, a habit or something in their manner. That was Devaney. The Irishman was really beginning to piss Hawkins off. Couldn't keep his big mouth shut.

A few more days more of this shit, and I'll end up throttling the bastard.

He decided Devaney needed to be taught a lesson.

The rest of the team stood near the gun table, looking on, while Hawkins took up a spot two metres from the targets. He snapped his weapon out of the belt holster and put down a couple of warmers on one of the paper bullseyes, getting his eye in. The bullets thumped into one of the sand-filled tyres behind the wooden posts. Hawkins backed up to a distance of four metres from the targetry, depressed the trigger twice again. Both rounds struck the same tyre as before. He repeated the same process at six, eight, ten and twelve metres.

Devaney looked on with amused disbelief.

'Fuck me. This is gonna be even easier than I thought. What are they teaching you cunts in the SAS these days? How to go begging to the Yanks for help, is it?'

Steyn said, 'Warm up is done, lads. Who's going first?'

'I'll go,' said Devaney. 'Let's get this shite over with.'

They both reloaded their weapons. Hawkins stuffed the USP Tactical back into the holster and retreated to a distance of ten metres from the paper targets. Close to the limit of the range.

Devaney tore his weapon free and aimed downrange at the central target. The Glock barked a dozen times in succession. A slow, controlled rhythm. Three of the shots struck the outer bull. The rest smacked into the inner circle a few inches from the bullseye.

Devaney stuffed the Glock back into his holster and stepped away. Grinning triumphantly.

'Not bad,' Martel said.

'Your turn, Geordie,' said Steyn.

Hawkins took up his position at the spot where Devaney had been standing a moment before. Steyn and the others had gathered to one side of the range, watching Hawkins as he raised the USP Tactical. He double-tapped at the target immediately left of Devaney's one, putting his shots deliberately wide. Aiming for a point on the tyre wall downstream from the paper bullseyes. A dozen rounds of .45 ACP hammered into the exact same point, the kinetic energy from each bullet absorbed by the sand and rubber.

He reholstered the USP Tactical. Walked up to the targets with Devaney and the rest of the gang.

'Terry wins,' Steyn declared.

'Can't even operate a pistol,' Devaney said, contemptuously. He jabbed a finger at Hawkins. 'Better watch your backs on this mission, fellas. More fucking chance of getting hit in the back by this twat than the Iranians.'

'Fuck it,' Hawkins said angrily. 'Let's go again. Double or quits.'

Steyn looked towards Devaney. 'You up for that, Terry?'

Devaney's lips stretched into a grin.

'Fuck it, I'll take that bet. Nothing better than fleecing an Englishman out of his daily bread.'

Steyn replaced the targets while Devaney and Hawkins put fresh rounds in their mags. Hawkins went first this time. He pointed the USP at the same spot on the bank of car tyres, lining it up with the sights. Emptied the magazine at that exact point. Deliberately missing his target. Devaney chuckled at his lame efforts, rolled up and did his thing with the Glock. Perforating the inner and outer rings in a fairly loose grouping.

'Fuck's sake,' Hawkins said. Shaking his head and frowning at the USP. 'This pistol is bloody useless. Sights are well off.'

'The tool ain't the fucking problem. It's the tosser holding it. Ain't that right, lads?' Devaney extended an arm inked with the tattoo of the Virgin Mary. 'Pay up, dickhead.'

Hawkins raised a hand. 'Tell you what. Give us one last chance. Double again. Four hundred bucks to the winner.'

Devaney shrugged. 'It's your money. But you ain't changing weapons. You stick with the one you've got.'

'Fine by me. Let's go.'

Devaney stepped up first. He loosed off twelve more rounds, studding the target with .40 S&W brass. The bullets struck a little further out than his earlier efforts. One punched through the inner ring; the rest pierced the outer bull. Not the worst shooting in the world. Acceptable for a green army recruit. Someone who didn't live and breathe soldiering. But well below the standard required of a Tier One operator.

'Your turn, cunt,' Devaney said as he wheeled away from the range. 'Better get ready to cough up that dough.'

'We'll see.'

'Might buy a Union Jack flag once this is done. Piss all over it. Have myself a little party.'

Hawkins told himself not to rise to the bait. He focused on his bullseye. Shutting out the background noise.

Pistol shooting took a reasonable degree of skill. Different, in some ways, from firing a long. The shortness of the barrel magnified the slightest error in aiming. If you were out by a millimetre across a distance of fifteen metres, that might equate to a round falling short or landing wide by several inches. But an SAS man never lost the ability to shoot. Hawkins had used a pistol so many times in his Regiment career that it had become deeply embedded in his motor cortex. A precise set of physical movements rehearsed and repeated tens of thousands of times. Like driving a car. Or learning how to swim. The sort of thing you never really forgot. If you were a bit rusty, you might struggle with your accuracy on the first couple of shots, but after that the old muscle memory would kick in, and you'd hit the target dead-on.

An ex-SF soldier would know that. Bald had seen Hawkins missing the targets with the first two dozen bullets and realised that his old colleague was playing Devaney. Tricking him into thinking that Hawkins had messed up because of his hangover, or general incompetence. Any half-decent operator would have grasped what was happening. But Devaney had failed to see the trap being set for him. A combination of arrogance and stupidity. Hatred for the Englishman colouring his judgement. Now Hawkins would make him pay.

He set himself at the ten-metre mark. Planted his feet firmly on the ground. Exhaled lightly. Snatched his USP from the belt holster, lined up the front and rear sights with the central point of his designated target. Double-tapped. Paused a half-beat and fired twice more. He chewed his way through the remaining eight rounds in the magazine until he got the dead man's click. Reseated the semi in his holster.

Bald, Martel, Moussa and Steyn approached his target. They stared at the ragged hole in the middle of the bullseye. The kind of irregular, keyhole shape produced when a series of bullets passed through the same point on the target.

'One-hole group,' Martel said, his harsh German accent tempered by a note of grudging admiration. 'Every round in the same hole. Dead centre.'

Devaney stared at the target, mouth agape. 'Fucking hell. It ain't possible. How did you manage that?'

'He was tricking you, bra,' Steyn said. 'Sticking his rounds on that same spot on the wall to make you think he couldn't shoot for shit. We all saw it coming.'

Moussa, Martel and Bald all burst into laughter, chests heaving up and down. Steyn joined in too. Devaney looked livid. His expression darkened. He stormed up to Hawkins, getting into the latter's grille.

'You fucking played us.'

'Aye,' said Hawkins. 'And you fell for it, you daft cunt. Now, are you paying up in cash or cheque?'

Devaney made a strained noise in his throat. His nostrils were so wide you could have rolled boulders up them. He dug out his wallet, handed over a thin wad of twenty-dollar bills. Hawkins pocketed the money. Devaney stared him down.

'I'll not forget this. You'll be fucking sorry.'

'Keep running that stupid mouth of yours,' said Hawkins, 'and you'll be picking your teeth off the ground before the job's done. Now get the fuck out of my face.'

Devaney fumed but kept his mouth shut. He backed away from Hawkins. Tactical withdrawal. The lizard part of his brain taking over, prioritising self-preservation. Hawkins had just made an enemy for life, but he didn't care. He had bigger problems in his in-tray. The plan to steal the HEU cylinders. His mission with Six. Making sure he didn't blow his cover. He wasn't going to spend the next several days listening to Devaney pulling the piss.

They spent another thirty minutes at the range. Then Steyn checked his watch and said, 'Rugger's on soon, lads. Let's head back to the lapa and get the beers in. Staff will fix us up some grub.'

They packed away the kit. Moussa put the weaponry back into the gun bags while Steyn gathered up the plywood-pasted targets from the range. He stowed them in the shed with the folded table, secured the padlock to the door. Then the team took the short path running westward to the lapa, passing between the walled garden and the golf clubhouse. The course with the Antonov AN-72 hidden somewhere on it. Moussa led the way, walking fifty metres ahead of the others, carrying one of the gun bags, saying nothing. Like a Buddhist monk observing a vow of silence. Only with much bigger pectoral muscles. Steyn trotted along in his wake with the other bag, chatting to Bald about the Lions's prospects in the upcoming series against South Africa. Martel was behind them, gazing round at the estate with a faintly amused smile. Then came Hawkins, with Devaney sulkily bringing up the rear.

Hawkins cast his mind back to the earlier briefing. The plan looked good on paper. But every plan looked good on paper. Any number of things could go south once they hit the ground. Unforeseen issues at the border crossing, perhaps. Or during the ambush itself. They were going to intercept a convoy carrying nuclear materials, on one of Iran's busiest highways. The soldiers might put up an unexpectedly hard fight. Or the Iranian general might be wrong on the strength of the infantry support for the convoy. The uranium cylinders could suffer damage during the firefight.

Even if the attack went perfectly to plan, they were going to have to leg it back across the border with Turkmenistan without getting intercepted by the Iranian security services.

A tough op.

One of the hardest I've ever had to pull off.

After two hundred metres they came round to the lapa. A white refuse truck had stopped outside the guest accommodation. A pot-bellied old-timer in a shabby brown uniform was chucking the rubbish left outside the bungalows into the back of the van. Waste collection service. Private contractors paid a pittance to collect the garbage from all the wealthy properties in this area. Manpower recruited from the slum up the road, probably. Little Zimbabwe.

Bin collection is due in an hour, Steyn had said before they'd made for the range. *Any rubbish, leave it outside your front door.*

Hawkins was fifty metres from the lapa when Devaney abruptly stopped in his tracks.

'Who the fuck is that?' he said in a startled tone, looking towards one of the bungalows.

Hawkins had put the brakes on. So had Bald and Steyn and Martel. All four of them staring in the same direction. A hundred metres away a scrawny youth, decked out in the same uniform as the old-timer and wearing a baseball cap, was climbing out of the small window on the side of the bungalow, clutching a bunch of tech gear in his right hand. What looked like a laptop and a tablet.

'Fucking thief,' Steyn said. He called out to the kid in the baseball cap, 'Hey! You!'

The kid landed beside the open window, the looted kit clattering around his feet. He heard the shout coming from Steyn a hundred metres away, looked down the path at the mercenaries – and froze.

Moussa was fifty metres ahead of the gang. Therefore the closest to the thief. He dropped the gun bag and broke into a sprint, barrelling towards the thief with astonishing speed.

The thief jerked into action. He spun away from the colossal Eritrean, sprinting past the bungalows and making for the main gate several hundred metres away. A hopeless plan. The kid was acting out of fear. But understandable when you had three hundred pounds of muscle bearing down on you. Possibly the kid had heard the stories about Moussa being a jinn. He tripped and almost fell, regained his balance, staggered on. Still clutching his plunder, ignoring the frantic gestures and cries from the old geezer at the truck.

Moussa quickly closed the gap. He was almost on top of the thief now. Legs working like pistons, propelling him forward. Like a bull chasing down a fighter. In another two strides he sprang forward and lunged at the kid, tackling him to the ground. The blow knocked the wind out of him, scattering the stolen tech across the front lawn.

Hawkins hurried past the lapa to catch up with Moussa. Martel, Steyn, Devaney and Bald jog-trotted after him. The old geezer was yelling at Moussa, throwing up his arms and generally making a lot of noise. A hundred metres away, Kettler charged out of the mansion, presumably having heard the commotion outside. He caught sight of Moussa and the kid and ran towards them, brushing past a maid scrubbing down the front steps.

Moussa was kneeling over the thief, thighs pinning him down while he rooted through his pockets. He retrieved a pair of phones from the kid's jacket, set them down next to the laptop and the tablet. Then he scraped the thief off the ground, sitting him upright.

The kid was groggy. He kept moaning at Moussa. Repeating the same words over and over. What sounded to Hawkins like a plea.

The Eritrean wrapped his left arm around the kid's neck, right hand gripping his chin. He made a sudden movement, twisting the kid's head sharply towards his left side and simultaneously jerking his chin in the opposite direction. There was a light snapping sound, like a stick being broken in two.

The sound of a human neck breaking.

The thief went limp. Moussa released his grip and climbed to his feet. The kid's lifeless body slumped on the grass in front of him.

Kettler reached the scene a few moments after Steyn and the others. He glanced at the dead kid with an expression of mild irritation. Not the look of a man overly perturbed by the death of a child on his grounds. More like he'd just realised the yoghurt in his fridge was past its use-by date.

Life is cheap here, bra.

The old-timer hobbled over from the truck, spared a glance for the limp body on the ground and started waving his arms at Kettler in protestations of innocence.

'I swear, boss, I don't have nothing to do with this. I swear on my life.'

Kettler dead-eyed the geezer. 'Who the fuck is he?'

'I don't know him, boss, I just gave him a job. I needed help. My back, boss. Gives me pain all the time. Not my fault.'

'Where is he from? Your village?'

'No, boss, not mine,' the refuse collector responded anxiously. 'He comes from another village. Many miles from here. This not his home.'

'Does he have any relatives here?'

'No, boss. No one knows him.'

Kettler nodded slowly. He dipped a hand into his back pocket and plucked out a clip of fifty-dollar bills. He peeled off four Grants from the wad, pressed them into the geezer's calloused palm.

'Put him in landfill,' Kettler said, flapping a hand at the dead kid. 'Make sure he disappears. Do that and another two hundred will come your way. Anyone asks questions, you say he didn't show up for work today. Is that clear?'

'Yes, boss,' the old man said. 'No problem. I take care of it. Don't worry.'

He closed his grip around the bills, shoving them into his jacket while Steyn and Martel lifted the body and hauled it over to the refuse truck. They threw the thief into the back with the mound of bin bags. The geezer would dispose of him in some municipal rubbish tip far away from the compound. Carrion for the wild dogs and birds. Hawkins wasn't surprised at the old-timer's reaction. He probably had a family to provide for, mouths to feed. Plus he had the extra two hundred bucks in his pocket, with the promise of more to come. He wasn't about to kick up a fuss over a dead thief.

The old-timer hustled back over to his truck. He gunned the engine and steered back round to the driveway, heading westward in the direction of the main gate, while Steyn and Martel started back across the grounds.

Kettler scooped up the phones and took a long look at them, his brow pouched. One of the handsets was turned off, Hawkins noticed. He caught a glimpse of the logo above the blackened screen. The same cheap Chinese no-name brand as his false-screen phone.

Something cold slithered snake-like down his spine.

Two phones, he thought.

A personal one.

Plus a secret one.

A question prodded at Hawkins.

Why the fuck would any of these lads have two phones? He could think of only one explanation that made any sense. Someone was using a covert handset, similar to his own device. Turning it on only when necessary to save on the battery life.

Hawkins recalled what Steyn had told him on the drive up from the airport.

The boss is concerned about leaks.

He doesn't trust anyone right now.

At his side, Devaney stood stock-still. Fear spreading across his face.

'Where did this wretch steal this from?' Kettler asked, calmly. Putting the question to the wider group.

'There, boss,' Moussa replied. The first time Hawkins had heard him speak. Maybe the first time the guy had uttered a word in his entire life. Hawkins felt like someone should erect a statue to commemorate the event.

The Eritrean pointed with a brick-sized finger.

Indicating the nearest unit.

Devaney's bungalow.

Fourteen

No one said a word for several moments. Devaney stood perfectly still. Putting down roots on the spot. Kettler slid his gaze from the bungalow to the Irishman, his lips pressed into a hard line. Hawkins could sense the ire simmering behind his features. It was there in the gleam of his eyes. The twitching of his cheek muscles.

'What the fuck are you doing with two phones, Terry?' he asked, quietly but sternly.

Devaney hesitated. He glanced round, as if hoping that whatever deity he believed in would appear to rescue him.

'Well, Terry?' Kettler pressed.

'It's just a burner, boss,' Devaney stammered. 'I use it to call Julie.'

'Who the fuck is Julie?'

'My girlfriend, boss. My bit on the side. It's so my wife doesn't find out. She's got a habit of checking my personal phone, like.'

Kettler didn't look convinced. 'So you brought your burner here to do what, exactly? Send naked selfies to each other while you wait for the job to go down? Is that it, Terry?'

Devaney shrugged helplessly. 'We've just been chatting, boss. There's no harm in it. Check for yourself if you don't believe me.'

Kettler dropped his gaze to the switched-off phone. Thinking hard.

He reached a decision.

'Take this cunt over to the lapa,' he ordered.

Moussa and Steyn clamped their hands around Devaney's biceps and frogmarched him up the path to the lapa. Martel retrieved the two gun bags and joined the rest of the gang at the lapa, Kettler bellowing at the bar workers to piss off. They hastened down the separate path towards the staff lodgings on the far side of the compound.

Steyn swiped the remote and punched buttons, turning off the rugby match showing on the big screen. Moussa seated Devaney on a chair near the fire-pit. The latter dropped into it without a struggle. The logical option. No point putting up a fight, not against Moussa. Devaney was a big guy, but next to the Eritrean he looked like a toy doll.

Steyn retrieved a dishrag from the sink next to the bar, a roll of duct tape from one of the cupboards. Moussa held Devaney's head in place while Steyn stuffed the rag into his piehole. The South African took the tape, tore off a strip, slapped it over his mouth. Shutting Devaney up for the first time in his life.

Kettler said, 'Give us that tape, Rory.'

Steyn handed over the duct tape. Kettler ripped off a small piece and placed it over the rear camera. He looked round carefully at the other team members. 'When I turn this thing on, nobody fucking talk. Not a word, not so much as a fart. We've got no idea who might be listening in.'

He approached Devaney, dropped to a knee in front of him, spoke to him in a strangely calm tone.

'Listen, Terry. In a moment, I'm going to turn on this secret phone of yours. When I do, you're going to put in the PIN code. Refuse, and I'll break every fucking bone in your body. Understood?'

Devaney nodded. He understood.

'Good man,' Kettler said.

He stretched to his full height.

Booted up the device.

Kettler offered the screen to Devaney. The Irishman still didn't look panicked. Either he was confident in his cover story, or he really was having an affair with someone called Julie. Trading raunchy texts while waiting for the tip-off from the Iranian general.

Devaney tapped in a six-digit number. Steyn and Moussa peered over his shoulder, making a note of the PIN. The phone unlocked with a diplomatic click. Kettler scrolled through a series of exchanges on the messaging app. The silence broken only by the sound of meat sizzling on the braai.

After a few minutes Kettler shut the device down again.

'Well, boss?' asked Steyn.

'Not much on there. Like the man says. Lots of texts to someone called Julie. No emails or photos. No social media.'

'So he's telling the truth?'

Kettler shook his head fiercely. 'I've seen these devices before. A couple of years back. At a military expo in Washington. Modified versions of a no-name Chinese import. Made to look like burners. The CIA use them, among others. What they call a false-screen phone.'

Kettler was staring at Hawkins as he spoke.

Hawkins stayed very still.

'Jesus Christ,' Steyn breathed.

'How does that even work?' Martel asked. 'I've never heard of such things.'

Kettler said, 'There are two channels. One acts like a normal phone. The second one gives you a direct line to Star City. Unbreakable encryption, or as close to it as you can get. The mic is always on and transmitting. The guys at the expo were raving about them.'

Hawkins suddenly realised why Kettler had wanted Devaney's mouth taped shut. Because of the false-screen phone. *The mic is always on.*

As soon as Kettler powered up the device, any chatter would be broadcast back to Devaney's handlers in real-time. The guy might try to alert them to his situation. Or he could shout out a code-word. Something to signify that his cover had been blown. Then the mission would go down the pan.

And my chances of finding out who's buying the cylinders would go the same way.

He briefly wondered if his own device had the same functionality. If so, Six hadn't mentioned it to him. Which got him thinking.

They didn't give me the heads-up about Bald being on the team.

They haven't told me if Bald is working for them or not.

What else aren't those bastards telling me?

Kettler reverted his gaze to Devaney.

'Take the rag out of his mouth,' he said.

Devaney let out a muffled cry of pain as Steyn yanked away the duct tape and removed the dishcloth. Devaney gasped for breath, taking in big gulps of air. As if someone had just given him mouth-to-mouth.

Kettler knelt in front of Devaney. Dropped his voice to a harsh whisper as he spoke again.

'Let's cut the bullshit. You're working for someone else, Terry. You've been spying on us and feeding them information using this false-screen phone. Don't waste your breath on this cock-and-bull story, son, I wasn't born yesterday. It's better for you if you come clean now. Otherwise, things will get very ugly, very fucking fast. I can promise you that.'

'Boss, I swear to God, I don't know what you're talking about,' Devaney said between ragged draws of breath.

'Bollocks.'

'It's just a stupid fucking burner. That's all it is. Jesus, I wouldn't lie to you, boss. I wouldn't.'

'But you are, Terry,' Kettler said. 'You're lying to my face right now.'

Devaney said nothing. Kettler spoke again.

'Enough with the games, Terry. Tell me who you're working for and what you've told them. Do that, and I give you my word that I won't kill you. Keep up with your lies and we'll do this the hard way. Moussa will break every finger in your right hand. Then he'll move on to your left. Then he'll take out your teeth and fingernails. By the time he's finished with you, son, life won't be worth living.'

Devaney didn't answer. He was starting to brick it now. Hawkins could see the struggle playing out on his big, dumb face. Did he stick to his cover story and take the pain that was coming his way? Or fess up to Kettler? Admit the truth and throw himself at his mercy?

'Last chance, Terry,' Kettler said.

'Boss, please,' Devaney begged, his voice trembling with fear. 'I haven't done nothing. On my life, it's just a burner.'

'Fetch the rope, Rory,' said Kettler. 'Tie this fucker up.'

Steyn returned to the bar. He rummaged through a set of utility drawers until he found several lengths of nylon rope. The sort of thing everybody stored in a lapa for one reason or another. For rigging up a hammock, or repairing damaged poles or braces after stormy weather. He paced back over to Devaney, looped the rope around his midriff, tethering him to the chair. Moussa kept him fixed in place, his huge paws pressing down on Devaney's shoulders.

Devaney protested in an increasingly panicky voice, directing his pleas at Kettler, his eyes wide with terror.

'Boss, you can't do this. Please. Jesus, I'm telling the truth.'

Kettler made no reply. He casually extracted a fresh Montecristo from his shirt pocket. He guillotined the cap, toasted the foot of the cigar with his pocket lighter and took a long draw, exhaling smoke, while Steyn bound Devaney's forearms to the armrests. Steyn pulled the knots tight, damn near cutting off the blood supply. Secured Devaney's legs with another piece of rope, tying them just below the knee.

'All done, boss,' Steyn said as he stood up.

'Talk, Terry,' Kettler said. 'Tell me the truth.'

Devaney didn't respond.

Kettler gave a nod. A slight inclining of the chin, directed at Moussa. As if to say, *You know what to do.*

The Eritrean read the signal. He manoeuvred his huge frame around the chair so that he was standing directly in front of Devaney. Moussa grabbed hold of the index finger on Devaney's right hand. Devaney was breathing hard now, his chest heaving up and down as he steeled himself for the coming pain. Moussa wrenched his finger backwards in one clean sharp motion. Bending it towards his wrist.

There was a sharp crack of splintering bone. Devaney's mouth went slack, forming a stunned 'O'. He let out an inhuman howl, his whole body convulsing with shock and pain.

Moussa moved on to the middle finger. He broke that one too. Devaney screamed in agony.

'That's enough, for now,' Kettler said.

He stepped towards Devaney, enjoying a few puffs on his stogie. Devaney was sobbing. Tears ran in veins down his cheeks, wetting his spade beard. A dark patch stained his combats, and Hawkins realised the guy had pissed himself.

'Talk, son, or Moussa will break the rest of them,' Kettler said. 'So help me God he will.'

'Boss,' Devaney groaned, despairingly. 'Don't do this. Christ, I'm begging you . . .'

'Again, Moussa,' Kettler said.

The Eritrean man-mountain got to work on Devaney's remaining fingers. Snapped the fingers on his left hand, then his thumbs. Devaney's sickening screams pierced the air, carrying across the estate. Hawkins looked round but he couldn't see any ground staff in sight. Probably they knew better than to go anywhere near the lapa right now. They would be staying in the main house, or their lodgings, minding their own business.

Moussa moved on to Devaney's upper body. Giving him a series of hard digs to the torso and face. Devaney's sobs grew weaker.

'Who are you working for? The Americans? Mossad?' Kettler demanded. 'Tell me, man. Spit it out.'

Devaney refused to answer.

'Get the hammer, Rory,' Kettler said. 'Break his fucking toes.'

Steyn made another trip to the storage area at the bar. He rooted around in the drawers, came back wielding a ball peen hammer. Moussa yanked off Devaney's boots and socks and held his leg firmly in place, toes planted on the floor. Steyn struck downward with the flat head of the hammer. As if he was striking the top of a chisel. Or minting a coin. The face crashed down on Devaney's big toe, mashing up bone and ligament.

Steyn hammered the rest of Devaney's toes. He smacked up his shoulders and jaw, gave him a few blows to the shins for good measure. Devaney groaned in agony. Blood dripped down from his busted nose and lips, staining the floor between his rag-order toes.

'Fuck me, boss,' said Steyn, rubbing the torn flesh of his knuckles. 'He's a tough one to crack.'

Kettler didn't say anything. He was contemplating Devaney. Head tilted to one side, pulling steadily on his Cuban cigar, his brow crinkled in thought above the hooded eyes. Like a guest at an art exhibition, trying to decipher a postmodern masterpiece.

'Get the whisky,' Kettler said. 'The strong stuff. Bring a jug of water, too.'

Steyn returned to the bar yet again. He fetched a bottle from the drinks shelf behind the counter. One-hundred-and-twenty proof whisky. Cask-strength. A higher alcohol content than some of the other brands. Therefore extremely flammable. Steyn brought the bottle over, handed it to Kettler. He made another trip across the lapa, seized a jug, filled it with ice and bottled water.

Kettler towered over Devaney, pouring the whisky over his thighs. Drenching him in the stuff.

'You're making me do this, Terry. This is on you. All you've got to do is say the word and this will all be over.'

The air reeked of whisky. Devaney lifted his battered head, watched fearfully as Kettler thumbed the flint wheel on his Zippo lighter. A flame sparked out of the wick. He relit his Montecristo, taking a long drag. Then he held the lighter to Devaney's booze-soaked legs.

Devaney screamed. Flames licked down past his knees, the foul stench of burning fabric, skin and hair mixing with the whisky and the aroma of grilling braai-meat. Devaney was shrieking hysterically, thrashing about wildly and begging for mercy.

Kettler puffed calmly on his Cuban.

Waited.

Devaney kept screaming.

Kettler said, 'Put the flames out, Rory.'

Steyn emptied the contents of the jug over Devaney's toasted legs. Water quenched the flames with a violent hiss. Smoke wreathed up from his incinerated combats. Devaney wept softly, head sagged, shoulders pistoning. He cut a pitiful sight. Most of his trouser material had burnt up, revealing patches of charred skin. His T-shirt was stained with blood. Hawkins became aware of a revolting smell in the air. Not the odour of cooked flesh, but something even worse. Shit. Human shit. Devaney had voided his bowels.

Kettler tapped off a seam of cigar ash and said, 'Start talking, Terry. I won't kill you. I give you my word on that. Just tell me the truth, and this will all be over.'

Devaney nodded. 'No more, please. I'll talk.'

He collapsed into a coughing fit, hacking and spluttering and gasping for air, choking on the putrid fumes of his own roasted skin and hair. Kettler waited for the episode to pass.

'Who the fuck are you working for, Terry?'

'Langley,' Devaney said, breathing shallowly. 'I'm working for Langley.'

Something shifted in Hawkins's bowels.

Langley.

The CIA.

Devaney carried on. Spewing it all out between shallow breaths.

'I didn't have a choice, boss. I swear to Christ. They had me by the short and curlies. If I didn't do what they told me, I would have ended up behind bars. That's the honest truth.'

'When did they approach you?'

'A month ago. I was living in Boston. Moved there from Wicklow a couple of years back. After I left the Ranger Wing. Got a job with one of my uncles over in Dorchester. Working for his construction firm. Shite money. Shite hours, too.

'One of my cousins, he had connections to a family in the drug business. Some guys who worked with the Nicaraguans. Cocaine and crystal meth. Load of other shite too. Fentanyl and such. I started working a corner for them. Low-level distribution. But enough to pad out my bank account. Worked my way up to running stash houses and distribution. Big business.

'Some fucker snitched on us. Never found out who did it. Police arrested me outside my house. Had their search warrants ready. Turned my house upside down and my fucking car, too. Took me in and booked me. Said they'd found bags of cocaine and fentanyl in my bedroom, in my car. Bastards had me bang to rights. Told me I was looking at fifteen years in Club Fed. I was up to my neck in the shit.

'That's when the fella from the CIA met with me. Told us he could make the charges disappear, but I'd have to do a job for the agency. I fucking leapt at it.'

'Why would they use you? Why not one of their own?'

Devaney spat out a globule of blood. 'He told us they couldn't put a Yank on the team. Too dangerous. Layers of separation or something. Whatever that meant. They said it had to be someone else. A foreigner. Someone you wouldn't suspect of working for Langley. But it had to be someone legit, with a track record of SF service.'

Hawkins listened keenly. He reckoned there was another reason the CIA would have wanted an outsider to infiltrate Kettler's team.

Because Devaney was expendable. If anything happened to him, no one would be asking questions. There would be no coffin coming back to Fort Bragg on the back of a C-130, Stars and Stripes draped over the lid.

Kettler said, 'How much do they know about the job?'

Devaney said, 'Next to nothing. God's truth. All they know is that you're planning something big, and you've been meeting with that Iranian general.'

'They must have *some* idea of what's going down. They wouldn't have gone to the hassle of planting you otherwise.'

Devaney grimaced and said, 'They believe the job is an assassination. Regime change.'

'Why the fuck would they think that?'

'The general is a popular figure in the country at large. The peasants love him. The Yanks think he's plotting to knock the Ayatollah on the head and install himself as leader. That's all I know.'

'Makes sense, boss,' Steyn opined. 'If the CIA thought we were involved in overthrowing the regime, they'd definitely want someone on the inside, relaying int. Make sure their man took over.'

That must have raised a question in Kettler's mind because he returned his attention to Devaney.

'What's their plan? Once they find out what we're doing? They can't have sent you in here blind, Terry.'

'They didn't say. They just told me to get on the team and report in whenever I had solid information. That's all I know.'

'What have you told them so far? The truth now.'

'Fuck all. I've only messaged them twice since we got in. Once to say I'd arrived, a second text to let them know the briefing was going down today. That's it. They don't know anything else.'

'The Americans must be getting sloppy,' Martel cut in. 'Sending this piece of shit out here with two phones. Stupid fucking move.'

Devaney shook his head slowly.

'That's on me. They told us to leave my personal phone at home.'

'So why bring it here?' Kettler asked.

'I've got a girlfriend. I wasn't lying about that side of it, see. Denise. That's her name. She's back in Wicklow. My sweetheart. Known each other since we was at school. We've been messaging lately on me personal phone. Sharing this and that.'

'What about the texts on the false-screen phone? The messages to Julie?'

'That's just cover. Some shite cooked up by a desk jockey at Langley. In case anyone asked questions about the burner. What they told me, anyhow.'

A phone with nothing on it would look shifty, Hawkins knew. Better to stick a few randy messages on it and pretend you were using it to sex-message your new squeeze. Devaney's cover story might have worked, but the guy had fucked up by travelling to Pretoria with both his phones. An obvious red flag. One that had immediately made Kettler suspicious. Devaney had made the classic mistake of dumb operators everywhere. Breaking his SOPs, ignoring the rules. Thinking he was the smartest bloke in the room. The kind of stupidity that got people killed.

A troubling thought stabbed at Hawkins. His phone looked identical to Devaney's false-screen device. The same cheap-as-chips Chinese manufacturer. Same model. If Kettler laid eyes on it, he would doubtless suspect Hawkins of being a plant.

Next time it will be me in the chair, getting the flame-grilled treatment.

Kettler indicated the false-screen phone. He said to Devaney, 'Tell me how to access the secret channel.'

Devaney told him. After which Steyn stuffed the cloth back in Devaney's pie-hole, sealing it with a strip of duct tape. The lapa fell pin-drop silent again as Kettler powered up the handset. He tapped open one of the preloaded apps on the home screen. Put in the correct sequence of numbers, following Devaney's instructions. The code must have worked, because Kettler spent a good minute reading through an exchange of encrypted messages, finger drawing slowly up the screen.

He stopped scrolling. Switched the phone off again.

Steyn ripped the tape from Devaney's mouth.

'What does it say, boss?' Steyn said.

Kettler said, 'Conversation between Devaney and his handler. Last message sent yesterday evening. Eleven o'clock. Asking if our man here had any more news.'

'That's before the briefing this morning,' Martel said.

'We're safe, then,' Steyn said. 'The Yanks can't know about the plan.'

'Unless Devaney deleted the latest transmission. There are ways of doing that.'

Bald said, 'We're in the clear. I'm sure of it. If the Americans were onto us, we wouldn't be having this conversation. Them fuckers would be on us like a rash. Black Hawks would be sweeping all over this place.'

Kettler said, 'I agree. Nevertheless, we should take steps to protect our position. A brief message to Devaney's handler should do the trick. Get those idiots off our backs.'

'What about him, boss?' Steyn asked. Waving a hand at Devaney.

Kettler skimmed his gaze towards Bald and Hawkins.

'You two. Take this worthless scum down to the river,' he said. 'Somewhere away from any witnesses. Then kill him.'

Fifteen

Devaney raised his head in a sudden jolt of terror. His eyes were wide as a couple of medallions. He looked from Kettler to Bald and back again, his voice tremoring with fear. 'But you – you gave me your word, boss. You said you wouldn't kill me.'

'I said *I* wouldn't kill you,' Kettler corrected. 'Didn't say anything about Bald and Hawkins, though.'

The colour drained from Devaney's face. He looked sheet-white. 'No, boss. Don't. Please. Don't fucking do this.'

Kettler blanked him and continued to address the two ex-Hereford men.

'Dispose of this thing while you're at it.' He handed the false-screen phone to Bald. 'Leave it turned off until you've given him the double-tap special. Then turn it on, put in the PIN and jump over to the secret screen.'

Kettler walked them through the steps. Practically the same ones Hawkins used to unlock the hidden screen on his own device, differing only in the numbers entered into the calculator app.

'Once you're on the covert channel, open the messaging app and reply to the last text. Write, "No news, not expecting any movement until next week." Switch the phone off, take out the SIM card and chuck everything in the water. Clear?'

'Yes, boss,' said Bald.

Kettler looked at the two ex-SAS men in turn. 'Either of you have a problem with your orders?'

Bald said, 'The guy is a fucking snitch. That's no problem, in my book. It's a pleasure. Up there with seeing Aberdeen beat Celtic in the cup final.'

Kettler smiled. 'You're a cold bastard, Jock. Geordie?'

'No problem, boss.'

'Good.'

He gave Hawkins directions to a local fishing spot along the river. A two-minute drive from the estate. Bald salvaged the Colt 1911 from one of the gun bags Martel had deposited on the long table facing the projector screen, wedged the pistol into the waistband of his jeans, pocketed an eight-round single-stack magazine of .45 ACP.

Steyn and Moussa untied Devaney from the rattan chair. They heaved him to his feet, stuffed the dishrag into his mouth and lashed his hands behind his back, the cord digging into his wrists. Then Bald and Hawkins took him by the arms and plotted a course for one of the Land Cruisers parked in front of the main residence.

They moved along at a Zimmer-frame shuffle. Devaney could barely walk. Because of the mangled toes and the torched legs. But also because of the fear. The guy was shaking in terror.

Hawkins took the wheel. He steered counter-clockwise round the fountain, motored down the tree-flanked avenue towards the front gate. Bald in the passenger seat, Devaney lying on his side in the back, the dirty cloth stifling his panicked cries for mercy. Blood staining the beige leather.

The drive gave Hawkins time to think over what had just happened. He had a lot to process.

His situation had become much more perilous. That much was clear. The Americans were sniffing around Kettler and his crew. If the CIA knew about the plan to lift the uranium, Hawkins and the other team members were in serious trouble. There would be a furious row with Whitehall, too, especially if Farrell learned that Six had been withholding vital int from their cousins at Star City. Had actually encouraged the Iranian general to lie to his handlers in Washington, stringing them along with a cock-and-bull story about regime change. Making sure that the plot to steal the uranium wouldn't be comprised.

All of which was several notches above Hawkins's paygrade. Fine by him. Other people were paid generous salaries to sit in air-conditioned offices and deal with that stuff. He was far more concerned with the situation in front of him.

Kettler knew he had a leaky ship. Therefore he would be scrutinising the others even more closely now. Looking for any suggestion that they might be working for the enemy.

The moment Kettler catches sight of my false-screen phone, I'm a dead man.

The phone had to go. No question about it. Hawkins resolved to ditch it as soon as they returned to the compound. That would mean he had no way of contacting Vauxhall, of course, but he couldn't worry about that. He had more pressing problems to deal with. First and foremost, the Irishman leaking blood all over the back of the Land Cruiser.

They passed through the front gate, the brown-uniformed guards armed with their AK-47s moving aside to make way for the wagon. Bald put the Land Cruiser on a northward trajectory. After two hundred metres he turned onto a dirt road running parallel with the river.

Devaney kept up his protests in the rear seat, screaming at Hawkins and Bald through the filthy cloth in his mouth, making all kinds of incomprehensible noises.

'We shouldn't be doing this, Jock,' said Hawkins.

'Doing what?'

'Him.' Hawkins threw a glance at the rear-view.

'Fuck off.'

'It's murder.'

Bald curled up his lips in disgust. 'This cunt was planning to shop us to the CIA. We could have ended up in prison if Kettler hadn't seen through that crap about his phone. Or they might have dropped a missile on us. Wiped us out. The guy is a traitor.'

'That's as may be, Jock. But I don't want his blood on my hands.'

'What's the problem? I thought you hated his guts.'

'If we kill him, and this job doesn't turn out the way we hope it does, we're looking at fifteen to twenty years.'

'Won't happen.'

'But what if it does? How many guys back home are getting prosecuted for stuff that went down thirty, forty years back?'

Bald said nothing. Hawkins tried again.

'There's a chance the mission goes south. You know that as well as I do. What happens then? There are four fuckers back at the compound who could easily sell us out to the authorities. Negotiate themselves a lower sentence in return for giving witness statements. We'll end up sharing cells with a bunch of long-bearded ISIS fanboys eager to avenge their Afghan brethren.'

Bald squinted hard at the horizon but said nothing. Hawkins didn't care about Devaney on a personal level. The guy was a rat. But he was thinking several steps ahead. The prospect of a murder charge hanging over him once he returned to Britain.

If I ever make it out of here alive.

Bald drove on for two hundred metres until they hit a patch of dirt set back from the riverbank. A local fishing spot, just like Kettler had described it. Long since fallen out of use. Bald eased off the accelerator, parked the Cruiser close to the river's edge.

A harsh wind greeted them as they dropped down from the wagon, whispering through the spiked ribbon grass, shaking the branches of the bushwillow trees hugging the bank. The harsh call of a hadeda interrupted the incessant chattering of grasshoppers. Hawkins looked round but the area was deserted. No pedestrians, no residents out for an afternoon jog. Not that kind of place. They were in an area of sparsely inhabited farmlands and game reserves, interspersed with the occasional sprawling estate. They had the riverside to themselves.

They pulled Devaney feet-first out of the wagon. Bald holding him by his mutilated feet, Hawkins with an arm wrapped around his flame-scarred legs, the pair of them heaving like two teammates yanking on a rope in a tug-of-war contest.

They stood Devaney fully upright. He put up a fight, struggling against his captors, wriggling from side to side in a futile attempt to break free. Bald dug out the Colt from his waistband, clobbered Devaney round the back of the head. The fight drained out of him.

They marched Devaney towards a point where the ground sloped down to a section of the river about twenty-five metres wide. The Irishman walked stiffly, Hawkins and Bald moving along either side of him, helping him navigate the rock-strewn bank. Like a couple of lads walking a drunken mate home after a night on the tiles. Hawkins tried to ignore the quivering in his guts.

We're about to kill a guy in cold blood.

Not any old idiot.

A CIA asset.

They stopped four metres up from the water's edge. Hawkins glanced round once more. No vehicles approaching from either direction on the dirt track. No locals rocking up for a spot of afternoon fishing or a family picnic. Bald ripped the duct tape from Devaney's mouth, pulled out the cloth. Hawkins untied the rope knotted around his wrists. Devaney wept pitifully. Pleading with Bald and Hawkins to spare him.

Bald said, 'How much money have you got on you, Geordie?'

Hawkins emptied his wallet. He had a little leftover travel cash, plus the wedge he had won from Devaney earlier that afternoon. Four hundred and fifty-eight dollars in total.

Bald took the bundle and thrust it at Devaney.

'Your lucky day, son. We're going to let you go. But if you talk to anyone, you'll die. It'll be my life's mission. Number one on my bucket list. Got it?'

Devaney blinked, nodded his assent.

'This is what you're going to do,' Bald carried on. He pointed out a gravel track on the far side of the river. 'Make your way over to that path. You'll be able to wade across, the river's not deep in these parts. Once you're across, follow the path for a couple of kilometres. You'll hit a camp before long. Farm hands. Seasonal labourers. Give them the money and tell them to put you up for a couple of weeks, no questions asked. You stay low, keep your head down.'

Devaney stared at Bald in unbelief. Unable to comprehend his sudden change in fortune.

'Get moving,' said Bald. 'Now. Before I change my mind.'

Devaney snatched the notes and limped on towards the river. He started wading across the murky brown waters, heading for the far bank forty metres away.

They were taking a risk in letting him go. Hawkins was conscious of that. Devaney might try to find some way of reaching out to his handlers. Let them know what had happened. But it seemed unlikely. A moment ago he had been steeling himself for death. The ultimate one-way trip. Now he'd won an unexpected reprieve. Eleventh-hour pardon. He wasn't about to throw that away. The team would be safe, for a couple of weeks anyway. After that, even if Devaney did alert Langley, it would be too late.

Devaney had made it no more than a few paces from the bank when the crocodile leapt out of the depths. It shot up in a hide-scaled blur, jaws snapping open. The croc trapped Devaney between serrated teeth and twisted sharply round, slapping him down on the water in a death roll. Three more crocs surged out of the water and joined the attack, swarming round Devaney. The Irishman screamed, thrashed wildly as the crocs tore at him, their heads jerking from side to side as they ripped off chunks of flesh. Two of them pulled Devaney round, dragging him further away from the bank, towards a deeper patch of reddening water. He let out a final frenzied howl. Then he vanished beneath the surface.

The water calmed.

Devaney was gone.

'Fuck,' Hawkins said. 'Jesus fuck.'

Bald stared at the spot where Devaney had gone under. 'Well, we gave him a chance.'

Something in his tone gave Hawkins a start. 'You knew they'd set on him. Didn't you?'

Bald grinned. 'Had a hunch they might. Them fuckers like to stay in their burrows when it's too cold. Conserving energy. River is crawling with them along this stretch. Why no fucker fishes here these days. Too dangerous.'

'Fucking hell, Jock.'

Bald said, caustically, 'Don't tell me you're in a flap over that useless prick. The guy would have compromised us. Good riddance. Should be thanking me, Geordie.'

Hawkins checked himself. He was supposed to be a ruthless mercenary, amoral, willing to steal Iran's nuclear stockpiles without question. Not the kind of person who would get worked up over Devaney's demise. Besides, the croc had provided a neat solution to their dilemma. No one could accuse Hawkins or Bald of murder now.

'I'm not angry about him,' Hawkins said. 'But you cost me my winnings. That bastard went down with my money.'

Bald laughed. 'Tight English bastard. You'll be making a lot more than that when we've pulled this one off. Especially with him out of the way. More dough to split between the rest of us now.'

They started towards the Land Cruiser. Bald stopped, remembering Devaney's false-screen phone in his front pocket. He followed the instructions Kettler had given them. Powered up the device, accessed the secret screen through the calculator app. The same sequence Hawkins used on his covert phone, only with a different access code. Bald drafted a new message to Devaney's handler, thumbs working the touchscreen. Telling Devaney's handlers that they wouldn't have any further news for several days.

Hawkins read through it, gave it the thumbs-up. Bald hit send. Then he extracted the SIM card, stamped it underfoot, grinding it to tiny silicon fragments. He tossed the handset into the water. It splashed down close to the spot where Devaney had disappeared underwater. The crocs would feed on their prize for a while, devouring chunks of soft tissue and muscle. Swallowed whole, because as everyone knew, crocs couldn't chew. Then they would cache Devaney somewhere along the bank, below the waterline. Wait for the carcass to rot before eating the rest of it. The juicy internal organs, hair and bone. A big feast. Several days' worth of chow for the croc float. By the time they were finished, there would be nothing left of Devaney except a few bones and scraps of clothing.

If I'm not careful, I'll end up the same way.

Food for the crocs.

Hawkins was under no illusions about the seriousness of his situation. He was working with a pit of vipers. First the thief, broken-necked and dumped in landfill. Now Devaney. If he fucked up – if Kettler suspected him of working for Six – they would kill him. No question of that. They would torture him first. A long and horrible death.

They jumped back in the wagon, backed out of the dirt patch. Away from the fishing spot and the scene of Devaney's death.

They drove in silence. Hawkins still had no idea whose side Bald was on. *Is he working for Vauxhall? Or is he just here for the money?* Even if Bald was on the Legoland payroll he would probably deny it. Hawkins could admit to his own dealings with Cruttwell and Jackson, tease the truth out of his old colleague. But he wasn't prepared to do that. Not while he had doubts over Bald's position.

'You really think we're in the clear?' he said at last.

Bald said, 'The Yanks would be on us already if they had the slightest clue about the job. Delta lads would be sweeping through this place like a dose of salts. We'd be on a rendition flight, getting the jumpsuit treatment. There's no way they know.'

'If you're wrong, we're fucked. We're complicit in torture, for Chrissakes. We could be walking into a trap.'

'I ain't wrong, Geordie. I'm more worried about them fuckers back at the compound.'

'You think there might be another plant?'

'We're playing high stakes here. Interfering with superpowers. If the Americans have been trying to infiltrate us, you can be sure that other countries are sniffing around too. Mossad. Iranian intelligence. Maybe even them tossers at Vauxhall.'

'What are we going to do?'

'We trust no one. Rule number one, that. Law of the jungle, Geordie. And if anyone else threatens the job, we'll dump them in the river too.'

Hawkins glanced at his one-time SAS comrade. Was Bald bluffing him? Putting on a show to disguise his own position as a Six asset? Or did he really just want to get the job done and settle down for an early retirement with his new-found riches? Hawkins couldn't tell. He decided to shift the conversation on.

'Who do you think is buying the stuff – the cylinders?'

'Fuck knows. Could be anyone with deep pockets.'

'But if you had to bet?'

Bald rubbed his jaw. 'ISIS in Somalia. That's my guess. They'd want to get their hands on this shit. Bankrolled by the Qataris or the Emirates, perhaps. Them, or one of the sides in the Yemeni civil war. But that ain't the big mystery.'

Hawkins asked what he meant.

Bald said, 'We're lifting two hundred kilos of sixty per cent enriched uranium. I'm no fucking scientist, but I know this much: uranium is no good for building a dirty bomb. Something to do with emitting radiation slowly and alpha particles. I read it in a book somewhere. You detonate this stuff, you won't be doing much damage. Hardly worth the effort.'

'Why would anyone want to buy it then?'

'No idea, Geordie. Long as their money is good, who cares?'

'It might be used against us. Or our allies.'

'And it might not. But it's not my problem. Secrets and memoirs.'

'What d'you mean?'

'Them rear-echelon bastards kick up a fuss whenever one of the Regiment lads comes out with a book. They start complaining that so-and-so is cashing in, selling secrets. But whenever Major General Toff-Toff gets a book deal and writes about some black op, it's a fucking memoir.

'Double standards, see. They want blokes like us to be lions in the Regiment, then go back to our little council estates and live off crumbs. Meanwhile, they're raking it in with non-exec board positions and book deals, seats in the House of Lords. So don't lecture me on morality. I'm well past that. You should be too. The Ruperts never give two shits about morality when it comes to lining their pockets. High time lads like us made our nut for a change. Fuck the rest of it.'

They rolled through the front gate. The eucalyptus trees and cypresses lining the driveway wavered gently in the strengthening wind as Hawkins ploughed up the driveway, over the crest in the land.

'Speaking of Ruperts,' he said.

Kettler was waiting for them at the foot of the steps, pacing up and down, gripping a chunky satphone in his right hand. A black Thuraya handset with a short stubby antenna, small glass display and a numeric keypad. Like a throwback phone.

Kettler stopped pacing as Hawkins drew the Land Cruiser to a halt beside the fountain. They got out. Kettler glanced at the blood-stained rear seat then brought his gaze back to Bald and Hawkins.

'Well? Did you get rid of the problem?' he asked.

'Aye, boss,' Bald said. 'It's done. That scumbag won't be talking to anybody from now on.'

Kettler didn't press them for the grisly details. He seemed in a big hurry about something. 'Sort your kit, wait at the lapa and be ready to move.'

'What the fuck's going on?' Bald asked.

'The general has heard from his subordinate. The colonel. The rising star of the Iranian military.'

'And?'

'The convoy is on high alert. Units are being mobilised. There's a possibility of a move tonight.'

Bald drew his head back in surprise. 'But they're not supposed to be leaving yet. Not for a few more days.'

Kettler said, 'The plans have changed. It's a fast-ball now. Air crew are running through their pre-flight checks.'

'Why the fuck would they bring the move forward?' Hawkins asked no one in particular.

'We don't know,' Kettler said. 'I'm waiting to hear back from the general. He'll let us know once the operation has been green-lit. Should have more details from him then. Now hurry up and get your stuff ready. The clock's ticking, gents.'

Sixteen

Hawkins and Bald hastened towards the bungalows. Behind them Kettler hurried purposefully back into the mansion. *Clock's ticking. There's a possibility of a move tonight.* In a few hours they were going to be wheels up and on the way to Turkmenistan. On a mission that would either end with them making millions or facing an Iranian firing squad. Over at the lapa, Martel, Steyn and Moussa were waiting with their go-bags already packed, sitting at the long table, sipping brews, grazing on sandwiches and protein bars while they studied the mapping. Steyn motioned to Bald and Hawkins, waving them over.

'Put these with your kit,' he said, dishing out a couple of blue United Nations identification vests. He handed one each to Hawkins and Bald. Emergency wear. In case they were stopped during the op. The guys could throw the bibs on, pass themselves off as friendlies. Hawkins doubted they would have to use them, but he approved of the principle. *Plan for the worst. Make sure we're covered for whatever might happen once we're on the ground.* It told him that the other guys were taking the job seriously.

Hawkins took the vest and said, 'What are we gonna do about Devaney?'

'What about him?' Steyn said.

'We're down to five men now. We've planned this op for six lads, working together in pairs.'

'Already taken care of, bra. The boss is coming with. He's gonna take Devaney's place.'

'At his age?' Hawkins failed to hide the surprise in his voice.

Steyn said, 'The boss knows the plan inside out. He's in good trim. Better shape than most fuckers half his age. We won't have to waste time bringing him up to speed. Not like we've got time to recruit anyone else, not this late in the day.'

'Better than going in half-cocked,' Bald said. 'I'd rather have an ex-Reg bloke on the team than that back-stabbing leprechaun. No fucking contest there.'

Steyn said, 'Leave your phones behind in your rooms. Any other personal equipment. We're going data black on this one. Soon as you're packed RV back here.'

Conflicting thoughts jostled for space in Hawksins's head as he made for his lodgings. He wondered about the sudden change in the Iranians' schedule. Bringing forward the departure time. He could think of three potential reasons. The Iranians might have planned to go early all along in order to confuse any external threats to the convoy. Classic misdirection. Or perhaps Tehran had intelligence suggesting that the Americans were preparing to send in the bombers ahead of Farrell's publicly stated deadline, and moving the uranium had become a matter of extreme urgency. Or the regime had been forewarned somehow of the gang's plot to steal the cylinders.

In which case we're heading straight into an ambush.

Nothing he could do about that now. Out of his hands.

Worry about the stuff you can control, forget about the rest.

Starting with that false-screen phone.

Hawkins knew he had to dispose of it immediately, in the next few minutes, at any rate before they boarded the cargo plane. Kettler might get one of his cronies to search through their rooms once they were airborne. Looking for anything suspicious the guys had left behind. A reasonable possibility, after that business with Devaney and the CIA. That false-screen phone had become a ticking bomb in Hawkins's life.

He headed into the bedroom. The phone was in the exact same place he'd left it that morning, plugged into the charger on the bedside table. He looked round, but there was no sign that anyone had rummaged through his belongings while he'd been feeding Devaney to the crocs. He entered the formula into the default calculator app, brought up the messaging app he'd been using to communicate with Vauxhall. He had a new text from Cruttwell – or was it Jackson? Delivered a little over half an hour ago. Demanding an update on the situation.

Hawkins dashed off a message, alerting them to the possible change in schedule. *Potential go. Awaiting confirmation.* He said nothing about Devaney's death or his part in it. He had no intention of giving Six more rope to hang him with later.

He jumped off the secret channel. Shut down the device, removed the microscopic SIM card. Crossed to the bathroom. He took a knee beside the toilet and reached into the bowl, forced the phone down the trap, past the swan-necked bend, the part that prevented vile odours from permeating the room. He stood up, chucked in the SIM card, flushed. Waited to make sure both items had been fully washed down the drainage pipe, into the nearby septic tank.

He towelled down his arm, drained his bladder, ducked back into the bedroom. Packed the UN vest into his rucksack, on top of the spare set of clothes he'd brought with him from Ventanola. The team would be travelling light. Everything else would be waiting for them at the airhead.

A minute later Hawkins quit the bungalow. He found Steyn, Martel, Bald and Moussa sitting round the table at the lapa, doing their map studies. Last-minute run-throughs of the plan. Kettler was there too. Steyn was right about his shape. He was in pretty good trim for a guy in his mid-fifties. Some noticeable wear and tear a little rust on the bones, but probably in better shape than most squaddies.

The guys all wore variations of the same kit. Drab-coloured mountaineering trousers, Solomon or Merrell walking boots, heavy canvas shackets over plain T-shirts. No need for any thermal fleeces or thick outer layers. The route from Turkmenistan to Iran would take them through desert plains, coastal highways, mountain foothills. Temperature in the high twenties or low thirties during the day, dropping to around twenty at night, less in some places. Minimal rainfall.

At least we won't freeze to death if we have to make an emergency extraction on foot.

Steyn distributed rations for their go-bags. Sandwiches, protein bars. Energy gels. Bottles of water. Juice. They had a thirty-hour trip ahead of them. Followed by a fourteen-hour exfil. Forty-eight hours surviving on minimal rations. A hardship for a desk-bound civilian used to the routine of three main meals a day. But nothing that the guys on the team hadn't faced before in their military careers.

They spent the next fifty minutes going through the plan. Refreshing their memories. Studying routes and procedures. Escape and evasion procedures. They went through the attack blow-by-blow. Positions on the slipway before the attack. The articulated truck manoeuvring side-on, blocking the freeway from emergency rest-stop area to central reservation. They looked at designated teams. Who would take out the lead vehicles, which guys would sweep up from behind to wallop the infantry at the rear of the convoy. The movements of the truck driver once the gang had taken command of the convoy vehicles, clearing a space for the team to pass through before closing the gap again. Every detail rehearsed and committed to memory, so that each man fully understood not just his own role, but the roles of the other team members too. Three-sixty-degree planning, leaving nothing to chance.

Steyn had marked out the spot on the map where they would make the handover of the uranium to the mysterious buyer. An abandoned cement factory seventy kilometres from Gorakan, near the foothills of the Kopet Dag mountain range. Twenty kilometres from the nearest village. The ideal spot for the exchange. The place had stood empty for years, Steyn said. They would shake hands, make the trade; the other party would commandeer the two Unimogs. The team would take the technical back to the airfield. Two guys in the cab, the other four on the rear bed.

At exactly five o'clock, Kettler's satphone vibrated. He unsheathed the antenna, walked away from the lapa to field the call. Hawkins realised he had gone almost twenty-four hours without a drop of alcohol passing his lips. A long time. Now the urge came on strongly once more.

Christ, I could do with a livener right now.

A little something before we board the plane.

Two minutes later, Kettler marched back over.

He said, 'That was the general. He's just received confirmation from the colonel. Convoy is on its way to Fordow now.'

Hawkins made a quick calculation. According to Kettler's int they had around thirty-four hours until the transports were outbound from Fordow. Because of the aforementioned security protocols. Bottlenecks. Safety procedures. Equipment checks. The colonel and his crew following the rules. Tehran was ninety minutes ahead of Pretoria. Therefore the trucks would leave the facility at approximately 04.30 Iranian time, the day after tomorrow. They would reach the ambush site at around 05.00.

He looked round at his fellow mercenaries. There was no hint of excitement or fear written on their faces, only expressions of grim determination. Men ready to do anything in order to get filthy rich.

'Does he know why the Iranians are moving so soon?' Hawkins asked.

Kettler said, 'Apparently Farrell is bringing the attack forward. The Iranians have got watchers at Whiteman Air Force Base in Missouri. The only permanent base for the B-2s. They've reported heightened activity. Lot of people rushing around.'

'Could mean anything,' Bald said. 'Might be a dry run. Training op.'

'That's not all,' Kettler said. 'There are other indicators. Security has been ramped up at American military installations in Qatar,

Abu Dhabi and Bahrain. Same deal with the US embassies in the region. There's also been a media blackout at the White House. A routine press conference for tomorrow morning has been cancelled without explanation.

'The general has also been tipped off by one of his friends at the CIA. A vague warning to make sure he's well clear of the enrichment sites tomorrow night.'

'That tracks,' Martel said. 'Especially if the CIA thinks the general is planning to topple the regime. They'd want to forewarn him of the attack. Make sure the new leader doesn't come to harm.'

'But why is Farrell sending in the bombers now? Why the mad rush?' Hawkins asked.

Kettler said, 'The general doesn't know. Best guess, the public deadline was a bluff. A red herring designed to catch the Iranians off-guard. Washington might have information about the planned movement of materials from the facilities at Natanz and Esfahan.'

'Either that,' said Steyn, 'or Farrell thinks he's gonna miss out on the Nobel Peace Prize and he's taking his rage out on the Iranians.'

'With that fucker,' Bald said, 'you never know.'

'The main thing,' Kettler said, 'is that the Americans still don't know the uranium is at Fordow. The general is one hundred per cent sure on that front. They're still under the impression that the uranium is at the holding site on the other side of the country. No one will be watching Fordow.'

Hawkins thought: a sixteen-hour flight to Turkmenistan, with a quick turnaround at Djibouti to refuel en route before taking to the skies again. Then a long drive from the airport at Gorakan to the ambush site in Iran. Journey time of around fourteen hours. Maybe longer, in traffic. They'd get into position at the slipway for around one o'clock in the morning. Roughly four hours before the trucks were due to hit the ambush site.

'We're cutting it tight,' he said. 'There's no margin for error on this one. If we're delayed for whatever reason, we're going to miss our chance.'

Bald laughed. 'When has it ever been any different? Story of our bloody lives.'

'Let's move, guys,' Kettler said. 'Plane's waiting. General will give us a further update once the convoy has reached Fordow.'

Martel folded up the mapping, stuffed it into his bag. They shouldered their light rucksacks and started down the grassy track leading towards Kettler's private golf course five hundred metres south-east of the lapa. Dusk was encroaching the land, the sun reduced to a pale glimmer on the horizon as they trekked past the small clubhouse and the line of parked golf caddies. They followed the cart path across a lush green fairway, Kettler marching at the head of the group, slipping back into his old life as a Regiment Rupert, leading his band of merry men into battle.

Kettler noticed Hawkins at his side and glanced sidelong at him. 'Ready for this one, Hawkins?'

'Yes, boss. I am.'

'I forgot to ask you yesterday. During our little tour. Do you keep in touch with any of your old colleagues at all?'

'Not really, boss,' Hawkins replied noncommittally.

'Why not? Were you blackballed?'

'Nothing like that. Just ain't my rag. Hanging out in Hereford, shooting the breeze about the good old days, slagging off the new intake. Don't see the point.'

'You're a lone wolf, then. Prefer your own company. Is that it, Hawkins?'

'Something like that, aye.'

Hawkins wondered where this conversation was going. He had the feeling that Kettler was probing for information.

'Some of the chaps from my squadron had the same attitude. Turned their backs on camp life. Thought they could make a stab of it in the civilian world. One or two ended up working for those chaps south of the Thames, actually.'

'Is that so, boss.'

'I suppose they hoped to find a new purpose in life. Six doesn't work like that, of course. One job and then they're done with you. Then you're on the scrapheap.' He paused. 'Don't suppose you know anyone who went the same way?'

'No, boss.'

'Never interested you, Hawkins? Working for Vauxhall? Getting involved in secret shows?'

'No, boss.'

Kettler lapsed into silence as they approached the golf course. A landscape of manicured greens stretched out in front of Hawkins, faintly illuminated by security lights in the gathering dusk. Clusters of large shrubs and leafy trees. Ponds and streams. Drainage systems. Hawkins guessed the cost of maintaining it must have been stratospheric. Another big item on the Kettler expenditure spreadsheet. He was beginning to understand why the guy might feel the need for a big cash injection.

The cart path meandered around a corridor of tall trees planted in a dogleg close to the putting green on the second hole, screening the third tee on the far side. Kettler continued in that direction, hurrying along at a quick trot. They rounded the edge of the tree-belt, and then Hawkins stopped in his tracks.

Ahead of him was a par-five hole. Which he knew was the longest hole on a regular golf course. Three shots from tee to green. The teeing off boxes faced a broad strip, six hundred metres from end to end, snooker-table-smooth, on an east-to-west axis, with a large sand trap on the north side of the fairway, a smaller bunker close to the hole.

A knackered old Antonov AN-72 was parked on the edge of the fairway. A Soviet-era transport plane, capable of taking off or landing on a short grassy strip. Engine ducts mounted like a pair of giant bazookas either side of the fuselage, emitting a distinctive pre-flight turbine-hum as they turned and burned.

A metal-framed hangar roofed with camouflage netting had been erected between the trees behind it. Another question resolved itself in Hawkins's mind. He had been wondering how Kettler had managed to hide a Russian aircraft on his golf course. Now he understood. The Antonov would have been stowed under the canopy, invisible to any drones or satellites, hidden from view of the surrounding estate by the treeline. With the runway strip landing disguised as the fairway.

From the look of it the Antonov had seen better days. Better decades, too. The paintwork was chipped and faded in places. Several panels had been repainted in a different colour, giving it a patchwork feel. Hydraulic fluid stained the wings, the underside of the fuselage.

'State of this fucking thing,' Bald muttered in dismay. 'Bloody hell. Are you sure this is going to get us to the airhead?'

'She might not look like much,' Kettler said, 'but she's a work-horse. The pilots swear by her. She'll get us there. Depend on it.'

'How long is that strip?' asked Hawkins. He was thinking that it looked a lot shorter than a standard runway.

'Six hundred and twenty metres exactly.'

He did a double-take. 'Christ, is that gonna be long enough?'

'The pilots will make it work. This isn't their first run with this old bird.'

A smell of jet exhaust fumes choked the air as they approached the loading ramp at the rear of the Antonov. An engineer in over-alls stood beside the control panel near the ramp entrance, wait-ing for the guys to ascend into the cargo hold. Hammocks hung from the mainframe. There was a toilet next to the cabin door with a curtain round it, rows of fold-down seats on the sidewalls. Not much else. A long way from the business-class luxuries Hawkins had enjoyed on the way in.

They dropped into the seats, secured their harnesses, wedged their rucksacks between their feet. The engineer toggled the selector switch to the 'UP' position, the ramp rose slowly upwards with a motorised whine, sealing the team inside the cargo compartment. The engineer pointed to an electric urn lashed to the sidewall. There was a canvas service box secured to a hardpoint next to it.

'Hot water if you need it, lads,' he said. 'Mugs, tea bags and instant coffee in the canvas box.'

'Roger that,' Kettler said.

The engineer gave the thumbs-up, disappeared through the cabin door leading into the cockpit.

This is it.

No going back now.

The engines roared. The Antonov shuddered violently. Hawkins felt it in his bones. Fittings shook and threatened to snap loose. The cargo compartment vibrated like a tuning fork. Hawkins half-expected the plane to break apart. The pilots were full-throttling it, keeping the brakes on, hammering the engine up to full revs before they shot down the grass strip. The turbofans roared, built up to a crescendo. Like an F1 car on the starting grid, ready to shoot forward as soon as the starting lights extinguished.

The pilots released the brakes. The Antonov steamed down the makeshift runway, hurtling across the par-five fairway. Hawkins hoped to fuck that the pilots knew what they were doing. Then the aircraft lifted, climbing higher, the pilots banked heavily to the right before straightening out, and suddenly they were on their way out of Pretoria. Out of South African airspace. Heading towards Turkmenistan, and Iran, and a do-or-die attack on a nuclear convoy.

Thirty-four hours to go.

Seventeen

The Antonov cruised north towards Djibouti. Eight hours for the first leg of their flight, according to the engineer when he'd poked his head through the flight deck door. With the empty cargo hold they were making good time. From Djibouti they were looking at another six-and-a-half hours in the air before they reached the airfield at Gorakan. Once they hit the airhead they were going to have to grab their kit double-fast, jump into their vehicles and race down to the border crossing at Incheh Borun. If everything went according to plan they would be in position on the slipway a couple of hours before the attack.

A very big 'if'.

Let's just pray there aren't any delays along the way.

Hawkins unwrapped a protein bar from his rucksack. He chewed on it and thought back to something that Bald had told him earlier. In the Land Cruiser, on the way back from feeding Devaney to the crocs. The point about the enriched uranium cylinders.

Uranium is no good for building a dirty bomb.

Doesn't spread very well.

Which prompted a question.

Why the fuck would the buyers want it?

Hawkins didn't know. Maybe a non-nuclear state wanted the uranium to accelerate its own ambitions. A crash programme to build a crude nuclear weapon. Could sixty per cent uranium be used with a conventional ballistic missile? Or could it be combined with some other type of delivery mechanism? Hawkins remembered reading somewhere that uranium had to be enriched to a level of ninety per cent before it could be considered weapons-grade. What was known as nuclear breakout. Presumably uranium at a lower level of enrichment could still be deployed in a less powerful device.

Whoever it is, they're paying big bucks for the HEU. Which means they intend to use it somehow.

He turned his mind from the HEU to the guys sitting opposite. Moussa. Steyn. Martel. Would the CIA have planted a second asset on the team? A backup in case Devaney fucked up? Moussa and Steyn both seemed outwardly loyal to Kettler. Martel was something of an unknown quantity – he and Hawkins had hardly spoken since he'd arrived at the compound. But the German seemed perfectly at ease with the plan. So did Bald. Nothing in their behaviour suggested they were working for foreign intelligence.

These lads are probably looking at me and thinking the same thing. Wondering about my loyalties.

Thoughts of the buyer brought Hawkins back to his secret mission. He had been left with no choice but to dispose of his false-screen phone back at the compound. But it gave him a massive problem.

How the fuck am I going to contact Six?

He recalled hearing from a mate that Bald had spent a couple of years on secondment with the Revolutionary Warfare Wing during his time in the Regiment. Also known simply as 'the Wing'. A covert unit within 22 SAS, working hand-in-glove with MI6. SF muscle. Kicking in doors, lifting targets. Doing all of Six's dirty work. Only the best Blades secured postings with the Wing.

Bald would know how to get in touch with Vauxhall, of course. A name or number from his time with the Wing. But that would mean Hawkins revealing his hand. Admitting to his mission for Vauxhall. Which could backfire on him in all kinds of ways.

His head was starting to hurt.

Steyn distributed sleeping tablets from a plastic pill container, along with pairs of noise-cancelling earplugs. Each man popped a tablet, chased it down with a mouthful of bottled water. Then they climbed into their hammocks. Following the oldest rule in warfare. *Get your head down while you've got the chance.* Once they touched down in Turkmenistan, they were going to be in a frantic race against time. They might have to go days without proper sleep. Besides, there was nothing else they could do. They were thirty thousand feet in the air. No comms.

Nothing to do but wait.

Hawkins pushed his troubles to the back of his mind. He plugged his ears with the foam buds, closed his eyes. Jesus, he was wiped. The stress of the past twenty-four hours. Infiltrating the gang, getting rid of Devaney, hoping his cover didn't get blown. Felt like a lifetime had passed since he'd departed Ventanola. Two lifetimes, maybe.

Soon the gentle rocking motion of the hammock and the effects of the pill had worked their magic, his eyelids felt heavy, and he slipped into the numbing black embrace of sleep.

* * *

Hawkins awoke to the engineer's harsh voice, announcing that they were making their final approach to Djibouti airport. Hawkins wriggled out of his hammock, took a piss in the toilet behind the curtain screen. The rest of the lads roused themselves, returned to their fold-down seats, buckled in for the landing.

The aircraft shuddered to a halt, the engines wound down. Hawkins heard voices outside the plane, the whir and clank of machinery as the ground crew got on with the business of refuelling the Antonov. The team stayed put in the cargo compartment. Kettler's orders. *We keep a low profile. No one leaves the bird while we're on the apron.* There was a major US military presence at Djibouti airport. Questions would definitely be asked if they saw half-a-dozen burly guys getting off the back of what was officially listed as a humanitarian flight.

The engineer opened the emergency access door, ducked outside to confer with the ground team. Bald took a mug from the canvas box, popped in a tea bag, filled it with hot water from the electric urn. He offered Hawkins a mug. Hawkins shook his head. He wasn't a tea man. Other lads at Hereford consumed gallons of the stuff, but he'd never developed the taste for it.

Martel got up to stretch his legs. Pacing up and down the compartment. Steyn wolfed down a ham-and-cheese sandwich. Hawkins studied the mapping. Only Moussa remained in his uncushioned seat. Staring at the sidewall as if he had a personal beef with it.

Kettler pulled out his satphone, drew out the antenna. A few moments later he wandered over to the rear ramp to field an incoming call, index finger plugged in his other ear to drown out the noise. He returned several beats later.

'Another update from the general. Convoy has arrived at Fordow.'

'When?' asked Bald.

'Half an hour ago. Three o'clock in the morning, Iranian time. Scheduled to leave Fordow twenty-four hours from now. Three o'clock the next morning.'

Steyn frowned. 'Shit. They're early. Running ahead of schedule.'

Kettler said, 'We'll still get to the target site a couple of hours before the convoy. Meanwhile the general will remain on standby next to his satphone. Keep us informed on the convoy's movements. I've told him to remain in position until the mission is over. Once the handover is complete, he'll get on the next flight out of the country. Him and the colonel.'

Hawkins listened. He doubted it would go down like that. Probably the general would throw the colonel under the bus. Set him up as the fall guy. *I'd do the same thing if I was in his position. Frame the colonel, make it look like the guy had been dealing with the CIA.* That would have the additional benefit of diverting suspicions away from the general, buying him precious time to get out of Iran. Board a flight to Dubai while the regime interrogators were still getting to work on the colonel.

Hawkins said, 'Are there any sets of NVGs with that pile of kit at the airhead?'

Steyn said, 'Two pairs of binos. All they could get at short notice. No time to source NVGs, my guys said.'

'Doesn't matter,' said Bald. 'Night-time ambush works in our favour, anyway. We'll be able to approach the slip road unseen, lose the enemy in the darkness and put some serious distance between us and the QRF before it's sun-up.'

The turnaround went smoothly. Twenty minutes after they had touched down at Djibouti they were back in their seats, strapped in for the second leg of their journey. The pilots revved the engine, the Antonov catapulted down the runway. Hawkins hoped it was longer than the fairway strip back at Kettler's compound. Three minutes later they were climbing into the sky above the Red Sea and heading to their final destination. Turkmenistan. Gorakan airfield. The airhead.

Twenty-four hours until the convoy was due to leave Fordow.

Twenty-four hours until the ambush.

Not long to go.

Eighteen

They slept for most of the flight and landed at Gorakan six-and-a-half hours later. Shortly after midday local time. 10.48 in Tehran. Roughly fifteen hours before they expected a follow-up call from the general, informing them that the convoy had departed Fordow with two hundred kilograms of highly enriched uranium.

The Antonov taxi-crawled across the runway before it shuddered to an abrupt halt. The noise petered out and the engineer reappeared from the front cabin to resume his duties as loadmaster, toggled the control panel. The loading ramp yawned open, like a jaw sagging in slow-motion. The operators adjusted their watches, debuckled and snatched up their rucksacks, checking to make sure they had left nothing behind.

The six mercenaries trooped down the ramp, the soles of their walking boots pounding against the roller tracks and drainage grooves. They walked straight into a wall of midday heat. The air felt thick and oppressive. It smothered Hawkins. As if it was physically weighing down on him. He figured the temperature had to be in the mid-thirties. Maybe higher.

Gorakan was as bleak as Kettler had described it back at the estate. *Place went to rack and ruin years ago.* Because of the abandoned gas fields. Testament to economic ruin.

They had parked on the stand on the eastern side of the taxiway. Runway to the east, two hundred metres away. There was a control tower on the edge of the apron, a steel-framed maintenance shed and a fire tender, a parking lot with a beat-up old Toyota Camry. Hawkins supposed that must belong to the fuel manager.

On the south side of the apron was a steel-framed hangar shaped like a barrel sliced in half. A smaller service road ran north from the apron to a separate entrance a couple of kilometres away. To ferry supplies from the apron to the old gas field. There was a radio rebroadcasting tower five hundred metres north of the ramp, to the west of the service road, with half a dozen aviation gas containers on the other side. Massive white cylinders set on beds of concrete with external metal stairs ascending to top-mounted access plat-forms. Large tanks, Hawkins noted. Tens of thousands of gallons of avgas in each cylinder, sufficient to top up any long-haul aircraft using the strip as a stopover.

Weeds poked through the tarmac. Piles of rubbish festered beneath the blowtorch sun. An access road ran west from the apron to the main road two kilometres away, flanked on either side by a chain-link security fence.

The airport was in the middle of nowhere. A desolate oasis, surrounded by an ocean of arid steppe pocked with rocky outcrops and the occasional clump of tamarisk or sagebrush.

A huge crater glowed in the distance, two kilometres away, in the same direction as the gas fields, set in a gentle depression in the ground. The Mouth of Hell.

Gouges of bright orange flame shot up from the collapsed crater basin, crested momentarily above the rim before expiring. The roar of hundreds of distant fires broke the dead silence of the desert. A handful of yurts had been set up in close proxim-ity to the crater. For the benefit of tourists, Hawkins presumed. Fire-worshippers and eco-hippies, chanting and dancing. Empty at the moment, according to Kettler. Because of the likelihood of sandstorms.

A rough track ran from the service road to the crater before it looped round the rim in a wide circle. *The President likes to fly in on his private jet. Doughnuts in his rally car around the edge.* Hawkins had the image of a playboy dictator. Gold-plated assault rifles, lux-ury palaces. Not someone overly concerned about the hardships of the peasantry.

A short, stout guy wearing maintenance overalls stepped out of the control tower and crossed the apron to greet the new arrivals. He had a round face framed by a frowsy beard, bushy eyebrows and dark oily hair, eyes the colour of walnuts. Hawkins figured he must be the fuel manager.

Kettler switched on his satphone, broke away from the gang to put in a call to the general, while the manager approached Steyn. He pumped the South African's hand in an exaggerated gesture, like he was drawing water from a well.

'Everything here, Mekan?' asked Steyn.

Mekan, the fuel manager, extended a chubby arm in the direction of the hangar. 'Delivered yesterday. In the trucks.'

Steyn said, 'Any unexpected visitors? Anyone snooping around?'

'Nobody. Just one cargo plane, yesterday. On way to Siberia,' he said in broken English. 'They saw nothing.'

'Anyone else due to come in?'

'Next plane lands two days. No one before then. You have place to yourselves.'

'We'll be leaving the plane in the hangar. Twenty-eight hours, then we're back in the air.'

'Pilots too?'

'They'll keep to the hangar. Don't worry. They'll stay out of your way.'

Steyn retrieved a band of money from his rucksack. US currency. Fifty-dollar bills. The wedge was about an inch thick. Several thousand dollars. He pressed it into Mekan's grubby palm.

'Where is rest?' he asked.

Steyn said, 'Ten thousand now, the other half later, once the job is done. That's what we agreed.'

Mekan shrugged and started back towards the ancient control tower.

'Come on,' said Steyn to the others.

A hot, dry wind wafted across the airfield as they walked at a quick clip towards the steel-framed hangar. Behind them Kettler loitered on the apron, deep in conversation with the general. Getting the latest report on the intelligence picture at Fordow. Times and movements.

The articulated lorry had been parked up beside the hangar, front end facing the apron. Inside the hangar they found the two Unimogs and a battered white Toyota Hilux pickup. Otherwise known as a technical. The front and sides were caked in dried mud and dirt. Both Unimogs had flat rear beds fitted behind the cabs, with two-foot-high panelling on the sides and rope hooks welded to the boardings to secure the tarpaulin covers.

Steyn said, 'Check the kit, guys. Supplies, fuel, weaponry. All of it.'

Martel peeled off towards the technical. Bald and Hawkins hooked round to the back of one of the Unimogs, Steyn and Moussa checking the other wagon.

Bald flipped down the rear loading hatch, Hawkins whipped away the sheet of dark green tarp covering the bed, revealing a stash of equipment laid out on the wagon floor. The hardware Steyn had acquired from the drug-traffickers. Some items had been wrapped in old blankets. Others were housed inside wooden crates with various markings on the sides and lids. Cyrillic lettering. Therefore Russian-manufactured. Army-issue kit. Presumably stolen from Russian military stores by corruptible NCOs before being sold on to Kettler for a hefty premium.

Bald and Hawkins climbed up onto the wagon bed, broke open the crates. Two of the coffins contained RPG-7s wrapped in waxed paper. Shoulder-mounted man-portable rocket launchers. One of the great inventions of the Soviet army. Two more wooden boxes contained pre-assembled missiles for the launch-tubes, four per box. A fifth box contained ten old F1 fragmentation grenades with their distinctive pineapple-patterned cast-iron casings.

They moved on to the blanketed weaponry. Unshrouded half a dozen AK-47 assault rifles, plus four Russian semi-automatic pistols. Two TT-30s and a couple of Makarovs, with a set of leather holsters. The TTs were chambered for the 7.62x25mm Tokarev round. Impressive stopping power. With the TT you could drop a target with a couple of well-aimed shots. Whereas the Makarovs used a smaller 9x18mm calibre. A lighter weapon, easier to carry and conceal. But it packed less of a punch. Mobility versus power. The oldest argument in warfare. The pistols came with three eight-round clips apiece, the AKs each had four twenty-round mags. There was also a box of tracer rounds.

On the back of the other Unimog, Steyn unwrapped a pair of Dragunov sniper rifles in 7.62mm, swaddled in thick cloth. Quartet of ten-round mags beside them. Moussa had taken the covers off a couple of belt-fed PKM machine guns. Both were bipod mounted, with three belts of two hundred rounds of link per weapon, stored in green lunchbox-sized metal ammo cases.

Hawkins thought: *Two PKMs. Four pistols. Half a dozen AK-47s. Plus the grenades, Dragunovs and RPGs.*

A lot of firepower.

More than enough to get the job done.

Bald inspected the other supplies on the back of the Unimog. Black masking tape, a Leatherman multi-tool, two sets of binos. Half a dozen camo-patterned ballistic vests, an equal number of cheap-looking walkie-talkies. The same type used by the Taliban in the bad old days of the Afghanistan war. Laycorn storage boxes for the HEU cylinders.

Next Hawkins found the box containing the explosives. Two kilograms of Russian plastique in four half-kilo lumps. The Eastern bloc version of C4. There was a clacker firing device alongside the charges, a Russian variation on the M57 firing device used for blowing Claymores. About the same size as a pair of stapling pliers. To detonate you rigged the clacker up to a spool of green-coated electrical wire, attached that to a pair of blasting caps fitted to the Claymore. When the clacker was squeezed it sent an electrical pulse shooting down the wire, initiating the primer and triggering the C4. The Russian model operated was essentially the same.

The explosives would come in handy for the op. They could rig up the artic with plastique, blow it up, creating an obstruction on the highway, impeding the progress of a pursuing Quick Reaction Force. Or they might need it later down the line during their escape. They could blow up an underpass, use it to set up a snap ambush.

The spool was kept in a separate foam-lined container, with 'AETOHATOP' stencilled down the side in big letters. Russian for 'detonator'. Hawkins recognised the word from the Regiment dems course. He'd handled the same stuff while running training packages in Africa, instructing students in the basic principles of bomb-making. The armed forces in those countries invariably used Russian-sourced kit. Cheaper than the Western models, and easier to procure.

Hawkins was about to break open the box to check the spool when Kettler called out from across the hangar.

'Everyone down here now! Drop your kit.'

Hawkins replaced the spool container. He swung down from the rear of the Unimog, jogged across the concrete-slabbed floor. Steyn, Moussa, Bald and Martel had gathered in front of the vehicles. Kettler stood in front of them, his face drawn tight, gripping the satphone in his white-knuckled right hand. A man trying very hard to stifle his emotions.

'What's going on, boss?' Steyn said.

'We have a problem,' Kettler said, tersely.

Steyn just stared dumbly at him. 'Boss?'

'The general has heard from his contact. He says there's been a last-minute change of plan.'

The words dropped like an anvil. Bald and Hawkins looked at one another. Steyn pulled at his horseshoe moustache. Martel ran a hand through his smooth blond hair. Moussa said nothing.

'What change, boss?' Steyn asked.

Kettler said, 'There's a new route. Convoy is going to avoid the main highways. Orders from the very top, the general says. They're going to stick to the B-roads instead. Departing Fordow at eleven o'clock tonight, Iranian time.'

'But that's just over twelve hours from now,' Hawkins said.

'They're in a big rush. All hands to the pumps. The B-2s could depart from Whiteman at any minute. Might have left already, for all we know. The Iranians need to move everything ultra fast.'

Bald said, 'That explains the timing. Doesn't explain the new route.'

'Could be any number of reasons. Maybe they planned to do this all along. Someone high up might have been twitchy about moving the uranium on a busy highway, and persuaded his bosses to take a more covert route out of Fordow. Keep it low profile.'

Steyn said, 'Either way, we're fucked. It's a fourteen-hour drive from here to Fordow. We'll never get there in time.'

Kettler didn't appear to have heard him. 'Paul, get the map out.'

Martel dug out the mapping from his go-bag, laid it flat on the hangar floor. The mercenaries gathered round while Kettler took a knee beside the map. A bony finger carefully traced the new route out of the Fordow facility.

'The general says the convoy will travel west for fifteen kilometres, mount the Old Tehran-Qom road and take that north for thirty kilometres, then make a left turn, cutting west through an area of steep-sided mountains. Destination is an old precious metal mine at a place called Baqram.'

Steyn stared at the map, brow slightly crumpled.

'Why the fuck is it heading there, boss?'

'Security,' said Kettler. 'According to the general the Iranians are worried that the Americans might know about the new storage site. The one they had planned to move the uranium to before the deadline. They're going to park the trucks up in that mine, wait there for forty-eight hours, until they're sure the bombing is over. See which facilities are left intact.'

'It's a good idea,' said Hawkins, grudgingly. He was studying the area around the Baqram mine. 'Place is empty. No camps or villages for miles around. Probably just a few local goat-herders. That mine won't be flashing up on any target list, that's for sure.'

'This is a fucking disaster,' said Steyn, bitterly. 'The plan's gone to shit. No slipways on that main road. Nowhere to hit the trucks.'

'Can't attack the mine, either,' Martel said. 'They'll have sent troops ahead to secure the site.'

'Shit.' Steyn banged a fist against his thigh in frustration.

Bald had stayed quiet. He had centred his attention on the map. Now he cleared his throat and said, 'We can hit the transports here. The job can still be done.'

He tapped his index finger at a spot thirty kilometres east of the mine, a sharp bend in the mountain pass. The contour lines to the left of the bend were squished together, rising sharply to the ridgeline above. Which told Hawkins that this was a steep slope, with a ravine on the right-hand side of the road, dropping down to the valley floor below.

Hawkins instantly grasped the plan.

'We'll park here,' Bald went on, pointing to the tarmac immediately left of the bend. 'That way they'll be out of sight of them wagons when they come tooling up the pass. We'll hit the convoy from the slope above, immobilise the vehicles, drop any security, load the goods onto the Unimogs, then get the fuck out of Dodge.'

Kettler said nothing. He was staring hard at the map. Working through the angles.

Steyn said, 'What about the Quick Reaction Force? Them bods at the mine. They'll be on us as soon as this goes noisy.'

'There's a way round that,' Hawkins said. He indicated the tightly bunched contours above the road. 'We can rig up the explosives above the pass. Plant them around any large boulders. Bound to be loads along that mountainside.

'The explosion will trigger a landslide, sweeping over the pass and pushing everything down over the side of that ravine. The trucks and bodies will be buried under an avalanche of rock and mud. The Iranians will think the convoy has been taken out in a landslide. It'll take them days to recover the wreckage and find out what really happened. Meanwhile, we're back across the border and getting the beers in.'

'It's a solid plan,' Martel agreed. 'Rough and ready, but we could do it.'

Bald said, 'Better than that fucking slipway attack. This way we'll have no witnesses.'

'Doesn't solve our other problem,' Steyn said. 'We've got to get there before that fucking convoy.'

Bald said, 'It can be done. If we floor it, we can shave a good ninety minutes off that road trip. Maybe more. We can be in position for around eleven or eleven thirty at night.'

'That convoy won't be in any great hurry once it's on the road,' Hawkins said. 'Because of the cargo. It'll take them another hour to reach that pass. At the very least. Around midnight.'

'We'll still need time to set that ambush up,' Martel pointed out. 'Half an hour, I'd say.'

Bald nodded. 'If there's no time, we'll just block the road with the Unimogs. Take the bastards on. Hit them hard. That's our Immediate Action plan. The Deliberate Action is the ambush. Sorted.'

'I'm down with that,' Martel said. 'We've come too far to give up now.'

Despite himself, Hawkins felt a hot thrill of excitement at the prospect of action. Finally. The chance to do some proper fighting. Hawkins had missed it. He had thought he could take off his Regiment uniform, slip into the clothes of a civilian without a problem. But he had been wrong.

In the Regiment you were encouraged to be a gambler. Or perhaps it was truer to say that Hereford appealed to those willing to take a calculated gamble with their lives. Crash through that door, and you're either going to take down the bad guy and be a hero or you'll end up with a bullet between your eyes. Black and white. Death or glory.

On Civvy Street it had been completely different. You were expected to change from a lion into a lamb. Hawkins had tried hard to adapt. Bloody hard.

Face it, Davey. There's no place for blokes like you in the civilian world.

Maybe you don't belong anywhere.

Then a thought slapped Hawkins hard in the face. He remembered his mission. *I'm working with a bunch of criminals.* If Hawkins somehow pulled this off, Kettler and his cronies were going to end up behind bars for the rest of their lives. Bald too, maybe.

'That's it, then.' Kettler stood up ramrod straight. 'That's what we'll do. We're leaving now. Jock, Steyn, have you checked the weapons?'

They both confirmed that everything was as it should be.

'Fuel, Paul?'

'Unimog tanks are full,' the German said. 'Vehicles gassed up, extra diesel tanks on the backs.'

'The technical?'

'Ten spare jerry cans. We've got plenty of water too.'

'Least we won't die of thirst out there,' Steyn quipped, darkly.

'Geordie, explosives?'

Hawkins had been checking everything when Kettler had announced the change of plan. There had been no time to look inside the box containing the spool, but he didn't need to get eyes on that. He knew the wire would be in there. The Russian lettering on the lid had told him as much. He had the plastique, the fuses, the electrical wire. Everything he needed to create a big bang and bring the mountainside crashing down.

'It's all good, boss,' Hawkins said. 'All there.'

Kettler said, 'Let's fucking move. Hurry.'

'What about the artic?' Steyn asked.

'Check it for fuel and kit. We won't be needing it now.'

They rushed to get the motors ready. Martel snatched up the map. Moussa sprinted outside to check the articulated truck cab. Everyone else raced over to the Unimogs, collected their AK-47s from the crates, taking four mags each. One in the rifle, three spares wedged into the pouches on the front of their chest-rigged plate hangers. Martel distributed the pistols, gave one TT to Bald, kept the other one for himself. Hawkins and Steyn took the lower-calibre Makarovs.

They replaced the Dragunovs in their blankets. Threw on their body armour. Russian army-issue crap, with Kevlar plates in the front and rear. Cheap as fuck. The same ones used by Russian cannon fodder in eastern Ukraine. Capable of stopping a nine-milli round but nothing bigger than that. Each man took a walkie-talkie, so they could stay in touch on the road. Kettler would keep the satphone switched on, staying in close contact with the general, in case the Iranians had any more tricks up their sleeves.

Moussa came jogging back into the hangar lugging two more jerry cans. He chucked them onto the back of the technical with the rest of the fuel and supplies of bottled water, ratcheted the load down, securing it to the floor, threw on a comically small ballistic vest. On his gigantic frame it looked more like a camo-patterned crop-top.

Bald, Steyn, Martel and Hawkins put the heavy stuff back in the crates. The RPGs, the explosives. The fragmentation grenades. The Unimogs wouldn't need any jerry cans. Both had auxiliary drums mounted on reinforced racks behind the front cabs. Flexible rubber hoses ran from the drum outlets, snaked along the chassis rail into the main tank. To top up the fuel, you simply stopped the vehicle, got out, twisted the hose valve, and gravity would do the rest, piping fuel from the drum into the tank.

They pulled the canvas sheets over the Unimog beds, fastening the rope cords to the dropside panel lashing points. Then Bald and Hawkins got into the cab of the Unimog carrying the RPGs. Hawkins with the wheel, Bald in the shotgun seat, AKs barrel-down beside their legs. Ready to snatch up and engage any fucker who tried to stop them. Steyn and Moussa took the second wagon, Martel and Kettler riding a short distance ahead in the technical.

They rolled out of the hangar, the Hilux in the lead, the two Unimogs gassing along behind. As soon as they were clear of the apron the pilots would guide the Antonov into the hangar, hiding it from view of any satellites or drones. After which they would wait for the team to return. A twenty-eight-hour stretch. Hundreds of thousands of dollars in return for sitting on their arses. Worse ways to earn a living.

Hawkins followed twenty metres behind the technical as it flew down the access road west of the control tower, Moussa and Steyn belting along in the rearmost wagon. They turned left off the approach road, tore south for a kilometre, dialled round at the roundabout, rocketed east on the highway. A route that would take them all the way to the border crossing at Incheh Borun.

Hawkins hammered the accelerator, glanced at the digital clock on the Unimog's instrument cluster.

12.28 local time.

Eleven o'clock in Iran.

Thirteen hours before the convoy would reach the mountain pass.

Thirteen hours until it goes noisy.

Nineteen

The mercenaries white-knuckled it on the highway east out of Gora-kan, Hawkins keeping the needle ticking around the ninety kilometres per mark as they raced past the foothills of the Kopet Dag range. Martel and Kettler a hundred metres ahead in the Hilux, ready to notify the others of any obstacles or threats over the walkie-talkies. Steyn and Moussa fifty metres back in the second Unimog. They flashed past a handful of impoverished villages, herders beating one-humped dromedaries with their sticks, goat-herders watching over their flocks. Hardy souls scraping a living on the edges of the great endless desert to the north. Rural Turkmenistan. Hardly a thriving economy. The only vehicles they passed were antiquated trucks transporting fresh goods down to the border.

After eighty kilometres the motorway abruptly cut south, funnelled them through a landscape of rolling green valleys and deep gullies flanked by steep-sided mountains, interrupted by salt flats and clumps of juniper trees or pistachio bushes. Hawkins kept checking the time on the Unimog display. 13.29. An hour since they had sped out of the airfield.

11.59 in Iran.

Eleven hours until the convoy departed Fordow with the uranium. Twelve hours until they reached the bend on the mountain pass. The sheer drop down to the valley floor.

We can still make it.

But it's going to be bloody close.

They carried on through the mountains for another hundred kilometres until the road swung round to the south-west, paralleling the course of the Atrak river that formed the natural border between Iran and Turkmenistan. They left the foothills behind, and the landscape became table-flat again. Chickens pecked in the dirt outside run-down compounds. Goats grazed on the patches of vegetation. Belts of wheat and barley shivered in the light breeze spilling down from the mountaintops.

Dark thoughts plagued Hawkins as they tooled on towards the crossing. He still had no idea how he was going to reach out to Six. Which prompted another question.

Even if I manage to get a mark-one eyeball on the buyers, how the fuck am I going to stop them from getting away with the cylinders? They could go underground before Six can react.

Without the false-screen phone he was out on a limb. Anger pounded between his temples. He cursed Six for sending him on this fool's errand of a mission.

Then Hawkins remembered his training. The long years of training at Hereford. The Regiment didn't just teach you how to kill. It taught you how to solve problems at light speed. Quicker than any slop-generating AI. The worst thing you could do was look too far ahead. That was how people got overwhelmed. Worry about the door you're about to kick in, not the one after that.

Hawkins zoomed in on his immediate difficulty. The ambush. He allowed himself to look no further than that.

'You reckon this will work, Jock?' he asked.

'The plan? Piece of piss,' Bald said. 'Easier than ambushing them trucks on a busy motorway. That's for fucking sure.'

'If the Iranians are onto us, we're shafted. We might be driving into a trap.'

'They don't know,' Bald said, with feeling. 'If they did, the general wouldn't be talking freely to Kettler on the satphone. He'd be in an interrogation cell somewhere in Tehran, begging his captors to put him out of his misery.'

'And if you're wrong?'

'Then we'll bug out. Emergency exfil. Make for the nearest border. Every fucker for himself.'

Hawkins ground his jaw. 'This ain't right. We're making it up as we go along, Jock. Half-cocked. That's how mistakes happen.'

Bald shot him a look of unfiltered contempt. 'Get over it, Geordie. This is the real world. Plans always go to shite. Nothing to do but grit our teeth and see the fucking thing through. Besides, the attack ain't our biggest worry. Not by a long shot.'

Hawkins glanced at the grizzled old warrior. 'How's that?'

'When it goes noisy, we'll be needing ice-skates to get out of here. I'm not talking about having the plod on our tails or the local green army. The world and his fucking dog will be after us. All the assets you care to name. We'll be on the news tonight.'

'What if we run into trouble on the exfil?'

'Then we're fucked. Plain and simple. There's no safety net on this job. We'll be out on our arses. Half a dozen lads versus every asset in the Western world. No surviving that.'

Hawkins gripped the steering wheel vice-tight. The Unimog cabin felt kiln-hot. Partly because there was no air-con. But also because of the anxiety stirring in his guts. The mission, the exfil. The problem of how to contact Six once Kettler had shaken hands with the buyers. Sweat ran freely down his front, staining the T-shirt under his Kevlar plating.

'Don't know about you, mate, but I could bloody murder a cold one right now.'

Bald said, scornfully, 'Word of advice, son. Lay off that crap. Get off it and stay off it for good.'

'You told us to drink more or cut it out.'

'You're English. Nation of famous lightweights. You can't function when you're on the piss. Not like us rock-hard Scots. Drink your tribe under the table. Better for you to ditch it.'

'Fuck off, Jock. I can handle my booze.'

'No, *you* fuck off. I've been there in the past. I know what you're doing. Drinking doesn't make you sleep any easier. Doesn't solve your problems. All it does is create a ton more.'

Hawkins said, tetchily, 'You ain't teetotal yourself, Jock. Fuck me, you were knocking it back the other night at the lapa.'

'Aye, but I've got a cut-off point. I keep my mind stable, I don't get pissed, and if I start blathering on about politics or religion, I pull the plug. I like the taste, but I can stop anytime. You're drinking yourself into oblivion. There's a big fucking difference.'

Hawkins stared at the empty road ahead, anger burning in the back of his throat. He hated to admit it, but Bald had a point. In his Regiment days he had never been a big boozer. Had no interest in the stuff. It had all started after Jacob's death – after the head shed had exiled him. A nightly measure to take the edge off, keep the hydra-headed monster of depression at bay. Since then it had got steadily worse. Now he was knocking back a hundred-plus units a week. He was out of control.

I've got a problem.

Bald spoke again.

'This life doesn't do reruns, Geordie. There's no afterlife. When the lights go out, that's it. You won't be going through the pearly gates and feasting at the big man's table.'

'What's your point?'

'You've got one life, and you're pissing it away. Keep up the boozing, and you're going to lose everything. Your daughter, whatever's left of your sad career. It will all go down the fucking pan. Especially in this line of work.'

'Meaning?'

'You're a mercenary now. This ain't like it used to be in the Regiment. Our line of work, we kill people for money. Some lads can't handle that. Messes with their heads. So they turn to the drink. But that just makes everything worse. You start emptying the whisky bottle to get through the day. Then you're looking for the job to pay for the next bottle. Spiral of fucking doom.'

Something in Bald's voice told Hawkins that the guy was speaking from personal experience. Hawkins glanced again at his old colleague. He had only ever heard one version of the Jock Bald myth. Bald the rogue warrior. Hereford's prodigal son. The brilliant soldier who had gone over to the dark side. Now Hawkins was beginning to see him in a new light. A hard-as-nails Blade, blackballed by the Regiment.

His life had been one long war. Against the world. Against himself.

Say what you like about Bald, but he's a fighter.

The guy had unquestionably lost his moral compass. But that wasn't entirely Bald's fault. The bosses at Hereford expected the lads to be like lions on a mission and sheep when they were back home. Like flicking a switch. Some men struggled with that. They couldn't stop being lions, even when the mission was over.

'Take a week,' Bald went on. 'Off the drink, like. You'll hate it for the first three days, but by the end of that first week you'll start feeling healthier. More fucking human. Stay off it for a month, and you'll be glowing. You'll never want to go back.'

Hawkins said, 'What are you gonna do? If this pans out.'

'Retire,' Bald said. 'See out my days in Dubai. Women and sunshine. Money on tap. No more worries. No more of this shit, either. Getting too old for soldiering.'

Hawkins didn't reply. But something told him that Bald wasn't the retiring type. Fighting was all the bloke had ever known. A month in Dubai soaking up the rays and he'd be climbing the walls.

They hurtled down the motorway for another hundred kilometres, flying past crumbling hovels, the occasional small town marked by whitewashed minarets, giant billboards and gleaming civic buildings. Twelve kilometres to the border crossing, according to the signs on the side of the road. They were making good time. 16.08. Four hours since they'd left the airfield. 14.38 in Iran.

Keep this up and we'll get to that pass well before the convoy.

Fifteen minutes later they hit the border on the Turkmen side, a cluster of prefabricated buildings on the side of the road. Directly ahead the three-lane motorway channelled towards the security checkpoint. Soldiers loitered aimlessly near the guardhouses. Out-of-shape blokes with protuberant bellies, packing AK-47s and holstered pistols, dressed in Soviet-era hand-me-downs. Two of the gates were operational. Long lines of traffic had formed in front of both of them, waiting for the border guards to check their papers.

A hundred metres ahead, Kettler and Martel lane-hopped and made for the third lane. Which was closed, apparently. A big red cross illuminated the display on the overhead gantry. Kettler's voice hissed over the scratchy walkie-talkie net, directing the rest of the team to follow their lead.

Bald and Hawkins stuck bumper-close to the Hilux, passing rows of stationary trucks and old bangers. The technical stopped in front of the boom barrier. Hawkins halted four metres behind, Steyn and Moussa in the second wagon pulling up an equal distance behind them.

A portly guy with a bushy moustache stepped out of the guard booth. The driver-side window buzzed down. An arm thrust out of the Hilux cab, passing the fat officer an envelope. Filled with cash, Hawkins presumed. The second part of a bribe, with the down payment made by Steyn days earlier. The deal would have been easy enough to arrange. In a rural backwater everyone had their price. Grease the right palms and you could get almost anything done.

The officer discreetly pocketed the envelope. The barrier arm lifted. The technical fired up, rolled on past the guardhouse, the Unimogs running close behind.

They went through the same routine on the Iranian side of the crossing. Drove past the queues of waiting cars, straight up to the closed booth. Kettler handed the guard a wadded envelope. The guy took the money, waved the three vehicles through. Smugglers bringing up fentanyl from Mexico used similar tactics, Bald explained. Skip the line, pay off someone at the crossing in advance. Get fast-tracked through customs, no questions asked.

First hurdle cleared, Hawkins thought.

We've still got a long way to go.

Six hundred and forty kilometres to our destination. Six hundred and forty kilometres to the mountain pass near Baqram.

Hawkins and Bald both changed the time on their watches. 15.12, Tehran time. Less than eight hours until the convoy departed the enrichment facility at Fordow. Roughly nine hours before it hit the pass. *Doable*, Hawkins thought.

As long as we don't run into any roadblocks on the way.

They stuck to the motorway running south from Incheh Borun to Gorgan, Hawkins and Bald maintaining a distance of a hundred metres from the Hilux. Hawkins kept the Unimog ticking along at a hundred and ten kilometres per, a shade under the national speed limit, so they wouldn't draw attention from any overzealous cops along the route.

After eighty kilometres they turned onto the coastal highway, rocketed west along the fertile plains and citrus groves fringing the southern shores of the Caspian Sea. Further on the route skirted counter-clockwise around the small city of Qaem Shahr. Hawkins dropped down to seventy per as they shuttled south through gloomy residential neighbourhoods. The streets were eerily quiet. Hawkins spotted the occasional patrol car, officers prowling the main junctions. But he saw few pedestrians, hardly any traffic. The place seemed tense. On edge.

'Where the fuck is everyone?' Hawkins said.

'The regime leaders are expecting the bombs to start dropping at any minute,' Bald said. 'They'll be tied up securing various sites, making sure all the clerics and officials are tucked up safe and sound in their bunkers. Rest will be protecting government buildings and national infrastructure, I imagine.'

'What for?'

'People might use the attacks as an excuse to take to the streets. Protest against the clerics. Wouldn't be the first time that's happened. Reckon they'll have switched off the internet for that same reason.'

'If they're not looking in our direction, that works in our favour. Those bastards will be running around like headless chickens instead of watching the roads.'

'For now. But it won't be like this on the way back out. It'll get fucking tasty then, Geordie.'

South of Qaem Shahr they joined Route 79 through the great chain of the Alborz mountains, taking them further inland, away from the coastal plains. Hawkins flicked his eyes to the instrument cluster again, made a quick back-of-fag-packet calculation. 18.48. They had been on the road for a little over seven and a half hours. Three hundred and fifty kilometres from their destination now.

They picked up speed again as they raced through the Alborz, driving as hard as they dared. Twice they stopped on the roadsides to take a piss-break and open the valves on the auxiliary fuel drums, topping up the main tanks on the Unimogs. In the Regiment they called it POL discipline. You had to work on the assumption that you might not get another chance to stop and refuel for a long time. A quick turnaround. Two minutes and they were back on the road again. Hurtling towards their destination.

Hawkins grazed on a snack from his rucksack, took a swig of tepid bottled water. He gripped the wheel hard, willing the Unimog to go faster. Praying that they would make it to the pass in time.

They descended from the foothills in bleary darkness. Tehran below them, a constellation of stars scattered like diamonds across the tableland. Hawkins stuck close to the Hilux as they coasted through the easternmost districts of the city. The streets were dark and quiet. The bombing campaign. Everyone would instinctively understood that something bad was about to go down. They had seen this movie before. People would be hunkering down at home, lights out, waiting for the bombs to start falling.

They passed massive billboards featuring AI-generated images of President Farrell, posters depicting rows of coffins draped in the Star of David and the US flag. Hawkins looked once more at the clock display, glowing orange in the blackness of the cabin. They were only a hundred and ten kilometres from the ambush point now. Hawkins felt a quickening in his veins. For the first time he started to believe that they might actually make it.

21.48.

Ninety minutes to the pass.

They took Route 7 running south through the outskirts of Eslamshahr, a stretch of worn blacktop, the highway lights switched off. An energy-rationing measure, maybe. Or a decision made by the clerics in advance of the B-2s. *The infidels are coming.* National blackout. Internet shutdown. Every police officer and soldier on high alert.

They scudded past Tehran international airport, carried on for another thirty kilometres. Rim of the salt lake at their ten o'clock. Mountains to their right, a dark mass rising like a clenched fist above the surrounding plateau, just about visible against the star-pricked sky.

Martel's voice came over the radio net, confirming that they were now twenty kilometres out from their destination. Hawkins kept white-knuckling the wheel, mashing the pedal so hard his leg muscles had started to ache. The speedometer needle around the hundred per mark.

At 11.04, Kettler's voice crackled over the walkie-talkie net.

'Update from the general.'

'Yes?' Bald said.

'Convoy has left Fordow. Repeat, convoy has left Fordow.'

Hawkins thought: *We'll get there ahead of them. Not by much, but enough time to set up the ambush on the slopes. Prepare the Deliberate Action plan. Rig the explosives.*

'How many vehicles are we facing?' Bald asked.

'Six,' came the reply from Kettler. 'We have a confirmation of six vehicles. Escorts front and rear, uranium transports in the middle.'

'Roger that, boss.'

Bald got off the net again. Keeping activity over the net to a minimum. The Iranian regime had state-of the-art surveillance systems. Chinese-sourced kit. The bad guys of the world clubbing together against the Evil Empire. Tehran had tools capable of getting around VPNs, breaking encryption, even tracking burners. They would definitely have the ability to pinpoint a simple walkie-talkie signal.

Hawkins said, 'We're not gonna have much time to get that ambush set up.'

Bald grunted his agreement. Both of them running through the plan in their heads, examining every angle, like they had been trained to do as Blades. They would have to move fast once they reached the ambush site. Park the wagons round the bend, so they were out of view of the approach, plant the explosives for the rock-slide, set up firing positions along the slope.

Bald smiled grimly. 'Flying by the seat of our pants, son. Just like being back in the Regiment.'

'Aye. Except this time, we're about to become criminals.'

'*Rich* criminals, Geordie. Richer than any of them fucking Ruperts.'

'We've got to survive the night first.'

Bald grunted his agreement. 'Get through it, and we'll celebrate in style once we're back home. Drinks are on me. I'll buy you a detox juice.'

'Piss off, Jock.'

Bald let out a laugh. Hawkins smiled too, easing the tension they had both been feeling on the mad rush down from Gorakan.

The Hilux suddenly dismounted the highway. Hawkins and the guys in the Unimog took the same slip road, the lead technical switching to full beams as it cut west on the secondary road for five hundred metres. Then they took a hard left onto the metalled road winding up the steep mountainside. 23.08. Eight minutes since the convoy had set off.

The Unimog engine growled throatily as it struggled up the mountain road behind the Hilux. Steep rockface on their left, sheer drop to their right. A height of some sixteen hundred metres from the roadside to the bottom of the ravine.

Half a kilometre further on they rounded a sharp left-hand bend in the road. The Hilux skidded to a halt fifty metres beyond the turn, Bald and Hawkins stopping just behind it. They snatched up their longs, sprang the door handles, leapt out of the cabs, muscles stiff from the long race across Iran.

23.19.

Nineteen minutes since the convoy had left Fordow.

Moussa and Steyn had parked up five metres to the rear of the Unimog. Hawkins and Bald gazed up at the mountainside, their eyesight gradually adjusting to the grainy darkness. A nearly full moon broadcast high above the slope. Hawkins scanned the area quantum-quick. Huge boulders littered the rockface, some of them the size of suburban houses. In other places Hawkins saw clumps of loose stones and rocks. Some of them teetered dangerously over the road, as if poised to collapse.

In the Alps, steel wire meshing was normally draped over road-side escarpments, anchored in place with rock bolts. To stabilise the face, prevent any large debris from tumbling down onto the road and causing an accident. But here, no effort had been made to secure the scarp. A lack of foresight, or money, or technical ineptitude. Or all three. The engineers had simply gouged out a section of the mountain, laid the road, and moved on. A few wedges of Russian-variant C4, rigged along the slope, would bring the whole mountainside crashing down.

Bald and Hawkins looked at one another, grinning broadly.

'Fuck me, Geordie. This is gonna be even easier than I thought.'

'Gather round, lads,' Kettler said, motioning for the others to join him in front of the bend. The ex-Rupert taking charge of the situation.

'Right, firing positions,' he went on hurriedly. 'Rory, Moussa, you're on the right cut-off. Paul, I'll be with you on the left cut-off. We'll take the Dragunovs. One RPG for each cut-off. Hawkins, Jock, you're in the middle with the kill group. That means you'll be on the PKMs.

'When that convoy comes up the pass, left cut-off will disable the front escort. Knock the tyre out. That'll confuse them and force the other drivers to bunch up close. On my signal right cut-off will fire an RPG into the rear truck. Then the kill group will engage the troop transports. Keep firing until every fucker stops moving, but whatever you do, be careful with the trucks with the metal containers. They're the ones transporting the uranium cylinders. Look for the wagons with the canvas-topped backs, those are the troop carriers. Concentrate your fire on those. Once we've walloped the troops we'll move forward, mop up any wounded and load the containers onto the Unimogs. Make sure they're tied down securely in the Laycorn boxes. Meanwhile, Hawkins, you'll set up the clackers and wire. Soon as we're ready to bug out, you'll blow the side of the mountain. Then we're back on the road. Questions?'

No one said a word. Everyone understood their role. Classic SF ambush tactics. The kill group would clobber the transports, with the left and right cut-offs knocking down anyone who tried to make a run for it back up or down the pass. The Iranians would be caught between three deadly arcs of fire. No escape.

'Get your kit ready,' Kettler said. 'Sort your firing positions. Once we've unloaded the hardware, we'll move the wagons forward. Get them hidden behind the bend. Arses into gear, guys.'

Hawkins and Bald broke round to the back of the lead Unimog. They released the cords lashed around the fastening points along the sideboards and tore off the tarp covering, started unloading the heavy stuff. The two RPGs, F1 grenades, the three boxes containing the explosive charges, detonators and wire. Steyn and Martel unpacked the PKMs from the rear bed on the other Unimog, the two canvas-wrapped Dragunovs.

Bald pocketed the Leatherman multi-tool, handed both sets of binos to Steyn and Moussa. As the right cut-off team they would have the job of observing the convoy as it approached the pass. Tracking its progress and alerting the others.

'Hawkins, Rory,' Kettler called out once the last items had been unpacked. 'In the Unimogs. Move them out of the way. Get those tanks topped up while you're at it.'

Bald, Martel and Moussa began lugging their equipment a short distance up the slope, setting up their firing positions, while Hawkins and Steyn jumped into the Unimogs, kickstarted the engines. Kettler arrowed the technical further up the pass, stopped again a hundred metres west of the bend, concealing them from view of anyone coming up the pass.

Hawkins pulled up immediately behind the Hilux. He grabbed the box of Russian plastique, left the crates with the spool and clackers on the Unimog – he wouldn't need them until the time came to rig up the explosives, after the ambush. He jogged back over to the kill zone, leaving Kettler and Steyn to refuel the pickup with the extra cans of diesel loaded on the rear bed. They would also top up the main tanks on the Unimogs, ensuring the team had full tanks for the exfil journey. Remembering their POL discipline.

Hawkins was sweating freely. He could feel the tension coursing through his bloodstream. By now his natural night vision had kicked in and he could easily distinguish the shapes of the other mercenaries as they scrambled up and down the rockface, getting their weaponry ready, racing to set up their positions. Martel was lugging one of the Dragunov rifles over to a boulder the size of a wrecking ball. Two hundred metres to the east, Moussa carried an RPG up to his firing point at the right cut-off, scaling the rockface in giant strides. Bald had taken one of the PKMs over to a dip screened by a mound of rocks, twenty metres up from the road, equidistant between the two cut-offs.

Hawkins climbed further up the slope, thirty metres above the firing points. He stopped beside a massive boulder, emplaced one lump of plastique into a crevice underneath it. When it detonated, the energy released by the resulting explosion would lift that boulder off the ground, along with everything else around it, sweeping the lot down the mountain and carrying away anything that happened to be on the road at the time.

He put the other three charges in similar spots along the length of the slope. Distributing them evenly, so that half the mountain would come down when the charges went off. He wasn't worried about the plastique accidentally detonating during the firefight. Russian derivative PVV-5A, like C4, was relatively stable. You could safely throw it against a wall, kick it, make a brew on it, and it wouldn't blow up. You could only trigger it by generating enough energy through a primary explosion. A stray bullet wouldn't set it off.

Hawkins picked his way back down to the roadside. Ahead of him, Steyn and Kettler were rushing towards their respective firing points. They distributed the frag grenades between the two cut-offs, five per team. Hawkins lifted the second PKM by the carry grip on the side of the receiver, hauled it up to a spot ten metres to the right of Bald. He laid his AK-47 flat beside the PKM, made two more trips back down the slope, bringing up the three boxes of two-hundred-round link. Hawkins set them down beside his firing point. Then he set up his machine gun. Opened the feed cover on top of the receiver, cracked open the nearest box of detachable link, took the belt of 7.62 and laid it over the tray, ready to discharge. Slapped the cover shut again.

Tugged on the firing bolt.

Ready.

23.39.

The convoy might only be ten or fifteen minutes away from the pass. A sixty-five-kilometre drive from Fordow. A journey time of between fifty and sixty minutes, depending on conditions.

Half an hour from now, if everything went to plan, the gang would be racing out of the pass with a load of stolen uranium on the backs of the Unimogs. Then things would get hairy.

The world and his fucking dog will be after us.

All the assets you care to name.

Steyn and Kettler had taken up their respective spots with the right and left cut-off teams. At Hawkins's three o'clock, Moussa and Steyn were watching the approach to the bend through their binos, scanning for the first sign of the enemy further down the mountain. In this dark, with no ambient light, the glow of the head-lamps would be clearly visible from several hundred metres away.

Each operator also had a walkie-talkie. Everyone waiting for the order from Kettler to go noisy. Unsecured net, so they would keep chatter to a bare minimum. Vital comms only. They wouldn't need night-sights or NVGs for the job, not at this distance, not for this kind of ambush. When the muzzles started lighting up, and the RPGs smashed into the trucks, it would be like broad daylight on the pass.

23.44.

Hawkins waited.

One minute passed.

Then another.

Then a third.

He war-gamed the attack in his head. The ambushers would remain silent, waiting in cover until the lead vehicle had rolled just past the central kill group. Then Martel would shoot up the driver-side front tyre. The wrecking-ball boulder would suppress the muzzle flash; the sharp crack of the rifle discharge would be drowned out by the rumble of half a dozen diesel engines straining up the pass.

The men in the lead vehicle would grind to a halt, naturally assuming they had suffered a puncture. The larger transports would be forced to stop behind them in close order, directly below the ambushers scattered in cover along the mountain slope.

Then the fire teams would let rip.

They were about to cross a red line. Men were going to die.

If we get caught, we'll be facing the death penalty.

Even if they pulled off the ambush and escaped from Iran, Hawkins wasn't necessarily in the clear. He might end up facing prosecution back home in the UK. Maybe not for a while. Maybe not for several years. But one day, there might be a knock at the door. His actions would be indefensible in a court of law. Six would be in no rush to protect him. Whitehall had previous for throwing good SF men to the wolves.

Nothing I can do about that now.

No choice but to see it through, and hope for the best.

23.49.

Almost time.

Any minute now.

Then Hawkins heard the noise.

Coming down the road.

Heading straight for the ambushers.

Twenty

The noise came from the west. Somewhere beyond the arc of the bend and the left cut-off. Not a car engine. Not a human noise, either. But something else. A soft chorus of bleating sounds, the irregular clopping of hooves on the tarmac.

Carrying sharply across the tepid night air.

A beat passed.

Kettler said over the net, 'Two guys walking down the track, heading towards our position. Herd of goats. Loads of the fuckers.'

'Shit,' Steyn said.

They swept into view a moment later, a rabble of twenty-odd underfed goats shambling round the bend. Behind them, a spindly old man in baggy trousers and a purple vest over a threadbare shirt, and a boy in a red woollen hat. Or at least Hawkins assumed he was a boy. He had reached that milestone in life where it became impossible to distinguish the age of people much younger than himself. The boy might have been twelve or twenty or anywhere in between.

'What the fuck are they doing up here?' Steyn asked over the radio.

Nobody replied. But Hawkins knew the answer. Mountain herders. Living up in the hills for part of the year with their flock. Taking them down to the valley floor for the local market at first light. A fifteen- or twenty-kilometre trek, with several stops along the way to water the flock. A routine that pre-dated recorded history, practised by mountain folk the world over.

The herders shuffled on.

'What do you think?' Kettler asked over the net.

Hawkins held down the Push-To-Talk button on the side of his walkie-talkie. 'Let them go. They haven't seen us.'

'Not yet,' Steyn butted in. 'But they might do. Why take the risk, boss?'

There was a pause of silence.

Then Kettler said, 'Paul. Deal with them. You know what to do.'

Martel sprang to his feet from behind the great big boulder at Hawkins's nine o'clock. He advanced steadily down the slope towards the old herdsman and his kid, holding up his hands in a universal gesture of peace.

The kid had spotted the approaching German. He called out to the old man in Farsi, shouting and pointing excitedly at Martel. The old man had also stopped. He turned towards Martel and said something. What sounded to Hawkins like a challenge.

Who are you? What are you doing here?

Martel walked closer. Hands raised, calling out to the herdsman in a cheerful tone. Acting like a friendly. The old man stood still, gripping his knobbly herder's staff, unsure what to make of the blond-haired stranger in the Western clothing.

Martel was two or three metres from the herders when he snatched out the TT-30 semi-auto concealed under his shirt. Drew the pistol level with the old man's face.

The TT barked.

The snout flamed twice.

Blood sprayed out of the back of the goat-herder's head in a carmine mist. He was still falling away as Martel trained his weapon on the kid and fired twice more.

The goats nearest to Martel promptly scattered, terrified by the gunshots. They stopped again a short way down the road, below the right cut-off team, bleating noisily and bumping against one another.

Hawkins fumed over the net, 'What the fuck did you do that for?'

'Had to be done,' Kettler said, stonily. 'They left us no choice. Hawkins, get down there and give Paul a hand. Get those bodies over the side.'

'What about the goats?' Steyn was saying over the walkie-talkie.

'Leave them. They're a bonus. Slow the trucks down. Move, Hawkins.'

'Fuck's sake,' Hawkins hissed under his breath as he broke down the slope, rocks crunching beneath the soles of his hiking boots. He couldn't believe what he had just seen. The herders had posed zero threat. They could have stayed put in their firing positions. Waited for the locals to wander past. Instead, Martel had executed them in cold blood. A reckless act. Unnecessary. More than that, it was depraved. Psychotic. Kettler and his gang were totally out of control.

'You take the kid,' Martel said as he stooped down beside the old man.

Hawkins bent down next to the boy, took one look at him, felt the anger pounding hammer-like against the wall of his chest. Half of the kid's face had been blown away. Hawkins fought off the bile in his throat, held his legs just below the knee, dragged the body over to the side of the road. He weighed almost nothing. Skin and bone.

Martel gave the old man a hard shove. His corpse tumbled down the nearly vertical rockface amid a clattering of loose stones, until he was lost to the blackness. Martel stepped back, and then Hawkins rolled the kid over the edge. His torn, bloodied corpse rolling down a short way, bumping and gashing against sharp rocks.

'It's done,' Martel reported over the comms. 'Heading back to our positions.'

Hawkins felt sickened. A hollowness spread through his stomach. His unease must have showed on his face, because Martel smirked and said, 'I thought you SAS soldiers are supposed to be rock hard. Not a bunch of girly men.'

'You shouldn't have done that.' Hawkins was struggling to suppress his fury. 'You could have let them go, for fuck's sake.'

Martel gave him a look of mock pity. 'Did I hurt your feelings, English?'

'Fuck off.'

The German sneered at him. 'Grow a pair, as they say in your country. Where's your backbone? This is what happens when you lose an empire, I guess. You lose the will to do what is necessary to survive.'

Martel about-turned, scrambled back over to his firing point. Hawkins picked his way up to his PKM near Bald, trembling bodily with rage. He dropped to his front in a prone position. Tried to clear his mind of the image of the dead kid, his head blown apart.

Fifty seconds later Steyn spoke over the radio channel.

'It's on, fellas. Convoy moving up the pass now. Seven hundred metres from our position. Heading straight for us.'

'Can you make out the vehicles?' said Kettler.

A beat of silence passed as Steyn observed the enemy through his binos.

Then Steyn said, 'Six of them. Just like your man said. Looks like a Nissan Patrol in the lead. Five military trucks behind. Second and third wagons have got rigid metal bodies. The other three have got canvas sides.'

'Those will be the troop carriers,' Kettler said. 'The hard bodies will be the transports for the cylinders. Listen up. When I give the order, the kill group will target the canvas-framed trucks. Keep firing until every one of those fuckers is dead. Right cut-off will tackle the rearmost wagon. No one fires before I give the command. Remember, be very careful where you're putting those rounds. Clear?'

'Clear, boss,' said Steyn.

'Roger that,' said Bald.

'Roger,' said Hawkins.

Kettler said, 'Keep watching, Rory. Weapons ready, everyone.'

Hawkins steadied his breathing. Index finger lightly feathering the trigger mechanism on the PKM. The appalling violence of a few moments ago already receding from his mind, sinking back beneath the surface as he steeled himself for the imminent firefight.

Forty seconds to go.

No one else spoke. Everyone kept the line clear while Steyn updated them on the convoy's progress. A few of the goats foraging amid the rocks pricked their ears and looked towards the road, alerted by the sounds of the approaching convoy.

'Six hundred metres,' said Steyn.

The engines grew louder. Hawkins felt his stomach muscles instinctively tense. His mouth was dry, as it always was in the seconds before a firefight.

'Five hundred.'

'Four hundred.'

'Three hundred out . . . Two hundred . . . Standby.'

Hawkins glanced down the road as the Nissan Patrol steamed towards the bend, headlamps burning. Line of transports a hundred metres further back, spaced out at fifty-metre intervals from one another, strung out like festoon lights on a cable. Hawkins counted three soft-skinned trucks, one in front of the rigid-bodied wagons, two more behind it. Providing maximum protection to the highly sensitive cargo sandwiched in the middle.

'One hundred metres,' said Steyn.

The trucks kept on coming. Hawkins had an irrational fear that the sight of the goat flock might spook the soldiers. At the very least they might wonder what had happened to the herders. But there was no reason why that should be the case. Flocks probably went astray all the time up in the hills.

The Nissan Patrol dropped its speed, the driver honking his horn at the goats. The flock quickly dispersed, tightly bunching the roadsides or cantering up the slopes, forcing the transports to move along at a slow creep.

The Patrol picked up speed again, carried on past Hawkins, towards the team on the left cut-off. There was a short crack, almost lost behind the roar of the trucks, the blaring of horns, the snorts and nickers of the goat-flock. The discharge of a Dragunov as Martel targeted the front left tyre.

Air shushed out of the punctured wheel. The Patrol struggled on, rubber slapping against the blacktop, and ground to a halt ten metres downstream from the bend. Directly below Kettler and Martel in the left cut-off.

The engine tapped out. The driver-side door flew open. A grey-bearded guy in camo fatigues swung out and went over to investigate the problem. By which time the second occupant had also disembarked. A tall, clean-shaven man in olive-green uniform, wearing a black beret. Therefore an officer. Riding in comparative luxury compared to the grunts in the wagons to the rear.

He joined the driver beside the busted tyre. The two of them having themselves a private confab, the officer resting his hands on his hips, the driver scratching his balding head. Puzzling over their situation. Neither of them seemed to have heard the shot or noticed the muzzle flash. They weren't panicking or looking at the slopes above them in anticipation of an ambush. They were focused on the problem of the flat.

The other vehicles stopped behind the Nissan, bunching up in the kill zone. Like concertina wire being compressed into a nest.

First came one of the soft-skinned trucks, canvas material pulled over the supporting tilt bows. The troop carriers. Then the two rigid bodies, followed by two more infantry transports. Green-army soldiers would be sitting on the rear benches, packed sardine-tight. Wondering why the fuck they had stopped on the pass.

Steyn said, 'Rear truck has just passed us, boss.'

Fifty metres away, the Iranian officer and his driver were still standing beside the Nissan Patrol's front left fender. Debating what to do about the ruptured tyre.

The rearmost transport came to a rest three or four metres aft of the canvas-skinned carrier in front. Engine running.

All six vehicles contained within the lethal kill zone.

23.58

Kettler's voice boomed over the net.

'Go, go, go! Fire! Now!'

Twenty-One

The attack kicked off a micro-beat after the order had left Kettler's mouth. Hawkins heard a sudden whoosh at his three o'clock as the right cut-off team fired an RPG into the rear truck. The vehicle burst into flames as the missile struck the diesel tank, lighting up the mountainside in a flickering apricot glow. The fire spread instantly over the canvas covering, incinerating the occupants and turning it into a raging inferno.

Trapping the rest of the convoy on the pass.

In the next quarter of a second Hawkins lined up his PKM with the troop carrier at his eleven o'clock. Squeezed the trigger.

Rounds spat out of the free-floating barrel, peppering the wagon with 7.62. Spent cases cascaded steadily out of the ejector, tinkling amid the scattered rocks. Hawkins fired in a continuous burst, pissing bullets, arcing the weapon from left to right on the bipod mount, raking the length of the canvas frame. Firing at such close range the tracers had no time to ignite. The soldiers in the back of that carrier didn't stand a chance.

In his peripheral vision, ten metres away, he glimpsed a white flash as Bald let rip with the other PKM. Plugging away at the transport immediately behind the two hard-bodied trucks. Half a dozen rounds glanced off the main chassis in a frenzy of sparks. Bald fired again, putting a hot burst in the tank. The truck exploded. A figure staggered out of the back, his torso on fire, waving his arms and running around in terror. Bald drilled him, putting six rounds in his belly.

Although he had no NVGs, Hawkins could see everything in front of him clearly. A combination of the seething blaze from the rear truck, the headlamps and the muzzle flashes of the six ambushers lying along the slope. Lighting up the mountain pass like a Seventies disco. At his nine o'clock Martel and Kettler were taking pot-shots with their Dragunovs, whacking the officer and the driver beside the Nissan Patrol, knocking them down like skittles.

To his right, some distance beyond Bald, came the discharge of assault rifle fire as Moussa and Steyn switched over their longs, cutting down targets to the rear of the formation. A couple of maimed figures staggered out of the burning wagon. Survivors of the RPG attack, stunned from the explosive impact. Moussa and Steyn must have set their AK-47 selectors to semi-automatic, Hawkins realised, because they were loosing controlled single shots at the two figures. Half a dozen bullets smacked into the Iranians. They jerked and fell away as a third figure climbed out from the front cab. The driver. He started running towards cover at the bottom of the rockface. Two rounds thumped into his guts. He collapsed in a bloodied heap at the edge of the road.

As Hawkins looked on another pair of silhouettes stumbled out from the transport Bald had been brassing up. They were both in a shit state. One of them limped heavily. The other guy's right arm was hanging off, like a piece of rope almost cut in half. They blundered forward, disorientated, heads turning this way and that. Looking for cover, or somewhere to escape. Big mistake. They were caught in the kill zone. Nowhere to take cover. No escape route, other than throwing yourself into the ravine. If the Iranians had been switched on, they would have understood that they had one option: run towards the enemy. Charge straight at the threat. That was what they taught you at Hereford. Engage the enemy. Never back down. But these guys weren't elite SF. They were poorly trained infantry. A month or two of basic fieldwork, drills and weapon handling. Against half a dozen elite operators they didn't stand a chance. Several cracks filled the air as Moussa and Steyn plugged the two injured soldiers. They went floppy and hit the ground, kissing tarmac.

Twenty seconds since it had gone noisy.

Hawkins kept on spraying the front troop carrier. Putting down more rounds in case anyone had survived the initial onslaught. The canvas had been shredded. Scraps of it flapped in the light breeze. No one emerged from the back. The PKMs had worked their magic.

To his left more single shots whipped through the air as Martel and Kettler engaged the drivers. The team hadn't paid any attention to those guys in the first seconds of the attack. All of their efforts had been concentrated on eliminating the biggest threat first. The armed infantry. But with the troops wiped out they could now turn on the rest of the detail. Bullets starred the windshield of the foremost troop carrier. Four Dragunov rounds punched through the glass and hit the driver. Blood spattered the spider-webbed glass.

Behind the front carrier, the two drivers in the hard-bodied wagons leapt out and darted round to the far side of the front cabs before the snipers could put the drop on them. Putting a solid structure between themselves and the ambushers. The driver of the carrier immediately to their rear reached the same conclusion. Flight instead of fight. He jumped down from his cab, dashed past the flaming wagon, hoping to make a run for it but went down under a flurry of single rounds from Moussa and Steyn.

'Cease fire!' Kettler yelled over the HF radio at the top of his lungs. 'Move forward. Clear positions. Drop anything still breathing.'

Everyone stopped shooting.

Hawkins relaxed his trigger finger. The PKM fell silent. He realised he had expended nearly a full belt. Two hundred rounds of ammunition had been poured into the front troop transport. Bald had put a similar amount of 7.62 calibre into the other wagon. Devastating. Like shooting turkeys. A classic Regiment ambush.

At once the six ambushers picked themselves up, snatched up their AK-47 longs and set off down the slope at a measured pace. Wooden stocks seated tight against their shoulders, scanning left to right, searching for any moving targets. There could be no survivors. A wounded soldier might identify the attackers or alert the authorities before they had a chance to get back over the border. Everyone had to go.

The familiar stench of burning flesh hung over the kill zone. Bodies littered the tarmac. Hawkins counted nine of them. The rest had been cut down before they could get off the wagons. Some were burnt to a crisp, others riddled with hot lead, blood puddling around their lifeless corpses. One or two of them were still moving in spite of the unrelenting fire that had rained down on them from above. Which wasn't wholly surprising. Hawkins had heard stories in Iraq and elsewhere of guys taking forty or fifty rounds and still drawing breath.

One Iranian soldier lay writhing on the ground at the foot of the slope. His guts were hanging out. He groaned miserably, trembling hands tried to staunch the flow of blood from the gash in his stomach. Moussa stopped beside him. The soldier lifted his eyes to the Eritrean. Got a good look at his killer a split-beat before Moussa shot him twice in the head.

Two more wounded soldiers were slumped close to the smouldering wreck of the rear carrier. Moussa and Steyn despatched them, while Hawkins, Bald, Martel and Kettler advanced across the road. Clearing the ground, searching for any remaining threats amid the decimated wagons and the bullet-riddled corpses.

Hawkins spied a blur of movement at his one o'clock. He shifted towards the two vehicles carrying the uranium. Four figures emerged slowly from behind the cab of the front truck, arms raised above their heads in a gesture of surrender.

Two were dressed in the same uniform as the infantry. Hawkins recognised them as the drivers. The other pair wore plain green uniforms. Hawkins guessed they must have been sitting in the front passenger seats of the wagons. They would have jumped out on the opposite side from the drivers, hit the tarmac out of sight of the ambushers. Staying behind cover while their mates were cut to pieces.

They looked too old to be soldiers. Late forties or early fifties. They had the soft, slabby build of lifelong desk jockeys. Engineers or scientists, therefore. Tasked with travelling with the uranium.

All four of them looked shocked. Fifty seconds ago they had been sitting comfortably in their wagons. Now their mates had been annihilated. At some point they had taken the decision to throw themselves at the mercy of their attackers. The most natural thing in the world for defeated soldiers. Raise the white flag and beg for your life. One of the drivers said something to Hawkins and Bald. His voice was cracking with fear.

Martel marched right up to them. He stopped two metres away, the business end of the AK barrel pointing at the surrenderers.

'Down,' he said. 'Get down. On your knees.'

The German made a gesture with his assault rifle, pointing to the tarmac. The soldiers seemed to understand in spite of the language barrier. They knelt down, visibly shaking, hands still in the air. Like believers at a revival meeting, praising Jesus for healing the sick.

Martel circled round, standing behind one of the kneeling captives. He lowered the AK-47, dug out his TT pistol from his waistband. Capped the man in the back of the head twice. He proceeded along the line, executing the three other Iranians in quick succession. The German casually stuffed the TT-30 away again, grinning at Bald and Hawkins.

Fucking hell, thought Hawkins. *This guy is a lunatic.*

The use of the pistol bothered him. There was something personal about killing someone with a handgun instead of a long. Intimate, almost. Martel had shot four unarmed Iranians at close range, with his TT, without batting an eyelid. That took a certain type of personality. The kind that relished murdering people.

Martel noticed Hawkins was staring at him. 'You have a problem, English?'

'No,' Hawkins said. 'No problem.'

'I hope not. Otherwise, me and you, we have a problem also.'

'Right,' said Kettler, taking control of the situation. Asserting his Rupert credentials. 'Rory, Hawkins, Jock. Bring the vehicles back over here. Fucking go!'

The team split up, moving fast. Everyone eager to transfer the goods and get down from the mountain as quickly as possible. The clock was ticking. No telling who might have heard the firefight. One of the drivers might have alerted the force at the mine. The Americans might have picked up something on their satellite coverage. Or Mossad.

Bald, Steyn and Hawkins dashed up the road, swerved round the bend west of the kill zone, ran past the empty jerry cans skittling the ground. Steyn dived into the Hilux, while Bald and Hawkins hurried over to the two Unimogs. Hawkins climbed into the nearest one, wrenched the key in the ignition, throttled the engine, released the handbrake. Pumped the gas. He steered hard to the left, braked, shifted into reverse, K-turning in the middle of the road so that he was facing the direction of the ambush. Then he cannoned back down the road, Bald at his six o'clock, Steyn bringing up the rear in the Hilux.

Hawkins screamed to a halt alongside the two box trucks, the Unimog facing downhill. He engaged the parking brake, kept the engine ticking. Jumped out as Bald pulled up behind him. Then came Steyn in the technical, tyres shrieking against the blacktop.

'You two,' Kettler said, pointing to Bald and Moussa. 'Start transferring the cylinders. Take one of the trucks. Paul, Rory, you'll unload the other one. Hawkins, start rigging up those charges. Let's get this shit on the wagons and get out of here.'

Steyn and Martel jogged round to the rear of the lead box truck. Bald and Moussa ran over to the second hard-bodied vehicle parked two metres behind it, wrenching open the rear swing doors. Kettler powered up his satphone and prowled up and down the road, alternating between checking his watch and waiting for a call from the general.

Hawkins left them to it and ran over to the back of the rearmost Unimog. He found the Russian variant clackers on the platform bed, removed them from the box. Reached for the second container. The foam-lined unit with 'AETOHATOP' stamped along the side. *Detonator.* The one with the spool of firing wire inside it.

Once Hawkins had unpacked the kit he would push back up the rockface, attach the wire and blasting caps to the four shaped charges. Then he would rush back down, wait for the team to finish loading the crates, move to a safe distance from the kill zone, depress the clacker. Initiating the explosion that would bring down the side of the mountain.

Hawkins unloaded the box, set it down near the wagon. Lifted the lid.

Froze.

There was no wire inside the box.

He was looking at a dozen long sticks with brass rods at the bottom. Like a set of pencils. Old-school firing devices. Time-delay switches. Hawkins had seen similar fuses on the Reg dems course. Second World War technology. The same kit used by the pioneers in L Detachment in North Africa. Sneaking onto airbases and blowing up Axis aircraft. The pencils contained a glass ampoule filled with acid. To set the fuse you crushed the container with a set of pliers, releasing the corrosive liquid inside. Which would then eat through a soft retaining wire over a certain period of time. Anything from five to fifteen minutes, depending on how far down the stem you crimped it.

When the wire broke, the internal striker would hit the detonator. That in turn triggered the primary explosion, setting off the bigger bang of the plastique charge.

Or rather, that was how the devices worked in theory. But time-delay pencils were notoriously unreliable. Theoretical fuse-time rarely corresponded to actual detonation.

The pencils looked ancient. Eastern bloc junk. Probably manufactured in a Soviet munitions factory decades ago. Gathering dust on a shelf in a remote army base ever since, until a beady-eyed Turkmen smuggler had pilfered them and sold them on to Steyn.

Would they even work after all this time? Hawkins had no idea. Anxiety flooded his guts.

The others had almost finished loading up the Unimogs. Over by the Hilux Kettler was tearing off strips of black masking tape, sticking them down on the bonnet to form the letters 'U' and 'N'. An extra precaution. But it might get them through a heavily guarded checkpoint. Or stop someone from dropping a bomb on them on the way out of the country.

Martel and Steyn carried over the last HEU cylinder to the Unimog nearest to Hawkins. The German climbed onto the cargo bed, carted up the twenty-five-kilo package, gently lowered it into the remaining Laycorn crate. He shut the lid, pulled a ratchet strap over the box and tightened it, securing the box to the platform floor. Martel swung down again, while Steyn pulled the canvas material across the rear cargo bed.

Hawkins said, 'We've got a problem, boss.'

'What the fuck is going on?' Kettler demanded as he marched over.

Hawkins showed him the box of pencil fuses. Kettler's face whitened with silent fury. He looked up at Hawkins, his lips knife-slash thin, his expression so tight Hawkins thought his skin might snap.

'You told me, Hawkins, that you had checked all this kit. You gave me your word.'

'There wasn't enough time,' Hawkins said, guardedly. 'We were in a big hurry. All the other kit checked out.'

'You idiot, Hawkins. Bloody fool, man. You've really fucked this one up.'

Moussa and Bald had finished tying down the last Laycorn box on the other Unimog. They quickened over to the rest of the group standing around the box of old pencil fuses. All of them at once grasping the implications. No det wire. No way to set off the charges with the clackers.

'What are we gonna do?' asked Steyn.

'There's no time to change the plan,' Kettler said, voice shaking with barely controlled rage and frustration. 'That mountain needs to come down one way or another. We'll just have to set the pencil fuses.'

'Will they work?' Steyn said.

'They'll work,' Bald said. 'It's chemicals and wiring. Basic circuitry. Basic as you can get. But the timings might be off. Depends on the integrity of them ampoules. Whoever ignites them is gonna have to crimp and run like hell.'

Steyn sucked the air between his stained teeth. 'I ain't doing it, boss. No fucking way. This shit went out with the Ark. If them things have gone bad, whoever sets them is gonna get blown apart before they can get away.'

No one spoke for a long beat.

Then Martel said, 'The Englishman fucked up. He should be the one to set the charges.'

'I agree,' Kettler said. 'You dropped the bollock, Hawkins. Your mistake. You own it.'

Hawkins felt his arsehole clench with fear. He hesitated, frantically trying to think of some way of squirming out of the task. Then Kettler did a thing with his eyes. Gesturing towards Martel. An unspoken command. The German dropped his hand to the TT-30 wedged down the front of his hiking pants. Fingers resting lightly on the rubber grip. A clear warning.

Kettler said, 'Do it, Hawkins. Or you can go over the edge with the rest of them. Your choice.'

Hawkins swallowed hard. Fear lodged in his throat. He said, shakily, 'I'll need a pair of pliers. Can't set the pencils off without them.'

Bald reached into his pocket, fished out the Leatherman. 'Here. Use this, Geordie.'

Hawkins took the tool. He pulled the handles outward, locking them in place. Gathered up the pencil sticks, left the clackers in the other box. He wouldn't be needing them now. They were useless without the firing wire.

'Everyone else in the wagons,' Kettler ordered. 'Leave the heavy stuff behind, but keep your longs and pistols and the ammo. Take the RPG too in case we run into a roadblock. Everything else is going down that mountain with the convoy.'

Kettler pointed out a spot two hundred metres east of their position, at a section of the pass with no overhanging boulders.

'Hawkins, we'll park there and wait for you. Once you've set those fuses, run over as fast as you can. Then we're getting out of here.'

Martel said, 'Be careful with those things. One mistake and bang! Bye-bye English.'

He did a little wave, lips pouting in a mock sad-face.

Hawkins tensed his jaw. The German was really beginning to piss him off. But there was no time to say anything else. The clock was ticking. *Every second counts. The Americans might be watching our every move. Waiting for clearance to drop a JDAM on our heads.*

Martel darted over to the technical with Kettler. The German lunged into the driver's seat, Kettler vaulting up on the passenger side. Steyn and Moussa scrambled into the rear Unimog. Bald mounted the wheel of the Unimog at the front of the formation. Engines thrummed. The three motors set off down the road, bypassing the ambushed convoy, headlights beaming through the semi-darkness. They came to a rest two hundred metres away. A safe distance from the det site, away from any loose rocks that might be set off by the explosion.

Hawkins scrabbled up the rocky slope with the box of pencil detonators, his heart hammering frenetically in his chest, blood rushing in his ears. He was shitting himself.

Four shaped charges, he thought. *Twelve decades-old pencil fuses.* His life now depended on the craftsmanship of a Soviet munitions manufacturer. A coin toss.

Heads, you survive.

Tails, you get blown limb from limb.

He decided he would have to move very quickly. No point trying to calculate det times. Just stick the fuses in the charges, crimp
them and leg it. He would use three pencils per charge, in case a
few of them turned out to be duds. Always a possibility when you
were dealing with antiquated kit.

Hawkins had never believed in luck. He had always been a make-
your-own-luck sort of bloke. They drummed that philosophy into
you at Hereford. The more you train, the more hours you put into
improving yourself, the less you needed to rely on God or good
fortune. Only crap soldiers put their faith in a higher power. But as
he beetled over to the first charge, Hawkins became a big convert.
I hope to Christ my luck is in today.

He dropped to his knees next to the first charge. The one set in
the crevice beneath the wrecking-ball-shaped boulder. He laid the
pliers down, took three pencils from the box, rammed them into
the Russian variant C4, inserting the brass ends fully.

Hawkins was sweating hard as he snatched up the pliers with his
shaking right hand. He wiped his brow, placed the serrated jaws
around the ampoule. His chest was beating so fast he thought his
heart might actually explode. He took a deep breath, squeezed the
Leatherman handles together. Crimped the fuse.

Nothing happened.

The fuse didn't detonate.

The liquid slowly ate through the copper wiring.

Thank fuck.

Keep going. You're on the clock.

Tick-tock, Davey boy.

He moved on to the second pencil, his throat constricted with
dread. His T-shirt was drenched with sweat now. Hawkins could
hardly breathe. He positioned the plier jaws around the stick at the
same height, his stomach involuntarily tightened as he crimped the
glass tube, releasing the acid. He shifted over to the next fuse-delay
wand, working speedily in spite of his trembling hands. He didn't

know how long he had before the detonators ignited. Could be five minutes. Could be ten. Could be a whole lot less than that. No way of knowing.

Hawkins compressed the Russian pencil.

Shot to his feet.

Sprinted over to the second plastique charge.

Three pencils down.

Nine to go.

Fear was dripping into his bowels. A terrible thought gnawed incessantly at Hawkins: *These things might blow up at any moment. Taking down the mountain, and me with it.* Every cell in his body screamed at him to ditch the pencils and get the fuck away. Before he got ripped limb from limb. But he couldn't. He had to look that fear in the eye. Acknowledge it. The Regiment way.

He scrambled over to the second charge in the sequence, moving sequentially from west to east, so that he would have less ground to cover to the Unimog after setting the final charge. He noted, absently, that the goats had vanished, figured they must have scattered into the hills once everything had gone noisy. Down below, the fire had gutted out the troop carrier at the back of the Iranian column. Acrid smoke billowed upwards from the twisted hulk, spiralling into the black infinity of sky.

He planted three fuses in the second charge. Crimped them one by one. Each time he half-expected the detonators to ignite, atomising his body. Nothing left but scraps of bone. But the pencils were stable. Thirty years of storage hadn't corroded the working parts. Soviet craftsmanship at its finest.

Hawkins put a trio of pencils in the third and fourth snowball-shaped explosives. He ditched the box and the Leatherman multi-tool, scuttled back down the scarp, almost slipping on a patch of loose rocks before he regained his balance. He hurried on, almost flying down the last few metres until he hit the roadside near the flamed-out wagon. Then he wheeled east, running towards the vehicles two hundred metres away. Motors running, fumes spewing out of exhaust pipes. Ready to get the hell out of the area.

Hurry.

Get a move on, Davey Boy.

He was eighty metres away when the ground shook.

There was an ear-splitting boom as one of the charges set off behind Hawkins. Then a second one. Then a third and fourth, the explosions coming almost on top of one another. BOOM-BOOM-BOOM-BOOM. Hawkins felt the earth move beneath him as a thousand tonnes of soil and rock came rushing down the rockface, surging towards the vehicles and bodies on the road below.

Hawkins chopped his stride, his lungs burning, running for all he was worth. Imploring his weary body to move faster.

Keep going. Push through it. Don't stop now.

He closed the gap to the technical to forty metres. Glanced over his shoulder as the avalanche of rock swept across the road, pushing the dead bodies and the trucks over the precipice, into the ravine below, and he knew then that their plan had worked.

Hawkins became aware of something hurtling rapidly towards him. The vibrations had dislodged a small boulder on the slope above. He had just enough time to register that thought before the rock struck him on the side of the head.

Pain rattled viciously through his skull. Like getting punched in the face by champion-era Mike Tyson. Hawkins stumbled, felt his legs give way beneath him. He fell on his front, face smacking against the blacktop. Grogginess settled like a fog over him. He couldn't move. Couldn't get up. Rocks and boulders rained down on him as the explosions displaced more material from the scarp above. The entire rockface was about to come crashing down. Hawkins had the strangely detached feeling that he was about to die.

Over.

It's over.

I'm going to get buried under the avalanche.

Then he glimpsed a silhouette to the east. Rushing towards him across the shaking earth. Bald was suddenly on top of him. Sinewy arms reached under his armpits, interlacing around his back. Bald pulled him upright, dragging him to his feet, slipped an arm around Hawkins's shoulder blades.

'Let's go, Geordie!' the old Scot bellowed above the downrush. 'Move it! This fucking thing is about to come down!'

Hawkins hobbled along, jaws cinched tight against the jarring pain in his head. Bald urged him to move faster, the two ex-soldiers hastening towards the front Unimog. Fifteen metres to the wagon now. Hawkins heard a louder crash at his back. He glanced round, saw the road behind him disappearing beneath a torrent of loose rock and dirt. He had been two or three seconds away from getting swept into the ravine.

Martel had stepped out of the technical. He was at the front Unimog. Peering inside the front cab on the driver's side. As if he was searching for something. Large rocks were tumbling down from the nearly vertical slope and showering the roadside, rattling against the Hilux bonnet. Hawkins staggered on. In three more strides they reached the Unimog.

The German stepped back from the vehicle and stabbed a finger at Bald. 'You took the keys. You could have got us all killed!'

'Fuck off!' Bald spat. 'You would have driven off and left us both for dead, you bastard.'

Martel said nothing. He shot Bald a black look, charged back over to the Hilux parked to the rear of the wagons.

'Get in, Geordie!' Bald yelled.

Hawkins collapsed into the front passenger seat. Bald climbed in on the other side, slotted the key into the ignition. He revved the engine, stamped on the pedal. The Unimog lurched forward, the two other vehicles accelerating after them, pulling clear of the pass a nanosecond before the mountainside came crashing down in a deluge of dust and debris.

'Fuck me, that was close,' Bald said, catching his breath.

Hawkins had started to reply when a blaring noise filled the air. He heard it over the ringing pain in his ears, the guttering rumble of the diesel engine. A long fluctuating wail, coming from somewhere in the distance.

The howl of an air raid siren.

Which could mean only one thing.

The B-2s are here.

The bombs are about to drop.

'Are there any other nuclear sites around this way?' he said, shaking off the dizziness clouding his mind.

'None,' Bald replied. 'Fordow is the only one.'

'What the fuck are they hitting it for? They've been told that place is empty.'

'Might be covering their bases. Hitting every site in the country.' Bald hesitated. 'That's one explanation.'

'What's the other?'

'The Yanks might have realised the general has been bullshitting them.'

'Shit.'

Silence. Hawkins's head felt lead-heavy. He became dimly aware of a throbbing pain above his brow. Blood runnelled down his face from the shallow cut to his forehead.

They raced on down the pass, the siren screaming into the night sky. The instrument clock glowing in the darkness of the front cab. 00.07. Nine minutes since everything had gone noisy.

'Thanks,' Hawkins managed. 'I owe you, mate.'

'Save it,' Bald said. 'Long way to go yet. We've got to get the fuck out of here first.'

Twenty-Two

They raced on down the pass. The dirge of the air raid warnings died away.

Hawkins gazed out of the side window, descried a faint plume of smoke in the distance, somewhere south of the salt lake crater, twenty or thirty kilometres from their position. Marking the site where the bombs had struck Fordow. Massive Ordnance Penetrators. Bunker-busters. Anxiety percolated through his guts.

If the Americans find out what we're carrying, that shit will be dropping on us next.

They hit the secondary road at the foot of the mountains, at which point they switched formation. The Hilux taking the lead in the forward scout position, Kettler scanning the road ahead with a pair of binoculars, looking out for potential threats. Bald and Hawkins in the middle, Moussa and Steyn as the tail-end Charlie, ten metres behind them in the second Unimog. The technical was carrying nothing incriminating. No heavy weaponry, no cylinders of looted uranium. Just spare cans of diesel taken from the artic, torpedoes of bottled water, the UN lettering taped to the bonnet. They had the best chance of getting through a roadblock. If Kettler spotted a checkpoint directly ahead he could warn the guys in the two Unimogs, giving them time to turn off the road, box their way round.

They kept the net free, Kettler occasionally talking, giving the other team members directions. Bald hung a left, shadowed the technical past a deserted campsite and a ramshackle garage. After which they mounted the Old Tehran-Qom Road, taking them on broadly the same trajectory as the main highway, but with fewer petrol stations and rest stops along the route. Therefore less chance of running into a roadblock. A simple fact of human nature. Soldiers on checkpoint duty liked to be within close proximity to basic amenities. A toilet, hot water, somewhere to sit and fix a brew.

At this late hour the road was quiet, and dark. They passed no civilian motors, just a couple of small-goods vehicles rumbling along in the opposite lane. Unofficial curfew. The country had just been bombed. Hardly anyone would be undertaking a car journey right now. Not unless it was absolutely essential.

Ten kilometres further north they passed a deserted checkpoint next to an isolated rest area. A pair of army trucks were parked up outside the building. Hawkins strained his eyes but he couldn't see any soldiers. No personnel flagging down motorists.

'Where the fuck is everyone?' Hawkins said as they rolled past.

'Night shift,' Bald answered. 'Them lads will be sitting inside where it's nice and cosy, having tea and a falafel sandwich. Passing the hours until it's time to clock off.'

Hawkins shook his head in professional contempt. 'They've just been attacked. These idiots should be on high alert.'

'Conscripts, Geordie. They're not motivated. Most of the elite troops will be tied down elsewhere. Tehran and the other big cities. Carrying out patrols and snuffing out any protests against the regime. Shotgunning young people with placards calling for the return of the Shah. Rest will have orders to secure key government buildings, banks, military bases. Anywhere that might get bombed in a follow-on attack.

'Besides,' Bald went on, 'no one's gonna be interested in us. The Iranians aren't on the lookout for a team smuggling this stuff out of the area. Not for a while yet.'

Hawkins nodded. By now the security force guarding the old mine would have grown extremely concerned. The nuclear convoy had failed to show up on time. Questions would be asked. *Where the fuck are those guys? Why aren't they answering their radios?* A detail would be despatched to the pass to investigate. There they would discover the landslide, the wagons buried under a mound of rocks and debris.

Their first instinct would be to retrieve the uranium. Priority number one. Get the excavators in and start clearing away the rubble. But they would have to move cautiously, because of the possibility of contamination. One mistake and they might have a mini-Chernobyl on their hands. It would take a day or two before they realised the transports were empty.

Meanwhile senior commanders would be sending specialist teams to the bombed nuclear sites across the country. Damage assessment. Searching for survivors and salvageable pieces of equipment, anything that might have survived the bunker busters. For the next several hours the regime would be distracted by events elsewhere. Total chaos.

No one will be looking in our direction.

'Long as we steer clear of Tehran and the other big cities, we should be gravy,' Bald was saying. 'But that's not our biggest problem. The biggest danger ain't from the Iranians. It's from up there.'

He pointed up at the sky.

Hawkins said, 'Do you think the Americans will have seen us?'

'They've definitely had eyes on Fordow for the past few hours. We know that much. They wouldn't have bombed it otherwise. Some smart analyst over at the NSA might have picked up on the attack at the pass.'

Hawkins considered. 'No,' he said after a pause. 'No way. If the Americans knew about the attack, they would have lobbed a missile at us.'

'Not necessarily.'

Hawkins glanced quizzically at the Scot.

Bald said, 'The Yanks might be more interested in following us, Geordie. See who's in on the deal. Who's pulling the strings. Where the product is going. That information is more valuable than the risk of someone setting off a dirty bomb.'

Hawkins tried to ignore the quivering in his stomach. The muscles around his neck were tightly corded with tension. He kept glancing at the digital clock. 00.54. Another nine hours until they hit the border. A longer drive than the infil route. Because of the need to avoid the major motorways and cities on the way out. They were adding an extra hundred kilometres to their journey time.

He wondered again about Bald. The guy had saved his life back at the pass, putting his own neck on the line to drag Hawkins away seconds before the rockface had swept across the road. That took serious courage. Martel and the others would have undoubtedly left him for dead. Maybe Hawkins had been wrong about him. Maybe Bald did have a moral compass.

He weighed up the possibility of coming cleaning to Bald once they were across the border. Fess up bout his secret mission with Six. If Bald was also working for them, he'd have a way of contacting his handlers.

And if I'm wrong? What if Bald is really only in it for the money?

Hawkins closed off that train of thought. Mental compartmentalisation. He refused to look any further ahead than the next few hours.

They stuck to the empty road as it made a wide easterly orbit of Tehran airport, carried on for twenty kilometres. They slowed down as they weaved their way through the south-eastern suburbs of Tehran, shuttling past rows of warehouses, petrol stations and car dealerships. Hawkins figured this must be some sort of industrial zone. The occasional light truck or motorcycle buzzed past, heading in the opposite direction.

A throng of police officers stood outside a grimy teahouse, sipping drinks or leaning against the sides of their vehicles. They paid the gang no attention. No reason to suspect them of anything. Just two small-goods vehicles and a pickup doing a late-night run through the suburbs.

Then Kettler reported over the net, 'Army vehicles ahead, lads. Heads-up.'

Hawkins gripped his long. The guys in the technical and the other Unimog would be going through the same drill. Heightened awareness. Like a stand-to at daybreak. If they were stopped, if the soldiers pulled them over, they would have to shoot their way through. But if that happened, the team would shortly have every police officer and soldier in the country on their backs. Hunting them down. They would almost certainly be captured before they could escape the country.

The Iranians were experts at inflicting torture. Fingernail crushing, waterboarding. Beatings. Hawkins, Bald and the other guys would face days of horrific pain before they were executed.

Bald reduced his speed to forty per as they drew closer to the wagons. Three personnel carriers parked along a lay-by. A group of bored-looking soldiers squatted on the rubbish-strewn verge, huddled around a forty-five-gallon steel drum cut in two with a fire blazing in it, puffing on cigarettes and chatting among themselves. Conscripts on the graveyard shift. Poor quality.

The soldiers made no move to flag down the vehicles. Bald drove on, the canvas-backed trucks shrinking from view in the side mirror. Hawkins relaxed his grip slightly on the assault rifle, breathed a sigh of relief.

They pushed on. Every passing minute induced a fresh wave of torment for the occupants of the Unimog. The fear that they might run into a group of switched-on soldiers. Or an American fighter jet might drop a payload on them from above. Blow them to pieces. Instant death. Hawkins started clock-watching like a bored kid on a long car journey. Counting down every minute of the drive. Willing time to go faster.

01.27.

A hundred and ten kilometres down.

Six hundred to go.

They motored north-east for another twelve kilometres, and then Kettler said over the HF frequency, 'Checkpoint ahead, lads. One kilometre from your position.'

'What's the plan, boss?' Steyn asked.

'There's a right turn two hundred metres from your position, next to an Indian car dealership. We're taking it now. Follow us and box round the checkpoint. We'll remount the main road four hundred metres north-east.'

Hawkins depressed the PTT button. 'Any news from the general? Do the Iranians know anything yet?'

Kettler paused. 'The general's not picking up.'

'Why the fuck not?'

'It's chaos over there. Iranian airspace has been closed down. All mobile phone and internet services have been switched off. Radio stations are down. TV networks too. Digital darkness. The Ayatollah is in a panic. The general's probably stuck in a briefing with the leadership. Figuring out how to respond to the attacks. Drawing up a list of US targets in the region. They'll be arguing over how far to push the envelope without encouraging further US retaliation.'

'Keep trying your man,' Hawkins urged. 'Keep hammering that fucking number until you get through. We need to know if that border is still open.'

'It will be,' Kettler said insistently. 'Count on it. If the Iranians suspected anything, the general would have sent us a warning message. Just focus on getting round that checkpoint. Weapons at the ready. Once we're clear of those bastards we'll take the right-sided slipway leading to the trunk road heading east. That will take us away from Tehran, towards the mountains.'

Bald made the next right off the strip, signposted by the car dealership. They steered down a blacked-out side road flanked by industrial units and garages, taking them towards a residential neighbourhood. The second Unimog made the same turn, lights blading through the deserted street. After four hundred metres Bald took a left turn, following the directions Kettler gave them over the net. They cantered down a decrepit thoroughfare, circled clockwise at a roundabout, took the second exit, pointing the wagon north-east. He rejoined the expressway beyond the checkpoint.

They continued for another five kilometres, boxed round a second checkpoint, hit a sprawling cloverleaf up ahead and took the slip road onto the highway. Taking them away from Tehran, towards the southern slopes of the Alborz mountain range. The landscape here was dotted sporadically with ranches and industrial units, rest stops and office blocks.

Minutes ticked past with agonising slowness. Hawkins felt a stiffness in his jaw, realised he must have been grinding his teeth hard for hours. Bald gripped the steering wheel so hard his knuckles were shaded white. The stress of the journey manifesting itself.

At four o'clock they hit another checkpoint west of Semnan. They bypassed it using the slipways, took the secondary roads through the city itself. Twice the team had to get off the main road to avoid army roadblocks, the detours ferrying them past crumbling residential blocks, the still deadness of the pre-dawn broken by the loudspeakers carrying the muezzin's call to prayer.

The first hint of the new day glimmered on the horizon as they broke clear of Semnan. A gas-flame-blue ribbon burnishing the sky behind the black hulk of the mountain range. The Unimog fuel indicator crept slowly downward. They were eating through a lot of gas. Because of the longer exfil route. They stopped on the hard shoulder to fill up the Unimog tanks once again, Martel refuelling the technical with a couple of jerry cans, pouring diesel into the tank with a plastic funnel. The other guys used the break to empty their bladders and scoff down protein bars. Then they were back on the road again.

The checkpoints thinned out as the team clawed their way further east. Just like Steyn had predicted back at the briefing in Pretoria. All the big events were happening elsewhere in the country.

The bombings. The convoy at the bottom of the pass. Unrest in the capital. Eastern Iran would be way down the list of the regime's priorities. They raced past a couple of unmanned checkpoints, turned off the expressway and steered onto a one-lane carriageway winding north through a chain of jagged mountains.

Dawn had spilled across the landscape. Hawkins alternated between checking the clock, searching the sky and glancing at the bonnet, looking for the tell-tale glint of a drone flying overhead. He found nothing, but he couldn't shake the feeling that they were being watched. It had him in a chokehold. Six hours into the journey, his nerves were totally shredded. His stomach felt knotted with tension, and fear.

Six o'clock.

Still there had been no news from the general. Hawkins operated the walkie-talkie, checking in with Kettler in the front Hilux.

'Nothing yet, Hawkins. I'll let you know as soon as I've heard back from him. Now get off the net.'

'Fuck off,' Bald hit back. 'We're not in the army now, mate. We need to know if that border is still clear. Give us a straight answer. Yes or no.'

'I'm not able to confirm it,' Kettler said, frostily. 'As I just told you, I'm awaiting an update from the general. Until I hear from him, there's nothing else I can do.'

'That guy must have a pad in Dubai. He'll have a cleaner there, or a cook. Household staff. Get on the blower. One of them is bound to pick up. See if he's arrived in town yet, or if he's on the way.'

Kettler fell silent for a beat.

'Two minutes,' he said.

They waited.

Hawkins was clenching his teeth so hard he could have split logs with them. 'Maybe the general just panicked. Maybe he upped sticks and left the country. Bolted before the situation goes pear-shaped.'

Bald said, 'He won't have skipped town, Geordie.'

'Why not?'

'That guy has only been paid part of his fee. He doesn't get the balance until the deal is done and dusted. He wouldn't leg it yet. No chance. He'd be left out of pocket.'

'So why isn't he answering his phone?'

Bald didn't reply.

The knot in Hawkins's stomach pulled a little tighter.

Something felt wrong.

Very wrong.

Two minutes later, Kettler spoke again on the HF net.

'I've heard from the general's cleaner in Dubai,' he said.

'Well?'

'The general isn't expected to get in until tomorrow morning. He's also checked with his personal chauffeur. Far as he knows there has been no change to the schedule.'

Bald said, 'It's obvious, then. The general's been compromised.'

'We don't know that, Jock. Speculation.'

'Bullshit. That guy isn't picking up his phone, and he's not out of the country. A tenner says he's in a prison cell right now, getting electric shock treatment to the bollocks.'

'What are we gonna do?' Steyn asked from the rear Unimog.

Kettler said, 'The plan stays the same. We head for the border. I'll keep trying the satphone. In the meantime, keep this line clear. That's a fucking order. Anyone could be listening in.'

They fell silent. Hawkins took a gulp of warm bottled water, fought to calm the feverish tapping in his chest. They were gambling now. Playing for high stakes. The highest imaginable. Betting their lives on being able to squeeze out of Iran before the general spilled his guts to his interrogators.

If this goes wrong, we're fucked.

Seven o'clock.

Three hours to the crossing.

A long time for someone to hold out under torture. But maybe not for a career soldier and a hardened veteran of the Iran–Iraq War.

As they continued east Hawkins made a silent promise to himself. The booze had to go. No ifs or buts this time. No excuses. *If I make it out of here alive, I'm cutting out the drink once and for all. Clean my shit up. Get my head straight.*

Jock was right. *This life doesn't do reruns.* You couldn't go through life feeling sorry for yourself, blaming the world for your own fuck-ups, hoping that something might turn up to change your fortunes. You had to attack it. Go through that door, take control of the situation. Don't stand outside, worrying about what might happen.

So he would miss his daughter's wedding. Look at it through the wider lens. That was one day out of many. He could still play a big part in Zoe's life. Watch her flourish.

We've got to get across that border first.

The sun had fully risen now. Hawkins was shattered. His eyes felt like coarse-grain sandpaper. His last kip had been on the flight from Djibouti to Gorakan. Twenty-four long hours ago. He hadn't eaten a morsel since the previous evening, but he had no appetite. Dread had twisted his stomach into a vicious knot.

At 10.07 Kettler reported over the comms, 'Approaching the crossing point. One kilometre ahead of your position.'

'What can you see, boss?' asked Steyn.

Hawkins listened anxiously. Kettler would be assessing the checkpoint through his binos. Watching for anything unusual. Any change in the security patterns they had seen when passing through the checkpoint on the way in. The presence of armoured cars, or a large number of infantry or police in the area. But a hand-ful of scabby-looking guards checking paperwork probably meant that they were safe.

'It's clear,' Kettler said at last. 'Four border guards. No other personnel in sight.'

'Thank fuck,' Steyn said with obvious relief.

'We ain't through yet,' Bald said back. 'Might be soldiers hidden behind one of them buildings. They might wait until we've come to a stop at the barrier, then swarm over us.'

Kettler said, 'Jock is right. This could still be a trap. Weapons at the ready. If this doesn't look right, for whatever reason, we'll have to shoot our way through.'

Hawkins had butterflies in his stomach. A kaleidoscope of them. Bald felt the same. Hawkins could sense the nervousness coming off his mucker in waves. He dropped his gun hand to the AK-47 trigger guard. Thumbed the fire selector to semi-automatic. Fingering the trigger.

Moment of truth.

Is the border chief still on our side? Has the general given chapter and verse to his interrogators?

Only one way to find out.

They skipped past the loose line of trucks and knackered civilian cars queuing at the two working checkpoints. The ones with the green ticks lighting up the gantry screens. The technical drove down the closed gate, halted in front of the lowered barrier arm. Bald and Hawkins came to a stop right behind it, the second Unimog pulling up at their six.

A thickset border guard wearing a field cap emerged from the gatehouse. Golden epaulettes on his shoulders denoted his rank as an officer of middling rank. Behind him marched a younger guy in shades, AK-47 slung over his shoulder. The guy in shades held back a few paces from the technical, gripping his assault rifle with intent, while the officer walked up to the driver-side door. Tapped his knuckles on the glass.

Martel stuck his head out, exchanged a few words with the officer. The Iranian responded by shaking his head and shouting at the two occupants, making a series of highly expressive gestures. He seemed unhappy about something.

The guards at the other booths were looking over at their boss, taking a keen interest in the heated exchange between the officer and the two lads in the pickup truck.

Hawkins felt a stab of fear.

Have we been compromised? Have we driven into a trap? Are they going to arrest us?

The argument dragged on for two minutes. Strong words were being exchanged. Hawkins tensed his index finger on the AK trigger. Then Martel thrust an arm out of the window, handed the officer a stuffed brown envelope. Presumably containing a wad of cash. The officer peeked inside, wedged the envelope into his back pocket. Then he adjusted his cap and stepped away from the Hilux, growling an order at the guy in the shades.

The barrier arm rose.

'What was that all about?' Hawkins said into his walkie-talkie as they trundled through the crossing point.

'Greedy bastard wanted another payment,' Kettler said bitterly. 'Treble the agreed price. Outrageous. Bloody cheek.'

'Who gives a shit,' Bald said. 'It's a few extra pennies. A chunk of change. This ain't the time for penny-pinching.'

'Say that when you've got my level of expenses, Jock. You'll be scrabbling down the back of the sofa then.'

'Twat,' Bald muttered to Hawkins. 'I'll be glad when we're out of this place, Geordie. Had enough of dealing with Ruperts to last me ten fucking lifetimes.'

Hawkins grinned weakly. 'You and me both.'

A few kilometres further on they reached the checkpoint on the Turkmen side of the crossing. Kettler palmed another wad of cash to the guard manning the closed gate. The guy pocketed his bonus, opened the barrier, and suddenly they were driving through Turkmenistan.

An enormous weight lifted from Hawkins's shoulders. All the strain he had been feeling over the past twenty-four hours sloughed off. He celebrated with a hunk of stale sandwich. Christ, that tasted good. The best meal he'd ever had. At his side Bald was grinning like a madman, slapping Hawkins on the shoulder, eyes aglow with the prospect of the fortune coming his way. Ten million. More, with Devaney out of the picture.

Three hundred kilometres to the airhead. Two hundred and thirty to the RV at the old cement factory. The meeting-place for the deal Kettler had brokered with the buyers. Three more hours on the road. But a less nervy drive than the exfil from Iran. The main threat had receded. No more checkpoints to evade, no risk of getting apprehended by Iranian militiamen.

Hawkins turned his exhausted mind to the problem of the handover. The deal brokered by Kettler with the mysterious third party. Two hundred kilos of highly enriched uranium, in exchange for two hundred million dollars wired to a bank account in Dubai. Somehow Hawkins needed to find a way to get eyes on the buyers. Establish their identities, and notify Six before they went underground.

The first part would be fairly straightforward. Kettler would want to surround himself with bodyguards at the meeting. The logical move. There was a chance the buyers might try to slay the gang, take off with the goods. Kettler needed to guard against that scenario. Hawkins felt sure he, and the other team members, would be in the room when the deal went down.

Which left the second part of his mission. Alerting Vauxhall. Hawkins had no phone, no direct line to his handlers. He racked his brains, but he couldn't see any obvious way round that problem. He would have to just play it by ear. Stay alert, keep his eyes peeled, wait to see if an opportunity presented itself to contact Six.

They tooled on through a featureless moonscape of rocky plains dotted with scraps of vegetation, the mountain range to the east demarcating the border with Iran. The team took a piss-break at eleven o'clock, stopped at a lay-by to replenish the Unimog tanks,

funnelled two more jerry cans into the technical. All six mercenaries taking the opportunity to stretch their legs after eleven-plus
hours of hard driving.

Martel wandered off to take a shit behind a derelict shack and
returned two minutes later. The guy looked edgy, Hawkins noted.
Tightly coiled. Probably eager to get the deal over and done with,
then hop back on the Antonov to Pretoria. *Same as the rest of us.*
None of them wanted to spend a minute longer than necessary in
Turkmenistan.

Thirty seconds later they were back on the highway.

At 12.54, Ketter spoke up on the comms once more.

'One kilometre out from the RV.'

'What's the plan when we get there?' Hawkins said.

'We'll park up behind the warehouses, so we'll be out of sight of
the highway. Buyers should already be in position. Paul and myself
will approach the meeting-point on foot. Rest of you stay with
the wagons in case we need to make a getaway. We'll bring you
forward only once we've established that it's safe.'

An invisible band tightened around Hawkins's chest. In a few
minutes they would be meeting the other party. The shadowy buyers. Terrorists, or go-betweens working for a state actor. Or ISIS
maniacs. Someone with a track record of financing terror. A group
with deep pockets and a burning desire to inflict great harm on
Britain and her allies.

The abandoned cement factory hove into view three hundred
metres to the north. A jumble of concrete silos, cooling towers,
dilapidated sheds and chimney stacks set a hundred metres back
from the roadside, half-hidden behind a clump of shrubs and small
trees. A paved spur ran from the trunk road to the front of the
cement works.

The Hilux just ahead of them eased off the accelerator. Bald did
the same in the lead Unimog.

They drew closer.

A hundred metres to the access spur. Hawkins could make out the entrance more clearly now. There was a haulage yard at the front of the plant complex; behind it stood dilapidated sheds and warehouses, mountains of gravel, rusted mixing machinery.

Then he saw the police lights.

Twenty-Three

Hawkins counted seven vehicles. They were parked up in loose semi-circle around the front of the haulage yard, lights flashing through the watery desert haze. Three police cars and four tactical personnel carriers. The place thronged with cops. In among them, a bunch of soldiers in camo kit, balaclavas and olive-green berets, packing assault rifles. Elite local troops. The guys wheeled out for special operations. Drugs busts and attacks on terrorist cells.

Swarming over the RV.

'Shit,' Hawkins said.

'What's going on, boss?' Steyn demanded over the net.

Kettler's voice bled out of Hawkins's walkie-talkie. 'The RV is blown. I repeat, the RV is blown. Keep driving.'

'Fuck's sake,' Bald muttered. 'Have we been compromised? What's going on over there?'

'Must have seen something,' Steyn said. 'Why else would they be all over that place?'

Kettler said, 'Let me worry about that. I'll speak to the buyers. Smooth things out. Just keep fucking going. Don't stop or slow down.'

They pushed further down the trunk road. The cluster of police lights shrivelled to flashing dots near the horizon. Priority number one. Get well away from the RV. The place was hot.

Kettler's voice intruded over the comms.

'Paul says there's a disused petrol station six kilometres from here, next exit off the highway. We'll pull up there. I'll speak with the buyer, get the lowdown on the situation at the cement works. Location of the new RV.'

'Let's hope there is one,' Bald groused.

'There will be,' Kettler said, sharply. 'I know the buyers. It'll take a lot more than a compromised RV to give them cold feet.'

Hawkins tried to place himself in Kettler's boots. He would be extremely worried right now. The RV had gone south. He needed to gather himself. Reach out to the buyers, find out what the fuck was going on. Establish the alternative RV. Hence the decision to convene at the old petrol station. A safe place, away from the trunk road, but not too far from their current position in case they had to double back on themselves to make the new rendezvous.

But Kettler wouldn't want to make that call on the side of the road. A bunch of blokes next to their vehicles on the hard shoulder, talking on their phones, would stand out like shits floating in a punchbowl. That was how drug dealers got rumbled. Russian spies had used the same tactics back in the day. Roadside meet-ups, with the agent under instructions to put their hazards on. If a police officer stopped to investigate, the agent would claim to have broken down.

'How the fuck did the local plod know about that RV?' Hawkins said.

Bald responded with a shrug. 'Maybe the buyers were slack about their personal security. One of the drivers might have been pissed behind the wheel and driving erratically, got himself pulled over. Or it could just be bad luck. Some nosy coppers taking an interest in the activity around the plant. Happens all the time.'

'Maybe.'

Hawkins remembered something Jacob had once told him. Several months before he had frozen to death on the Brecons. *Bad luck happens when you least need it.*

'You think there's something else going on?' asked Bald.

'The police might have been tipped off.'

Bald chewed on the thought. 'No. Doesn't make sense. The only fuckers who know about the RV are the six of us, and the buyers. We haven't even got a phone, apart from Kettler.'

'So maybe the buyers got sloppy with their counter-surveillance measures. Someone might have been listening in. Or watching them. Could be anyone.'

'As long as that fucking deal is still on,' said Bald. 'All that matters in my book, son.'

'You're not worried about where this stuff is going?'

'We're in this for the money. Life-changing sums, Geordie. It's a bit fucking late in the day to start moralising.'

Hawkins said, 'If these cylinders end up in the hands of ISIS, or another group, there are going to be consequences. We both know that. We'll end up with blood on our hands.'

He was trying to suss out Bald. Testing his loyalties. *Is he a Six asset, or a rogue mercenary?*

'I don't give a monkey's where it's going,' Bald said. 'For all we know it could be someone wanting to do the world a favour, buying up the uranium so they can destroy it.'

'You don't seriously believe that, do you?'

Bald didn't reply.

They ploughed on for five kilometres, reached the next off-ramp without running into any more blue lights. They took the slipway, hooked round onto a minor road and motored on for half a kilometre before they found the petrol station, set down in the middle of a dustblown plain. Rusted pumps baked beneath the furnace-hot sun. Weeds sprouted through cracks on the forecourt. There was a station store with boarded-up windows, a mound of old car tyres to one side of a dumpster. Like something out of a spaghetti western.

The technical and the wagons rocked to a halt on the forecourt. Hawkins, climbing out, shook the deadness out of his muscles. He left his AK-47 in the footwell, the Makarov pistol holstered down the front of his shacket. The day was dry and airless. Heat swamp-water thick. Hawkins had to physically wade through it.

He felt like shit. His threads were caked in dust. The bruise to his forehead throbbed painfully, a low dull ache. His hands were greasy with firearm residue. He sipped water while Kettler walked away several paces to make the private call on his satphone. Martel dug out the mapping from his rucksack, spread it across the ground beside the lead Unimog, then disappeared round the back of the store to take a piss. Moussa fetched the last diesel can from the back of the technical, popped open the fuel cap, seated the funnel in the filler neck. He started pouring diesel into the Hilux while Hawkins, Steyn and Bald gathered round the map.

They were doing a seat-of-the-pants map study. Looking for turn-around points on the trunk road, potential drop-off positions. As soon as they had information on the new RV they could start plotting out routes from the station. Factoring in logistical hurdles. Depending on the distance to the alternative meeting-point they might be looking at an extra journey time of eight or nine hours. That would mean sourcing more fuel for the technical, possibly the Unimogs too. Someone would have to notify the fuel manager and the pilots at the airhead. Notify them about the possible delay to their departure.

A few paces away Kettler was speaking to someone on the other end of the line in a low, almost inaudible, voice. The buyer, Hawkins guessed. Kettler seemed to be doing most of the talking. The ex-Hereford Rupert, rising to the occasion. Taking a firm grip of the situation. Reasserting himself.

Yes, we're here. We had to evade the RV. What the hell is going on?

Moussa was tipping the last of the diesel into the Hilux. Martel walked back over from behind the closed-down office, rejoining the gang after his piss-break. Steyn gulped down water, wiped sweat from his brow. Bald and Hawkins focused their attention on the map.

Behind them, Kettler had stopped pacing up and down the forecourt.

'What the fuck?' he said.

Then a gunshot ripped through the air.

Twenty-Four

Hawkins reacted fast. Tens of thousands of hours of Tier One training hard-wired into his genome. He whipped round in the fraction of a second after the discharge, reaching for the Makarov tucked under his shacket, brain processing the scene before him.

Kettler lay slumped on the forecourt, mouth hanging open, limbs twisted at unnatural angles. Like he was doing a drunken impression of a John Doe chalk outline at a crime scene.

Martel stood six paces away, right arm outstretched, hand clasped around the TT-30 semi-automatic. Barrel pointed at the spot where Kettler had been standing upright a moment earlier, back when he had been a living member of the human race.

Moussa, unweaponed, had spun away from the Hilux, dropping the jerry can as he broke into a run towards Martel. Head tucked tight to his chin, raging at the German like a bull charging at a torero, determined to avenge the death of his boss. Martel clipped him with two quick shots of 7.62mm Tokarev to the face. Blood squirted out of the back of Moussa's skull. A mountain of dead muscle thudded to the ground with a hard slap. Like a rhino being hit by a poacher on safari.

At the same time Bald and Steyn pinwheeled round to face Martel. Steyn had dug out his pistol. The lower-calibre Makarov. Bald had drawn his TT-30. Both of them lined up their pistols with the German. So did Hawkins.

Martel slowly lowered his gun arm to his side.

'Never liked that prick anyway,' he said, staring at Kettler.

'What the fuck did you just do?' Steyn screamed.

'A favour,' Martel said evenly. 'I've done you all a big favour.'

He seemed supernaturally calm for a guy with three pistols trained on him. Hawkins wondered about that.

'Lose the weapon,' he said, keeping his Makarov fixed on the German. 'Lose it, or you're getting dropped.'

Martel worked his mouth into a smug grin.

'Easy, English. Don't do anything you might regret. A minute from now, you'll be thanking me for this. Now stop pointing that fucking pea-shooter at me and let me explain.'

'Not gonna happen.'

The grin spread like cancer across Martel's smooth face.

'Kill me, and you're going to piss away a golden opportunity to get incredibly rich. The one chance any of us have got for a big payday.'

'What the fuck are you talking about?' Bald said.

'These wretches were going to betray you.'

Martel pointed with his eyes at the two dead bodies. Diesel fuel sloshed out of the jerry can, mixing with the blood puddling on the forecourt.

He went on.

'Moussa wasn't an Eritrean mercenary. That was just a cover story cooked up by Kettler. He was in fact an officer. In the Yemeni army. The guy had deep links to the Houthis. They were going to sell the shit to Moussa's Houthi contact, pocket the money and kill us all.'

'The Houthis?' Steyn furrowed his brow. 'Why the fuck would they want to be complicit in stealing the uranium from Iran? They're on the same side.'

'That's the line Tehran likes to peddle in public. The truth is very different. The Houthis have gone rogue. They've grown tired of dancing to the Ayatollah's tune, being told what to do and when. Being drip-fed equipment and money. They're prepared to blow up that relationship if it means getting their hands on the material for a nuclear weapon.'

'How do you know all this?' asked Hawkins.

'I knew Moussa. From back in the Emirates. We were running a training package together. He reached out to me a few weeks back. Out of the blue. Told me there was a heavy lift job going, asked if I was interested. Big money. Then he let me in on the real plan. Day before the Englishman showed up, in fact. Told me they were going to sell everything to an old army friend in the Houthis and put you three in an early grave.'

'Bullshit,' spat Steyn. 'I know the boss man. He wouldn't do that.'

Martel chuckled. 'If you believe that, my friend, you're even thicker than you look.'

'Don't make sense.' Steyn looked wounded. His voice began to crepitate. 'Why the fuck would they drop us? We had a deal. It was all lined up.'

Martel said, 'Your boss was selling nuclear-grade material to a proscribed terrorist group. Any leaks and he could find himself taking the stand at the Hague. He needed to cover his tracks. You were all loose ends, as far as he was concerned.'

There was a curious look in his eyes. Something that made Hawkins think the German wasn't being entirely honest with them.

'Even if that's all true, you've scuppered our chances of a deal,' Bald flared. 'Kettler was the brains behind that sale. Moussa had the contacts. Without them two, we're royally fucked.'

'I have arranged a better deal,' said Martel. 'One that is going to make us much richer.'

'Who's the buyer?'

'First, tell your friends to lower their pistols.'

'Bollocks to that,' Hawkins spat.

'Do it, Geordie,' Bald said. 'You too, Rory. Let's hear him out.'

Steyn looked at him with raised eyebrows. 'You can't be serious. Bra. This guy fucked us. We had a deal.'

'That deal is dead,' Martel said. 'Forget about the Yemenis. Even if you wanted to resurrect it, they'll have been spooked by the compromised RV. When you hear what my buyer has got to say, the sums of money coming to each of you, trust me. You'll be celebrating like you've just won the World Cup.'

'Lower your weapons,' Bald repeated. 'Do it. Let's sort this out between us.'

'But—' Steyn began.

'But nothing. We're all in this for the money, right? That's why we're here. This guy says there's a new offer on the table. We should at least hear what he's got to say for himself.'

'Forget about your old boss, Rory,' Martel said. 'You don't owe him shit. He was going to double-cross all of you.'

Steyn relented. Pointed his Makarov down. Hawkins still kept his pistol lined up with Martel. Finger tense on the trigger.

'You too, English,' said Martel.

Hawkins didn't trust Bald. But he respected the guy as one of the Old and Bold. Besides, he had to consider his mission. The new destination for the uranium. Six would definitely be interested in where that was going, who was paying for it, and why. All the big questions.

He had to consider a third point too. With Kettler out of the picture he had no other means of escape from Turkmenistan. He was boxed in.

No choice.

Nothing I can do except go along with it.

Hawkins lowered his pistol.

'Give me a hand with those two first,' Martel said.

He indicated the bodies.

'You do it,' Hawkins said. 'Your fucking mess. You clean it up.'

Martel gave him a savage look. 'You're upset. I can see that. But a police car might flash down that road at any moment. Do you really want to take that risk?'

'Fuck's sake.' Bald set his face hard. 'Come on, Geordie. Rory. Let's get it done.'

Hawkins stuffed the Makarov down the back of his hiking trousers, tramped over to Kettler's lifeless body, grabbed hold of him by the arms. Bald took the legs, the two ex-Blades dragging the dead Rupert the short distance across the forecourt to the dumpster. Steyn and Martel had the job of moving Moussa. The short straw. Like trying to carry a sack full of rubble. In the end, it needed all four of them to tip Moussa's body into the container. He landed on top of Kettler, amid the scraps of cardboard, plastic bottles and bags of festering rubbish.

Martel snatched up the satphone Kettler had dropped on the forecourt. He tossed it into the waste container with the other trash. Slammed the lid shut.

Bald caught his breath and said, 'Start talking. What's the craic with this new buyer?'

'The money is coming from Selina Gechter. Bavarian. Traces her ancestry back to an old noble house. Very well connected. Sole heir to one of Europe's biggest pharmaceutical firms. She's worth billions. Tens of.'

'Never heard of her.'

'You wouldn't. Selina is strictly low profile. Stays in the shadows. No social media accounts. Doesn't give media interviews. Something of a recluse.'

'What the fuck does some German aristo want with the cylinders?'

'Gechter isn't buying the uranium for herself. She's acquiring it for the New Patriotic Front.'

'Who the fuck are they?' Hawkins asked.

'A group of proud Germans. Public figures, high-ranking soldiers, academics and businessmen. United by a common belief in the tragedy of Germany's national decline, and a desire to reverse it. My old commanding officer in the KSK is a member. I orchestrated the deal through him.'

Hawkins shook his head furiously. 'You're selling the shit to a bunch of fringe far-right nutters?'

Martel looked at him darkly. 'The Front is more powerful than you might think, English. They have many supporters within Germany, and friends abroad. Britain, the US. Other places also. Those who share their concern with the direction of travel in Europe.'

'How much dough are we talking?' Bald asked.

'Selina has agreed to pay us four hundred million dollars for the uranium. Transferrable upon delivery of the goods to an airstrip outside Casablanca.'

Bald and Steyn exchanged greedy looks.

Hawkins thought: *Four hundred million dollars. Split four ways.*

A hundred million each.

A lot more than the offer Kettler had secured from the Houthis. Hell of a lot more.

Steyn frowned at the German, eyes shrinking to points.

'How can we trust you? You just capped the boss man and Moussa. What's to stop you plugging us when our backs are turned?'

Martel gave a smile so thin you could have carved a melon with it.

'You'll just have to trust me.'

'Fuck that.'

'If you don't believe me, perhaps you'll believe Selina herself. I can get her on the phone right now, let her outline the terms of the deal.'

'Fine. Do it,' Bald said.

Martel reached into his trouser pocket, produced a slim handset housed in a rugged black casing. It looked identical to a regular smartphone, except the device had a chunky antenna poking out of the top edge. Hawkins recognised it as one of the newer generation of satellite phones, with dual satellite and 5G connectivity.

Hawkins thought back a few hours. The piss-break, shortly after they had crossed into Turkmenistan. Martel had taken a shit-break. The guy had been out of sight for two-plus minutes.

And he had a satphone.

He said, 'You're the one who blew the RV. You alerted the local security services.'

Martel lifted an eyebrow. A smile teased out of the left corner of his mouth. 'I'm impressed, English. It seems you're not completely thick after all.'

'Fuck off.'

'Don't look so angry. You should be grateful. If I hadn't put in that call to the police, tipping them off about the RV, you and your friends would be dead right now.'

Martel worked the screen, fingers swiping and tapping and dancing. He put the call on speaker as the phone rang and rang. A young-sounding female voice answered. 'Hallo? Paul?'

Martel and the woman exchanged a few words in German. Classical music played softly in the background on the other end of the line. Hawkins imagined a turreted castle in Bavaria. Perched on a mountainside facing the Alps.

Martel seemed to be confirming something with the woman. The deaths of Kettler and Moussa, maybe. Then he said, in stilted English, 'Selina, you're on speaker. I've got the other guys here. They're interested in your proposal, but they're looking for reassurances before they commit to anything.'

'OK,' said Gechter. She cleared her throat noisily, then spoke more loudly. For the benefit of her other listeners. 'Well, I can certainly confirm what Paul has already told you. The deal is four hundred million. A hundred to be paid to each of you, in US dollar currency, once the goods have been delivered to our people.'

'Where's the money coming from?' Steyn asked.

'Right now, funds are in a holding account in the British Virgin Islands. I won't go into details, but it's clean. A series of tortuously complicated transactions, involving numerous shell companies. All you need to know is that it's completely untraceable.'

Bald said, 'How do we get paid?'

'We'll set up secure accounts for each of you upon your arrival in Morocco. We have a man on the ground waiting there. He'll remotely open four accounts at a respected Dubai bank and complete the transfers electronically. It's a fairly simple process. Once you have confirmation of delivery of funds, you'll make your way to Dubai via private jet. Onward transportation from Morocco has been arranged at our end.'

'What about customs staff at the airfield?'

'Paid off in advance. A commercial cargo plane, registered to a charity providing medical supplies, will fly the package on to a private strip outside Munich. Then it's our problem. Nothing that could be traced back to you.'

Hawkins said, 'What are you and your mates planning to do with it? Build a dirty bomb?'

'What difference does it make?' Gechter replied bitingly. 'You'll get your money. What we do with it is our business.'

'It matters to me, lass. I want to know if we're going to end up looking over our shoulders for the rest of our fucking lives. I'll do it, but you need to level with us first.'

'I'm with Geordie,' Bald put in. 'I ain't lifting a finger until you tell us what you plan to do with this shit.'

There was a long beat of silence as Gechter weighed things up. She sighed audibly over the line.

'Very well. The uranium will be used to manufacture IND. Improvised nuclear device. Gun-type detonator. Several of them, actually.'

Something shifted knife-like through Hawkins's guts.

INDs.

He'd heard of such weapons in the past. A new type of threat. Home-brewed nuclear bombs built using gun-type detonator systems. They worked by firing a sub-critical piece of enriched uranium down a high-strength barrel, smashing it into another lump of HEU, creating a super-critical mass. The resulting explosion was equivalent to a low-yield nuclear bomb. One or two kilotons. A fraction of the size of Fat Boy. Big enough to destroy several blocks of a city, small enough to smuggle across borders in the back of a truck.

The ultimate weapon. The experts reckoned such things only existed in theory.

He recalled what Bald had told him back in Pretoria.

Uranium is no good for building a dirty bomb.

Doesn't spread very well.

'Christ. You're going to set off a load of nukes.'

'One low-yield bomb. The rest may or may not be used, depending on circumstances. You shouldn't be too bothered about the target. We're using it against a common enemy.'

'Who?'

'Russia. The target is the city of Kaliningrad. Or Königsberg, as it used to be known in the days when it belonged to our people. Members of the Front are going to smuggle an IND across the Polish border and set it off in the city.'

Kaliningrad. The Russian enclave on the Baltic coast. Home to a major Russian naval base.

An IND detonated in the middle of the city.

Tens of thousands of casualties.

Utter devastation.

Hawkins stared at the satphone. Dumbfounded.

'Why?'

'To make an announcement to the German people. We will show them that the New Patriotic Front is the only political force capable of defending the fatherland from her enemies.'

'By blowing up a fucking city?'

'If anything, you should be elated,' said Gechter. She was warming to her theme now. Bragging about her big plan.

'Germany has endured eighty years of national humiliation. Our country's army has been enfeebled. We suck on the teat of cheap

Russian oil and gas, and we do not even have our own nuclear weapons. That is a travesty. By attacking Kaliningrad, we are going to prove to the country that the Front will do whatever it takes to advance the interests of the German race. Then we shall encourage our supporters to rise up against the government. We'll remove those spineless leaders and take control of the country.'

'You'll provoke World War Three, for fuck's sake,' Hawkins said. 'The Russians will respond.'

'For sure, but what can Moscow realistically hope to achieve? Their army is bogged down in Ukraine. At the very most Putin might threaten to retaliate with a low-yield bomb. But that is to our advantage. It will press home to the people of Germany the need for a new leadership, able to stand firm against our enemies. Once we have taken over the country, we shall embark on a new era of militarisation. Nuclear weapons, a vast army. In this way we shall create a new, more powerful Germany. One capable of standing alone in the world.'

'You're fucking insane. Out of your minds.'

'I think not. The mad person is the one who refuses to see the world for how it really is.'

'Fuck does that mean?'

'Look around you. The old order is dead. In the new world, the future shall belong to the strong, and the weak will become mere slaves of the great powers of the age. The time has come for Germany to rediscover her muscularity, the great military tradition of von Bismarck, Arminius and Rommel. Only then can we claim our rightful place among the first nations of the world. You English would be wise to do the same. Those countries who continue to play by the rules will get eaten up.'

Bald said, 'You'd need a small army to build them bombs. Scientists and all sorts. You can't make that shit out of toilet tubes.'

'Less people than you think,' said Gechter. 'We have a team on standby in a secure location. Machinists. Physicists. Explosive experts. It's a small group.'

Martel said, 'We've wasted enough time here. If we're going to do this, we need to go now. Selina, I'll call you back once we're at the airhead.'

He killed the line.

Bald said, 'It's a good deal. We won't get better.'

Hawkins looked at him aghast.

'You can't be serious, mate. We can't do it. We'll be complicit.'

Bald said, 'Think it through, Geordie. We've just committed an international crime. What are our options? We've got a quantity of highly enriched uranium and no buyer, and we can't exactly flog this shite online. It's this or nothing.'

Hawkins tried to think clearly. His chances of reaching out to Six before the exchange happened were minimal. If he couldn't stop the handover, a few days from now, the Patriotic Front would detonate a nuclear device in Kaliningrad, and many thousands of people were going to die. The plan was mad. Utterly mad. But he saw that he had no other choice. All he could do was go along with it. Delaying tactics. Agree to the plan, buy himself time until he could find some way of stopping the deal.

'Fuck it,' Steyn said. 'I'm in. Who gives a shit about a load of dead Russians anyway.'

'I'm in, too,' Bald said. 'On one condition.'

'What's that?' asked Martel.

'No more fucking surprises from now on. If you try to pull a fast one on us, the last thing you'll ever see will be me putting a round between your eyes.'

'Agreed.' Martel skimmed his cold eyes towards Hawkins. 'Well, English? Do we have a deal?'

'Aye. We do.'

'What's the plan for getting out of here?' Bald asked.

Martel said, 'The exfil plan stays the same. We'll drive to the airhead, load the stuff on the back of the Antonov, direct the pilots to the new destination. The landing point outside Casablanca.'

Bald said, 'Before we do anything, I've got to take a shit.'

'Now?'

'Can't be helped, son. When you've got to go, you've got to go. Get to my fucking age, you'll know what I mean.'

He disappeared round the back of the service store before Martel could stop him. Hawkins tried to control his rising anxiety. Every minute they spent in Turkmenistan increased the likelihood that someone might catch up with them. The Iranians, or the threat from the skies. The CIA. Mossad.

Martel checked the time, fretting. A man on the cusp of pulling off the most audacious deal in history. Steyn closed the flap on the fuel filler, took the empty jerry can and threw it into the dumpster with the other rubbish.

A couple of beats later Bald swung back into view, pacing across the forecourt, fastening the belt around his hiking trousers.

'All set?' Martel asked him.

'Aye,' said Bald. 'Ready.'

'Get in the back Unimog with English. Me and Rory will take the front wagon. You two follow after.'

'What about the technical?' Hawkins said.

'We'll leave it here. No need for it now. Get moving.'

The early afternoon sun beat down mercilessly on the mercenaries as they piled into the two wagons. Hawkins and Bald stuck close to Steyn and Martel in front as they steered out of the petrol station, barrelled back up the secondary road and took the next on-ramp to the highway cutting north-west through the foothills of the mountains.

Sixty kilometres to the airhead.

Fifty minutes from now, we're on that plane.

Almost out of time, Davey Boy.

From the moment Martel had ended the call with Selina Gechter, Hawkins had been wrestling with the problem of how to raise the alarm with Vauxhall. His situation looked hopeless.

He knew only one thing. He had to stop that package from taking off.

Only one person can help me now.

'Jock.'

Bald glanced at him, hands clasped around the wheel. He was staying bumper-close to the Unimog in front, keeping the speed to seventy kilometres per hour.

'Aye, Geordie?'

Hawkins opened his mouth to reply. Ready to come clean to Bald. Disclose the truth about his dealings with Six. *I need your help.*

Then an object swooped down towards them.

An aircraft.

Hawkins became aware of it an instant before it buzzed over the highway in front of them. It was flying dangerously low, perhaps a hundred feet above the Unimog, the snarl of its engines blaring over the chugging noise of the Unimog, startling Bald and Hawkins.

At first Hawkins figured it must be a fighter jet. *The Americans are here. They're about to drop heavy ordnance on our heads. We're finished.* Then the object banked round to the east of the highway before it came on again, gliding towards them, wingtips glinting in the cloudless sky, and suddenly he understood.

Not a fighter jet.

A drone.

Twenty-Five

The drone flew over the road again, buzzing the Unimogs a second time. Hawkins peeked out of the side window as the drone banked round over the plain to the west before it settled into a circling pattern a few hundred feet above the highway. Like a vulture waiting for its prey to expire. It circled twice, then dipped its wings and sheered off to the south.

Bald said, 'Shit. We've been located.'

'How?'

Before Bald could respond Martel's voice rattled over the radio frequency.

'Who the fuck was that?'

'Iranians,' Bald asseverated. 'Got to be. Them drones have a fairly short range on fuel. Four or five hundred kilometres at best. They'll be heading back across the border.'

Steyn said, 'How did they know where to find us? They should still be clearing rubble from those trucks in the ravine right now.'

'It's the general. Got to be. No other explanation. He must have caved in under the torture. Told them what really happened at the mountain pass. They'll have flooded this entire area with drones, telling the pilots to look for a two- or three-vehicle convoy with a couple of Unimog wagons in a rear bed configuration, heading away from the border.'

'But if they've located us, why didn't they attack?'

'They can't. They'll want the uranium package intact. That drone will be sending imagery back to base. Giving the heads-up for a ground force to follow up. Won't be the only ones watching us, either. They'll have other drones flying at a higher altitude, ones we can't see, tracking our progress.'

'No problem,' Martel said. 'Everyone chill the fuck out. We're fifty kilometres from the airhead. The Iranians will never catch up with us in time. We'll be airborne long before their troops get across the border.'

Bald fumed, 'Use your noggin, man. It ain't just the Iranians we've got to worry about. That problem is way down the list.'

'How so?'

'The Iranians are tight with Turkmenistan. Thirty seconds from now, the top commander in Tehran will be getting on the blower to his Turkmen counterpart, ordering any forces in the area to carry out an immediate vehicle interdiction on our arses.'

'They might refuse to co-operate.'

'The Iranians will tell them that we're extremists. Anti-government forces planning to carry out an attack elsewhere in Turkmenistan. That'll get their attention. You can bet that the Iranians will be pulling every lever to pressure them into action. We could have a horde of soldiers breathing down our necks before long.'

'You overestimate the threat, I think,' Martel insisted. 'At this short notice they could rustle up some poorly trained militia, perhaps. They won't have time to mobilise anyone else.'

'They don't have to be good troops. All they've got to do is tie us down until the Iranians rock up. It's a numbers game.'

Hawkins said, 'Does the general know about the airhead?'

'No,' Steyn came back. 'We deliberately excluded him from the detailed planning. Kettler's orders. He knows we're exfilling through Turkmenistan, but nothing more than that.'

Hawkins breathed a little easier. That meant the Iranians would be unaware of their destination. They wouldn't be able to pre-position forces at the airhead to ambush the vehicles.

Steyn said, 'What the fuck are we gonna do?'

Hawkins scented the fear in the South African's voice, even over the crappy HF net.

'We push on,' Bald said. 'Race to the airfield. Our only escape route is that Antonov. If we miss that, we're knackered.'

'The Scot is right,' Martel said. 'When we arrive, we'll have to move fast. Load the goods and get that bird in the air before any ground troops can close with us. A few hours from now this will all be behind us.'

The line fell silent.

Martel and Steyn in the front Unimog pulled ahead, picking up speed. Bald hammered the accelerator, speedometer needle hovering around the ninety kilometres mark.

Forty-five kilometres to go.

Thirty minutes to Gorakan airfield. The Turkmen commanders would be scrambling to mobilise any forces in the vicinity. Units of poorly trained local militia, probably. Low quality. But fifty or a hundred troops would be sufficient to overrun the four mercenaries. Or fix them in place until the Iranians could catch up with them.

With a great will of effort Hawkins forced himself to refocus on his mission.

'Jock,' he began. 'I need to tell you something.'

He swallowed thickly.

'What is it, Geordie? Tell us, man.'

'I'm working for Six. They sent me here. To spy on – on the team.'

Hawkins laid it all out. How Cruttwell and Jackson had co-opted him after he'd lost his job at DeepSpear. The plan to get him on the team by leaning on his friendship with Steyn. His mission to follow the uranium trail to the buyer. The false-screen phone he'd been forced to flush away back at the compound.

Bald didn't interrupt or question him. He just listened in stony silence, his eyes pinned to the road ahead. But there was the slightest tautening of the facial muscles, a barely perceptible tightening around the jaw. His face was a picture of tightly controlled fury.

Hawkins kept secretly hoping that Bald would cough up. *Yeah, I'm with Six too, son.* But he didn't. Which confirmed what Hawkins had already suspected. Jock wasn't an MI6 plant. He had joined the team for reasons of greed, pure and simple. The guy was no different to Steyn and Martel. Hawkins realised his mission was hanging in the balance. Somehow he had to persuade Bald to change sides and work with him. If not, everything would be lost.

'We've got to stop them,' he said. 'There are bigger things at stake than the money. Surely you can see that. It's not just about one bomb going off in Kaliningrad. These nutjobs are planning to build several of them. Multiple attacks, Jock. We could be looking at hundreds of thousands of deaths. More, if Putin decides to respond with nukes of his own. Christ, they might even inspire a few copycat attacks. Give them lot in ISIS a few ideas. We can't let this happen.'

Bald didn't say a word. Hawkins didn't know if that was a good thing or not. He pressed on anyway.

'You know he'll cap us. The German. That money isn't coming our way. We'll never see a penny of it. There's no payday at the end of this road, Jock. The only thing we're getting is a double-tap tap to the nut. Me, you and Steyn. That rich Bavarian wouldn't have told us about the Kaliningrad plan unless they were planning to eliminate us.'

Bald still said nothing.

'Jock.'

'Fuck's sake, Geordie. I'm trying to think. Give us a minute.'

Hawkins gave him a minute. Then another.

'If we're going to stop the German,' Bald said slowly, thinking aloud, 'we need to do it before we put them cylinders on the back of the Antonov. Once we've done that, you, me and Steyn are surplus to requirements. If we get on that plane, we'll be taking a tumble from thirty thousand feet. That's fucking guaranteed.'

Hawkins was taken aback at how swiftly Bald had come round to his way of thinking. At the petrol station, the guy had seemed eager to go along with the new arrangement Martel had put together. Dollar signs had been flashing in his eyes. Now Bald had changed his tune. That puzzled Hawkins. Possibly the involvement of Vauxhall had changed his assessment of the situation. He might have decided to help Hawkins in the expectation of avoiding prosecution down the line. Or he might have disbelieved the story Martel had fed them.

Another possibility occurred to Hawkins. *What if Bald is biding his time while he works out how to get rid of me?* He might have suspected Hawkins of playing a double game, pretending to confess to Bald in order to lure him into exposing his own dealings with Vauxhall.

He had no time to worry about any of that. He would just have to trust Bald. And watch him closely. Eyes in the back of his head.

Forty kilometres to go until we hit the airhead.

Twenty-five minutes.

'If we had some way of getting hold of Six, they might be able to stop that plane from taking off.'

'That,' Bald said, 'is the absolute last thing we should be doing.'

Hawkins looked at him in surprise. 'Why not?'

'Think about it, Geordie. The moment we contact Six and tell them that the uranium is about to be put on a plane and disappear, they'll tip off their mates at Star City. The Americans have already got assets in the area because of the strikes on the enrichment sites. Ten minutes after that call from London they'll drop a Tomahawk on us.'

'You don't know that.'

'Aye, I do. I've worked with those slippery cunts before. Back in the Wing. I know what they're like. You can't trust them an inch. All they're interested in is keeping that uranium off the black market. You and me, we're expendable.'

'What should we do?'

'We'll have to take Martel on. At the airhead. First chance we get. Slot him. Steyn too. Stop them before they can load the cargo. Two on two. Good odds. We should be able to overpower them.'

'Martel might be making the same offer to Steyn. They might be planning to put the drop on us.'

'Aye, but there's one thing in our favour.'

'What's that?'

'We're ex-Reg. They're not. We can take them two fuckers down with our eyes closed.'

'That still leaves us the problem of what to do with the cylinders.'

'One thing at a time,' Bald said. 'Let's focus on stopping the Boer and his neo-Nazi mate first. But we ain't putting a call to Six about any of this. Not yet.'

Hawkins dropped his gaze to the instrument cluster. 14.04.

Thirty kilometres.

'Think we'll make it to that strip before the militia catch us?' he asked.

'If we do, it's going to be close. The Turkmens will have rallied every army and militia unit in this area. They're probably in contact with any other drones the Iranians will have deployed to track our progress. Everyone will be in a big hurry to stop us. These guys have got a vested interest in making sure that package doesn't leave Turkmenistan. Not just because they're pals with the Iranians.'

'How d'you mean?'

'We've just made the local security forces look like mugs. We landed here, smuggled a load of illegal weaponry into Iran from their side of the border. None of this would have happened if the Turkmens had their shit sorted. This is on them as much as the Iranians. They'll know that. They'll want to get hold of that package, put themselves back in favour with Tehran.'

They raced on. The four most wanted men in the world. Even if they escaped Turkmenistan, their immediate prospects looked desperate, Hawkins knew. The CIA and Mossad had eyes and ears in Iran. It wouldn't be long before they learned of the uranium heist. An international warrant would be issued for the gang. The Americans would be after them. MI6, too. They would unquestionably want to cover up their knowledge of Kettler's plan. Their inolvement in the theft. A face-saving exercise. Preservation of the transatlantic alliance over the lives of a couple of ex-Blades.

Everybody will be looking for us. Nowhere will be safe.

We're not going to get away with this one.

In the space of a week Hawkins had gone from knocking back pints in a grimy London boozer to having his face plastered all over the FBI's Most Wanted list. Had to be some sort of record.

They hit the roundabout south of the airfield, took the first exit running north for a kilometre. Then Steyn and Martel swerved off to the right, bucketed down the access road. Bald made the same turn, burning rubber, the back end of the Unimog fishtailing before it straightened out. They shot east for two kilometres, hared through the ruined guard booth fronting the apron. Screeched to a halt near the hangar. The bi-panel doors were closed, as per Kettler's previous orders. Keeping the Antonov hidden from sight of any other planes that might unexpectedly land at the airfield to refuel.

Bald jerked the handbrake up. Left the engine puttering.

He said, 'We'll wait until the pilots have gone through their pre-flight checks and moved the aircraft out of the hangar. Then we'll do the pair of them. Let's make sure that bird is ready to get airbourne before we start dropping bodies.'

'Roger that.'

They both got out. Steyn and Martel were rushing over to the personnel door built into one of the sliding panels at the front of the hangar, both wielding their AK-47s.

Hawkins and Bald followed Steyn and the German through the service door. A voice travelled across the apron as the fuel manager came trotting over from the control tower, flapping his arms and calling out to the mercenaries. Panicking, no doubt, that they might bug out before he could collect the rest of his bribe money.

The cabin access door on the side of the Antonov had hinged open. A set of airstairs trailed down from the cockpit. The engineer stood at the bottom of the steps, alerted by the sound of the wagons pulling up on the tarmac apron, blinking and staring in puzzlement at the four dirt-crusted faces in front of him.

'What's going on?' he asked, warily. His eyes tightened. 'Where are the other fellas?'

'No time for that,' Martel said. 'We're leaving now. Get this plane on the stand and we'll load everything up. New destination.'

'What about Pretoria?'

'Forget Pretoria. That place is burned. We're flying to Morocco. Airfield outside Casablanca. I'll give you the exact co-ordinates for the airfield once we're off the ground.'

One of the pilots appeared at the top of the flight stairs, staring at the team with a wrinkled brow. 'What's going on here? Where's the boss?'

'I'll explain later. We've got to move right this fucking minute.'

Behind them the fuel manager continued his one-man protest. Throwing his arms up and yelling at the gang. Demanding his money.

The pilot said, 'We can't go yet.'

'Why not? Haven't you refuelled?'

'It's not that. The tanks are full. But we need to do our checks first. We can't just take off. It's protocol.'

'Fuck the protocol. We're leaving now. Right this minute. Tell the pilots.'

The pilot started to reply.

Then they heard the gunshots.

Twenty-Six

Hawkins spun round. He brushed past the fuel manager, shoving him aside as he sprinted breathlessly out of the personnel door at the front of the hangar, heart beating double-fast. Shading his eyes beneath the blazing sun, he snapped his attention to the approach road to the west. Three pickups were pelting towards the airfield. A bright blue Isuzu D-Max truck in the lead, with a pair of Toyota Hiluxes to the rear. No more than fifteen hundred metres from the wrecked guard booth, but closing fast. Multiple bods on the back of each truck. Too far away for Hawkins to get an accurate head-count. One of the Toyotas also had a machine gun mounted on a tripod on the rear platform. The operator standing upright, spray-ing bursts at the rusted Camry in the parking lot. Bullets slapped into the control tower, the maintenance sheds. He wasn't aim-ing at individual targets, just putting rounds down to give himself confidence.

More rounds hammered against the hangar, glancing off the double-skinned metal frame. Like the sound of hailstones patter-ing against a tin roof.

Bald, Steyn and Martel had rushed out of the service door after Hawkins, wielding their AK-47s, sporadic gunfire splashing down around them. They followed the instincts of every elite warfighter when they found themselves in a firefight. Run towards the enemy. Engage them without hesitation. Neutralise the threat. Don't waste a second.

Hawkins took control, mind rapidly cycling through the plan he'd formulated approximately half a second earlier.

'Get into firing positions facing that access road,' he yelled, slinging the AK across his chest. 'Rory, Paul, you cover the left side of the road. Jock, you'll hit them from the right. Hold off until I stick an RPG in that first wagon. Then I'll join you, Jock, and we'll hammer them from both sides with crossfire. Remember, don't put down any rounds until that rocket hits. Go!'

Bald, Martel and Steyn pounded across the apron, made for firing points either side of the access road. Steyn and Martel raced towards the fire tender a hundred metres to the west, Bald made for the maintenance shed to the east. Covering the ground both sides of the access road due south of the apron.

Another volley of poorly aimed machine gun rounds ricocheted off the side of the hangar as Hawkins scrambled over to the nearest of the two Unimogs, hoping to fuck that the enemy didn't get lucky. Any time you had to leg it across exposed ground you were playing the lottery with your life. Hawkins reached the wagon, picked up the RPG tube from the rear bed, tore a missile free from the crate. The rockets had already been pre-assembled, so he didn't have to waste valuable seconds screwing the booster to the warhead.

Ten metres away the engineer stood frozen in the service doorway, his face pale with terror.

'Tell the pilots to get that bird ready,' Hawkins ordered him. 'Stay in the hangar and don't open them fucking doors until we've sorted these fuckers. Get moving!'

The engineer snapped out of his stupor and hurried back into the hangar, slamming the door shut behind him. More rounds pounded against the double-skinned metal frame. Another burst whacked into the fuel manager as he fled towards the control tower, caving in his face. He wouldn't be needing the second half of his bribe.

Hawkins grabbed the RPG and the missile and zigzagged back across the apron, bullets firecracking on the ground a few inches either side of him. He ran on for six more paces, dived for cover behind an electric junction box. Steadied his breathing as he assessed the situation. The lead Isuzu was nine hundred metres from their position now. Six hundred metres from the derelict checkpoint. To his left, at the fire tender, Steyn was crouching beside the rear wheelbase, while Martel had taken up a position beside the front fender. Both had their AK-47s sighted on the ground west of the approach road, waiting for the enemy to draw within effective firing range.

On Hawkins's right, a hundred metres to the north, Bald had dropped to a knee at the corner of the maintenance hut. Assault rifle at shoulder height, peering down the iron sights, ready to hammer the attackers on the right side of the approach road.

Hawkins took the missile tube, pushed it into the muzzle until he heard the click confirming that the weapon was properly loaded. He flipped up the sights, stepped out from behind cover with the RPG on his right shoulder and took up a kneeling firing position next to the junction box. Hawkins was dangerously exposed now. A burst of 7.62 narrowly missed him, passing overhead, so close he could feel the heat from the velocity of the rounds.

Once Hawkins had knocked out the first vehicle the two Hiluxes to the rear would get rammed up behind it, blocking their route into the operational area. The gunmen would have no choice but to debus on either side of the approach road and continue their advance on foot. At which point the two fire teams positioned around the apron to the east would let rip. The enemy would be trapped between the destroyed vehicle in front and the security fence on either side.

Hawkins lined up the notch and rear post with the inbound Isuzu. Right hand on the trigger guard, left hand clasping the rear grip. The pickup was four hundred metres from their position. A hundred metres from the old guard booth. At this distance Hawkins couldn't miss. Another torrent of machine gun fire splattered the ground an inch in front of him. Three more rounds struck the junction box housing in a flurry of sparks.

Three hundred and fifty metres.

Three forty.

Hawkins depressed the trigger.

The warhead hissed out of the tube, streaking through the air. It struck the Isuzu on the grille, engulfing it in a thick plume of flame and smoke. The vehicle skewed round and juddered to a standstill thirty metres west of the old guard booth. Smoke gushing out from under the bonnet.

Hawkins was already on his skates, ditching the RPG and darting across the apron, taking up a firing position beside another junction box five metres from Bald. He deslung his rifle, centred it on the approach road. The two Toyotas had stopped behind the stricken Isuzu, jamming up the ground due west of the old checkpoint. Figures deboarded from the rear beds of both vehicles, shouting in alarm, dropping down to the left and right, scrambling for cover in the three-metre gap between the tarmac and the security fencing on either side. Four bods dismounted from the back of the front truck. Six more from the wagon to the rear with the mounted machine gun. Plus the gunner and the guys in the front cabs, two apiece. Fourteen targets.

Hawkins, Martel and Bald each had four full twenty-round mags. Steyn had emptied a few rounds with his AK-47 back at the mountain pass, but they still had enough to deal with the attackers spilling out of the trucks.

'Now!' Hawkins bellowed. 'Open fire!'

The defenders opened fire simultaneously. Steyn and Martel peppering the sliver of ground between the fence and pickups on the left side of the road, Hawkins and Bald putting down aimed shots on the targets jumping down on the right side. Turning that stretch of blacktop into a turkey shoot.

Hawkins put a couple of controlled shots into a guy wearing a black shemagh as he struggled out of the cab of the front Toyota. His head exploded, torn inside out by the kinetic energy of the round. He belly-flopped to the ground in a tangle of slack limbs. At his two o'clock, Bald was drilling the other bloke in the front cab. Three rounds of 7.62. The Jock Bald special. The guy was dead before he could clamber out of the vehicle.

Hawkins arced his weapon across, scanning for his next target. Martel and Steyn had slotted the two guys in the cab of the second truck; bullet holes starred the windscreen. Another figure in white sneakers and a green headwrap went down next to the fence north of the road, sparks flying off the chain-link fence as Hawkins gave him the good news.

He glimpsed a flicker of movement as a pair of attackers scurried for cover behind the second lead Toyota. Three more shooters were kneeling on Hawkins's side of the road, tucking tight beside the vehicles, decked out in mismatched clothing. That left four gunmen on the left side of the road. Hawkins couldn't see them from his vantage point, but he knew Martel and Steyn would be tearing into them with their longs.

One of the shooters on the right-hand side of the road had a black full-face mask. The second guy wore a red bandana tied around his neck. Next to him knelt a bloke dressed in baggy green trousers and sandals. They weren't bothering to seek cover or aim properly at the defenders. They were fighting on instinct and fear, lifting their assault rifles above their heads and loosing off wild bursts. Hoping for the best.

These guys weren't reacting like highly trained soldiers. Probably Turkmen militia, Hawkins supposed. Low-quality cannon fodder. Thrown into the fight to keep the mercenaries bogged down at the airstrip until the cavalry arrived.

A fifth guy manned the machine gun on the rear Hilux, dressed in head-to-toe black. He kept up a furious rate of fire on the apron. Bullets smacked against the junction box and the maintenance hut, forcing Bald and Hawkins to scurry back behind cover. More rounds gouged out chunks of the control tower, struck the tarmac closer to the hangar. Hawkins wasn't worried about the wagons getting hit in the firefight. The cylinders were safely encased in their Laycorn crates; the enemy would be under strict orders not to hit the package. A stray round or two might scratch the Unimogs, but they wouldn't damage the cargo.

Hawkins drew his sights on the operator in all black, fired three times. One round deflected off the machine gun. The second two landed short, fracturing the windshield and slapping into the corpses in the front cab. Hawkins shrank back again as he took a volley of incoming. There was a brief lull. Then he eased out a breath, popped out from behind the junction box, squeezed the trigger twice more. This time he was on the money. The gunman fell back, arms dancing like an inflatable tube man. Hawkins caught him with a headshot on the way down to earth. The guy in the sandals started to climb up onto the bed to take his dead mate's place. Hawkins put a trio of bullets into his breadbasket.

Bald had made quick work of the two remaining gunmen on the right side of the Toyotas. Bandana and Face Mask were both down, faces buried in the patch of bare dirt between the roadside and the perimeter fence, like they were in practice for the face-planting world championship. At his ten o'clock Martel and Steyn had stopped firing as they killed the last of the targets to the left of the approach road. Which left the two figures Hawkins had seen scrabbling behind the rear technical.

Over at the maintenance hut Bald was reloading his AK. Hawkins called out for Bald to cover him and broke forward. Fire and move tactics. The time-honoured method of advancing to contact with an enemy. Bald putting down suppressive fire on the rearmost wagon while Hawkins moved across open ground. He stopped five metres further on, dropped low next to the wheelbase of the shot-up Camry, started looking under the axle of the rear technical. He spied two legs, a knee.

Hawkins raked the ground with single shots and heard a piercing scream as one of the guys rolled out from behind the vehicle, clawing at his bullet-shredded ankle. Hawkins capped him twice, put two more in the back of the last gunman as he lay prone on the ground, got the dead man's click as he reached the end of his clip.

Twenty rounds down.

Sixty left.

Hawkins ejected the spent mag, took a fresh one from the sleeves on the front of his Russian body armour and paid it into the underside of the receiver. He picked himself up, started yelling hoarsely.

'Move forward! Make sure no one is alive! Gather any serviceable ammo!'

Hawkins pounded across the apron, sweeping his AK-47 left to right, the other guys doing the same as they approached the killing field from their respective firing points. Everyone scanning their arcs for any signs of life.

Ahead of him Martel, Steyn and Bald were double-tapping the wounded, checking the dead bodies, patting them down for spare clips of 7.62 for their AKs. The attack had been surgical. Fourteen targets chopped down in a matter of minutes.

Hawkins had almost drawn level with the others when he saw the dust cloud.

It rose up from the south. Towards the highway. A forest of swirling dust pluming above the road. Hawkins stopped and looked again across the rock-strewn plain.

A column of vehicles was racing north towards the approach road. A mixture of Toyotas and Isuzus. Hawkins did a very fast count. Six of them. Equivalent to thirty or possibly forty enemies. A miniature army. The second wave. Rushing towards the airfield.

'Shit,' Martel said.

Steyn said, 'How did they get here so fast?'

No one answered. They were all in a state of shock. Hawkins looked on as the column stopped briefly at the turn-off for the fence-lined approach road a kilometre to the west. For a cold beat he thought they might start bounding down the road, following in the footsteps of the first attack wave. A sequel to the turkey shoot but with a much larger attacking force.

'One of you get over to the hangar,' Hawkins said. 'Tell the pilots to get that plane up and running on the taxiway. Loading ramp down. We're getting the fuck out of here. No way we can hold this lot off.'

Martel left the group, darting across the stand towards the hangar on the north-eastern edge. Hawkins made a split-second estimation of times and distances, speeds. His Regiment-trained brain working the angles. A minute to get the hangar panel doors open. Two more for the Antonov to manoeuvre down the taxiway to the runway.

Going to be close.

Too close.

To the west, the column had started up again. It was running further north now, past the access road. Hawkins wondered what they were doing. Bald and Steyn were looking in the same direction, the South African scratching his head in perplexity.

'Fuck's going on? Have they missed us, bra?'

Hawkins didn't get a chance to reply.

The column stopped once more.

Six hundred metres north of the approach road. At a point where the perimeter security fence had collapsed. Decades of rust and neglect. The old airfield gone to rack and ruin. A pile of uprooted steel posts and strips of chain-link fabric blocked the fallen-in part of the fencing facing the column.

Hawkins felt his guts turn to ice.

'They haven't missed us,' he said. 'They're going to break through the fence. They're coming right at us.'

Twenty-Seven

'Get moving!' Hawkins roared at Bald and Steyn. 'You two, get into a defensive position covering that service road to the north. They'll be sweeping in from that side. I'll try and delay them with the machine gun. Go!'

Bald and Steyn started back across the tarmac, hastening towards the control tower north of the apron edge. A drainage ditch surrounded the tower, like a drained moat around a castle, providing them with firing positions overlooking the service road running north of the operational area. They wouldn't start firing until the enemy had breached the perimeter and drawn to within four or five hundred metres. Hawkins hoped it wouldn't come to that. They needed to be on the Antonov before the enemy could close with them.

Otherwise we're knackered.

He hotfooted it over to the rearmost Toyota down from the wreckage of the checkpoint. He scaled up the side of the Hilux, pushed aside the dead guy in the baggy green trousers slumped over the tripod-mounted PKM machine gun. A belt of 7.62mm link hung like a brass tongue out of the side of the weapon receiver.

Half a belt. Hawkins had half a belt left. Roughly a hundred rounds.

Shit.

He frantically searched the floor, looking for any spare belts or ammo cases amid the carnage. Found nothing. He just had the hundred-odd rounds left in the PKM. His only ammo.

A bleak realisation seeped through his guts. There was no way he could fend off the incoming force, not for long, not with only half a belt of ammunition.

Hawkins pointed the PKM at the enemy column to the north-west. A distance of sixteen hundred metres. Well within the maximum range of the machine gun.

Two ant-like figures had descended from the truck in the van-guard. They were migrating towards the fence. Hawkins read their intentions at once. Someone must have spotted the bodies and vehicles jamming up the approach road and made an executive decision to burn the original plan of attack. Instead, the attackers would sweep in from the north. But they wouldn't take the service road entrance because that was too far away from the apron. Valuable minutes would be lost driving around the perimeter of the airfield. They needed to engage the defenders immediately, before they could make their escape on the Antonov. A forward-thinking individual must have spotted the collapsed section of fencing and ordered the column to stop there. The soldiers would clear away the debris, drive through the opening and mount the service road a kilometre to the east, then cut south and charge at the apron.

Front assault. Overwhelming firepower.

Whoever these guys are, they're more switched-on than the last wave.

Hawkins sighted the machine gun on the two figures beside the fencing, pulled on the trigger. Combing the area with lead. He wasn't aiming at individual targets, not at this range. One of the enemies fell like a collapsed domino. The second guy scuttled towards cover behind the front of the truck.

Three more figures scampered forwards, running past their mates to take over the job of clearing away the collapsed fence. The machine guns on the three middle vehicles started flaming, shooting over the front cabs of the wagons behind them as they put down sporadic fire on Hawkins and the figures diving into the control-tower ditch. Rounds winged inches past Hawkins, close enough to feel the heat from the carriage of the bullets. Four more banged against the side of the Hilux. Another perforated the rear tyre.

At his one o'clock, seventy metres away, Bald and Steyn stayed low as rounds pelted the ground above them, throwing up clods of earth and disintegrated rock.

Hawkins fired another burst at the three figures moving away the debris, using up more of his precious link. One man dropped. The two others went prone, making themselves smaller targets.

In the corner of Hawkins's eye, he saw Martel running from the hangar to the ditch encircling the control tower, criss-crossing across the open ground as rounds zipped past him. The hangar panel doors were sliding open on their mounted rails. From within came a low hum as the pilots fired up the Antonov engines preliminary to take-off.

More enemies were converging on the collapsed fence. Six guys, working in pairs to shift the remaining posts and strips. Hawkins put another burst on them, more out of desperation than any realistic hope of killing them. He glanced down. He'd chopped through half the belt. Fifty rounds left.

The gunmen hopped back into their pickup trucks. Occasional bursts were flying in from the machine guns in the middle of the column, strafing the control-tower ditch, clattering against the chassis below Hawkins. The vehicles steamed through the passage, bulldozing across the plain towards the service road a kilometre east of the fence.

They'll be on top of us in less than a minute.

We're done for.

Hawkins glanced at the service road. At the point four hundred metres north of the control tower, where the blacktop ran between the rebro tower to the west and the avgas tanks on the opposite side of the road. The road would funnel the enemy through that gap, towards the apron.

An idea suddenly took shape.

A long shot. Last-chance saloon.

But his only hope.

Hawkins shunted the PKM down at an angle, aiming at the avgas tanks. Four hundred metres north of the guys at the control tower. Tens of thousands of gallons of highly flammable aviation fuel. Six tanks. Sufficient to restock the tanks on a long-haul cargo plane. Set that alight, and they could put a great wall of flame between themselves and the enemy. Use the confusion to make their getaway on the plane before the attackers could organise themselves.

Hawkins depressed the trigger, emptied a stream of bullets at the gleaming white cylinders, putting holes in all six of them. Fluid pissed out of the tanks, spilled across the two-hundred-metre-wide gap between the avgas tanks and the rebro tower.

Hawkins pointed the machine gun barrel at the nearest burst tank. A couple of rounds into the tank could ignite the liquid.

He fired.

A burst of 7.62 hit the cylinder.

Nothing happened.

The fuel didn't ignite.

Hawkins put another burst into it. Then a third.

Same result.

He was out of link. End of the belt.

A kilometre to the north the enemy column came off the dirt and mounted the service road, tyres churning up great fists of dust and debris as they swerved round. They started south, moving almost line abreast, with one of the Hiluxes riding just ahead in the van, the rear gunners discharging bursts over the cabs at the control tower. A volley of rounds whumped into the ground above the ditch, throwing up fountains of dirt above the drainage ditch.

In another twenty seconds or so the trucks would pass through that puddle of avgas. Then it would be all over.

Hawkins seized his AK-47 rifle, vaulted down from the technical. He started back down the ramp towards the control tower, filling his lungs as he shouted at Bald at the top of his voice.

'Jock! Get that fucking box of tracer. Start putting rounds into them fuel tanks. Now!'

Hawkins ran on, weaving from side to side to avoid the bullets bee-stinging across the airfield in three- or four-round bursts as the rear-gunners continued firing at the apron. At his three o'clock the automated hangar doors had now fully slid back on their rails; the Antonov began slowly rolling out of the steel structure onto the tarmac ramp.

Two minutes to take-off.

Hawkins kept running, muscles burning with the strain. He was now forty metres from the control tower. Another bullet zipped past, missing him by inches.

Bald was kneeling in the ditch, AK-47 propped on the earth beside him as he furiously thumbed rounds from a box of tracer into a curved mag. Steyn was lying a couple of paces away, his face unrecognisable. The impact of a 7.62 burst to the head, overpressure turning his skull inside out. Martel was there too, constantly glancing over his shoulder at the cargo plane crawling out of the hangar.

Rounds glanced off the stand a couple of paces in front of Hawkins. Four of them. Something smacked him hard on the side of the head. The impact knocked him off his feet; he landed on his side on the bullet-streaked tarmac, assault rifle tumbling from his stunned grip. Hawkins put his left hand to his head. Blood. He was bleeding heavily above the left eye.

Shot, Hawkins thought.

I've been shot.

He felt around the area, checking for damage. His skull seemed intact. Flesh wound, Hawkins realised. It hurt like fuck, but nothing serious. A round must have ricocheted up from the apron and cut across his face, grazing him.

He looked over at the ditch. Bald had finished loading the mag of tracer into the AK-47 receiver. He re-cocked his weapon, brought it up to his shoulder, took aim at the avgas cylinders four hundred metres away.

The truck in the vanguard of the enemy column was a hundred metres north of the rebro tower now. A hundred metres away from the flood of avgas pooling across the ground. Five or six more seconds and it was over.

Bald shot.

The AK ca-racked.

Nothing.

Bald shot again.

Nothing happened.

Bald fired a third shot at the leaking tanks. Still nothing.

The truck in the van had pushed on through the spillage area. In a few seconds the rest of the formation would have passed through the funnel.

Last chance. Live or die.

Time for one more shot.

Bald emptied a fourth shot of tracer at the nearest tank.

There was a roar as the thousands of gallons of puddled avgas burst into flames. A napalm-orange fireball mushrooming above the road, mixed in with clouds of rancid black smoke, singeing Hawkins's hair. Like a front-row seat to a volcanic eruption. Or watching the Trinity test in the New Mexican desert. The heat coming off the burning fuel was intense. Hawkins had never experienced anything like it.

The wagon in the vanguard rolled on out of the inferno, the tyres ablaze, tendrils of smoke rising out from the front grille, before it came to a stop. Two of the guys fell out of the rear bed, bodies mantled in flames. They lay flailing on the ground, screaming in agony. The other occupants had been fragged.

Ten metres further back another Hilux trundled out of the wall of flames, momentum carrying it forward. Hawkins heard several deep thunderclaps as the engines on the other vehicles exploded under the suffocating pressure of the fires. Tyres popped. Men squealed. The two burning figures next to the front truck had stopped moving. The scale of the destruction astonished Hawkins. No way anyone could have survived that.

Then the small voice piped up in his head.

We've got to get moving.

Before the next wave rocks up.

Which it undoubtedly would. More attackers would be en route to the airfield at that very minute. The surest thing in the world. The first group would have fed comms back to their commanders. *We've located the thieves. On the airfield. Getting ready to escape.* Orders would be flowing down to individual units. *Everyone, converge on that airfield immediately.* The head shed throwing the kitchen sink at the gang. Doing everything in their power to stop them from getting away.

Hawkins started to scrape himself off the tarmac. Bald rushed over from the ditch, dropped down beside him.

'Geordie? You all right, son?'

Hawkins grunted a response. Claret gushed down his face.

Eight metres away, Martel had climbed out of the ditch.

His AK-47 raised.

Putting a bead on Bald's back.

'Jock!' Hawkins cried.

Bald sprang up, wheeled round to face Martel.

Flames licked out of the mouth of the AK barrel. Two rounds punched into Bald's stomach. The Scot gasped in pain as he dropped to the apron. Martel switched targets, bringing his weapon to bear on Hawkins.

In the same movement Hawkins lunged for his AK-47, snatching up the weapon and pointing at Martel. He was a fraction quicker than the German. But a fraction was all he needed. He had no time to aim. Hawkins just lined up the snout with Martel's central mass and fired twice.

The German spasmed. His legs buckled. Like a piece of collapsible furniture. Hawkins put a third shot into Martel's frame on the way down to earth. He back-slapped against the ground beside the ditch.

Hawkins rose wearily to his feet. He trudged over to Martel.

Blood frothed and bubbled around the perforations in the German's upper chest. His breathing was strangulated; a strange sucking noise emanated with each gulp of air. Hawkins figured Martel had a punctured lung. Maybe both. Death wouldn't be far off. A few minutes at the most.

'Rich,' Martel managed. 'I can – can make you rich.'

Hawkins drew the AK barrel level with his head. Martel looked at him with hate in his eyes.

'Fuck you,' he said. 'Fuck—'

Hawkins shot him twice in the face.

He de-shouldered his rifle, hastened back over to Bald. The guy was groaning in pain, hands clawing his lead-stitched belly. Gut wound. Not a fatal injury. Hawkins had known a lad in the Regiment who had once driven a wagon hundreds of miles across enemy territory with a stomach wound. But worse than a flesh wound. Bald needed urgent medical attention.

He coughed hard, spat out blood and said, in a wheezing voice, 'Geordie. Listen. The cylinders. You have to get rid of them.'

'I know.'

'Do it, Geordie. Before the next lot get here.'

'I'm not leaving you here, Jock.'

'Fuck that. Don't worry about me. I'll be fine. Just destroy the stuff. I'll see you on the plane.'

Hawkins lingered a moment longer. He was reluctant to leave his mucker but he saw that Bald was right. Every second they remained at the airfield only delayed their escape.

He said, 'Get on the bird. We'll sort you out once we're wheels up.'

'Fine. Now fuck off out of here, Geordie. Go!'

Hawkins shot upright, hastened back across the apron. He kept glancing at the highway to the south, looking for dust clouds, anything that might premonish the arrival of more gunmen. The Antonov was facing the taxiway now, the loading ramp in the lowered position. The engineer stood at the edge of the rear cargo compartment, working the ramp controls. Hawkins shouted at him.

'Tell the pilots to get on the runway and wait for us. Then get down here.'

The engineer briefly disappeared while he relayed the message to the cockpit. He emerged from the cabin access door, started down the ramp, eyes wide as pucks, darting anxiously left and right. As if he expected another horde of attackers to come pouring out from behind cover at any moment.

'Hurry the fuck up!' Hawkins thundered.

The engineer picked up the pace, jogged down the ramp. Hawkins gestured towards the nearest Unimog and said, 'Get behind the wheel. Keys are in the ignition. I'll take the other. Follow me.'

The engineer stole a worried glance back at the Antonov. The guy was shitting bricks.

'Where are we going?' he asked nervously.

'No fucking time for questions. Just get in.'

The engineer nodded meekly. He wasn't about to argue with an ex-SAS man packing an assault rifle. He dived into the rear wagon. Hawkins took the front Unimog, dumped his AK on the passenger seat, cranked up the motor and put his foot to the floor, upshifting through the gears as he sped east along the apron, passing the front end of the Antonov. Engineer running close behind. Hawkins hard-turned to the left before he hit the ditch running parallel with the taxiway, belted north for eight hundred metres, circumventing the pierced fuel tanks and the monstrous wall of flame.

He joined the service road half a kilometre up from the avgas inferno, bulleted north, away from the airfield. Towards the service entrance on the northern side of the perimeter fence. He passed through the mound of rubble where the service road checkpoint had once stood, continued along for three hundred metres, then slalomed left onto the rough track running towards the gas crater.

The Mouth of Hell.

Hawkins hit the brakes six metres from the crater with the Unimog pointing straight at the rim. The engineer skidded to a halt at his rear. Hawkins left the engine running, leapt down from the cabin, signalled for the engineer to get out. They were close enough to the crater to feel the heatwaves emanating from the hundreds of fires raging inside it. The roar was deafening. Like standing next to an Apollo rocket at lift-off. Hawkins figured the temperature had to be in excess of a thousand degrees Celsius. Hotter than molten lava. Hot enough to melt steel, or incinerate a human.

Or destroy a load of highly enriched uranium.

'Give us a hand,' he said above the gas roar as he hastened round to the back of the Unimog driven by the engineer, untying the canvas sheeting fastened over the top of the rear bed.

'Get these crates into the back of the other wagon,' he went on. 'Make it quick. We'll send this thing over the edge, take the other vehicle back to the runway.'

The engineer looked at him in horror, eyes like a couple of frisbees.

'What if it blows us up? We'll be killed.'

'It won't happen. The stuff will just melt. Trust me.'

He wasn't absolutely certain of that. But he had to take the risk. He knew he couldn't leave the uranium behind. It would only end up back in the hands of the Iranians.

They worked fast, transferring the Laycorn crates to the other Unimog. Hawkins felt broken. A spent force. More tired than he'd ever felt in his life. He had to dig deep to summon one last effort. One last mile to cross. Always the hardest, in his experience. The sheer discipline and strength of mind needed to keep going when you had nothing left in the tank.

They loaded up the last container. Then Hawkins said, 'Back in the other wagon. I'll send this thing over the edge, then we're back to the runway.'

The engineer had stopped listening. He was staring back at the airfield. Transfixed.

Hawkins looked in the same direction. Then he saw it too. The billowing dust cloud due south of the strip. On the highway. A bigger cloud than the second wave.

A larger fighting force.

Inbound to the airfield.

'Get in,' Hawkins said, urgently. He thrust the engineer towards the empty wagon. They had minutes to spare before the third wave swarmed over the airfield.

Hawkins jumped back into the Unimog loaded up with eight cylinders of HEU. Iran's uranium stockpile. He left the driver-side door yawning open and did a quick visual sweep of the cabin, making sure that his clothing wouldn't catch on the handbrake or seatbelt or anything else.

Hawkins depressed the clutch, shifted into second gear, disengaged the parking brake. He crushed the gas pedal. The Unimog cantered forward. Hawkins dive-rolled out of the cab, hitting the ground a moment before the vehicle tipped over the edge.

The wagon plummeted. Gouts of flame spurted out from the Mouth of Hell. There was a deep crash from within the gas crater as the Unimog gas tank exploded. Then Hawkins was picking himself up and hurrying towards the second wagon, two hundred kilos of uranium burning up in the crater at his back, scorching his clothes.

'Drive! Drive!' Hawkins yelled as he threw himself into the passenger seat.

They accelerated back down the dirt track, then took the service road south, Hawkins tracking the progress of the dust cloud in the distance. The third column. They had almost drawn level with the roundabout south of the approach road. Another two or three minutes and it would be too late. *Those bastards will be all over us then.*

The wall of flame was still burning, cooking the attackers in the second wave as Hawkins and the engineer came tearing down the plain towards the runway. The Antonov was waiting at the end of the strip, ramp down, cockpit pointing south. Preparing for a tactical take-off. Same deal as the fairway strip back at Kettler's estate in Pretoria. Pilots cranking up the engines, ready to propel forward as soon as the brakes were off.

Hawkins glanced again at the cloud. He could see the vehicles now. A dozen of them streaming towards the breach in the chain-link fence north of the approach road. Seventy or eighty bods. The cavalry, racing forward to avenge their dead comrades.

Two minutes.

They pulled up in the slipstream of the aircraft. The jet turbulence hit Hawkins as he flew out of the Unimog, tugging at his clothes, whipping up a storm of sand and dirt. The Antonov revs were at their maximum now. Hawkins and the engineer had to physically claw their way towards the ramp. Like running underwater.

Machine gun fire rumbled thunder-like across the airfield, dimly audible over the noise of the turbofan engines. Hawkins glanced at his three o'clock. The trucks at the head of the third wave had burst through the gap in the perimeter fence. They were gunning straight across the airfield towards the runway, bypassing the apron and the fire wall. Rear-mounted gunners spraying long bursts in a forlorn effort to keep the Antonov grounded. Bullets slapped into the tarmac a metre or so from the wingtips. Another seventy or eighty seconds and they were finished.

Hawkins stopped midway up the ramp. Stared at the empty cargo compartment in confusion.

The engineer waded past him, manoeuvred round to the cabin door. Looked back at Hawkins. Shouted at him over the engine noise and the rattling of components.

'What are you waiting for? Christ, come on!'

'The other Brit,' Hawkins called back. 'He's not here. Where the fuck is he?'

'No time,' the engineer implored. 'We've got to go! They're almost on top of us!'

A volley of rounds struck the ground dangerously close to the ramp. One bullet struck the tail fin. Hawkins glanced over his shoulder. The vehicles were less than a kilometre away now, dust swirling in the wake of the lead pickups. Machineguns flaring. He couldn't see Bald anywhere.

'Let's go!' the engineer cried. 'Now!'

Hawkins clambered up the ramp. The engineer stood at the other end of the compartment, seized hold of the cargo restraint net, shouted at the pilots to get them airborne. Hawkins wrapped his hand tightly around one of the seat strappings, bracing himself as the Antonov launched horribly forward, the fuselage shaking like hell. The plane jolted, and then they were climbing through the air, rapidly gaining height, the ground below them lighting up like a firework display as the enemy gunners poured down a hail of lead on the runway.

The Antonov soared higher. Hawkins felt his guts lurch as the pilots banked sharply to the left, the old engines screaming, the fuselage quaking so violently it seemed as if it might break apart in mid-air. Hawkins held onto the strapping and gazed out past the lowered ramp, searching the ground below for any sign of Bald. Hoping to catch one last sight of his mate.

He saw Martel on the tarmac, Steyn over by the drainage ditch.

Bald wasn't there.

The guy had vanished.

The third wave of attackers swept into view, halting at the end of the runway. A teeming mass of gunmen dismounted, fanning out in search of survivors amid the carnage.

Then the ground exploded.

White-hot blasts rippled across the airfield, pumping thick bulging smoke into the desert air. Dozens of them. Huge explosions, triggered by something far, far bigger than a grenade or an RPG rocket. Like the universe at the point of creation. An aerial bombardment, Hawkins realised. Pounding the approach road, the entrance. The trucks strewn across the runway. Obliterating the third wave beneath a shower of heavy ordnance.

The engineer stared in astonishment and fear at the shockwaves detonating far below. 'What the fuck is going on?'

'Missiles,' Hawkins said. 'Someone's just dropped a load of them on that place. Hellfires or something similar.'

'Who?'

Hawkins made no answer. *Have the Iranians done this?* he asked himself. *Have they bombed the airfield in one last nugatory attempt to prevent the Antonov from taking off?*

Or is this the Americans?

Or someone else?

He didn't know, and no longer cared. He cared about only one thing. Bald was somewhere down there, amid the earth-shuddering destruction. Jock. His old colleague. One of the all-time Hereford greats. The guy had perished. No way he could have survived that firestorm.

Hawkins felt a prick of guilt. He'd left his mate behind. The appalling truth. He tried to tell himself that he'd been left with no choice. Bald had been badly wounded. Hawkins had needed to get rid of the uranium before they were overrun. They had both been in agreement on that. *Destroy the stuff,* Bald had said to him, blood leaking out of his belly. *I'll see you on the plane.* Then Hawkins had raced back from the crater, Bald had disappeared, and there had been no time to go looking for him.

Hawkins repeated this to himself. But it didn't lessen the guilt plaguing his mind. Didn't silence the voice. The one that told him, *You left Jock there.*

That guy saved your life back at the mountain pass, and this is how you repay him? You should have helped him onto the plane.

His death is on you, Davey Boy.

The engineer punched the controls, raising the ramp. More explosions were pulverising the airfield. Everything – buildings, vehicles, bodies – disappeared behind a curtain of smoke and raining debris.

The ramp shut.

The Antonov levelled out.

Hawkins dropped into a fold-down seat, exhausted. The engineer ducked into the cockpit and confabbed with the pilots. A short time later he returned to the cargo compartment.

'The pilots want to know where we're going,' he said. 'Is it Morocco?'

'Morocco is off,' Hawkins said.

'Where, then?'

Hawkins thought for a beat.

Then he said, 'Shobdon. Tell them to plot a course for Shobdon airfield.'

He was going home.

Twenty-Eight

Vauxhall, London. Three days later

The rain was falling slantwise across the street, thin needles drumming faintly against the raised umbrella canopies of the crowd waiting at the bus stop. Hawkins weaved past them, pulling his Belstaff leather jacket tight across his front. He swerved past the steps leading down to the Underground and crossed the road, making for the bulky structure brooding on the southern fringes of the Thames. The headquarters of MI6.

The building must have looked like a vision of the future at one time. Back in the distant past, when people still believed in rules-based orders and free trade. Now it just looked ugly and dated, a relic of an extinct world. A hulking monstrosity of concrete panelling and green-tinted windows enclosed behind a low perimeter wall topped with anti-climb fencing, surrounded by a clutter of gleaming new steel-and-glass high-rises, a drab monument to Britain's diminished status.

Three days had passed since Hawkins had forced the Antonov to land at Shobdon, a small airfield twenty kilometres north of Hereford. The pilots had put up a fight about the new destination – the distance was at the very threshold of the plane's range without stopping to refuel. Then Hawkins had pointed the AK-47 at them, and the pilots quickly changed their minds.

They had touched down in Herefordshire at five o'clock in the afternoon local time, a full seven hours after the missiles had struck the airfield, blowing up the militia column, and Jock Bald. Two figures stood waiting for Hawkins as he descended the loading ramp. Parchment and Shovel Hands. The two UKNs who had frogmarched him out of the Golden Fleece several centuries earlier. The Vauxhall welcoming committee.

Their presence wasn't completely unexpected. Someone at GCHQ would have obviously picked up the Antonov entering UK airspace and passed on the urgent message from the pilots to ground control.

We've got a package on board. Inbound from Gorakan airfield. Notify MI6.

The two UKNs had settled matters with the manager at Shobdon. They took the pilots and engineer into custody and gave Hawkins the keys to a safe house on the outskirts of Hereford.

There's food in the fridge, Parchment had told him. *Coffee and tea. Everything you need.*

Don't leave the house, don't talk to anybody.

Stay there and wait for a call.

Hawkins had walked on foot to the address. A nondescript flat in a post-war council estate on the western bank of the River Wye. The last place on earth anyone would think to look for him. Drawn curtains, tinned soup in the kitchen cupboard, own-brand cereals, processed junk in the fridge. The dank, musty smell of a home that hadn't been lived in for a long time. Burner phone on charge on the scuffed dining room table.

Hawkins spent two days in the flat. Watching TV, eating microwaved ready meals, replacing the bloodied dressing covering the flesh wound on the side of his head. Waiting for the phone to buzz.

He had plenty of time to mull over the events in Iran and Turkmenistan. His own private post-op debrief. He doubted Six would care one way or the other about his involvement in the ambush on the mountain pass. The cold-blooded murder of the goat-herders and the torture of Devaney, the CIA plant, bothered him, but in both cases the witnesses to those crimes were dead. Only Hawkins had survived. Kettler and Moussa were rotting in a dumpster at a derelict petrol station. Steyn had gone down in the firefight at the airfield. Hawkins had killed Martel himself.

Which left Bald.

Had Jock died at Gorakan? That had been Hawkins's initial conclusion. But now he began to reconsider. He remembered looking down from the back of the Antonov as they lifted off the ground. The moment before the missiles had impacted. Bald had vanished from the apron. He must have moved away from that spot. So where had he gone? Maybe the Scot had seen the enemy jets approaching and crawled into the basement of the control tower, or one of the sheds. A last-ditch bid to find cover.

Or maybe that was just wishful thinking. A way for Hawkins to avoid confronting the truth. He had failed Bald. Left his mucker to die at Gorakan to save his own neck.

He still didn't know who had lodged the ordnance over the airfield, or why. Or how much Six knew about Devaney and the CIA's interest in Lance Kettler. He had a ton of unanswered questions.

Hawkins spent two days going round in circles.

On the third day, he got tired of waiting.

The younger version of his self would have sat tight in the council flat, waiting patiently beside the burner. Being the good soldier. Following orders. But Hawkins was done with being pushed around.

He left the safe house that morning. Paid a visit to a mate who owned a garage in Widemarsh, borrowed a hundred quid and bought a ticket for the next direct train from Hereford to Paddington. Three hours later he jumped on the Bakerloo line to Oxford Street, switched over to the Victoria line, got off at Vauxhall in the late afternoon.

Time to get some answers.

Hawkins negotiated traffic islands and zebra crossings, headed down Vauxhall Bridge in the direction of the river, until he found the opening in the perimeter wall. He trotted down the gang-tagged stairs leading to the pedestrian entrance to MI6, stopped in front of a solid-looking steel door with a sign fixed to it warning against unauthorised access. Next to it was a turnstile with a keypad and a card reader. Cameras stared down at Hawkins from atop the tall security fencing.

Hawkins banged his fist against the door twice, stepped back. Waited. The rain had started to fall more heavily, stirring the murky brown waters of the Thames.

There was the clack of a bolt being unlocked on the other side. A security guard with pig eyes set in a round flabby face stepped out from a squat guardhouse. He looked at Hawkins with cold indifference, and sighed.

'Yes, sir?'

Hawkins said, 'I need to get inside, mate.'

'Do you work here, sir?' the guard asked, in a tone that suggested he regarded the idea of Hawkins as a Six employee as vanishingly remote. Up there with the existence of the Loch Ness Monster.

'No,' Hawkins replied. 'But I've been working for your lot off the books. I'm ex-SAS.'

''Course you are, sir.'

The guard looked bored, or disappointed. Maybe both. Hawkins wondered how many Walter Mittys the guy had to deal with on a daily basis. More than a few, he was willing to bet.

The guard pointed to the sign on the wall.

'Authorised personnel only, sir. Now clear off or you'll be escorted off the premises.'

He started to close the door.

'Wait.' Hawkins wedged his Timberland between door and frame. 'Look, mate, I'm telling you the truth. My name is David Hawkins. I've been reporting to two of your people. Peter Cruttwell and Chantelle Jackson. Check your list, they'll be on there. Get hold of them two, tell them my name. They'll know what this is all about.'

The guard studied him with narrowed eyes.

'Hawkins, you say.'

'Aye. David Hawkins.'

'Reporting to Cruttwell and Jackson.'

'That's right.'

'Wait here, sir.'

Hawkins drew his foot back.

The door slammed shut.

Hawkins was left standing in the pouring rain.

Minutes ticked by.

A queue of dull-suited office workers had started to form outside the turnstile entrance. Night-shift employees, waiting their turn to swipe their ID cards and key in their access codes. A two-step verification process. None of them paid Hawkins the slightest attention. He was just another anonymous face. A nobody.

Presently the side door clanged open again.

Peter Cruttwell stepped through the opening, dressed in a dark blue three-piece and a rose-pink tie. The corner of a neatly folded handkerchief poked out of the top of his breast pocket, matching the colour of his tie. A variation on the tweed suit he'd worn back at the private members' club.

Rain beaded his balding ginger pate. There was a glassy look in the blue-green eyes; the thin lips were pressed shut with tightly repressed anger. Cruttwell threw a glance in the direction of the night-shift workers, took Hawkins by the upper arm and marched him away from the turnstile. He spoke in a low rasp laced with menace.

'What in Christ's name are you doing here?'

Hawkins bristled. 'I haven't heard from you lot. Not a fucking peep. I've done what you asked, and you left me sitting on my arse in that grotty flat, twiddling my fucking thumbs.'

'I don't care. You were given clear orders to stay out of sight until further notice. Debrief to follow in due course. What part of that doesn't your Geordie brain understand?'

Hawkins stifled his rage and said, 'Someone else knows about the op. Someone outside this building. They put a load of missiles onto that airfield, right after we took off. We're exposed.'

'We know,' Cruttwell replied, irritably.

Hawkins jerked his head back, eyebrows squishing together. 'What the fuck are you talking about?'

Cruttwell said, 'Our cousins at Star City were watching you. They had eyes on you the whole time, as a matter of fact.'

'I – I don't understand.'

His voice drifted away to nothing.

'The CIA approached us a couple of days ago. Told us that they had a plant on the team. A British operative. One-time colleague of yours by the name of John Bald.'

Hawkins felt his mouth fall open.

'Jock? Hold on. You mean—'

'Your friend – Jock, as you so charmingly call him – was working for Langley. They co-opted him some weeks earlier, we understand. About the time he quit DeepSpear. He tipped off his handlers. Notified them about your presence on the team. The Americans wanted to know whether we had anything to do with that. And whether you were a problem.'

'What did you tell them?'

Cruttwell snorted derisively. 'What do you bloody think? We had to play innocent, of course. Told them you were a rogue operator, disillusioned with the system, and you had obviously decided to betray your country in return for making a quick buck on the Circuit. We could hardly admit to planning a mission behind the backs of Washington. They seemed to buy the story, thank God.'

Several things clicked inside Hawkins's head at once. Back at Kettler's compound Devaney had admitted to working for the agency, but in the intelligence game you always doubled up on everything. Like a crew carrying an extra life vest on a ship. The CIA would have factored in the possibility that one of their guys might be killed in the uranium robbery, or during the escape from Iran. But Devaney wouldn't have known about Bald's mission. The CIA would have siloed their assets. Standard practice in the business.

'So the Americans were watching us? All this time?'

'It appears so, yes,' said Cruttwell. 'They had drones in Iranian airspace, monitoring the operation from afar. We understand that your chum, Bald, sent a warning to Langley. Some hours after you crossed the border. He told them that the goods were being flown to a new destination and to prepare for an attack on the airfield at Gorakan. When they didn't hear back from Bald, they took the decision to go ahead and destroy everything at that location. Apparently, the Americans didn't want to take any chances on that stuff being smuggled out of Turkmenistan.'

Hawkins had stopped listening. He realised something else. He cast his mind back to the old petrol station. Martel laying out the new plan. *I have arranged a better deal. One that is going to make us even richer.* Bald had disappeared behind the service station to take a dump. The guy must have had a satphone on him. Direct line to Star City. He could have put in a hurried call to his handler.

The situation has changed. Get the bombers ready in case we can't stop them.

But then Bald had taken two to the guts; the CIA would have seen the live footage of the enemy gunmen sweeping across the airfield and ordered the Reaper pilots to start hammering the place with Hellfires. They wouldn't have vectored in that Hawkins had had already disposed of the HEU cylinders in the gas pit.

More Vauxhall workers were filing down the stairs, joining the line outside the turnstile. Cruttwell glanced round, dropped his voice so low it was practically subterranean.

'Look, I can't say any more. Not here. This one is supposed to be off the books. We'll have to meet later.'

'Where?'

Cruttwell ruckled his brow in thought.

'Do you know the Peace Pagoda at Battersea Park?'

'Aye.'

'I'll see you there. Tonight. Seven o'clock. I'll explain everything then. Don't be late.'

He gave his back to Hawkins without waiting for a response. Cruttwell skipped the queue, rapped his knuckles on the side door and slipped through the opening.

Hawkins climbed the stairs and started north down Vauxhall Bridge. He had a few hours to kill until the meeting. He wandered through the depressing backstreets of Pimlico, running through his conversation with Cruttwell. The revelation that Bald had been a CIA asset. So that was why Bald had agreed so readily to Hawkins's plan to stop Martel and Steyn. Because they were both working for the same side. Different teams, but with the same wider goal.

Bald had ordered the bombing of the airfield. He would have known that the Reapers were inbound. Lying there, on the ground, with a couple of bullet wounds to his guts, Bald would have given himself low odds of getting onto the Antonov before the bombs started falling. In which case he might have dragged himself over to cover instead. Somewhere that could have shielded him from the blasts. There was a possibility, however slim, that Bald had survived the attack on Gorakan.

Hawkins understood why Bald had kept quiet about his involvement with Langley. He would have been under explicit orders from his handlers. *Tell no one about your mission. Trust no one.* Even when Hawkins had admitted to working for Six, Bald might have suspected a trap, intended to wheedle the truth out of him.

But that raised another question.

Why had Bald argued against contacting MI6 when Hawkins had confessed to his secret op? *That is the absolute last thing we should be doing,* Bald had said after they had left the petrol station.

According to what Cruttwell had told him, Bald had already alerted his handlers by that point. *He sent a warning to Langley. Some hours after you crossed the border.*

Hawkins could think of only one explanation that made any sense. Bald must have given a selective version of the truth to the CIA. He'd want them to hold off their attack until the very last minute. Delay the bombing until the money had been transferred to his account.

That seemed to fit with what Hawkins knew about Jock. The guy was an old pro. Decades of soldiering under his belt. The kind of bloke who could see round corners. He would have known, or at least suspected, that the Americans wouldn't give a shit about recovering the money being paid out by the New Patriotic Front. They were only interested in the uranium. Bald had spied an opportunity to get paid while sticking to his orders. Get the goods over to Morocco, wait for the millions to drop into his account before sending a message to his handler. *Destroy this place.* Martel had planned to kill the others and keep the money, of course, but Bald would have backed himself in that situation. Then the Americans had decided to go ahead with the attack anyway.

A sinister thought squirmed through Hawkins's guts. *What if the CIA had wanted to get rid of us too? Send in the Reapers so they could get rid of the mercenaries and the uranium at the same time?*

No witnesses.

No loose lips.

Are they after me now?

He shrugged off this line of thinking, stopped at a dingy pub off Lupus Street. He ordered fish and chips and a Diet Coke, planted himself at an empty table. Passed the time grazing on his food while he watched the news.

President Farrell was holding a press conference at his Florida mega-palace. He stood over a lectern. Chandeliers hung from the ceiling behind him, a room dripping in gold. The kind of décor that would have met with Kettler's approval. Farrell was flanked by a pair of sober-looking cabinet members in dark suits. Hawkins vaguely recognised one of them as the Secretary of War. The third bloke was the Secretary of State.

'We destroyed everything,' Farrell was saying. 'Iran's nuclear enrichment has been obliterated. It was beautiful. One hundred per cent success. Very beautiful, maybe the most incredible mission in the history of this great nation. People said we couldn't do it, but we did.'

Hawkins permitted himself a wry smile. *No you didn't, pal.*

The real reason Iran's nuclear ambitions lay in tatters had nothing to do with strategic bombers or bunker-busters. It had only worked because of a couple of desperate old Blades on the ground, doing the dirty work. But no one would ever know that. *Secrets and memoirs*, Bald said, and the guy had been right. History wasn't written by the likes of Hawkins. It belonged to those with the power and wealth to control the narrative. The truth was whatever Farrell and his cronies wanted it to be.

The rain grudgingly abated as Hawkins set off for Battersea Park. He tramped along Grosvenor Road, crossed the bridge east of Ranelagh Gardens, stepped through the gate to the park, started down the promenade running parallel with the southern bank. He walked on for five hundred metres, stopped in front of the pagoda. Consulted his Mudmaster. He was early. A few minutes before seven o'clock.

The car park to the east was two-thirds empty. Just a handful of SUVs and motorbikes, a stack of dumped electric rental bikes. A pair of joggers hustled past the pagoda, a young guy in a flat cap walking his golden retriever. Two young women stood posing for selfies in front of the parapet wall overlooking the Thames. Behind them a service barge drifted lazily past.

He heard the sudden chainsaw-growl of a motorbike at his right. Hawkins looked towards the car park as a Triumph Tiger rolled down the walkway. Coming towards him. A crash-helmeted rider decked out in a one-piece black leather suit, and a passenger wearing a full-face helmet. They weaved past a couple out with a stroller, the man shouting at them with a raised fist. Presumably because bikes weren't permitted on the promenade.

The bike came on towards Hawkins, drew level with him.

Stopped in front of the pagoda.

The passenger raised their left arm. There was an object in the figure's hand, Hawkins realised. Something dark and bulky.

A gun.

Pointing at his head.